ChiZine Publica

A COLLECTION

OF SHORT STORIES

BY RAY CLULEY

PROBABLY MONSTERS

Distributed in Canada by
Publishers Group Canada
76 Stafford Street, Unit 300
Toronto, Ontario, M6J 2S1
Toll Free: 800-747-8147
e-mail: info@pgcbooks.ca

Distributed in the U.S. by
Diamond Comic Distributors, Inc.
10150 York Road, Suite 300
Hunt Valley, MD 21030
Phone: (443) 318-8500
e-mail: books@diamondbookdistributors.com

Library and Archives Canada Cataloguing in Publication

Cluley, Ray, 1976-, author

    Probably monsters / Ray Cluley.

Short stories.

Issued in print and electronic formats.

ISBN 978-1-77148-334-6 (pbk.).--ISBN 978-1-77148-335-3

(ebook)

    I. Title.

PR6103.L84P76 2015   823'.92   C2015-900090-4

                          C2015-900091-2

A **free** eBook edition is available
with the purchase of this print book.

CHIZINE PUBLICATIONS
Toronto, Canada
www.chizinepub.com
info@chizinepub.com

Edited by Courtney Kelly
Proofread by Dominik Parisien

CLEARLY PRINT YOUR NAME ABOVE IN UPPER CASE
Instructions to claim your free eBook edition:
1. Download the BitLit app for Android or.iOS
2. Write your name in **UPPER CASE** on the line
3. Use the BitLit app to submit a photo
4. Download your eBook to any device

Canada Council Conseil des arts
for the Arts   du Canada

We acknowledge the support of the Canada Council for the Arts which last year invested $20.1 million in writing and publishing throughout Canada.

ONTARIO ARTS COUNCIL
CONSEIL DES ARTS DE L'ONTARIO
an Ontario government agency
un organisme du gouvernement de l'Ontario

Published with the generous assistance of the Ontario Arts Council.

Printed in Canada

PROBABLY

MONSTERS

*For everyone who said I could
then waited for me to believe them.*

Especially my mother. She fought monsters and, for a long time, won.

PROBABLY MONSTERS:
a brief explanation

The title of this collection comes from the imagination of a little girl called Isabella. She asked what had made the hole she'd discovered in the floor and we didn't know, so with the straightforward simplicity only childhood seems to allow she provided her own answer: "Probably monsters."

Nowadays, when people ask me what I'm writing about, I tend to say "probably monsters." Sometimes the monsters are blood-sucking fiends with fleshy wings, and sometimes they're shambling dead things that won't rest. *Sometimes*. Sometimes they're people, people like you and me (well, maybe *you*, certainly not me) and these ones are *everywhere*. But sometimes they're worse than any of these. They're the things that make us howl in the darkness, hoping no one hears—monsters we've perhaps made ourselves and struggle to overcome. Despite what our parents may have told us, there *are* such things as monsters. Lots of them. We discover that quickly, growing up. So enjoy the book. You'll find a lot of different monsters here, including yours.

Probably.

Ray Cluley, February 2015

For Mark
Beware the monsters!
All the best
Ray Cluley

"'It's poor judgment', said Grandpa, 'to call anything by a name. We don't know what a hobgoblin or a vampire or a troll is. Could be lots of things. You can't heave them into categories with labels and say they'll act one way or another. That'd be silly. They're people. People who do things. Yes, that's the way to put it. People who do things.'"

Ray Bradbury, "The Man Upstairs"

CONTENTS

ALL CHANGE

Robert had become one of those people who ran for the train, huffing his way along the platform, briefcase in hand and heart struggling to keep up because he was getting bloody old. Well, sort of running; seventy-six, and feeling twice that. He knew people were making silent bets as to whether he would make it or not. To hell with them if he didn't.

"The *train* now approaching *plat*form *three* is the *six*-six*teen* service for . . ."

"Excuse me, excuse me, coming through please."

". . . calling at . . ."

"Miss? Thank you. Excuse me."

But he was too late. The people spilling from the carriages had become people heading for other platforms, heading for exits, greeting loved ones, buying coffee, and the one he was looking for was likely already gone.

"Oh, Chri—"

The full extent of his blasphemy was lost to the sharp blast of a whistle and the reprimanding hiss of closing doors. He scanned the people quickly, looking for loners, but everyone was in such a rush, criss-crossing each other's paths, pushing, pausing, that he couldn't get a decent fix on anyone or anything.

The train pulled away leaving Robert to wonder why they were never late when you needed them to be.

He closed his eyes and concentrated.

It had all been so much easier when he was young. Now there were too many trains, too many more platforms, too many new points to start and finish from. The only thing that didn't change was the fact that they always came through here. Wherever they were heading, wherever they had come from, this was where they came to at some point in their journey. Strangers passing through, unnoticed by most. Usually he was ready to meet them, had already sensed who or what they were, but not today. Today, just a feeling that he was meant to be here, and then a feeling as to which platform, and that was all.

"Is this right platform for six thirty-four?" a young Asian lady asked, clutching his arm.

Robert shrugged off her hand with a, "How should I know?" adding, "I don't work here."

Though of course it looked like he did. That was why he wore the blue trousers, the blue blazer, the awful tie. Not quite the uniform but close enough, and people barely noticed the briefcase.

The woman said something in her own language to an older lady beside her and they left him. The older woman looked back, but they were already too far for Robert to hear whatever curses she threw back at him.

They weren't *real* curses. Just an offloading of foreign syllables. He let them go.

"Where?" he muttered. "Where?"

There was a man, by the kiosk, looking around, maybe searching for—No. He had a coffee cup stuffed with an empty crisp packet; he was only looking for a bin. There, coming down the stairs, a woman, awkward in her steps because perhaps she—No. Just walking too fast in new heels. That one, though, the young lad looking up at the screen—something felt right about him. Or rather, it felt wrong. Yes, yes, it was getting stronger as Robert made his way over. A man in his early twenties, dark hair, brooding looks, pale—No. Not him. It was the screen he was looking at. Robert was feeling the screen. The arrival time. The *next* train.

He didn't know who or what he was after yet, but he knew the train they'd be on. He hoped he could kill them quick and get home before dark.

§

He was going to have to get on the train. It wouldn't be the first time, but those days had been in his youth, when he was less confident. Once, when he'd just started, he'd followed one all the way up to Scotland to make sure he was right about them. He had been, and he'd done what he had to, but his caution had meant another long uncomfortable journey back again. Plus there was the expense to consider. It was cheaper back then, of course, riding the train, much cheaper (*and* with a better chance of a seat) but at the time it had still emptied his wallet. These days he usually managed to get it done at the station. Usually. Often it happened in one of the toilet blocks, or far enough down the platform, near enough to the lines, that he was able to drag whatever was left to the edge and roll it on to the rails. It depended on what he was dealing with. Some he could do away with even in a crowd, confident nobody would know what had happened.

"Excuse me, mate, where's the gents'?"

Robert raised the briefcase to point because his other hand was clutching the knife in his pocket. The lad looked feral, but then a lot of them did these days.

"Cheers."

He watched to see if the young man actually went there, if it had been a genuine enquiry and not an attempt to glean something from Robert's actions or demeanour. But the lad headed right for the toilets, with some degree of urgency in fact. It seemed genuine enough.

Robert remembered one particular encounter in those toilets. He always remembered the pretty ones. She'd looked like a backpacker but the bag was there to conceal a large gelatinous hump, the weak spot Robert lunged for as soon as he'd identified the type. After that it was just a case of scooping handfuls of water from the sink to wash the ooze down the drain set in the floor. He'd bagged the clothes and binned them.

A man on the platform checked his watch, checked the screen, looked around. His gaze settled briefly on the tunnel down the track but from where Robert stood he couldn't tell if it was with impatience for the train or with a longing for the darkness he saw inside. If the man moved that way, Robert would have to follow. He hated working in the tunnel now that the lines were electrified, but such hazards had their uses. Still, it had all been so much simpler in the old days.

Old days? Young days, more like. *These* were the old days.

The rails made a quiet *tsst-tsst*, whispering the train's imminent arrival (*tsst-tsst*) moments before the voiced announcement declared it. Six twenty-five. He still didn't have his target; he'd have to get on board with the crowd.

People shuffled closer to the platform, some of them moving further up its length as if they could tell where the doors would stop, though they hadn't seemed able to do so before when they'd had all that time waiting. People picked up bags and cases and extended the handles of their wheeled luggage. One man shouldered a guitar case that could have really been anything of a number of things. Robert was getting his feeling from all around but couldn't pinpoint a target. He would have to get on the train with whatever it was he was here for and worry about locating it later.

§

The train had three carriages. Robert wanted to seat himself at the furthest end but it was remarkably full. All the seats were taken except one that was wet with something pungent. The man in the next seat, asleep against the greasy glass of the window, didn't seem to mind it though. Maybe it was his. Robert let him keep it, turning his body sideways and moving further up the aisle. Despite his care, his case bumped the armrests and elbows of a few passengers but they accepted his apologies with the familiarity of seasoned rail users.

"Here you go, you can sit here."

"Oh no," Robert said, though it would be a good spot. He hated the fact that he looked old enough for the young lady to give up her seat.

"Really," she said. "I won't need it much longer." She had beautiful eyes, green like go.

"Well if you don't mind," he conceded, already sitting down. Before he could complete the action the train pulled away and he had to steady himself with an arm against the fold-up table of the seat in front. He fell into his seat with the lurch of movement. The fold-up table opened in front of him. A newspaper had been tucked there, folded open to a page he knew was the third one because of the picture.

Robert sighed, turned the paper over, and settled himself. He put his briefcase by his feet to the annoyance of the teenager lounging in the adjacent seat who had to move his own feet out of the space. For a moment Robert thought the lad's ears were bleeding but it wasn't blood, it was a red wire leading to an iP3 M-pod thing somewhere in a pocket. Still, from the sounds of how loud it was, Robert was surprised there wasn't blood as well. It was suddenly clear why the young woman had been so eager to move.

He was feeling something from the kid, but it might have just been teenage angst and rage and hatred at the world, judging from the band that screamed at him, yelling directly into his brain. In fact, the feeling could've been coming from anyone around him; the carriage was so full it was difficult to tell. His plan had been to work his way slowly up the train but he was already in the right carriage, he knew that much. Robert was getting old but he could still go to the toilet on his own, it just took him a little longer; this would be no different.

He feigned getting comfortable so he could fidget a few looks at other passengers.

Opposite him, reading something from a tiny screen that wanted to be a book, was a swarthy fellow in business clothes. Suit, trousers, shirt open at the neck with no sign of a tie. He wore a tiny crucifix, so that narrowed the possibilities down one. His chest and throat were rather hairy, though. His nails were long; Robert saw them whenever he pressed a button on his toy. Next to him was a woman in a burka that could have been disguising all manner of signs; Robert thought perhaps a body wrapped in thin crisp bandages, skin tight and leathery, a skeletal figure held together with cobwebs. In front of them, a pair sat talking in quiet tones, whispers, and maybe they—

The teenager beside Robert shifted in his seat, turning away from Robert to face the window. He traced lines in the condensation. Nothing arcane, not an ancient script, just faces. Reminders of previous victims? Maybe it wasn't music he listened to, maybe it really was the screaming it sounded like, something to remember his prey by. Or maybe the faces were something voodoo he could spit a hex at. No. He wiped them away.

The countryside was out there somewhere, rushing past the window, but it was dark and all Robert saw were streetlights where he wanted trees, and the red rear lights of cars like evil eyes in the early night. He noticed his fellow passenger had a reflection in its surface. And he noticed the teenager notice him notice.

"What are you looking at?"

Robert didn't answer but turned away.

"Tickets, please."

Robert settled back into his seat and patted his pockets for his wallet, found it, folded it open. There was a library card in the plastic window where the photo of a loved one should have been. He caressed it briefly, as he might a lost wife. When Robert was a child he loved spending time in the library. As he grew older, to escape the horrors of the war that terrified his country, he buried himself in books. From boys' adventure stories he went on to Stoker, Poe, and M.R. James. By the time he was old enough for the war there was no part for him to play in it, but he was old enough for Lovecraft and Machen and Clark Ashton Smith. The library had taught him a lot. It taught him how to fight a different war, different to the one his father had died in but a war just the same, and just as dangerous. More so, because the enemy was always changing and had a variety of strengths. Fortunately most had a variety of weaknesses, too. The books had taught him that.

He needed to clear his mind for a moment before trying to focus again. As nice as Nikki (19, a student from Middlesbrough) looked in bikini pants and oil, Robert decided to read a book of his own rather than the newspaper. He rested his case on his lap, flipped the catches, and rummaged around inside without opening it more than he had to. He would feel what he wanted easily enough, avoiding the bottles and the vials and the cold metal, the leaves, the chalk, the holy symbols. The first book he found was old and brittle and ribbon-bound, sealed with a silver clasp, but the next had the comfortable warm flexibility of a second hand novel and he withdrew it eagerly. It was Ray Bradbury's *The October Country*. He would read "The Jar" again, take comfort from its familiarity and regain a sense of who he was, what he was doing.

"Tickets?"

"Return, please," Robert asked, pulling out a handful of notes. "End of the line."

The conductor tapped at a device he wore strapped across his chest. His actions were slow and weak and Robert thought maybe he could detect a faint odour coming from the man. Something chemical, something . . . earthy. He looked carefully at the man's face, his hands, and thought maybe they were too pale. He had the complexion that was referred to as ashen, or wan, depending who you were reading. When the man saw him looking and offered a hesitant smile, the teeth Robert saw were crooked and yellow and there was something caught between the front ones. Spinach, maybe. Maybe something else. Then the machine was spitting out an orange ticket, cutting it with a robotic hiccup as the man took Robert's money. He shambled away to the next row of seats. "Tickets."

A couple of the other passengers were looking at Robert. He wondered how odd he must have looked, scrutinizing the conductor. One of them, a woman with braided hair who kept licking her lips like she was tasting the air, gave him a nod and then turned away. The other, a middle-aged man with a receding hairline and poorly fitted suit, chuckled to himself and said something to a companion Robert couldn't see.

Maybe.

A dead baby, a tumoured brain, or glistening things both fat and pale; the night, the swamp, or the in-between; anything and everything was in that jar, it only depended on who was looking.

Robert loved Ray Bradbury.

Fiction is where we find our fiends, that's what Robert knew. And none of that *un*conscious or *sub*conscious rubbish; we knew what we were doing when we created such things. We put them in stories to be told around campfires, and later we put them in books, lots of them in lots of books, and that way people would know. Robert's greatest weapon was his library card. At least, it used to be. Recently he wasn't so sure. Monsters wore hockey masks, gloves with blades, something white-faced with a stretched open-jaw. Now, at his age, he was thankful that they sparkled, was glad to fight noseless foes with a curious grasp of Latin and a name that shouldn't be spoken. Diluted devils. Paper scarecrows. Easy.

Robert read a few paragraphs, enough to relax, and then he only *pretended* to read. With most books these days that was okay because these days most people only pretended to write, but it didn't seem fair to Bradbury. So he slotted his ticket between the pages as a bookmark. That was how he noticed he'd only been sold a single.

"There's been a mistake," he said, leaning out into the aisle for the conductor's attention. He held up his ticket. "Excuse me? I asked for a return."

The conductor faced him, said "Ticket," and continued up the train.

Robert began to stand. It *was* the conductor, hidden in plain sight. A purloined letter no one else could read. A ghost no one else could see. Robert reached down for his case but the teenager beside him put a clammy hand on his.

"There's no coming back from where we're going," it said. "The line terminates with us."

The way the young man kept wiping at the window as he spoke told

Robert he needed the condensation. He realized now that the wetness of the man's t-shirt came not from sweat but from the skin beneath that leaked moisture as much as it craved it. He had probably been sitting in the seat with the damp patch earlier. His voice was thick and bubbly, his words like gas escaping marshland.

"Found what you're looking for?"

Robert didn't know if the creature was referring to itself, or to the fact that Robert was carefully rummaging in his briefcase.

"As soon as you find your stake or silver bullet or whatever," — it burped, and a thick fluid rose and fell in its throat— "you'll need something else, and then something else, and something else. Look."

The teenager that wasn't a teenager pointed carelessly at other seats in the carriage. Everybody was looking at Robert. No, *everything* was looking at Robert. There was a woman with a sabre-toothed smile. There was a man who shimmered when he moved, fading into the upholstery, and beside him a boy with a lap that writhed. A woman with a skin of stitches and scraps of shroud or bridal gown. And others. Lots of others. An old man knitting at a furious pace. It looked like wool, but the line descended to somewhere unseen, a bulge around the midriff that could have been a sack of something silky.

A fox with bright green eyes, green like go, padded down the aisle, pausing to nod its snout at Robert and to sniff briefly at the seat it had given him. A green-eyed monster jealous of nothing Robert had to offer. With a sweep of tail it was gone, brushing past a pale man in a suit dark as night, a man who stood and moved forward, a blur of ink in clothes made of what you see with your eyes closed.

"Hello Robert," the man said, with a voice from under the bed. With a whisper from outside the window.

"Hello Robert," said something that hurt to look at, something that lived in uninvented corners.

"Hello Robert" and "Hello Robert," "Hello Robert." Words from fur and from fangs, words grunted, squealed, howled, growled, and gibbered. Their collective breath was one of blood and bile and burial soil, chewed worms and rotten fungus.

The pale man in tailored gloom came towards Robert. Each soft step on the well-worn carpet was the sound a promise makes as it breaks. "You found us all," it said with a mouthful of ash.

"Alright," said Robert. "Okay."

He closed his briefcase and then his eyes. Would it be teeth or claws he felt opening his throat? Would he be torn by spiny talons, falling away in fleshy pieces, or would they drink his spinal fluid, liquefy his bones, let him leak his last in a poison-swollen agony?

"None of those things," said a tiny man above him. He was nestled in amongst the luggage in the overhead carry space. He closed his eyes at Robert and a new one opened in his forehead. It was a colour Robert had never seen before. "We're not going to kill you."

He knew that these things lied: he knew that these things told the truth.

Maybe they would possess him.

"Maybe we already do."

One of them had tried back in '82. Lingering at the station platform, it had decorated many trains with human colours, leaping and splashing. It had pushed Robert from inside, but he'd pushed it right back. A tug o' war he wasn't sure he'd won.

"She had been playful, full of fun," said the little man-thing, wriggling into a more comfortable position, "she liked to run and skip and jump. Run from you, or so she tried, but you knew what to do, and so she died."

"I don't like poetry."

"Not true," said the man, "you do. You do. Coleridge, Keats, and Rossetti too."

"What are you—"

"*One had a cat's face, one whisked a tail, one tramped at a rat's pace, one crawled like a snail.*"

"How do you—"

"*Barking, mewing, hissing, mocking, tore her gown and soiled her stocking.*"

"Shut up!"

The little man closed his eye and opened his others, opened more, opened all of them. "I. See. *You.*"

Robert lunged up from his seat. He didn't bring a weapon out from his briefcase; he intended to use the case itself to mash the tiny little bastard into paste.

Several hundred hands seemed to grab him. Claws tore his jacket, hooks ripped it, long multi-knuckled fingers folded around his arm, something ropey and wet snared his waist, and a hand of bone forced him back, forced him down. Something cloven kicked him, something slimy whipped him, and something that wasn't there, something that was only air, held him in his seat. His briefcase was taken by something in yellow sleeves. The cuffs spewed things that crawled and fluttered and they scuttled across Robert's lap.

"Sit," they told him. As the train hurtled into the darkening night, the carriage he was in seemed to writhe and pulsate with things that shouldn't be but were. Things he knew.

The monsters have changed, said the tiny man without speaking. *Look.*

The newspaper before him fluttered open, pages turned by invisible hands. He saw wars and child porn and riots and terror and rapes and murders and tumours that couldn't be cured.

"And look."

A story had been circled with blotty blue biro. It told of a body discovered on a railway embankment, found by rail-workers carrying out emergency repairs. Police were treating the death as suspicious. It didn't mention why, but Robert thought maybe it was because the woman's wounds had been sown with salt. He'd hoped to rely on the city's urban scavengers after that but even they weren't desperate enough to feast from such remains.

"You don't need to worry," said the boy beside him. He was wet with a substance thicker than sweat, now. Part of his lap had burst and his t-shirt had dispersed into rotten patches of cotton that clung to a withered chest.

Robert covered his eyes with his fists—

He thrusts his fists against the posts and still insists he sees the ghosts.

—then brought them down on the chair in front. He did it again. And again. Again-again-again.

"You're not helping."

The words fell upon Robert like bee-stings. "Where are you taking me?"

"Carcosa."

"Innsmouth."

"The House of Pain."

Robert shook his head.

"Into the closet."

"Under the stairs."

"Endsville, old hoss. Where all rail service terminates."

But where was that?

"Somewhere over the fucking rainbow," said the little man amongst the luggage, "my pretty." It smiled with bloody teeth.

"Where the wild things are," Robert muttered. His breath fogged the air in the carriage. It was getting cold.

"Where we're going isn't important. Do you know who we are?"

Robert saw many he could give names to. Others he knew only by type.

"You're the monsters."

"That's *what* we are. Do you know *who*?"

He knew what they wanted to tell him. They would quote Nietzsche, talk about struggling with monsters or staring into the abyss. One of them might mention different sides of the same coin, or something like that.

"Do you know who *you* are?"

They were definitely going to give him Nietzsche.

"*We* know who you are. We all do."

Robert sighed. "I am legend, am I?" It was meant to be dry, a wry comment to die by, but a laugh built inside and he bellowed with it, he cackled, and he wiped away tears that had already been there.

Monsters change, but you don't want to.

"You do like the pretty ones."

. . . and still insists he sees the ghosts.

Robert thought he might be sick. The train rocked, side to side, and the things on board swayed with it, more used to its movement than he was. It lurched with brief bursts of speed, like a serpent lunging for prey, and sometimes it seemed to plunge, as if they were hurtling down somewhere deep and endless.

"You're coming with us."

It was a pointless thing to say because Robert already knew. Most of the others thought so too and turned away, sitting back down, coiling into their seats, gathering themselves into cocoons. Forgetting him. For now.

Beside him the seat was vacant. The cushion was damp and squelched at his touch. He wiped his hand on his trousers and stared out at the October country. He didn't see it. Instead he focussed on the reflection he saw in the glass. For now it was his, whatever may lie beneath. He hoped it didn't change into anything else.

What are you looking at?

The faint image of himself was fading from the glass. "Nothing," said Robert. He said it until it was true, and all there was to see was darkness.

I HAVE HEARD
THE MERMAIDS SINGING

I have a fragment of poetry in my mind, looping like a snippet of song, when I go to meet Eliot at the mission. Maybe it's because of his name, maybe it's because of the stories, but it resonates so appropriately with everything that I can't help but think it's something more. Maybe not God, but something neat and ordered in the universe telling me this is all as it should be, me being here.

I have heard the mermaids singing, each to each. That's the bit that has lodged in my mind, but it's the following line that I exhale with the last of my cigarette smoke.

"I do not think that they will sing to me."

I'm looking out onto a sea that is darker than the night sky above it, standing on a stretch of beach that says *shush* with each gentle wave that washes it clean. My clothes are stuck to my skin even now. There are two seasons here; wet and dry. Both seasons are hot seasons.

I sigh, like the waves, and flick my cigarette butt to the sand, then stoop to pick it up again; such casual littering isn't like me, even at home, and this certainly isn't home. This is Nicaragua, about six thousand miles from home.

This is the Miskito Coast.

The people here fish for lobsters. Eliot doesn't call them lobsters, though. He calls them gold.

"Red gold," he says. "And this is a gold rush."

I nod. I'm on my third cigarette but I'll stop now that Eliot has joined me on the sand.

"And do you know what else is red, my friend? Blood. Blood is red, and here it clots thick and starves the brain and that is too dear a cost."

He's lost me a little with the metaphors, but I know that he is talking about decompression sickness. The bends.

Eliot says something too fast and too Spanish for me to understand, but the tone is clear enough, and the palms-out shrug he directs at the busy people around us tells me even more about his frustration.

It's early in the morning or late at night, and my jetlag isn't helping me decide either way. I'm probably supposed to be tired, but I'm not. It isn't *all* jetlag. Some of it is being somewhere new, and some of it is all the strong Central American coffee, but most of it comes from Eliot. He talks with such passion, such earnest concern for his fellow man, that he keeps me more alert than any coffee in the world.

"Look," he says, pointing out to sea. The lights of the lobster boats bob up and down like fallen stars afloat on the ocean, their glow diffused by the night (or morning) mist. It would be a beautiful sight if I didn't know what it meant, although the sounding of the horns goes a long way towards ruining it too. Around us, entire families shove *cayucas* through the sand and into the surf. The dugout boats roll across chopped lengths of palm tree until, with enthusiastic cries of "Wop, wop!" the men launch themselves into their *cayucas* and paddle out to the waiting boats whilst their wives and children watch from the shore.

"Look," Eliot says again. He points, first to one boat, then another, shaking his head. "Not all of the children stay to watch."

He's right. Boys, maybe ten or eleven years old, are paddling out there with their fathers and brothers. Some cry out with joy and excitement as if they are at play, whilst others are all too serious and business-like in their manner, older in their minds than in their bodies. They are the men of the family, earning money the only way they know how.

Eliot has read my piece about the sweatshops. He thinks he can only persuade me to write a story if there's a child angle. It would make for a more striking article, but he should know that my being here means I'm already persuaded. Besides, I would write his story if only because he asked. He was there for my mother right to the end; well, right until her condition twisted the appreciation out of her, bending her into a bitter bitch with everyone but me. I owed him something for that.

Here, Eliot is a missionary. Back home he had been a priest. He looks better as a missionary. The white cotton trousers and open shirt go well with his part-Spanish features. A gold crucifix replaces the medallion his hairy chest suggests he should wear, but he has the dark oiled hair that is according to stereotype. Knowing his age, I know he must dye his hair.

"Shall we have some breakfast?" I ask him, taking a gamble with the time.

He sighs, but the sound is quickly lost beneath the slap of the waves and the way the wind flutters the edges of our clothes. Behind us, the village huts glimmer in faint candlelight, waiting for the dawn. If people are stirring for breakfast, they are doing it quietly. Perhaps they have gone back to bed.

Eliot kicks idly at one of the palm logs on the beach. He scuffs up sand in a half-hearted attempt to bury it.

"Yes," he says eventually. "Let us have some breakfast."

There is a picture of Christ on one of Eliot's walls, but I'm only taking Eliot's word for it. "He's there somewhere," he'd said when I asked. I find myself playing an odd version of Where's Wally, looking for the long-haired bearded son of God amongst all the other photographs while Eliot roots around in the tiny fridge. I hear only the tinkle-clink of bottles, so it's no surprise when he apologizes and says, "I only have beer. Beer for breakfast?" He laughs, briefly.

Beer for breakfast is fine by me. It doesn't feel like breakfast time anyway.

I discover a picture I did not expect to find. Nestled between a photograph of a tiny grinning Miskito boy, and one of a man in a wheelchair who nevertheless smiles for the camera, is a photograph of my mother. She is able to sit up in bed, and there's even some warmth in her eyes and lopsided smile. Her hand is at her necklace, but I don't know if she draws strength from the cross or from the fact that Eliot gave it to her. I remember taking the photograph. Maybe she hides the cross from me, knowing how I raged against God back then.

The bottle Eliot hands me is cool and wet. I use it to point at the picture. "I didn't know you had that."

Eliot nods and drinks. "She had always wanted to come to Nicaragua. She gave that to me when she knew her time was coming. She knew about my collection." He uses his beer to turn a small circle in the air, indicating the walls around us, and I realize all the people there are dead.

"Shall we drink these outside?"

He nods, and scrapes two chairs out to the porch. We can watch the sea ease in . . . and leave. Ease in . . . and leave. The lights of the boats, the bigger boats, are still distant watery stars.

"There is a reef out there. It used to be packed full with lobsters. Those spiny little treasures people die for here. There were so many, you could pluck them up with your eyes closed. Like this."

For some reason he feels compelled to close his eyes and mime picking them up, grabbing imaginary lobsters from around our chairs. When he opens his eyes again he laughs. "You only needed a snorkel in those days. Then came big boats and scuba diving and the reef was picked clean. No more red gold."

My watch beeps an hour I don't want to know.

"Tomorrow I will take you to someone who remembers this. Gabriela, she remembers this." He points absently at the room behind us and I know one of the pictures somewhere there comes from her. She will have a sadder story than disappearing lobsters, though the two will be inextricably linked.

"Today is what I mean. I will take you today."

"Why me, Eliot?" I haven't written anything for nearly two years. I've barely existed, one day at a time.

Eliot meets my eyes in the way he always used to. I feel strangely scared and safe at the same time. He holds my gaze as if looking for the answer there, not because he doesn't have one but because he believes I already do.

"People listen to you," he says.

I'm surprised and appalled at his certainty. I think of my mother, her gurgling-drain cough. The way she rolled her cigarettes even as she struggled to breathe, and rolled her eyes when I said anything about it. I will let him down again.

I finish my breakfast deciding to make it my supper. Eliot has a spare cot for me and I will lie on it, staring at the ceiling, trying to sleep.

Eliot wishes me, "Pleasant dreams." He is looking to sea when he says it and I wonder if he's thinking of when the lobster roamed closer to the shore. He has a faraway nostalgic look.

Then again, maybe he thinks of the same woman I do.

I have seen them riding seaward on the waves, combing the white hair of the waves blown back when the wind blows the water white and black.

I am staring at the *cayucas* on the beach, thinking of earlier when I'd seen them dragged and paddled out to sea, and I'm thinking of these lines from T.S. Eliot while I wait for a different Eliot to wake and take me to the clinic. I have more people to meet today than the Gabriela he has already mentioned. Each of them is tied somehow to the sea before me. It does not look like the place for mermaids.

I am separated from my home by a distance I cannot visualize, miles upon miles of ocean between me and my tiny flat above the newsagents. Sharif, the man who owns it, likes having a journalist live above his shop, though my work rarely appears in his stock. His wares are strictly daily papers and women's magazines and a top shelf of plastic-wrapped publications boasting star-nippled tits and mock-sultry mouths. No *National Geographic*, no *Focus*, no *New Scientist*. His is a shop where beer is sold by the individual can, a place to buy cigarettes and scratch cards. I imagine the people buying them dream of coming here, to the Caribbean, but this is not the Caribbean they'd imagine.

I take a breath of fresh ocean air, listening to the susurrus of waves and sand, and then I take a breath of cigarette smoke, filling myself alternately with salt and nicotine. I shouldn't smoke. My mother smoked. I think that's maybe why I do.

I do not get a "good morning" from Eliot when he wakes. Instead, he joins me on the porch with, "The lobsters have retreated to where the water is deeper, trying to escape the grabbing hands. It is like you, yes?"

I wonder if he's been thinking of something like that to say all morning.

"I'm here because you asked me."

He waves that away. It's not what he meant, and he knows I know. But he says nothing more about it.

"Today, you will see the clinic. And I will take you to see friends of mine. They will tell you about the mermaids."

He is wearing the same clothes he met me in at the airport. So am I. But then I haven't slept yet, so it feels like the same day anyway.

"Will I see the decompression chamber?"

He nods.

"And the boats?"

"Tomorrow. We will need an authority different to mine for that." He looks skyward as if apologizing to his authority, but I'm sure God knows we'll need an official to visit the boats. He'll forgive him. It's what He does.

"Do you want to freshen up first?"

I've never heard "freshen up" used in real life and it makes me smile. "It is the right expression?"

I clasp Eliot by the shoulder and tell him yes, it is, but I'm as fresh as I get these days. He clasps me back, and it's the embrace we didn't have at the airport. My mother was still between us then, at least for me.

"Let us go then, you and I."

Eliot is curious at my grammatical arrangement and I tell him a different Eliot wrote those lines at the beginning of a poem. He shakes his head in a gesture that is dismissive and amused.

"Poems," he says. He quotes me something in Spanish as he leads me to his truck but doesn't tell me what it's from. "It's beautiful," is all he says.

I think of those Spanish lines as he drives us from his place on the beach to various small communities up and down the coast; I don't understand this place, not yet, but there is a beauty to it. The buildings aren't as primitive as I'd imagined, not quite huts, but they're close. However small the settlement, there are people everywhere. They wear bright colours and baseball caps and they smile more than I thought they would. They know about the dangers that lie beneath the surface of the sea, and still they smile. Mermaids be damned.

After my mother's stroke they gave her an MRI scan and I expect the same sort of apparatus for a decompression chamber. The decompression chamber is actually quite large, though. At least, the one Eliot shows me is. The one I'm looking at in the clinic is only one of three in the entire region, despite the widespread problem. Hyperbaric oxygen therapy in a decompression chamber is the only way to treat the bends.

Eliot makes introductions as he and the doctor share a warm embrace and an exchange in Spanish. Dr. Kervin Mendoza and I simply shake hands. He holds my hand in his grip for a moment then he brings in the other and holds my one between his two. His hands are as warm as his smile. I hope Eliot hasn't built his hopes up about me.

"Do you know about decompression sickness?"

I do. I read about it on the plane coming over. Central Nervous System Decompression Disease, also decompression sickness, also the bends. But I want to hear it from this man, so I only say, "A little."

"When you go deep in the water for a long time, the pressure of the air you breathe increases and your body dissolves more nitrogen."

His English is excellent. I shouldn't be surprised—it's as widely spoken here as Spanish—but I am.

"The deeper or longer the dive, the more gas is absorbed into the tissue in higher concentrations than normal, and the faster the ascent, the less time between dives, the less time there is for this nitrogen to be offloaded safely, normally, through the lungs. When you come up quickly," he makes a quick upward motion with one hand, "the pressure drops rapidly and the dissolved nitrogen comes out of solution as bubbles. They expand and they clot the blood, which stops oxygen reaching the brain and spinal cord. The nerve cells in the brain and spinal cord."

"Like beer."

I think for a moment Eliot is making a poor joke, but Dr. Mendoza immediately agrees. "Yes, like a beer." He mimes opening one and makes a sharp "pssht" sound. "Fizzy blood. The bubbles stop oxygen reaching the cells that need it and they die. It damages the nervous system, like having a stroke."

Eliot exchanges a quick glance with me that is apologetic, but I had already made the comparison myself during my research. It's not a surprise.

"This chamber raises the pressure, the surrounding air pressure, so that the nitrogen bubbles dissolve back into solution. Then we lower the pressure, slowwwwwly," he flashes his teeth in a smile, "and the nitrogen returns to its normal state as if the diver has made a controlled and gradual ascent."

"So it saves lives," is my summary.

"Yes."

"And you only have three."

"Yes." That smile again, but sharper. "They are expensive."

Dr. Mendoza gestures for me to move into the next room. It's a small room, with a single small sofa. People can be in the chamber for hours and hours and relatives can wait here. The thread of the sofa has been pulled away by nervous fingers and stuffing presses to spit out but doesn't yet. None of us sit because it won't fit all three of us but the doctor says, "Please," so we do. Eliot and I lean forward, elbows on knees, feeling awkward sitting while Dr. Mendoza stands. It's a position that makes him seem enormous, probably a mighty reassuring force to those waiting to hear about loved ones, but with us he feels as awkward as we do so he scatters magazines and papers from a tiny table and sits on it like a stool.

"The people we see here have gone through a tremendous amount of pain," he says. Eliot nods beside me and I see he has put his hands together as if for prayer. I don't think he realizes he's done it. "They are often choking for air and can experience blindness, crippling back pain, as well as severe abdominal agony, all before they reach us. They lose the feeling in their legs and for many it will be permanent. They are paralyzed." He allows a second to pass and says that again. "Many are paralyzed. Many die. If they don't get here quickly. Even if they show no immediate symptoms, rapid pressure change can cause permanent bone injury; something called dysbaric osteonecrosis can develop from just a single exposure to rapid decompression.

"The only way to treat them, the *only* way, is in one of these chambers."

"They need more than their St. Andrews and St. Peters," says Eliot.

My job is to write about what's happening, raise awareness, maybe claw in some money for a new decompression chamber. If *Geographic* picks it up, maybe that will happen, but otherwise it's unlikely. I think both of them know this, they're just hoping the piece will move someone rich with as much heart as money. Maybe they even hope for another doctor or two. Hope, and pray.

"Is it true you have only three doctors here?" Too late I realize the question sounds like I doubt Eliot's email, but he doesn't seem offended.

"Oh, we have lots of doctors. Lots. We have herbalists and we have doctors."

"Witch doctors," Eliot explains.

I laugh, but he only smiles. "Are you joking?"

Dr. Mendoza looks to the floor.

Maybe I misheard and Eliot was asking, "which doctors?" but . . .

"We have four people with actual medical training and qualifications, including your friend." Dr. Kervin Mendoza points with both hands at Eliot. "The rest are local 'traditional' doctors."

Eliot continues. "To awaken the legs of a paralyzed diver they burn the spine. When it doesn't work it's because the water demon has already eaten the backbone, sucked out the spinal fluid like juice from a mango."

Dr. Mendoza spreads his hands and nods. "They have songs about it."

"What happens to these people?"

Eliot gets up, smoothes the wrinkles in his trouser legs. "Come. I will show you."

§

Gabriela is an African-Nicaraguan. Her skin is the same colour as the coffee she serves me, and her smile as bright as the sugar she adds to it. She smiles a lot, though I can only wonder what she has to smile about.

Eliot has driven us north to a sparsely populated area off the coast. Most of the people here descend from shipwrecked or escaped slaves and conditions haven't improved a great deal for them since. Houses are made of boards, three rooms held three feet off the ground on sturdy stilts. Many of the houses have swapped their front steps for ramps. I stopped counting the people in wheelchairs or on crutches when I got to thirty. Most of the wheelchairs were homemade affairs, little more than boards with wheels.

Gabriela is not in a wheelchair; she never dived, but her son does. He dives even though "the mermaids took his father." He risks a wheelchair, or worse, every time. Risks hearing the mermaids singing.

"I am better here, yes? On the land, my life is better."

After her husband's death, Gabriela, like so many women here, became the breadwinner of the family. For most women there is only one sure means of employment. That she considers prostitution better than diving for lobsters tells me how seriously the people here take the threat of water demons.

"Can you tell us about the fishing when you were young?" Eliot asks.

"I am still young," she says, and they laugh in such a way that I know it is a shared joke.

"When I was young," again she shares a smile with Eliot, "Americans came. They brought . . . mouth hoses—"

"Snorkels."

"Yes. Snorkels. And air you wear on your back. Like turtle. They wanted us to find spinys. There were lots of them then. You could see them at night." She holds her hands to her head and waggles the fingers like antennae.

"They glow," explains Eliot. "Phosphorescence."

"Spirit light," says Gabriela, and she chuckles. It's a thick deep sound in her throat, like the noise my mother made in her last days instead of coughing. I can't tell if Gabriela laughs because Eliot is foolish enough to think it natural, or because she mocks her own comment about spirit light.

"Now, no more lobster. The lobster were called deeper, so people go deeper."

She drinks all of her coffee down at once and I realize mine is cool enough to do the same. It feels strange, drinking it from a tin cup, but it tastes good.

"My husband, he dive. His boat the *Azul Celeste*. He make a lot of money."

She is clearly proud of her home. In my country we keep our bicycles and lawnmowers in better places. There is a photograph she shows me of her husband. It has been cut from a newspaper, a group of men standing around the biggest lobster I have ever seen. It's the size of a small dog. Its claws have been bound with what looks to be an entire roll of tape. Everyone is smiling and pointing. Behind them, rows of *cayucas* line the beach, waiting to go out again. Whatever story went with the picture has been cut away or folded behind the photograph.

"Richard Gere," she says, giving us that ambiguous throaty chuckle again, tapping one of the faces behind the glass. I doubt she knows who Richard Gere is, but I understand the sentiment and nod politely, either at her opinion or her joke.

"He look good to mermaid. One day . . ." Her eyes are wet, but she shrugs instead of crying.

"I'm sorry."

I remember how hollow those words had sounded when people said them to me, but we say them anyway, don't we? With my mother I wasn't even sure if the words were true, unless it was short for "I'm sorry it didn't happen sooner." For their own sakes as much as hers.

"He saw the mermaid," Gabriela says. "He tried to tell them, but she filled his mouth with water."

Eliot introduces me to dozens of people like Gabriela and all of them have similar stories. Some know the medical terms and conditions, but they offer them like alternatives to an already established fact: the mermaids came. I meet many widows and many men who have lost the use of limbs to paralysis. Some seem able-bodied and will not talk to me, but Eliot confides what he knows. "They say the demon came and took their seed. They are impotent." I see many men in wheelchairs, their homes still ridiculously perched on stilts, children dragging them backwards up the steps. Those not in chairs are on crutches. Eliot has made it his duty to visit daily, cleaning the ulcerous bedsores of one man in an attempt to stop the wounds festering in the tropical heat and turning sceptic. "There is no home care but me. A local doctor will spit in the sores and chant a backwards song, maybe throw fish bones."

As the day goes on, Eliot becomes angrier. I think before I came he stored it all, bottled his rage until, like nitrogen in the blood, it diffused back into calm. With me here it comes out too quick. I'm his chance to rant and he gives me words he wants rephrased for the article. He reels off statistics, high percentages living in poverty, the numbers of malnourished. Nicaragua is the second poorest country in the Americas. He takes hope from a growing improvement in people's literacy, but despairs at their tendency to cling to folklore and tradition. "We are nearly in a new century, the millennium, and still—" He gives up with an angry gesture.

Driving back to his own wooden hut, he takes us along coastal roads. His anger and the helplessness fall away with our speed, like he's racing away from it all, and he points out various places. When he parks on one of the elevated coastal roads he's something like the man I remember my mother meeting in Spain. He's the happy priest who taught me about the good in the world before he'd ever seen so much of the bad. "Look," he says, getting out of the truck.

The journey has shaken my bones, and the broken air conditioning has done little to cool the sweat on my skin, but up here there's a breeze to enjoy and even a tangy smell that is almost taste. I admire the view. Much of the Miskito coastline is a winding broken mass of lagoons and deltas. The ocean is a bright wild blue. It's beautiful. Here we look down on a magnificent curve of it.

"There are too many problems," he says. "There has been revolution, earthquakes, floods. There is unemployment, poverty, a lack of education. Don't write of those. Just write about the red gold. People will care about the animals and stop the diving, do you think? They will help the divers."

"Maybe."

We look at the sea rolling in, rolling out, itself a siren's call to those who need the things Eliot has told me they lack. Tourism is growing, but it's still nowhere near rivalling lobster fishing.

"People think different things about the name of this country, where it comes from." His hands are in his pockets. The sun is low but not yet setting and it casts little flashes of light from the crucifix he wears. I stand close to him and look out the same way, trying to see what he sees. "Some think it means 'surrounded by water', which is not good news if you believe in mermaids. The one I like best is that it means 'sweet sea.'"

I had heard the same thing. I think perhaps it was in the in-flight magazine, referring to the country's freshwater lakes.

"When you write what you write, remember it is beautiful here. Whatever you have to write, try to get some of that in, too."

§

Back at Eliot's, I still can't sleep. I stay up, sitting on the beach for a while. Sometimes I smoke. Sometimes I help myself to another drink from Eliot's fridge. My eyes feel like there's sand in them and I rub at them constantly. They're gritty, but not with sand. I want to close them, but they stay open. I try to yawn, but my body knows I'm faking. I try to remember my mother how she was before, but all I get is the sickness and bitchiness.

If I can't sleep, I can try to wake up; I go inside for a shower.

Eliot's bathroom is a freestanding tub with a sink beside the toilet. He has rigged a shower hose to the taps of the bath and a shower curtain hangs limp on a leaning rail. I strip out of my damp clothes, piling them on the toilet seat, and step into the tub. I turn the taps and step under the spray without waiting for it to warm up.

The first blast is a shock that makes me gasp and speeds my breathing but I soon get used to it. I turn the hot off completely but even with just the cold running I feel tired. The curtain keeps clinging to my right side and I feel colder down one half of my body. Eventually I stop peeling it away. I close my eyes and lean my head against the wall.

When I open them my mother is sitting in the tub with me. She has pushed herself into the far corner, naked flesh as pale as fish belly, and her hands are curled into claws that reach into the air.

I open my eyes again, properly this time, fully awake, and turn off the taps. I towel myself dry knowing I'll be sweating again in a few minutes.

I go back out to the beach.

§

When I go out to the lobster boats I don't use a canoe. I'm with Officer

Warner Lopez in a twenty foot launch. The sea is choppy and we bounce from peak to peak with no time for the troughs. It reminds me of yesterday's trip in Eliot's truck, but with the added splash of sea spray. I'm regretting the *gallo pinto* Eliot served for breakfast, *carne asada*, salad, and fried cheese churning in my stomach. I keep tasting the *plantains* that came after.

Eliot has not come with me and I feel relieved he has work to do. He's told me of some trouble he's been having with boat owners who don't like him educating the people around here about diving safety. I have no doubt that the situation is as terrible as he tells me, and although he helped the locals open up to me I feel better about him being elsewhere. Besides, I'm with an official who will be more persuasive than Eliot with these particular locals, albeit persuasive in a different way.

We rise up out of the water and for a moment we are airborne. We don't so much land as let the waves come up to meet us. Lopez is casual in his steering but clearly in a rush, kind enough to do a favour for Eliot but wanting it done quickly. His haste is evident in our speed, and the efficient way he handles the boat. When he speaks to me his sentences are clipped short, and his answers to questions are often a nod or shake of the head with one or two additional words if necessary. The lilt of his accent also makes his speech seem hurried, his English not quite as good as Dr. Mendoza's.

"This boat we're heading to," I call over the roar of the outboard, the thump of hull against water, "is it American?"

"Americans gone now."

"But they buy the lobsters?"

He nods once, then points.

There are many boats. The fleet expanded in the eighties and now the nineties sees a rapid expansion in lobster exports. The boats work the Caribbean and take their catch to processing plants at Puerto Cabezas, Bluefields and Laguna de Perlas. We're heading for a boat called *Rojo Tesoro*. It's a large, steel vessel the colour of dried blood. Closer, I realize this colour is rust. The entire body of the boat is a corroded flaking mess with only the faintest evidence of a blue colour beneath. The white lettering of its name is peeling where it isn't turning brown. Other vessels nearby are much the same.

"How do they stay afloat?"

Lopez doesn't have an answer for me. He cuts the engine and we come down hard on the surface of the sea, drifting to our destination. I can hear the calls of men working onboard. From another boat, one called *Roland B*, comes the sound of chanted song as men sort through their catch. Lively *Palo de Mayo* music fades in and out from a radio on another boat I can't see.

One of the men on the deck of the *Rojo Tesoro* raises his hands and says something in Spanish with mock fright. Don't shoot. The other men laugh and one or two imitate him.

Instead of humouring them, Lopez turns the launch broadside and tosses the man a rope. He catches it reluctantly and says something else, fast and angry, to which Lopez barks something back. The man begins wrapping the rope around a cleat.

"They do not want us onboard," Lopez says to me, giving me a first smile. I feel like someone he has arrested, that's the kind of smile it is. "It means I want to go onboard even more," he says.

"I thought all this had been arranged?"

Lopez shrugs. "I take you to a boat, *that* was arranged. Which boat, I have only just decided."

Great.

Lopez boards them first, quick and agile, and I clamber after him. There are about a dozen other men jostling for space here, stepping over plastic tubs of spiny lobster that fidget in their own forced crowd, or squeezing around stacked canoes and pallet racks of breathing apparatus. The masts and other beams are little more than scaffolding poles. They've been scraped of whatever colour they were once painted and are now metallic where they aren't washed orange, red, or brown with rust. The hand rail I clutch when the boat lurches actually crumbles against my palm and two of my fingers press a hole into the hollow metal. Ropes crisscross the air above my head and thrum in the breeze.

The men are mostly Mestizos, mixed Amerindian and white, though a couple are African-Nicaraguan, their hair fashioned into tight cornrows. They wear grubby white vests or torn t-shirts if they wear anything at all above their long shorts. About half of them wear baseball caps. Eliot has told me it's a popular sport here. Lopez stands out in his uniform. I expect I do, too, in my sweat and tourist clothes.

I guess that the man hurling words at Lopez is the captain. He's tightly muscled and square-toothed around the gaps and I'm reminded of the second most popular sport in this country: boxing. He gesticulates wildly around him, and prods Lopez's chest. I see Lopez's hand go calmly to his gun, probably a reflex that reassures him. It does little to reassure me.

"I just want to talk," I tell the man. It seems to get everyone's attention except his, so I say it again, adding, "Just talk."

The man throws his hands up to the sky and returns to hauling a rope up from the water. Lopez looks at me and turns his index finger around quickly like miming the rotor blades of a helicopter. I'm either free to talk to everybody or he wants me to wind things up quickly, or both.

I turn to the closest, a brown-toothed man with a moustache that grows sporadically despite the fullness of the beard around it, and ask him if he can tell me about the mermaids. He doesn't seem to understand what I'm saying.

"English?"

He nods, and he grins, and he looks around to see which of his friends sees him grinning. "English," he says.

"Tell me about the mermaids."

He nods, but doesn't add anything to it.

Lopez calls over in Spanish and the man nods again.

"*Si, si, sirena.* Be-autiful demons." He holds his hands out in front of his chest and laughs, and a couple nearby join him.

I offer him money, letting the others see. He becomes serious and takes it, but all he says is *sirena* again, this time refraining from the indication of breasts.

"That's Luis, he's an idiot, don't give him money."

The man who tells me this is sorting oxygen canisters. He's looking at me and smiling around a cigarette.

"Are you supposed to smoke around those things?" I point at the canisters behind him and at his feet.

The man shrugs and returns to his task. "I can tell you what you need to know, and then you can go," he says. The cigarette is bent and twisted in his mouth, bouncing as he speaks and dangling precariously at times from his bottom lip. The others have turned away, returning to their work, so maybe I was wrong about who's captain.

I duck under a rope and make my way across loose boards to where he tests each tank for air.

"That's a lot of oxygen."

"It's a lot of tanks. It's not a lot of oxygen. Fifteen minutes each, maybe thirty."

I look around for the rest of the equipment and he glances at me looking for it. He smiles to himself but offers nothing else.

"Where are the masks?"

He points briefly and I see a bundle of them in a plastic barrel. A wooden crate, the sort used for fruit or vegetables, sits beside it filled with the black tubes of breathing apparatus. They look like rigid snakes. Some are lined with tape like you'd get in a puncture repair kit for your bicycle.

"How do you catch them? The lobsters."

He mimes a spear thrust, then confirms it. "Spears. Back there." He only indicates where with a turn of his head. "Do you want to try?"

I'm surprised by the offer but not by the mocking tone.

"Yeah."

He becomes as serious as Luis did when I gave him money.

"Yeah," I say again. "Why not?"

Lopez comes over when he sees me shrugging on one of the canisters.

"You done this before? You have certificates?"

"Do they?"

He shakes his head, points to the box of coiled tubing.

"These are not good." Something catches his eye and he pulls it up from the tangle of pipes. "Look."

He is showing me the mouthpiece of a regulator which is secured only by a piece of tightly knotted string.

"We do not use that one," says the man helping me, but his voice has that same mocking tone that suggests of course they do.

Lopez picks up on that too. He starts yelling in Spanish and the man who'd prodded him earlier hurries over. While he's making his way to us, Lopez turns back to me. "Wait."

I nod, but I kick off my shoes and stuff the sweaty socks inside. In shorts and t-shirt I'm wearing exactly what the locals wear when they dive.

"He worries you will meet the mermaid and he will be in trouble." The man takes what remains of his cigarette from his mouth and offers it to me. I decline. As much as I'd like one, I'll wait. He spits into my facemask, rubs the saliva around.

"Who's that man?"

I'm talking about the man currently exchanging fast words with Lopez.

"That man is Pablo. This is his boat."

"He's the captain?"

The man shrugs. "It is his boat," he says, and I come to understand a little bit about how it works here.

"And you?"

"I am Carlos."

The other men are still working, but they watch us. They're done with diving for the day and the mermaids have let them be, but now it is late and there are fewer divers and maybe the mermaids will notice a foreigner like me.

I check my pockets. I've already crammed what there was into my shoes, but I check again anyway as Lopez and the man exchange more than words. It's not the blows I had feared were coming but money, Lopez taking a fistful of notes from the man. Afterwards, the boat owner, Pablo, makes the same hands-to-the-sky gesture he'd made earlier and backs away to the stern.

Lopez pockets the notes looking at me and says, "This is cheap equipment. You have no watch, no pressure gauge, no depth gauge. When you run out of air it will be sudden and surprising."

Isn't it that way for everyone?

I don't say that. I give his comments due seriousness and finally nod. "I'm buying a car without brakes." They're words from Eliot's email, the one that brought me here. The problem, to continue the analogy, is that the people in these small communities that depend on lobsters don't even know a car should *have* brakes. They dive with shitty equipment and not enough equipment and of course the boat owners don't tell them. It's cheaper for them to buy bare regulators without all the other gear. It's a violation of human rights that allows Caribbean spiny lobsters to compete with the more expensive American type, divers paying the price so the big companies don't have to.

"Alright," Lopez says. "So you know. You can go."

Carlos is barefoot and bare-chested, a tank on his back. He takes a last puff on his cigarette and tosses it overboard. Then he escorts me to where a section of railing is missing.

I realize then that we should have done all this in one of the canoes, closer to the surface of the sea. That would be the usual way. Instead, I have been tricked into proving myself to a crew of poorly educated, poorly prepared, divers.

Carlos presses his facemask hard against his face, says, "Like this," and pushes the respirator into his mouth, holding it firm. Then he steps from the boat and plunges into the sea. One moment he is there, the next he is nothing but bubbles and a dark shape, going down.

With one hand on my mask, the other holding the mouthpiece hard against my teeth, I jump down after him with little thought but for what I might find there.

§

When my mother got sick, it wasn't sudden. She had the usual warnings from doctors first, not to mention the advertising campaigns, and then not one or even two but three strokes. The first two were little ones, but enough to scare her, and me. The third one was enough to slacken one side of her face for a little while. She stopped smoking after each one, but obviously they didn't frighten her as much as they frightened me because soon enough she'd be sparking up again. In fact, she went from filtered to loose tobacco, rolling her own because it was cheaper. Maybe she was in some sort of rush to die; smokers triple their chance of a stroke.

I was working for a paper at the time, but managing to sell occasional features freelance to magazines. I didn't win any awards or anything, but people read them and noticed things for a while; I made a little difference. Sweatshops in India; a stretch of road in Australia that was particularly dangerous for backpackers; a piece on the use of fossil fuel in China. My point is, I wasn't always around. After my mother's first stroke, I took time off to stay with her. She didn't particularly need me, but I thought she might want me there. That was when I met Eliot. I was suspicious at first, of course, the first man not my father (especially as he looked so much the stereotype) but it turned out he really was a priest and, what's more, really did love my mother.

After the second stroke, I visited but I didn't stick around. She had Eliot, and I had my work. I was also working on sorting my own love life at the time, but that didn't turn into anything. On top of everything else it was just too much pressure.

Things between Eliot and my mother didn't work out either. His religion meant it was never going to be anything more than good friendship anyway, but they both felt the loss of it. He's a good man, a kind man, but eventually she managed to drive him away. It wasn't the self-pity and bitterness she cocooned herself in that he couldn't endure, it was that she did it because she didn't want him around. I promised him I would take good care of her. I moved closer. I promised to visit more often. I promised I'd keep her off the damn cigarettes. I promised a lot of things, both to Eliot and to myself, even to God.

My mother died. A stroke is caused by an interruption of blood to the brain and it causes a sudden loss of brain function. Smoking narrows the arteries and it makes blood more likely to clot. My mother's stroke was an ischemic stroke, which means it was caused by a blood clot. The same stroke that put her under water to drown in the bath one day also caused her to pull the plug from the drain by a wild kick to its chain. By the time the water had drained away, she was gone.

So, my mother died and I took up smoking. I took up drinking for a little while but wasn't very good at it.

Everything else I quit.

The water is only cold for a moment, but I barely notice. I hold on frantically to my mask and mouthpiece as I plummet through the rush of bubbles I've made. My t-shirt rides up my chest but I leave it, too busy holding on to my means of breathing. I've closed my eyes instinctively, despite the mask. It will not help in my search for a pair of ragged claws scuttling across the floors of silent seas. But the sea is not silent, not like in the poem. I can hear the pulse of boat engines, dull and heavy in the water. They beat with the same regularity of an MRI scan. Everything seems louder, like when you dunk under in the bath and let your ears fill. I can hear . . .

I open my eyes.

The sea is incredibly clear. Carlos is swimming below me, waiting for me to pull myself together. I keep one hand spread across my mask and regulator but with the other I put my forefinger to thumb and raise the other fingers in an okay. He returns it. Then he turns about on himself and dives.

I take my hand from my facemask slowly. Everything seems to be all right. Behind me, above me, the rusting hulk of the boat is a dark metal whale tethered to the ocean floor by a length of oxidized chain. If I stick close I won't lose my bearings.

Below me, Carlos is little more than a pair of red shorts and kicking legs. The soles of his feet are much lighter than his skin. I follow them down.

We must be thirty metres or so down when he starts turning rocks, sending up swirls of sand in his search for red gold. I realize we don't have the spears, but then I don't think Carlos had really expected me to go through with the dive. I swim close behind, watching him.

Eventually, Carlos turns and beckons me before jabbing his finger spear-like at the seabed below him. He points to a creature more mottled brown than red and when he flips it over I see a hardened underbelly as pale as corpse skin. Its tail beats a Morse code of distress at the ground, raising clouds of dirt around it as spiny front limbs grasp at nothing but water. Antennae waver and legs kick and again Carlos stabs in its direction with a pointing finger, eager for me to make a catch. I scissor my legs once, twice, and I'm there, reaching for the lobster before it can right itself, grabbing it around the body with unprotected hands.

Its legs wrap around my wrist and forearm. The forked tail that had been beating at the sea floor now pounds against the inside of my arm. I'm thinking of the facehugger creature from the *Alien* films as it clings to me, sharp points scratching my skin in panic or anger, and I shake my arm, shake it, *shake it*, trying to get the damn thing off. Its long front spiny claws slice the water around it blindly, conducting crazed music I can't hear, and I'm afraid to bring my other hand in to pull the creature off. I swim back to where the *Rojo Tesoro* chain rises from its anchor. The lobster is wrapped around my forearm. I'm sucking anxious breaths now through my regulator. I move my legs in quick nervous kicks and at the chain I scrape the lobster against the rusting metal. Flakes fall like scabs, but so does the lobster. It twists as it descends, landing feet first, and immediately scuttles to the safety offered by a split volcanic rock.

A sea-salt sting of fire and I notice the lobster's tail or maybe one of its legs has drawn a long line of blood from my forearm. It disperses into the water like thin red ink.

Carlos dives to where the lobster has disappeared and reaches in blindly, either brave or foolish. He pulls it from hiding by its tail and, taking up another rock from the seabed, bashes it once, twice. Broken, limp, he brings it up to me. He is smiling. I can tell from the way his mask is lifted on his cheeks, the delight in his eyes. If it wasn't for his mouthpiece, he'd be laughing. I'm suddenly thankful we don't have spears, not when there's a policeman up on the boat.

The Nicaraguan points up, directing me to make my ascent, then frog-legs his way to where his friends wait, no doubt eager to tell them of the tourist's fright.

If it's meant to goad me into following, it doesn't work. I don't have the same complacent disregard for decompression sickness, or the ignorance of it. I'll be heading up at the recommended rate of ten metres per minute. My story will not need a firsthand account of mermaid song.

A glance at my wrist reminds me I have no watch. It's tucked in my sock in my shoe on the deck. It's waterproof, so I don't know why I took it off. Without it, I count down from sixty, spiralling my way up and thinking of how safe the lobster must have felt for a brief moment, hidden away from the world.

It falls past me. The armour of its head has been caved in and its spread legs are limp in the current it makes going down. It lands in a cloud of silt and suddenly the water around me is very cold.

Above me Carlos is wide-eyed, fighting with something I can't see. He wraps himself around nothing but water, clutching his stomach. He strains his neck and spits his mouthpiece out in a rush of bubbles.

I can swim to him if I make a rapid ascent myself, but before I can even decide I feel my own limbs freeze. Dr. Mendoza said nothing of temperature change. Nor the sensation of being held. Yet I feel something, someone, wrap cold limbs around my own, someone who is a wet net of long hair and clammy skin and sagging breasts and my inhalations carry the taste of smoke. Like a cigarette burns somewhere in my oxygen tank or mouth hose.

The sensation is easy to give in to. I curl around myself, taking a position I knew for the first nine months of my life.

Above me, a bubbled cry from Carlos reminds me of his pain. I look to see him still struggling and suddenly it's easy to pull away from whatever holds me.

I swim to him, grab him, and bring him up out of the water.

As soon as I surface there are shouts and overlapped voices of alarm from the crew of the *Rojo Tesoro*. Everyone is leaning over the side, and four men have their arms outstretched, reaching for Carlos. I strip him of his mask and tank, letting it sink, as two, three men jump into the water. I sweep the mask off my own face and knock aside the mouthpiece. Between the group of us in the water we manage to raise him enough that the others can get a hold. Two men have one of his arms, another has his other arm by the wrist, and someone unseen on the deck is hauling him up the side of the boat by a rope.

Carlos is screaming. When they heave him over the gunwales his legs swing limply up and over. I hear them thud to the deck even from where I tread water, even over the urgent cries of the men and Carlos's pain. Or at least I think I do. I imagine I do.

A rope ladder clings to the rusting hulk of the boat like strange symmetrical seaweed, green and forever wet from always being down. I pull my way up, which is no easy task with the oxygen canister on my back. The adrenaline spurs me onward and upward.

"Lopez!"

I can't see him. I shrug out of the straps and the regulator whips up against my face as it all drops. The men surround Carlos, each of his limbs in several hands. He's being carried from one side of the boat to the other like a soaked sack of grain.

The motor launch roars to loud life and Lopez beckons me to hurry.

One of the men grabs me before I can pass.

"*Sirena! Sirena!*" he says. "Did you see it? Mer-maid?"

Carlos is dropped into Lopez's boat and he doubles up with a mournful sound of anguish, knees to his chest, arms around his abdomen.

The man who has my arm holds me with a lobster grip – he's seen part of an answer in my face – but I manage to shake him off.

Lopez leans on the throttle and the lurch sends me sprawling beside Carlos. He is arching his back, turning on his side, curling up, trying to get a position where the pain can't find him.

"Now you can write your story," says Lopez over the roar. He means no insult by it.

I have no reply other than to ask where we're going. Lopez tells me the same clinic I visited yesterday and then neither of us say anything more. He keeps us running with the waves, cutting a desperate channel towards land. We leave the *Rojo Tesoro* behind but bring a mermaid with us, buried in the flesh of Carlos. It twists him into various agonies the entire way.

From surfacing to clinic takes little more than two hours. There is a good chance Carlos will be all right.

I'm put in the chamber with him. I'm okay, but I surfaced quickly too. Even trained navy divers who ascend properly go through decompression every year, just in case. Besides, the damage isn't always visible.

Carlos is in a great deal of pain for much of the process, but it subsides. Eventually he speaks to me. He tells me he saw her.

"She told me it was goodbye. But it was not goodbye."

He has a thank you in his eyes but seems without the English to express it. What he says is, "And you did not say goodbye."

He refers, no doubt, to my presence in the chamber with him, or maybe he saw something of my own struggle, but he thinks only of mermaids. I nod, for he would not understand my disagreement.

The answer seems to please him and I'm thankful when he turns away. The ocean I'm filled with leaks from me in quiet tears. My whole body feels gritty with dried sea water. I rub it all away with my palms, shedding salt like a skin I no longer need, and settle back against the curvature of the chamber wall and finally manage to sleep.

§

Back at Eliot's, I watch the white lines of the sea push up to the sand, and then push up to the sand. I don't see the waves retreat. Sitting in one of his creaky old chairs, I smoke the last of my cigarettes. The last of the packet, and the last I will ever taste. It's a promise I feel able to keep.

"Lopez took money from Pablo." Eliot glances at me and I explain, "The owner of the *Rojo Tesoro*."

He nods and passes me a drink, sitting down beside me. "He gives the money to me."

"What's it for?"

Eliot takes a deep gulp from his drink. He looks exhausted and I realize I haven't been the only one feeling tired.

"They have a demon for everything in this country. For mental illness, for bad weather, for poor harvest." He makes a gesture to indicate there are many others. "The problems are real ones. *La Llorona* of legend weeps for her drowned son, but so do many real women. The demons are real but they are unemployment, poor medical care, lack of education." He makes that same gesture; there are many others. "People give Lopez money to not do things. Lopez gives *me* money to do what I can. To get rid of these demons."

"Then Lopez is a good man."

"He is." Eliot makes the sign of the cross in the air before him with his beer bottle. "I thank God for him."

It's not enough for me, so Eliot gives me more.

"When Lopez was a boy, his father went out to dive and didn't come back. At first, people said he finished work as normal. Then they said he did not show up and must have run away and left his family. One day, a man explained what really happened. The water demon. They didn't take Warner's father to a clinic because there weren't any and they didn't take him to a hospital because they couldn't spare anyone; they were all diving. They held him on board and later, when the others were gone, cast him back into the sea. The man was quadriplegic by then."

Eliot doesn't look at me. My reaction is obvious enough without seeing it. After a few moments, I ask, "Is his picture in there?"

Eliot nods. "Kervin Mendoza's father, too."

"How you can live surrounded by all of them?"

"I'd see them anyway, even if they weren't there. Hear them, too. But I can go on when they can't. They make me go on."

And I realize, he hasn't brought me out here to write a story. Or he has, but it's not only that. He's brought me here to show me those walls, to introduce me to others who have suffered, and lost, and who get on afterwards.

He confirms it.

"When I met your mother she was an angry woman because your father left, but she was a funny woman too. It was like losing her husband made her more determined to be happy. This is like that, in a way."

I nod politely, but I can only remember—

"When she became bitter," Eliot continues, voicing my thoughts, "it was to push people away. I didn't realize at first, and then I did and it hurt. But she did it because she didn't want to pull people down with her. Like a ship, when it sinks, pulls down the survivors if they don't swim far enough away."

He looks at me, and it's that look I don't like but do at the same time. "You didn't swim far enough afterwards, and you still haven't. Not quite."

If I hadn't already realized this in the decompression chamber, I'd be doing it now. Eliot has waited for me to do it slowly, taking away the last of the pressure by telling me how I feel, albeit more eloquently than I ever could.

I smile, a genuine smile, a grateful smile, and despite my time in the clinic there are still a couple of tears left.

"Ah," he says. "There."

I laugh, wiping them away, and we look out at the sea together.

Moving forwards, moving forwards, up the sand.

"That poem you like, how does it end?"

He knows how it ends. He's looked it up by now, that's why he asks. But I answer him anyway.

"'We have lingered in the chambers of the sea, by sea-girls wreathed with seaweed red and brown, till human voices wake us, and we drown.'"

Eliot shakes his head. "It does not need the last three words. The last three words are wrong."

I laugh at his correcting a Nobel prize-winning poet, but I agree. I know what drowning feels like. It doesn't need water. And human voices, if they say the right things, can save you.

"Eliot, do you have a pen I can borrow?"

I can feel him smiling in the dark, and we watch the sea caress the sand.

"That man in the poem, Mr. Prufrock, he was a coward, wasn't he?" Eliot says.

My answer to his question is the same as his answer to mine.

THE FESTERING

Ever since she was a little girl, Ruby had whispered her secrets into the top drawer of her desk. It had been a present from her dad, somewhere for her to make things because that was what she liked doing. He'd taught her how to make papier-mâché masks. They were easy to make. You mixed flour and water and dipped strips of newspaper in and then stuck them on a balloon and when it dried—pop!—you had a curved solid shell for a mask. Cut it to shape, add more papier-mâché lumps and bumps for facial features, maybe cut eyeholes, and then decorate it with paints, glitter, stickers, whatever. She had lots of craft stuff. There was a cupboard under the desk next to where her legs went where she kept old newspapers and phone directories, and there were three normal drawers on the other side for her pens and scissors and everything else, but best of all there was the secret drawer that pulled out from underneath the desktop. That was what her dad called it, the secret drawer, so that was what she used it for.

Now in her early teens, Ruby still used it for her secrets. Sitting at the desk, head bowed, it was easy to pull out the drawer and quietly drop her words into it. And as she spoke, the thing inside it grew. Not much, but enough that she noticed.

She noticed it more and more these days because it was getting too big for the drawer.

Mum had made her a sandwich to take to school. The crusts were still in good shape, probably because the bread was getting old, but the middle had been squashed by attempts to cling-film it and jam pressed against the wrapping in wet smears. It did not look appetizing. She'd throw it away at school. Mum would never know.

"I'm off," Ruby said.

A sound came from the bedroom that might have been goodbye.

"Maybe you could go get a job or something," Ruby added quietly. She was less careful with the door, slamming it shut behind her.

The corridor was stale with the smells of old dinners cooked by people in the other flats, and there was no natural light until you got to the stairwell, just the dingy dry flicker-light from dusty fluorescent bulbs. One of the doors, number fourteen, had a grubby area around the handle as if the occupant never used it, only pushed the door with dirty hands. Ruby didn't know who lived there. She didn't know any of them really, except for Mr. Browning at number twelve. She'd *seen* the others, though. Most of them looked like weirdoes and she wondered if she lived in a place that housed mental people who weren't mental enough for hospital, or rehabilitated criminals or something.

There was a line of post-boxes by the front door and Mr. Browning was checking his. He sang to her his usual hello, "Ruby Ruby Ruby *Ruby*," as if knowing the song proved he was still young, though he must've been thirty-something. Ruby didn't like the Kaiser Chiefs but she never said so. She smiled, because Mr. Browning was all right. She knew him pretty well because he looked after her when her mum went out. Mum still called it babysitting.

"Morning Mr. Browning."

"Phil."

"Yeah, Phil. Sorry."

It was a recent thing, this change from Mr. Browning to Phil. Ruby liked it. It made her feel older.

"Off for another great day at school?"

Mr. Browning—Phil—was a teacher. At a different school, thank God. That would have been well embarrassing.

"Yeah. They'll fill my brain with knowledge and I'll have to wipe over it later with YouTube and *Hollyoaks*."

He laughed. "Couple more years and it will all be over."

"Can't wait."

He opened the door for her. "Bingo night tonight," he said.

"Yep."

He smiled at her in a way that made her want to go back upstairs and whisper to her drawer.

"Did you eat your sandwich?"

"Yeah. Thanks, Mum."

"What was in it?"

"Jam."

She often tested Ruby like this, which meant she knew the sandwiches were crap. She released twin streams of smoke from her nostrils. "And?"

Ruby had opened the sandwiches and peered between the bread to check before throwing them away, just in case. "And nothing," she said. "Flora." Satisfied, Mum said, "Chip butties tonight."

"Chip shop or oven?"

"Oven, Rubes. I ain't made of money."

Ruby nodded. There was a new bottle of Tesco's own in the fridge, though, and always plenty of fags. She poured herself a squash, diluting it to little more than coloured water because Mum was watching.

"Got homework?"

"I've always got homework."

"Hard life, being at school."

Ruby drank her squash quickly, ready to retreat to her room.

"I'm out tonight," Mum said.

"I know."

"Mr. Browning will look after you."

"I know."

"Knows everything, don'tchya."

Ruby wiped her mouth instead of answering. "I'm going to do my homework."

"*Glass.*"

Ruby rinsed the glass even though a load of dirty dishes were still stacked beside the sink. Then she went to her room, closing the door behind her.

She loved her room. All right, it was small, and there was a damp patch that returned whenever she scrubbed it away, but it was hers and all her stuff was there. Her wall of masks, her bed, her desk.

She opened the secret drawer and whispered, "I hate her."

The thing in the drawer pulsed. Red and gelatinous, it was a parcel of flesh in spasm. A fresh wetness glistened on its skin. Tiny bubbles rose like spit from open slits. It was changing. Growing. Strings like dried glue criss-crossed the meaty shape, thick mucousy strands that allowed it to expand but kept it secure in the drawer's corner. Ruby had never touched it, not ever, but she knew somehow that it would be cold and slick like uncooked liver or how she imagined shark skin. She did know it was soft and pulpy, like chewed food, because she'd pushed a pencil into it once. The pencil had sagged afterwards, sodden and greyed at one end, rotting, so she threw it away.

"I chucked her sandwiches," she told the drawer, changing out of her school uniform, "and I cheated in maths today. I hate maths. I told Becky I still liked Steve but I don't."

That was all for now. She was bound to have more to tell it later.

Мr. Browning said it like he believed her, though they all knew Ruby's mother wouldn't come home until after the pubs kicked out.

"I'll be back by ten, half-ten."

"That's fine."

"Right. Well, wish me luck."

"Luck," said Mr Browning.

"Break a leg," said Ruby.

Her mother chose to ignore the tone that came with that, but pulled at the hem of her embarrassingly short skirt. "I got two of them," she said, looking down and then looking up to check Mr. Browning had noticed. "Legs eleven." She even turned one foot as if modelling new shoes, even though the strappy sandals had seen better days and even then they were fucking horrible.

"All right," she said, when no other comments came. "See you soon." She hugged Ruby, swallowing her into a bosom that strained the buttons she'd bothered to do up. She made as if to hug Mr. Browning too, then laughed. He laughed with her as if the almost "accident" hadn't been a joke many times before.

"Bye then," she said, staggering a little as she went. She blamed her heels with another laugh, though it had been obvious from the smell of her breath that there was more to it than that.

"Quite a character," said Mr. Browning when she was gone.

"That's a polite way of putting it."

This time his laugh was more genuine. He stepped back from the door to let her inside.

They always watched films. Usually horrors or thrillers, some sort of 18 certificate anyway, and Ruby got a thrill out of how it would horrify her mother to know. It was her way of rebelling against having a babysitter. Mr. Browning—Phil—had lots of films.

"Have you seen this one?"

The cover was all reds and blacks with writing that dripped.

"Have we watched it here?"

"I don't think so."

"Then no. The only DVDs we have is a complete set of James Bond Mum won at Bingo."

She didn't like to say Mum in front of Mr. Browning. It made her sound like a kid. Plus it highlighted the fact that they were related.

"The name's Bond . . ." Phil said, but he didn't finish it.

Ruby opened the popcorn and tipped it into a bowl as he put the film in. She offered him some as he settled beside her on the sofa but he waved it away. He always did. He probably knew she didn't get treats like this at home. There was a bottle of Coke, too. The real thing.

"Here we go."

The film seemed to be about a woman killing off her lovers using some kind of magic so that they exploded into a fine mist of blood which she sucked right out of the air. Ruby had a hard time following the plot because she and Mr. Browning always talked through the first film. He asked her about school and her friends and life in general. It was good, even though she didn't have much to say.

"Oops," he said. "Forgot about this bit."

The woman on screen was having sex. Lots of sex. They'd watched similar scenes before but this one was rather more graphic. And drawn out.

Ruby laughed.

"I'd fast forward it, but I think that'll make it worse."

Ruby laughed some more, then sat through an awkward quiet as they waited for the scene to finish. She picked popcorn from her braces.

"My mum fancies you, you know," she said.

Mr. Browning said nothing. Just watched the woman panting on screen. If he was uncomfortable, the only way he showed it was through his silence.

"She wants to win big at Bingo so she can get her hair done and pay you for babysitting and buy you a drink."

"Did she say that?"

"Sometimes."

"When she's drunk."

Ruby looked at him, surprised but not shocked by his honesty. "Yeah."

"Does that bother you?"

"Not any more. I'm used to her drinking. It's pretty harmless."

"No, I meant the other thing."

Ruby watched him carefully, wondering how to answer.

"She's a bit old for me," Mr. Browning explained.

Ruby still only watched him, saying nothing. It made the woman on the screen seem louder as she built to her inevitably bloody climax.

Finally, Mr. Browni—Phil—took the bowl of popcorn from her lap and leaned in close and at last they did what Ruby had been waiting for since, like, ages ago.

Ruby whispered into her drawer, "It was quick at first but then he went for ages and it was much better than with Steve."

The thing in the drawer knew all about Steve and how Ruby lost her virginity, just as it knew how disappointing the second and third time had been, though she'd told her friends and Steve that it was great. Now it throbbed with new secrets. The thin crimson skin pulsated, inflated, and it settled into a new size. It was darker in the middle, brown like rotten fruit, almost black. As she spoke, one tapered end of it spewed a string of fluid that curled upon itself in jellified coils that quickly solidified, cementing it more securely to the bottom on the drawer.

Mum was banging cupboards and drawers in the kitchen. She was looking for a bottle of wine she was sure she had, or trying to find the corkscrew, or something. Ruby still whispered, just in case, and tore newspaper pages into strips to hide any noise, smiling as she told the drawer *everything* she'd done that evening.

She'd made quite a nest of paper by the time she was finished.

"We better get dressed," Mr. Browning said. "Your mum will be here soon."

They lay in his bed this time. Ruby was still tingling, still glowing with the rosy warmth of what had just happened. She felt bigger.

"She's only thirty," Ruby said.

"What? Who is?"

Ruby turned to face him. He was looking at her, which was good. "You said she was too old for you. She's only thirty."

"*Really*?"

He was so shocked that she laughed.

"Doesn't look it, does she?"

"No, I mean, it's, yes, but . . . well, just . . ."

Ruby laughed again.

"She must have had you young."

"*Very* young. But that's not it—you think she looks *older*."

Ruby watched him think about whether to admit it or not. She smiled. He had a good looking face, especially for a grown-up, but his thoughts were always so obvious.

"It's okay, she does. She's got those awful roots and her hair's always frizzy anyway because she doesn't take care of it."

Ruby swept her own hair back as if it was in the way.

"And she's put on weight because of the drinking."

"Can we not talk about her please?"

Ruby zipped her smiling lips and leant in to kiss him. At first he pulled away but then he was kissing her and touching her and everything else, even though they'd just agreed to get dressed.

Before Ruby could get to the bit she liked best, just as she was finding it difficult to breathe in that way she liked, Mr. Browning began rushing. Ruby tried to catch up but he muffled his cry against her chest. Then he was getting up and stepping into his trousers.

"Come on, Ruby."

"What did I do?"

"Your mum will be here soon." He looked so serious that she said nothing, just did as she was told.

They sat on the sofa and watched another film, waiting. Ruby knew she was sulking but she couldn't help it, and Mr. Browning seemed lost in thoughts of his own.

When the door finally went, it was almost twelve. The film was nearly finished.

"We could have had ages longer," Ruby said. It was the first thing she'd said since they'd put the film on.

"I didn't know she'd be late."

She went with him to the door.

"Was she good?" her mum asked. She was holding the doorframe for support but still leaning.

"She was great."

"You have a good time sweetheart? What films did you watch?"

"We didn't finish," Ruby said.

"Well, maybe next time."

"Where have you been?"

"Sorry." The apology was aimed at Mr. Browning. "There was a *bit* of a do afterwards. Rude not to stay for a couple."

"It's okay."

"I'm a bit *pissed*, to be honest."

"*Mum . . .*"

"It's okay," Mr. Browning said again.

Ruby tried to steer her mother the few metres home.

"Steady on, darlin, there's no rush." Her mum staggered and had to put a hand against the wall to stop from falling. "I'm a *little bit* pissed," she said. "Who's going to tuck me in?"

"Come *on*, Mum, you're embarrassing me."

"Oh, *am* I? I'm *embarrassing* you? Don't talk to me like that in front of Mr. Browning."

Ruby didn't want to look at him. She fumbled her key at the lock as if she was the one who'd had a few drinks.

"Kids, eh? Bet you don't have any like Ruby at *your* school."

"Not really."

"Bet they're all respec . . . respecerful of their elders."

Hard to respect a woman who can't even say it, Ruby thought. She managed to get the door open and guided her mother inside. She turned to face Mr. Browning, to smile an apology or thanks or goodnight or something, but he looked kind of sad. It made it hard for her to shut the door on him.

"What the hell are you *playin* at? Answering back like that. You'll scare him off—"

Ruby went to her room.

"—just like all the others. You always fuck things up, Rubes."

It was something Ruby had heard before. She was just going through the motions. Like pouring a pint of water she wouldn't drink, or tying her hair back for when she puked her guts up.

Ruby shut her door on it all, sat at her desk, and opened the secret drawer. She was still warm between her legs, wet with what Mr. Browning had given her. Twice. She put her hand there and enjoyed how it felt on her fingers. "He said I was great," she whispered, and used the slick of his mess to finish what he'd started. She tried to find a mask on the wall to represent him but they were all too feminine or frightening so she closed her eyes. She tried to be quiet, even though the sounds she made were swallowed up by the open drawer, and as she finished she bowed her head to where she kept her secrets and spoke his name. She remembered to call him Phil.

From the bathroom down the hall came the sound of her mother throwing up.

<hr>

"The first time was really good," Ruby told the drawer afterwards, "but the second time he didn't wait for me."

She was making another mask. She grabbed another handful of shredded newspaper and wiped her sticky fingers with it until her hands were black with smeared newsprint. She slathered the soggy strips over the balloon.

"I think he liked it, though. He must have, because there's so much . . . *stuff*."

She wiped the last of it from her hands, squeezing newspaper into sodden shapes before flattening them over the balloon.

"Seriously, there's *loads*."

She wiped between her legs with more handfuls of paper and spread the moist mess across the balloon, smiling as it took shape.

"I left him my underwear," she said.

"I think I love him," she said.

<hr>

Mr. Browning greeted them at the door in tracksuit bottoms and a t-shirt. Ruby tried to hide her disappointment, especially as she'd made a special effort. Not that he'd paid her any attention yet, thanks to Mum.

"Yeah, well, I don't really do tutoring."

"It's just her first exams are next year and she's already struggling—"

"*Mum . . .*"

"—and maybe you could help her? I'll pay you."

"It's not that, it's—"

"I got a new cleaning job. Only once a week, but it's a bit of cash no one needs to know about."

"Mum, he said he doesn't do tutoring."

"Just a bit of English? Maybe some maths?"

"I teach drama."

"Oh. Is there an *exam* in that?"

"I'll ask around," Mr. Browning said. "About a tutor."

"Thanks. I'd be very grateful."

It was obvious how grateful she'd be because of the way she smiled. Ruby made no attempt to disguise her sigh and pushed passed them to wait in the front room.

She sprawled on the sofa. The popcorn was already in a bowl on the table. She put it in her lap and tried throwing pieces into her mouth as she waited. She stopped when she heard the front door close and sat up straight because it pulled her blouse tight.

When Mr. Browning returned, he barely looked at her. He had her underwear bunched in his hand.

"You left these," he said.

Ruby smiled. "You can keep them."

"You can't just leave these around my flat," he said. He sat at the end of the sofa and put her knickers and bra on the table.

"Why not?" And before he could give an answer she might not like, "Don't you like them?"

They weren't anything special. Pretty, flowery, but a bit girly and faded now from too many washes.

"That's not the point, Ruby. We can't—"

"What about these? Do you like these?"

She unfastened some buttons. At first he turned away, "Ruby . . ." but he turned back as she spread the blouse open to show him the new bra she'd shoplifted at the weekend.

Mr. Browning cleared his throat. "And under the skirt?"

She showed him.

"Ruby, Ruby, Ruby . . ."

He was moving closer now. When the popcorn toppled from her lap they were both too busy to stop it, or even notice.

"Oh God."

"Yeah," Ruby said.

"No, did you hear something?"

There was a knocking at the door, loud in the way that said someone had tried once already, and then her mother's voice, "Phil?"

Ruby said, "Oh fuck," because it felt grown up. Mr. Browning called, "Coming!" and Ruby laughed because that was hilarious, even if he didn't mean it yet. A moment later he was up, pulling on his tracksuit bottoms and putting his t-shirt back on as he went to the door. Nothing with buttons or zips, Ruby realized.

She pulled her new knickers back on quickly and buttoned her blouse. She grabbed the remote control from the floor and pressed play on whatever film was in, forwarding it a couple of scenes.

Her mother yelled, "Full house!" as soon as the door was opened.

"Excuse me?"

"I won! Two hundred and thirty pounds!"

"That's great, Mrs. Haze, well done."

"So I thought I'd come back early and we could celebrate or something. Maybe we could—"

"Ruby! Your mum's here!"

Ruby was picking up the popcorn, sweeping handfuls back into the bowl, picking individual pieces from the carpet.

"Hey, Rubes, guess who—what the hell?"

Ruby only glanced at her. "It was an accident," she said. "I'm clearing it up, Mum, look." She held up a piece of popcorn and placed it in the bowl with exaggerated deliberateness before realizing her mum was not looking at the mess on the floor. She was looking at the table. She was looking at Ruby's knickers and Ruby's bra on the table.

"What the fucking *hell*?"

"What? They're not *mine*." It was a terrible lie, her mum had seen them tons of times, washed them, hung them on the radiators. "They're *not*!"

"Whose are they, then?" She grabbed them, shook them. "Mr. Browning's?"

"I don't know, do I?"

Phil returned. "What's going on?"

"You tell me, you fucking *pervert*."

"Mum!"

"You fuckin *peedo*."

"Mum! They're not mine!"

"Shut it!"

"I'm fucking *wearing* mine!" Ruby tore her blouse open, buttons flying to lie with the scattered popcorn. "Look!" She wanted her to see how grown up she was. She wanted her embarrassed. She wanted her to stop before everything was ruined.

"Christ, Rubes, what *is* that? Where did you *get* that? You're too fucking *young* for something like that."

"Steve gave it to me." It was a lie she regretted immediately because she'd have to explain the name to Mr. Browning later.

"Those are mine," he said, pointing to the other set. "Well, not *mine*. They belong to my girlfriend." He tried to take the underwear but Ruby's mother threw them at him. He avoided them. "I'm sorry," he said.

Ruby's mum wasn't listening. She grabbed Ruby's arm and yanked her out of the front room.

"Mum!"

"Come with me. *Now*. And cover yourself up."

Ruby couldn't. She was moving too fast.

"Mrs. Haze—"

"*Miss.*"

They were in the corridor.

"Mum, I didn't do nothing!"

"Miss Haze, I don't know—"

"Shut it!"

Ruby turned to signal an apology or to implore for help, she wasn't sure which, but Mr. Browning's door was already closing. She heard him hook the chain on and then she was shoved into their own flat.

"Don't push me, Mum."

"Get to your room."

"Don't tell me what—"

"Get to your fuckin room!"

Ruby was glad to. She slammed the door hard enough to knock a mask from her wall (a white one with flowers), and sat at her desk. The new mask was there, still cupped around its balloon, but she wasn't in the mood to add to it, not now, so she snatched up a new balloon and inflated it with angry breaths. When it was full, she pinched it closed ready to tie and opened the drawer and said, "I hate her."

The thing in the drawer had developed some sort of fungal scab, furred like a moist flannel, and a run of sporadic sores had formed a bumpy ridge like bubble wrap along one length. As she watched, one of the sores split and leaked a clear pus while another sank back into the membrane from which it had expanded. Ruby was always surprised at the lack of smell. It looked like it should stink, a pungent wet sweaty smell or the rancid whiff of something rotten.

Ruby leant closer.

Something dark and jellied moved inside the mass of flesh, a darker colour spreading and changing like the shape trapped in a lava lamp. The grains in the wood of the drawer had filled with red and black fibres, spreading out from the organic lump like veins. In one place the wood had split because of this growth and a downy line rose from it like spores of mould.

"He called me his girlfriend," Ruby said. "But then Mum—"

She shoved the drawer shut just as the door to her room swung open.

"Don't you slam your door young lady."

It was a stupid thing to say now because the moment had passed while she'd been pouring herself a glass of something.

"Doing your arts and crafts? Old enough for slutty undies but not too old for glue and glitter? Maybe you should stuff those balloons down your top, eh? Give yourself some proper tits."

Ruby stretched the balloon neck, twisted it around her finger, and said, "I've already got proper tits, Mum."

The balloon was snatched from her hands before Ruby could tie it, but it spat out its air before Mum could do anything with it either and escaped, blowing itself around the room with a wet belch. Ruby's mum grabbed for the masked balloon instead, quicker than Ruby could stop her. She squeezed before Ruby could wrestle it away, pushed her painted nails into the skin, and it burst.

Ruby stood up so quickly that her chair toppled. "You pissed-up fat old woman, I hate you! You're *pathetic*, fuckin' *mutton*."

It sent her mother retreating with her hand up. "I can't be bothered with you anymore," she said, but that wasn't what the hand meant, the hand meant stop, and Ruby couldn't.

Ruby wouldn't.

"You fucked things up with Dad and you've fucked things up with every man since, every single one of them, and there's been a lot, Mum, hasn't there?" She was following her out of the room now. "But never the one you want, which is basically just anyone who will have you."

Still her mum retreated.

"That's it, go and have another drink."

The kitchen door slammed.

"There's a secret bottle stashed under the sink!"

With that, Ruby returned to her own room and slammed the door a second time. She used both hands. "Bitch!" She righted the chair. She picked up the limp loose skin of the burst balloon, hating how dead it felt in her hands, and retrieved the other from the floor, inflating it again with breaths that failed to calm her.

The masks on her wall watched—flowered ones, sparkly ones, stars, butterflies, stripes, fangs, some with bunched wool for hair, some with fringes of macaroni—and Ruby looked back, stretching the neck of the balloon into an open slit so that the air came out in a long thin scream.

She dropped the empty balloon and swept the masks from the wall with a scream of her own. A dozen faces looked up at her from the floor, most of them smiling, so she stomped them flat. She imagined each was her mother's face and smiled back at them as they disintegrated under her feet.

Ruby woke in the night to a quiet voice in her room. There was a figure sitting at her desk. She couldn't see if the drawer was open, but for a moment she thought the thing inside had grown into this new shape, that it was her whispered secrets distorted into massive proportions. But the ember glow of a cigarette came up out of the dark and flared its red circle, casting shadows away from a face that was a grotesque mess of make-up. Dark streaks ran from her mother's eyes, and her lipstick was smeared across one cheek where she'd wiped her mouth. Her face was a hideous mask, but one that showed everything instead of hiding it.

"And that's not even the worst part," she said softly.

Ruby wondered how much she'd missed, and whether her mother knew she was awake. She closed her eyes and pretended not to be.

"I could have done things. I could have gone places. And I'm not stupid, I could have gone to college." The gentle clink of a bottle against a glass in the dark marked a pause. "Could have got married, too, if you hadn't come along."

Ruby heard her swallow.

"You know, when you were born you had a layer of skin all over your face. A cowl or a caul or something. All shiny with blood. You really *really* fucking hurt to get out, but there you were. My precious little thing. My bloody red jewel."

She poured another drink.

"You weren't breathing at first. I don't know if it was that thing on your face or because you were so small because, you know, you were early. I thought you were dead, that I'd crushed you dead with all the tight clothes I wore to keep you secret. Because I had to hide it, didn't I? The lump I was carrying around. Knowing I was pregnant would've killed her, and then she would have killed *me*. You think *I'm* a bitch? You should've met your grandma. I thought if you were dead then she'd never have to know. But you weren't dead."

There was a pause for cigarette smoke to be sucked in. Puffed out.

"Sometimes I wish you were."

Ruby turned the noise she'd made into a murmur and fidgeted a little as if dreaming. She bit down on the inside of her cheek.

"I didn't get rid of you or nothing, didn't get an abortion or get you adopted, even though I could have, and I thought maybe you not breathing was my reward for not doing those things."

Ruby clenched her eyes shut tighter and made tiny fists under the covers.

"And now you give me shit all the time about how great your dad was and how I chased him off and all that bollocks and none of that's true, Rubes. I never told your dad about you. He would have cared even less than I did. You hear me?"

Ruby held her breath.

"I know you're awake."

Ruby said nothing.

"I'm sick of all your bullshit. Danny was a good dad, I'll give you that, but he *wasn't* your dad. So there you go. The dad I "*chased off*" was just some bloke who looked after you for a while."

Ruby reached out for the lamp at her bedside and turned it on. She stared at her mother for a moment before finally saying, "That's a lie."

Her mum brought the cigarette down on the desktop suddenly, two, three times, crushed it out against the wood, and said, "Fine. It's a lie. Whatever you say, sweetheart."

"Get out of my room."

"Good night, Ruby."

"Get out!"

The door opened and a slice of light came in from the hall. Ruby's mother left without looking back and without looking at the papier-mâché masks she stepped on to leave. Ruby had to get up to close the door so she was in the dark once more.

The next day, as she tidied the ruined faces away, Ruby shared her plans with the open drawer. She spoke quietly.

"...doesn't matter where, as long as it isn't *here*," she said. "With *her*. I could work in a club, like Kelly's sister, or get a job down the market. And in a couple of years me and Mr. Browning, me and *Phil*, can get married."

She dumped the last of the papier-mâché in the bin. For a moment she liked how the different fragments lay against each other, a new face of varied parts, and she contemplated, briefly, assembling a massive monstrosity of them for her wall. But she had decided she was too old for such things. She would finish the one she was working on but that was all, and even that she would hide in the drawer.

It lay on the desk, half formed. At the moment it was just a dry curved crust of dirty paper and sex, but she would add facial features over the next few weeks. She'd mould a nose, the ridge of a brow, open lips, and then she'd paint it.

She pulled the drawer open wider to hide the mask and only then did she see the mess inside.

"Oh..."

The end wedged in the corner of the drawer was still fat with what it hadn't managed to expel but the rest of it lay flat in a dried pool of tar-like fluid, mottled red and black and brown. It was a wrinkled skin that had curled open so that folds of its flesh lay exposed, as if some internal organ had been suddenly turned inside out. There were lumps in it, knots of sticky red mucus like clotted blood, and splatters against the opposite edges of the drawer. Edges she had hoped to see it reach one day.

"No..."

She reached in as if to pick it up before remembering the soggy pencil ends, the way they rotted.

"*Why?*"

Last night. It must have been last night. She hadn't looked in the drawer this morning, but last night she had watched it writhe and fidget as it filled with each new secret. And then . . .

Mum had come in. Ruby had yelled. She'd said things aloud, things she'd once whispered as secrets, but it wasn't her fault. If her mother hadn't come in . . .

And she'd come in twice. In the middle of the night she'd crept in to whisper her lies, and some of them must have seeped into the drawer. Yeah, that was it.

The bitch.

"I'll kill her," Ruby said. "I'll fucking turn *her* inside out."

The remains glistened with a fresh wetness, but even as Ruby swore more oaths and wept her secret pain, the flaps of skin merely fluttered in the breeze of her words. Part of it puckered open and closed but that was all, and eventually even that stopped.

Mr. Browning moved away.

Ruby spent a long time giving her tears to the drawer, but except for a few sticky red smears in the wood, there was nothing left of the thing inside to take them. Instead, the drawer held the mask she'd made. And beneath that . . .

"Mum made him go," Ruby said. "I know she did."

They'd never mentioned the underwear. Ruby thought her mum had forgotten it, like she forgot lots of things when she was drunk, but when she didn't go to Bingo the next week and then Mr. Browning moved away, Ruby knew something had happened.

She lifted the mask out of the drawer, kissed it, and put it to one side. There was a box underneath it. Just a small box, but it was her biggest secret ever. She didn't need to check inside—her blood had stopped, and that told her all she needed to know—but she checked again anyway.

"It's just for a little while," she said.

The mask on her desk stared at the ceiling. She'd threaded string through its ears; it would never hear her. It didn't matter. She was speaking to the little plastic stick in her hand.

"He'll come back for us."

She put it back in the box, trying to be just as positive.

"You want me to put this on?"

Steve turned the mask over in his hands. Ruby had painted it with pale pinks and browns, suitable flesh colours. She'd even added freckles in the right places, but Steve wouldn't know that. She knew he'd wear it; his tracksuit bottoms were sticking out around his erection.

Ruby nodded. Sitting on the bed, all she had to do was open her legs a little to encourage him. Just enough that her skirt hitched up.

"What about your mum?"

"You can do her too, if you want, I don't care."

Steve laughed.

"She's got a cleaning job once a week," Ruby said. "She's not in. And she thinks I'm at school."

"You can't say nothing," Steve said. "I'm going with Tracy now."

Tracy was a slutty townie, but Ruby didn't care. She pulled her knickers off. Steve put the mask to his face and approached her.

"Put it on properly," she said.

"It smells funny."

But he did as he was told and as he pulled the strings tight she pulled at his waist band and by the time he said, "Condom," he was already inside her.

"Don't worry about it," she said.

"You can't say nothing," he said again. His voice was flat behind the papier-mâché mask. "You kinky little bitch," he said. "Our secret, yeah?"

Mr. Browning looked down at her with Steve's eyes but sometimes he closed them and it was okay.

"Yeah," Ruby said. "Yeah."

That night, Ruby crept into her mother's room. She was slumped on the bed, fully dressed, smelling of sweat and booze and cheap perfume. There was a half-empty cup of wine on the bedside table.

"No clean glasses, eh Mum?" Ruby said. "Must be too tired to wash them after one whole day of work."

Her mother made no reply.

Ruby sat beside her and leaned close.

"I had sex with Mr. Browning," she whispered.

A little drool escaped her mother's mouth, but that was all. Ruby imagined her secret wriggling inside somewhere, finding a place to settle.

She tucked her mother's hair aside to expose more of her ear and said, "I'm pregnant."

Her mother murmured, fidgeted, and was still.

"I'm keeping it," Ruby said.

"I'm going to tell Steve it's his," Ruby said.

She stroked her mother's hair, soothing her as she whispered all her secrets. She quietly dropped them into her mother's ear, pausing between each one so that whatever held them had a chance to grow. She imagined something dark and wet expanding inside, festering in its new habitat, and knew that all she had to do was admit the truth of what she'd done one day to make it burst.

Ruby spoke until her throat was dry, pausing only to take a sip from her mother's cup before starting all over again.

AT NIGHT, WHEN
THE DEMONS COME

You'll notice these records have no dates. I don't think anyone really knows what the year is these days anyway. The last one I remember is 2020. Everyone remembers 2020, but my point is I didn't keep track after. Why bother? I only write this because of what happened recently, because someone taught me that others might learn if only I provided the opportunity.

There were four of us when Cassie came and she made six because she didn't come alone and naturally we counted her last. She was female, next to useless, and a little girl at that, so totally useless. But the man she was with, he was worth having around. We had a couple of guys on our college football team, back when things like that mattered, who were as big as this man. A couple, as in put them together and you had the right size. Fuck knows where he got his clothes. If he wasn't on your side your side was going to lose, and I'm not talking football any more. His name was Frances, can you believe that? Jones called him a walking Johnny Cash song. I was never a fan, but I knew what he meant.

If it hadn't been for the demon we probably would have hidden like we usually did and waited for the strangers to move on. We probably missed out on a lot of good people that way, but we sure missed out on a lot of bad ones too and that was fine by all of us. This time, though, we came out and stood in the road until they were near enough to talk to. Not that we knew they were a they at that time. We thought it was just him. Frances.

"Hello traveller," Jones said. It sounded stupid, like he was pretending to be someone else. We'd not had much practice talking to anyone but each other, and there was never much need for hello with us.

The man who would later tell us he had a girl's name just stood, assessing the situation. He made no try to hide it. He looked Jones up and down, then Frank next to him. He saw me easy enough, over by

AT NIGHT, WHEN THE DEMONS COME

the pump, and he took in both windows looking for others. There was only George, who he saw up on the roof. George knew he'd been seen. He stood up, put one foot on the wall, leaned over and spat. Then he raised his rifle, just enough for it to be visible. George always acted like he was cool and calm, like some kind of movie hero. He did it with us even though we knew better. Even though nobody gave a shit about movies anymore.

"Just the four of you?" the big man asked.

Frank seemed surprised. "Yeah."

"So no trouble."

"That's right," Frank said, but I reckon he misunderstood. Frances meant he'd find the four of us no trouble, that's what I reckon.

"What does he want?" George called down.

"Water, if you have it. Food, if you can spare it. Somewhere to sleep, either way." He said it quietly, addressing those who had spoken to him directly. "The wind's picking up and this place looks like it might have a storm cellar."

"It does," said Jones. "Only we haven't been in there yet."

The man waited for more but neither Jones nor Frank were eager to spill it. They looked at each other instead, then looked over to me. I was already heading over, breaking the shotgun open to show myself harmless.

"There was a demon," I told him.

I swear he didn't move, yet suddenly his empty hands weren't empty anymore. It was like the guns just appeared there. Both were cylinder loaders and looked to be full, unless he'd fashioned fakes to make it seem that way. Fakes wouldn't be much good against a winged bitch, though, which said to me the bullets were real.

"Quiet," he said. Not to us. Then I thought I heard something else but he covered it with words of his own.

"When was it here?" he asked.

Me, I put my hand up to shield my eyes from the sun he was walking from and said, "Still is."

Just like that, one of the guns was gone. "Dead?"

I nodded. Heard that something else again.

"Ssh," said the giant. Then, "You?"

I was flattered he'd think so. I was also glad George couldn't hear else there'd be some preening and showmanship before we could cut to the honest answer. "No. She was dead when we got here."

There was no need to ask if we were sure. We wouldn't still be here otherwise.

"Show me," he said.

"Alright," said Jones, "But do you want to put that gun away first?"

"No. Not yet."

"It's dead."

I thought I heard an echo of that, and judging from Jones and Frank and the way they frowned, so did they.

"Who you got with you?" I asked.

He said nothing, so it was up to her to make the introductions.

"I'm Cassie," she called out from behind him. Her voice was high, with the enthusiasm of someone about to play. "This man is my friend. He's called Frances."

Frances squatted down in the road. There was the sound of metal on metal, the sound buckles make, and he stood again. From behind him emerged Cassie. A little girl about six years old. She reached up and his hand was there for her.

I stepped behind the man Frances but he recoiled to keep his back facing away from me. It was only a reflex action. He turned back after and I could see a system of harnesses strapped around him. The girl had been fixed in, completely out of our sight back there and protected by the mass of muscle that was Frances in front.

"This is Jones, Frank, that there's George," I said. "My name's Charlie."

Nobody shook hands.

We'd found the place at around twelve. It took the best part of an hour to get close enough to see it seemed empty, and another hour on that to make sure it was. A two pump gas station, dust-blown and sun-baked, with a workshop and store and a single shell sign squeaking in a building breeze. That building breeze was why we'd risked an approach in the first place. Oklahoma was not a nice place to be out in the open, unless you liked flying kites. Tornado Alley, this stretch used to be called. I doubt there's much of anyone left to call it anything any more, but that wouldn't stop the tornadoes from coming.

"Empty," Frank had said and we'd all hushed him immediately. George slapped him across the back of his head.

"Idiot."

"Sorry."

Frank said "empty" last time, right before three women popped up from behind the sofa and started shooting. Lucky for us we were quicker, though Jones got some splinters from an exploding picture frame. The time before that, someone was hiding in the refrigerator. I got a gun rammed into my mouth because of that, which is why the front teeth aren't pretty. I drew my knife and that stopped things getting worse. I knew I could save my bullets because I knew he had none, and I knew *that* because there was still a gun in my mouth and not my brains on the wall. After two seconds he was backing away with his hands up and I was feeling in my bloody mouth to straighten my teeth. When Frank said empty it meant it wasn't and that someone who wasn't Frank was going to get hurt. To be fair, though, there was food or water to be had both times.

"You go first," Jones said to Frank.

And to be fair, Frank always did.

He came out from round the back of the building backing up. His gun was out but he wasn't really pointing it at anything.

"Frank?"

"You should come and see," he said. He pointed with his weapon. It trembled in his hand.

He showed us a demon nailed to a door.

She was an ugly bitch. None of us had ever seen one up close before. Obviously, because we were still alive. But we'd all seen them in the skies at some point, and I saw the carcass of one once in a ditch at the roadside but its wings had been pulled off and taken and so had the head and claws, so it wasn't much more than a mutilated female torso. Seen that way the purple skin isn't much different to mottled bruising. This one, the one Frank found, its skin still had a vibrant brightness even though it was dead, the pale lavender colour of its body darkening into violet at the arms and legs. The wings were stretched out to full span and pinned to the door with knives, railroad spikes, and even a couple of forks. They were a rich purple. The claws, two big scoops where the hands should've been, were a plum colour so dark it was almost black. She was the colours of dusk given fleshy form, hairless and vile.

"Nice tits," said George, trying to sound like the movie star tough guy he wanted to be.

The tits were plump and round and firm-looking but they were hellish in that they were hers. All that suckled there was demon or doomed.

"She looks like your momma," said Jones. I guess he was tired of George's shit.

George knew better than to fight with Jones, though. "She's got better teeth."

Its teeth were like a shark's, sharp triangles folding back from the gums in double rows. Too many teeth.

"What should we do with it?" Frank asked.

The door it had been impaled on had long ago been torn from its hinges and rested now against the sloping hatch of a storm cellar, maybe as some kind of warning, maybe as some kind of victory mark. Jones and I took a side each and pulled it face down into the dirt.

George jumped on it and we heard her bones crack. He lost his balance and fell on his ass and something else broke in the bitch under him. It was pretty funny.

"How did it die?" the big man asked, following us round.

"Various shots to the chest," Jones was telling him. "A couple very close range."

"You showing him our demon?" George called down from the roof, trying to take credit.

"Yeah."

I waved him down.

"Here she is," said Frank. He took hold of one edge and flipped it over, though that makes it sound easier than it was.

A bone stuck from its flank and its nose was broken flat, otherwise it looked much as it had. The skin had picked up some of the sandy dust from the ground. I thought the stranger might shelter the girl from the sight, but he actually steered her towards it. They looked at it together.

"See," said Jones, pointing to the chest area. Just beneath the breasts was a mess of bullet holes of different calibres. He pointed to where the skin was puffed and scorched. "Close range."

George was with us by then. "Nice tits, huh?"

Everybody ignored him. He spat on the body. He liked to spit. "Give you nightmares, little girl."

Frances pointed to the cellar doors. "You've not been in there?"

Frank shook his head.

"The demon was on it," I said.

"You think there's another one in there?"

It sounded ridiculous when he said it. "Maybe."

George pulled back the slide of what he liked to call his piece, just for the dramatic impact of the noise. "Only one way to find out, eh?"

Jones said, "You weren't so eager before."

"If it's loaded you can come," said the giant. He was checking the barrels of his weapons, spinning them, snapping them shut. "That shotgun would be handy close range, too."

I offered it to him.

"Going to have my hands full," he said, raising his revolvers.

"God damn it," I muttered, but I went to the doors.

"I'll stay with the girl," said Frank.

"Me too," said Jones.

"Good," said Frances. "Stick close to her down there, but keep her behind us."

Frank looked at Jones. "She's going too?"

Jones merely shrugged and turned the cylinder of his own thirty-eight, lining it up so the four shots he had left were ready to fire.

"I have to," said the girl. "Frances might need me."

Frank went to the left door, Jones to the right. Each grabbed a handle. Frances stood in the middle, both guns pointing down at where the stairs would be. George and I were on either side of him doing the same. The girl was behind us.

"Alright," Frances said, "on three."

But they were already opening the doors.

"Shit." I brought the barrel close to aim, panicked by the sudden opening, and caught myself in the cheek with the stock.

Stairs led down into gloom. Nothing came out. Nothing moved. There was no noise.

Frances went in.

"Shit," I said again and followed him down into the dark.

There were beds. About a dozen of them. We stood in the slant of sunlight that had come down with us, but the room went way back into a darkness black as oil. The beds we could see clearly were occupied. There was a woman bound to each of them.

"Penitentary," Frances said.

"What?"

We walked slowly, inspecting each bed just enough to tell us the person on it was dead. I said, "What?" again but nobody else said anything.

The women were drawn and wasted, skin over bone, dressed only in shadows where the flesh was sunken. They'd starved down here. All of them were manacled with homemade cuffs and chains, and all of them had deep dry lacerations that spoke of attempts to escape. One woman I saw had scraped her flesh down to the bone trying to pull her way out and I stopped looking at the others after that.

The girl—I'd forgotten her name—was muttering prayers for them.

Pushed against one wall was a plastic crate filled with bottled water, the huge types that refilled office coolers. I hadn't seen one in years and here there was four of them, plus one half-empty on its stand. Or half-full, depending on your philosophy.

"Whoo!" George cried, and he did a little dance step, "jackpot! Look at all that!"

At that moment we were attacked.

A woman leapt up from the foot of the cooler, not at all hidden but missed because of the distraction water is to thirsty men. I yelled for George. Jones grabbed at him, pulling him round just as the woman's nails raked at his face. She'd been going for the eyes but thanks to Jones only managed to scratch thin strips across his cheeks.

"Fuck!"

"Don't!" Frances called. I'm not sure who to.

I barrelled forward, pushed the shotgun firm into her stomach, and fired. Her back splashed against the wall and she flopped down in two pieces near enough.

"Was it one of them?" George cried, "Was it a demon?" He was patting at his wounds, probably hoping he weren't poisoned.

"No," said Frances, slipping his guns away and rubbing his face with his hands. "Just a woman."

"Oh. Good."

"Just a woman," Cassie repeated, looking at me where I leant against the wall taking shaky breaths.

Fucked if I was going to feel guilty.

The cellar doors had a place to slide a bar across but no bar. Up in the store section of the gas station we took down a regular door to saw into pieces the right size. The wind had picked up some by then. I'd started to clean up the mess I'd made but Frances pushed me away and said he'd do it. He was very firm about it. I think he was pissed with me for some reason.

"What if they're taking the water?" George asked, laying the door in place across the counter. The slices down his face had dried into crusty lines.

"They're not taking the water," I said.

"He's got that harness, he'd get one in that alright."

"I don't think even a guy his size would want to carry one of those on his back," said Jones. "And Frank's with him."

"Oh, Frank. Great. Everything will be fine then."

Just a woman. I kept hearing that in my head. The way the girl said it.

"She must have been crazy," said Jones. "Down in the dark like that when she could have come out. Doors weren't locked."

"The demon was leaning on them." George pushed and pulled at the saw. It bit its way through the wood reluctantly. It was old, that saw. We'd been carrying it around a while, blunt teeth and all.

"It don't weigh so much you can't push it down opening them doors out."

"Maybe she was too weak," I said, holding the door steady. "They looked starved."

"She was just a woman," George said. As if that explained everything. Or as if it didn't matter so why keep talking about it.

These last unnumbered years have been hard for everyone of course, but the women got it hardest once the demons came. Maybe before then.

There was a group I used to belong to. They stuck together like we did, safety in numbers, and they gathered up women they found along the way. Mostly it was the purpose I alluded to earlier, but sometimes it wasn't only that. There were other ways to fuck a woman, like calling her demon. They were always female, see, the demons, so it made sense that they were once women. Women who turned into hellish carnivores that flew with the wind-blown ash. Accuse a woman of turning, smack her around a bit for some convincing purple, and you had Salem all over again. I've seen women strung up worse than the demon we found on the door. Shit, I even believed it once.

"Hey, Charlie, where you going?"

I ignored George, but I told Jones on the way out I was going to speak with Frances.

Frances had seen places like this before but he wouldn't tell me anything more until we had the place secure. That meant tossing the bodies outside, making barricades of the rusty metal bed frames, and taking an inventory of remaining ammunition. I thought that was a little pointless. I was the only one who'd fired.

"He does it every time we stop," Cassie told me.

George and Jones managed to make a sturdy beam for the doors, halving the door from the store and binding the pieces together. I helped them carry it.

"Oh, now you decide to help," said George.

"I've been busy," I said. I pointed to the pile of bodies as Frances shrugged another two from his shoulders. We were going to burn them, the best funeral we could manage and more than most people got these days. The wind tossed his hair back with the tail of his long coat in a way I knew George must have envied. It was getting so we had to shout to be heard or our voices were snatched away too quickly. The gas sign rocked back and forth, screeching a rusty protest.

"How many more?" I called, but Frances ignored it. He stood looking up at the sky, letting the wind do its thing, and I thought oh shit, another George.

Cassie came up out of the cellar. She was dragging one of the bodies (just a woman). I heard it bump, bump, bump, up the steps. Jesus, she was five years old.

"Frances," she said.

"I know."

All of us turned to see.

Jones wasted nothing, not even words. "Oh. Shit."

Back the way we'd come from, criss-crossing the road in angry sweeps, was a twister. It span its dust with quiet violence for now but it was going to be on us quick and then we'd hear it scream.

I ran to the girl and took the ankles from her hands. I dragged the corpse up the last steps and dropped it to the side of the doors.

"No, over here. We don't want them feeding that close to the door."

"What?"

Frances pointed again.

"Oh shit. Shit."

Sailing in the winds of the storm were two demons. They dived and arced as if the cyclone was a large pet they played with.

I dragged the body over at a run. "Have they seen us?"

"Not yet."

Frances grabbed me by the shoulder and ran me back to the doors.

"How can you tell?" I yelled against the wind.

"They're still over there instead of here."

George was feeding the door-block down into the cellar. "Quickly, quickly."

Cassie was standing and clutching herself like she needed to pee. She stepped from one foot to the other in the rising dust, looking to where hell flew at us.

"Inside, little heart," Frances said.

We followed her down and George pulled the doors shut behind us.

Sitting in the dark, we listened to the wind howl. It wasn't long before the howls were those of the things flying with it.

"I thought they only came at night?" Frank whispered. We all shushed him quiet.

Above us, something landed on the roof with a heavy thump. We heard it even in the cellar. It screamed, and the winds pulled the sound round and round in echo. To me it sounded like a woman in labour, giving birth to something stillborn. Jones said later it sounded like the slaughterhouse. I guess we hear what we can relate to.

"Maybe the other one will—"

Jones, whispering so quiet it was like I was thinking the words, was cut off by the sound of something landing on the dry ground outside. It, too, screamed. It screamed in short sharp shreds. This was no bestial cry of the hunt. It was communicating with the one on the roof. It was scratching its way around the pile we'd made out there.

The doors shook. I cried out but my throat was parched and the noise I made was only a cracked nothing. Frank stifled a yelp. The doors thumped. It was only the wind, lifting and dropping them in its frantic wrath.

There came next a wailing shriek I never in whatever life I've got left ever want to hear again. If that rooftop scream was a woman birthing death, this one sounded like the demon clawed her own abortion. The shards of it went through you like jagged porcelain and as it trailed off it thinned to a fiery hot needle in your ears. The way the wind whipped it into a ricochet pulled it through you like infected thread, yanking the line tight till you clutched your head against the pain. When the other one joined in I wished for death just so the chorus would end.

It stopped eventually, though the reverberations of those screams will be with me forever as a tortured background noise as permanent as thought. I can still hear it now when I close my eyes, finding myself in the same darkness.

"They've found their sister," said Frances.

When the doors thundered again in their frames it was not the wind.

"Oh Jesus," Jones moaned.

"Ssh," said Frances, "they don't know we're here."

"Sounds like they know," said George.

"Ssh."

Sure enough, after a while of pounding the doors we heard them demolishing the store above.

"They'll tear the place apart just in case, but those doors are strong and we have water, even some tinned food. If we keep quiet, we can wait them out if we have to."

"You know what else we got?" I said. I pointed to the bodies we hadn't shifted yet. "Think they smell good now, wait a few days."

"Good," said Frances. "They'll smell it too and figure the only humans down here are dead ones."

The destruction above ceased. The only sounds we heard then were those of the wind as it tore its way over us.

"Think they've gone?"

"Maybe," said Frances, but we could tell he didn't think so.

"No," whispered Cassie. "They're still here."

They stayed long after the cyclone had passed. The new quiet allowed us to hear the occasional heavy dragging outside. When the sounds became wet, thick, and guttural we knew they were feeding.

"There's bodies plenty out there," Frank whispered, "they could eat here for weeks."

Nobody liked that idea.

Frances nodded his agreement and pointed across the room. We trod our way silently to the far end and huddled so we could talk quietly.

"There are only two of them," Frances said.

"Only?"

He spared me a glance but otherwise ignored my comment.

"There are six of us," he said. "If we're quick, we can take them."

Six. He'd counted the girl.

"Frances, you're a big man," said Jones. "You've probably survived by being a big man. Quick, too. But me, us, we've survived by keeping low, hiding out. Playing it safe, you could say, as safe as this new world allows. We're not about to go at it with two demon bitches."

It was a speech for Jones.

"Shit, Jones, you're chicken."

"Yeah, George, I am. Only a stupid person wouldn't be."

"I'm not," George replied, apparently missing the implication.

Frances counted off our advantages on his fingers. "They're feeding, so they're distracted. They're close, so we won't miss. There's only two of them, so they're outnumbered. There's a few hours of sun left, so they're weak."

I think he may have been making up the sunlight bit.

"Good enough for me," said George, already moving to the doors.

Frances saw an opportunity for visual emphasis and moved over with him, the girl going too, leaving just three of us cowering in the shadows. Frank said, "I go where the big man goes," and went.

"What about you, Charlie?"

I shrugged. "You make more sense," I said.

"But you want to take them down."

"Yeah."

Jones sighed. "Yeah," he repeated. "Me too."

We joined the others. It took only a minute to plan our tactics.

Frank checked his gun in the light that slanted down from between the doors. "We're all going to die," he said.

He was wrong about that. They only got two of us.

Four days after that fight at the gas station, Frances told me about the demon he and Cassie had seen in Colorado. We were camping at the side of the road eating beans from a can.

"Her parents were still with us then," he said.

Cassie nodded to herself, scraping at the sides of her tin.

"What happened to them?"

"People on the road," said Cassie. "They tried to take my mom for their penitentary."

"Penitentiary," I said, pronouncing the "sh."

Frances said, "No, she's right. They call it a penitentary."

I remembered he'd said the word in the cellar. Back when the others were still with us.

"Places where women are kept prisoner," Frances explained. "Sometimes by religious nuts, sometimes by men who are scared. Sometimes by those who just like an excuse to hurt women."

I nodded and put my can aside. Frances pointed at it with his spoon.

"Not hungry," I said.

He gave the rest of my beans to the girl.

"Anyway, we'd crossed the Rockies hoping things would be different on this side of the mountains. They weren't. We found a scrap yard, figured we might find a car. What we found was one of those things. It was flapping only in bursts, wings beating against the ground and hiding most of what it was hunched over."

"It was Brenda," said Cassie, as if I should know who she meant. I could guess why she wasn't with them now. "She looked like she was having a bad dream with her eyes open."

"We thought it was eating her at first but it wasn't."

"Was it turning her into a demon?" I asked.

The girl shook her head. "It was doing what adults do."

I looked to Frances but he only nodded.

"It was fucking her?"

The girl sucked in a breath.

"What?" I reached for my gun.

"You said a bad word."

"Oh. Yeah. Sorry."

Frances smiled and nodded again. "It was doing what adults do."

"But . . ."

"They're not all women," Frances said. "Whatever you've heard, or maybe even seen, there's at least one out there that isn't female."

"If we tell people they'll stop hurting each other," Cassie said, "they'll be nice again and just hate demons if someone tells them."

"You sure?"

Cassie misunderstood. "I saw its thing," she said.

Frances held his hands out about a foot apart. He shook his head, either appalled or impressed.

"What did you do?"

"We hid and it flew away."

"With the woman?"

"No, she came with us."

Before I could ask, Cassie said, "She died having a baby." She burped and covered her mouth.

Frances told Cassie to bury the cans a little way off and added quietly, "We did what we had to when we saw what was coming out of her."

I thought of my poor Beth. All that futile pushing, a labour of pain that brought only death.

"Do you think we should give him something to eat?" Cassie asked, coming back before I could ask any questions.

We all looked at where Frank lay, his broken body strapped as tight as he could bear it. He was asleep, the only retreat he had from the pain.

"Wait until he wakes," I said, knowing that he wouldn't.

Cassie simply nodded. Maybe she knew it too.

"Why didn't he shoot?" Frances asked, but I still didn't have an answer for him.

We'd burst out of the cellar as one, but that was as much of the plan we stuck to. After that, all tactics were abandoned in our response to the horror before us. We knew what we'd see, but confronted by it we could only react. Our reaction was to fire, fire, and fire again. We fired until our guns were empty, which didn't take long. We all fired at the same one.

She was standing over a body, one clawed foot buried in the cavity of its chest while the other clawed at what flesh remained of the stomach. A line of entrails stretched up from the corpse to the creature's mouth, its talon hands hooking more and more into a gathered mouthful as if balling twine. Its leathery wings beat just enough to add strength to its pulling.

We surprised it; that bit went to plan. Its mouth was a bloody slop of guts and when it screamed at us, chewed stinking mouthfuls dropped down its chest. It released the corpse anchoring it and took to the sky, managing only one sweep of its wings before we hit it. I ran to it firing and was satisfied to see a good chunk of purple thigh vanish in a spray of blood, the rest of the leg severed by the creature's own attempts to flee, hooked in the body that had been its meal. Shots from George and Jones and Frank peppered the demon's torso, each round a splash of blood and bile that hammered it back, back. Frances was more deliberate with his guns, hitting it three times in the head. Another blast from my shotgun blew its wing into tatters but it was already falling then.

The other one had been scooping handfuls of flesh from higher up the body pile and retreated behind the corpses the moment we started firing. Part of me registered that. Part of me knew it was there even as part of me knew the one on the ground was dead, yet that was the one I approached. I broke the shotgun open and reloaded as the demon body jumped and shivered with wasted rounds from the others. They were clicking empty when I put the barrel against the head and burst it like a melon.

"Charlie!"

I dropped turned and fired all in one action but missed as the other one sailed over my head. It caught a tangle of my hair by chance, even short as it was, and tore it from my scalp as it passed.

Frances dropped his gun behind him and Cassie crouched to reload it while he fired with the other. It was a smooth operation that suggested practice and I wondered how many fire fights this little girl had been in. Her hands weren't even shaking.

The demon wheeled in the air. A hole appeared in its wing but that seemed to be the only hit and it didn't slow it down none. It dove towards us screaming.

That was enough to send me and George back to the cellar. We crouched on the steps and saw Jones fumble for his knife. He raised it quick enough to lunge once and then the demon had him, lifting him up with her talons as she shredded his legs and bowels with clawed feet. He screamed his agony till something broke in his throat. She cast him away, flying back and up as Jones flew forwards. He smacked into the corner of the building with a crack that broke his spine.

"Come here, you bitch!" George yelled, then ran out to her before she could take him up on the offer. He fired all the way, quick for a man with a rifle, but she only soared higher, a twisting shape in silhouette against the darkening sky.

"Reload!" Frances shouted. "While it's up there! Quick, reload!" He swapped his gun for the one Cassie offered.

Frank stood, shielding his eyes from the dying sun, watching as the creature hovered.

"Reload, Frank!" I told him, pushing two cartridges into mine. When that was done I ran to him and snatched his weapon from a limp grip. I ejected the magazine and slapped his arm for a fresh one.

"We made them," he said, "when we did what we did to ourselves. They were born from the ashes that came after." He pointed. "We made them."

It was something I'd heard before, but not from Frank. Religious bullshit, like we didn't have enough to feel guilty about. I shook him, keeping an eye on the demon. It arced left and right but remained distant.

"Get some more fucking bullets in this and *unmake* it then," I said.

When he looked at me his eyes were empty, but he did as he was told.

"Spread out," Frances called. He'd shrugged out of his coat and harness. If the demon grabbed any of us, I hoped it grabbed him. With his bulk he wasn't being thrown anywhere, and with those arms he could tear this thing apart. Maybe that was why he only used crappy revolvers.

I put distance between me and Frank. George, for reasons known only to him, scrambled up the pile of corpses. He stood atop them with his arms out, daring the bitch to attack.

It did. It dived for Frank.

Frank levelled his gun at it calmly and had plenty of time to fire. But he didn't. He faced his doom as it flew down at him. George popped a few shots, making more tiny holes in the membrane of its wing. Frances took one careful shot but only clipped it as far as I could tell. I didn't dare from where I stood. It hurtled straight and hard, hitting Frank across the upper body and tugging him into the sky as it pulled up and away. I saw it rake a claw across his gun hand. The other sank into Frank's fleshy shoulder and he swung one arc of a pendulum before the creature's momentum took them both high.

I ran to where Frank had dropped his gun. A few of his fingers lay scattered around it like bloody commas.

Above us the demon screamed in play and tossed Frank away. He cartwheeled and fell a short distance but the bitch snatched him up again before he really began any descent, clutching him sharply around the ankle. A line of blood splashed down across my upturned face.

"Fucking shoot it," I yelled. My own weapon was useless at this range.

"Might hit Frank," said George. He was taking aim.

"I don't think it matters now," said Frances, also lining up for a steady shot. "Might be better."

The demon swooped low, dragging Frank so he hit the ground and broke somewhere. Then it was diving away in an abrupt turn and Frank was thrown into our midst. He struck George across the legs and the two of them fell in a tumble of female corpses.

I fired both barrels as it passed me. A chunk of its hip blew out and it spun, only for Frances to hit it once, twice, three times in the side and breast. It crashed down into the dirt and flopped in a writhing mass of purple flesh.

I was reloading as I ran. Frances was still shooting as he came at it.

The creature was rolling and flapping and spraying its blood, clouds of dust billowing in the gusts of its attempted flight. Part of its sleek violet skull erupted, then another as Frances aligned his second shot by the success of his first.

I raised the shotgun to my shoulder but Frances, beside me, lowered it with his hand. "Save your ammunition," he said.

We watched it twitch and spasm until it was still. Then Frances tore it to pieces with only his hands.

George, taken down by the thrown body of Frank, had fired another shot as he fell. It went in under his chin and opened the top of his head. Not the movie star end he would have wanted. Not the end many would have wanted, though I've known a few that have taken a similar route. I've thought about it myself from time to time. Only my fear that the demons will still come has kept me from that darkness.

George was dead. Jones was dead. Frank had lost a lot of one hand, which we bandaged, and most of one foot, which we amputated. Didn't take much but a snip here and there. He was a crooked tangle of limbs, each one broken more than once. His chest rose and fell in an awkward shape as he made rasping shallow breaths. He only screamed once with the pain of moving him and that pain was enough to make him pass out. He was easier to handle after that.

"He's my friend," I said, "but he's gone, Frances."

"That's not up to us," he said.

We made a stretcher for Frank. It was agreed without conversation that we'd leave the gas station behind as soon as we could.

Cassie gathered our supplies. When the stretcher was done I went through the pockets of the dead and said my goodbyes.

We didn't bury anybody.

Four days later they told me about demons with dicks, devil babies, and a mercy killing. I took a moral from the tale and smothered Frank that same night and in the morning we left him by the road still strapped to his stretcher.

We travelled south all morning. I learned that Frances was a mechanic, and that for a short while he and Cassie had travelled by car. I learned that Cassie had owned sixteen dolls and teddies and I was told each of their names. I learned her father had been a school teacher and her mother a police officer, back when we needed such things.

I didn't tell them anything about me other than a few stories about the others I'd travelled with. They figured it out on their own, though. Well, Cassie did. I'd travelled with Jones, George and Frank for the best part of a year and they never found out. Five days with this little girl and I'm asked, "Is Charlie short for Charlotte?"

Frances was as surprised as I was, and after the surprise it was too obvious to deny.

"Yeah."

"Charlotte's pretty," she said.

"Charlotte doesn't want to be pretty," I said back.

Which was why I'd cropped my hair right down to my scalp and let it grow everywhere else. I farted, belched, and scratched my crotch. Strapping down my chest wasn't much of a problem because there wasn't much there to begin with.

"Why don't you want to be pretty?" Cassie asked. "My mom was pretty."

Frances knew the answer. He told Cassie not to pry. Already he was looking at me different.

I didn't know what these penitentary places were, but I knew places like them, and probably a few places worse. Before Jones and George and Frank I belonged to a group who used me by night and called me demon by day to feel better about it. Sometimes, when we met others, I'd be loaned out in exchange for food, water, ammunition. It wasn't until I got pregnant that it stopped. Poor little Beth, spat from my poisoned loins in a flood of blood, reluctant to live in the world we'd given her.

They left me to die with her, and so I did.

And then Cassie came and reminded me of how things were, and how they could be.

"Left corner," said Frances.

Another fucking gas station. Like the one where we'd met, this one had a store and a bay for vehicle repair and two pumps out front, though one had been knocked down and lay like a blocky corpse in a dusty shroud. Unlike the other gas station, this one had people in it that were alive. One of them was leaning in the corner of the walled roof, a rifle pointing to where we stood in the road. The sun shone from his weapon in little winks of light, otherwise it was a good position.

"Seen," I said, though there wasn't much I could do about it from here.

Cassie was strapped in behind Frances, unseen. "We could move on," she said softly.

"There's another one in the repair well," I said, watching the man carefully adjust the angle of his rifle so it pointed up for a head shot if he needed it.

"Charlotte, we could move on."

I hissed at Cassie, "Ssh."

From behind the standing pump emerged a bearded man. He held a pistol down by his knee and raised his other hand slowly in greeting.

"What do you think?"

Frances looked around. "I think there's a few more, maybe laying in ditches we can't see. I think the ones we can see are distractions. But we'll see what he has to say. Maybe they're just careful, like us."

"We ain't careful if we stick around."

"We need food."

"And what are you thinking of trading for it?"

He met my stare. "Guns. We got empty guns they probably have bullets for. Even if they don't, a man will miss a meal or two for another gun."

"Hello!" the man called, nearing. His beard grew to the left as if blown by a wind we couldn't feel. His shirt was open, his scrawny chest the canvas for a large drawn cross. Jesus sagged in tattooed crucifixion and behind him rose the purple form of a demon, wings open to full span creating a bruised background for Christ's death.

"Not a word, little heart," Frances warned.

From where I stood I saw her mime a lip-zipping gesture. She smiled at me. I'll always remember that.

"I'll talk to him, keep him away from you and the girl."

I broke open my weapon and approached with it hooked over one arm. I could snap it closed quick enough if I had to. It was a gesture, that was all.

The tattooed man responded by holstering his.

"Dangerous road to be travelling in twos," the man said, "Unless you're seeking some Noah I know a nothing about." He laughed, though he'd clearly thought it up on his walk over.

"It is," I said. I gestured to my waist pocket and he nodded, making a lowering motion with one hand which I hoped was a signal to the others not to panic. I reached in and showed him what I had.

"Impressive," he said. "You must walk the righteous path."

"I do."

I returned the talons to my pocket.

"So do we," he said. "Got one of the bitches back there a way. She'd sniffed us out, found our haven."

"Too bad."

"Inevitable. What do you want, you want shelter?"

"Food, if you have spare."

"No such thing, but we can spare some of what we have. What you got to spare us?"

I had something better than guns.

The food he traded took me into Texas and there I hooked up with some people heading east. I'll go at least as far as Mississippi with them, depending how things go. They have paper and pens and keep leaving messages for others along the way, telling people where they're going. I started writing this down so others might learn the truth when they got there, only I'm not sure what truth it is I want to tell. That some demons are men, there's that, though I doubt you'll believe me. I never seen one of those things that weren't a bitch with wings, and I've seen a few now. Not all women are demons, but some are. I should admit that.

The men at that gas station thought so. They took me to the cellar and showed me.

"You have to whip them," the man with the tattoo explained. "It stops the wings from growing."

The women were tied face down over boards, their backs laced with red lines that ran in ribbons. He showed me what they'd done to stop demons being born, and then he showed me where the food was, piled high in tin towers. I began stuffing my pack with it, not sure how long I'd have before Frances tried something.

"They'll find us again," the bearded man said. "Sniff us out. When you take their chicks, the mothers come hunting. But people need to learn, and we provide the opportunity here. We can't stop in our work."

No, I didn't think he could. And all the time there were groups like this, the person who Cassie called Charlotte would be in danger. It was only a matter of time before Frances saw me as a means to feed and clothe his adopted daughter, and who knew what he'd do to *her* when she got older.

"He's going to be trouble, isn't he?" the man with me said.

"If you give him time to be."

He hadn't believed me at first, this man, when I told him Frances was my prisoner. "He looks a little big for you to manage," he'd said, "and he looks armed."

"He is. But so am I and I walk behind."

"And he carries his demon on his back," the man added, liking the symbolism.

"You don't need to take it," the man said now as I forced my bag closed and hefted it over my shoulder. "You could stay."

They'd had enough from me already.

"No. Thanks. I need to keep moving."

"Alright."

He walked me outside where Frances stood patient, trusting and careful.

"Want to say anything?" the man asked me.

"No."

"Forgive him, Lord," said the man. He signalled and Frances fell, for a moment looking as if the man's quick point had thrown him down. Then came the crack of the roof man's rifle.

Cassie called for Frances from where she lay under him. The men around me heard a girl's voice calling a man a girl's name. If she later called me Charlotte they'd dismiss it as something the same.

"You want to stay for her cleansing at least?"

I shook my head, more to clear it of its images than as answer.

"Alright," said the man, and clasped my hand.

I made sure my grip was hard and firm, then walked away.

There are demons everywhere. That's what I've seen. That's what the clarity of post-2020 vision shows me. You don't need a harness to carry them, either. They come at night, tormenting my darkest hours and screaming when I try to sleep. I have a strip of wire for when they come and I whip my back to keep the wings away, lashing at my skin, scouring my flesh until they're satisfied by the pain. They come and they scream and they know me for what I am, and they know it's not just a woman.

NIGHT FISHING

Terrence leaned the throttle forward and the *Siren Cisco* lurched over a swell, coming down in the trough with a bump that did little to shake the feeling of dread that had settled like bilge in his heart. He knew what he would find today and there'd be no setting his nets until he'd hauled it aboard.

The moon was full; he'd see it easily enough. He'd see it as clearly as he could see the bridge spanning the bay ahead, though perhaps that wouldn't be for long; a low fog was coming in. It always did on nights like these.

Glancing behind, he saw that Laura had joined him at last. She was always the first and she always came in at the stern. Stern Laura, with the sky in her eyes and seaweed in her hair. She was staring past him and he wondered, as he always did, if she stared at the bridge or into the darkness of the waves that had failed to claim her.

Three hours earlier, Terrence had been pushing his shopping cart down one aisle and up another, filling it with his usual fare. An easy catch: crackers, gherkins, spaghetti in tomato sauce, cheese, beer. Some meat, maybe. Never fish.

"Tertle," came a voice from behind, then—*clisch!*—her cart had rammed into his.

"Hey, Jill."

Jill's cart was filled with various soon-to-expire goods. "How's you?"

"Oh, you know," said Terrence, "slick as an oil spill—"

"—and twice as dark."

They smiled awkwardly at each other for a moment, remembering the poem.

"The tiramisu's good for another day," Jill said eventually, reaching into her cart. "You ever had tiramisu?"

Terrence shook his head. He may have been the wild man of Castro, but Bobby was the adventurous one when it came to food. Jill took out the dessert. "You'll like it," she said, and put it in his cart. She eyed the rest of his shopping. "Wanna come over for dinner tonight? Suzie misses you. Way she carries on, sometimes I wonder if she's really gay."

Terrence smiled.

"Well? Come on, we haven't seen you in ages."

He wasn't able to answer; the sea had found its way in. It surged ankle-deep from the top of the aisle down to the checkout and washed up in a sudden wave that splashed the tills. The operators swiped grocery after grocery—*bleep! bleep!*—and the water receded without them knowing it was there, leaving lines of sand and pebbles in its wake. A crab scuttled beneath the shelves of cereal.

"You know, most men would love a home-cooked dinner with two women all to themselves, but if it's the company," —her voice became cautious— "then there's this guy I know . . ."

Terrence closed his eyes but he could still smell the brine of the wet floor and somewhere he could hear a fish as it flopped for breath. Or maybe it was his own struggle to breathe as he tried to wake up. Jill's voice had faded entirely. He knew, if he were to open his eyes, he'd find she was gone. The aisle would be empty. Or Laura would be there instead.

"This is a customer announcement," the speakers began. The voice bubbled and choked as if the throat was filling with water. "Terrence Shelby to the Golden Gate Bridge. That's Terrence Shelby to the Golden Gate Bridge."

He opened his eyes. Laura stood broken and limp at the foot of his bed, pointing.

"What time is it?" Terrence asked, rubbing the sleep from his eyes. He knew she couldn't answer.

Laura spoke a dribble of ocean, all she ever spoke, and went from the room on legs that folded too much, twisting at the hips as if her spine were made of shingle.

Terrence followed her out, the carpet squelching beneath his feet whenever he found the wet prints she'd left behind.

He eased off the speed when he caught sight of something pale bobbing port-side. His seemed the only boat out this late at night, but it wouldn't be long before others were leaving the bay to trawl for the day's specials. His catch of the day would be of a different sort, though.

The water rose and fell slowly, a welcome relief to the steepness of the city streets. "You're a city fish," Bobby had said once, "but you wish it was on the water instead of next to it." He'd been right about that, as he'd been right about so many things. They'd been on Telegraph Hill, watching the fishermen come and go. The "city fish" line, and much of the view they were admiring, found its way into Bobby's "Night Fishing." Sometimes Terrence still went to the hill and watched the ferry come in and he'd think of Bobby, entering the city in the same way as his hero, Thom Gunn. Bobby, who would wonder at a snail's fury and peer at the world through the keyholes of hotel rooms. But as good a view as the hill offered, Terrence preferred to be on the bay itself. His favourite days were when the sea was an open flatness spoiled only by the churning engines of other boats.

The pale bobbing thing in the water was nothing.

Nothing, the wanton name that nightly I rehearse till led away to a dark sleep.

He wasn't sure he remembered it right—was it supposed to be present tense? He didn't read poetry much anymore, Gunn or anyone else. He didn't want the patterns they promised; he was already living in a rhythm he didn't like.

In the water, the pale pages of an open city map rose and fell. Rose and fell.

"You lost?" Terrence had asked, more right than he knew. And Bobby, fresh from the ferry, had smiled and said, "Not anymore." His poise had hooked Terrence but the smile brought him up out of the water, gasping for air. Bobby was looking for Castro on a map that forced his arms to full length. Terrence had pointed it out gladly, said he went there a lot himself. Testing the waters.

Closer, Terrence saw it wasn't a map at all in the water but the open spread of a newspaper page that sank away with his memory. Thoughts of Bobby had fooled him, forced a reminiscence that was still as sharp as a fishhook.

Something else in the water caught his eye. It was another nothing: a sea-filled plastic bag, fat as a jellyfish. He took down a boathook to scoop it aboard; it wouldn't do to keep seeing it, wasting time wondering who it could be.

The bag came up easily, dripping.

A bloated pink face came right up after it.

Terrence fumbled the boathook as he stumbled backwards. He managed to juggle it back into his grasp as the rest of the body surfaced, the skin puckered and fish-nibbled. He stared, getting his breath back, merely startled, then calmly hooked the folds of an "I heart San Francisco" shirt and pulled the body closer.

"Hello Matthew."

He wasn't startled when the eyes opened and the man smiled the frothy smile of the drowned. Blood-tinged bubbles spilled from his lips in a careless vomit of foam, just as they had the first time Terrence found him.

"You coming aboard too?" Terrence asked, knowing the answer.

Instead of bumping against the boat's hull, the man passed through, disappearing into the vessel.

By the time Terrence had thrown out the tattered plastic bag, the drowned man was standing with Laura. His chin rested on his chest at an angle that had him forever looking down, but his waist had folded backwards on impact with the water, straightening his gaze a little. Matthew was an engineering student, stressed with his studies and finances and the certainty that he'd fail.

"How many more are coming?"

But of course, they didn't answer him.

"Come on," Terrence said, "I can take it."

Terrence and Bobby were in bed, naked, eating Japanese food from boxes and talking about why Bobby's family disapproved of his recent life choice.

Bobby tangled some squid with noodles and gave the reasons. "Your age, your colour, and your 'inclination'."

"You have the same inclination."

"Yeah. But it wasn't real to them until you."

Bobby did not play the gay scene. He went to the clubs, made a lot of friends, but resisted the casual sex with a strength Terrence only had because he'd been there and done that. Terrence used to worry they'd met too soon upon Bobby's arrival. Taking him to Castro, fresh from the ferry, he'd thought that Bobby would want to experiment, live a little, like *he* had at Bobby's age. But Bobby didn't want to live a little.

Falling hook, line and sinker for Terrence, Bobby had written him a copy of Gunn's "Tamer and Hawk" to prove as much, sticking it on the fridge with an alphabet letter the morning after they'd sealed their love (omitting the final stanza, Terrence learnt later). Not long after, Bobby had moved in.

His family did not approve.

Terrence scooped noodles to his mouth, then speared a prawn for Bobby.

"So they don't mind that I'm just a lowly fisherman?"

"Nah, Christ was a fisherman so they're good with that. Your lack of religion, though . . ." Bobby tut-tut-tutted.

Terrence had grinned, chewing his food. "Means you're the only one going to Hell."

Looking up at the bridge, buffeted by a chill wind and rocked in the chop of an irritable sea, Terrence hoped there was no such place, but he knew there was because he was in it most days. Those gathering at the prow only proved it. Laura, Matt, and now the shin-splintered Lee holding himself up by the gunwales; Terrence had pulled all of them from the water over the last year, pulled others out after, and none of them would leave him alone.

The three stood, as best as they could, looking out at the bridge they had jumped from.

The Golden Gate Bridge was once the world's longest suspension bridge and was declared a modern wonder. With the exception of London's Tower Bridge, it was the most-photographed bridge in the world. It was also the world's most popular suicide spot. "From the golden gates to the pearly ones," Bobby had joked once, back before his own dive from its heights. "People come from all over to do it. A permanent solution to their temporary problems."

Statistics varied. One jumped every two weeks or thirty jumped per year, and Terrence had read somewhere else that every month saw as many as five people drop to their deaths. The only thing that didn't vary was the fact that from that height, three hundred feet or so, hitting the water was like hitting concrete. Some survived, but not many. And usually not for long.

Terrence only ever found the dead ones.

Except Bobby.

"You should write something that's more you."

Bobby was struggling with a new poem. A new poem about one of Thom Gunn's poems.

"Like 'Fisherman', you mean?" He screwed up the piece of paper he'd been scratching away at and threw it behind him. It landed nowhere near the trash can, rolling to a stop among brothers of balled up paper sitting in crumpled crowds around the lamp stand.

"Fisherman" had been a flop, according to Bobby, which only meant his buddies at the open mic didn't like it. They didn't like it because it offered them no familiar landmark to comment on, no reference to another poet with which to expound their knowledge, display their intellect like birds spreading feathers to attract a mate. They'd loved "In Praise of Our City" because of how it played with Gunn's poem, personifying the city into the masculine without losing any of the eroticism and altering the sense of entrapment. "Fisherman," on the other hand, had been all Bobby and it was beautiful. Perhaps it was too personal for critical appreciation, but Bobby had told him poetry was all about sound, and "Fisherman" had turned his words into music.

Terrence loved it.

It would be useless to say as much with Bobby in one of his moods so he only watched as Bobby mouthed words quietly to himself, testing their shape and texture, tasting them without quite swallowing like an expert judging wine.

"Which one are you using this time?" he asked eventually. He knew it would be another Gunn.

"'On the Move'," said Bobby, confirming it. "Problem is it isn't going anywhere."

Terrence laughed. Bobby scowled, deciding whether to be hurt or not, then leaned back in his chair and laughed with him.

"Let's go out for some dinner," Terrence suggested when the laughter subsided.

Bobby's laugh became a smile which became an apology. "I can't. I need something for tomorrow night."

He reached for the book in his pocket, a collected volume of poems that was always there, though surely he knew it by heart. Terrence said that he carried the book like it was both his shield and his sword at once, something to hide behind while making his own poetic jabs. Bobby's eyes had glittered with a smile, and then he'd sulked, claiming later after some make-up sex that he'd been jealous. "You're poetic without even trying," he'd explained. Then he stole the line for "Night Fishing."

"Night Fishing" was Bobby's poem about the gay scene, his family, his poetry. It was about how hard he found it to fit in; about how he'd looked for lovers and failed; about the hooks his family had in him; about how he'd deliver his rhyming lines fishing for compliments, hoping for applause that was more than polite, and getting it only if he stole from someone else. He was Gunn's wayward bullet (a metaphor Terrence had never liked), casting his lines blindly in the dark.

"I want to go out," Terrence said.

"Okay."

For a moment Terrence thought he'd agreed but realized quickly he'd only offered permission, already lost in bastardized rhythm and rhyme.

Terrence went out, with no idea where he was going.

His ghastly crew pointed as one. Nine of them now had been drawn to the boat, stretching their arms as best they could to direct his gaze, gargling salt water and their own frothed mucus to get his attention.

Not a bag this time.

He gunned the engine just enough to turn, then cut it, drifting to where the woman rose and fell with the tide beneath the bridge. As he neared, the dead he carried with him left one by one. Some disappeared into moonlight. Others wavered like reflections on water and were gone. One or two threw themselves overboard, replaying their own end. They were gone before any splash could mark their absence.

Terrence was left with the woman in the water, the skirts of her dress billowing around her like a lily pad, she the grotesque flower. Her stomach was large and round, and he felt his usual horror that she might have been pregnant, but it would be gas. He hoped it was gas. It built up in the intestines, bringing a body to the surface after about two weeks. He'd come to know a lot about it. He knew her skin would be puckered like a washerwoman's hands. Her eyes would be missing and the softest of her flesh eaten away, but otherwise she'd be remarkably well preserved thanks to the temperature of the water. Bones would be broken from the impact. Sometimes the impact didn't kill a person, though, and they'd drown. Their violent attempts to breathe would whip the water and mucus in their lungs to a foamy froth, tinged with blood from ruptured vessels. Sometimes the sudden shock of impact and cold gave them a heart attack. Sometimes, paralyzed, they lived long enough to die from hypothermia. If they managed to do it at night, with no one watching.

This one was mottled and bloated, grinning a lipless smile at the bridge above them. In the shadows of its structure her teeth shone bright in a grimace of bitter triumph.

Terrence radioed it in.

There was the usual poor joke about his alibi but they let him haul her out of the water. They knew him well enough now.

He hooked her under the right arm and dragged her close, then leaned over to grab a handful of sodden dress, polka-dotted and clammy as flannel. She was Japanese, or Vietnamese, or Asian anyway. It was hard to tell now. It made him think of Aokigahara. With a grunt of effort he hauled her up over the gunwales. There was a wet ripping and a button flew free, ricocheting with a sharp *ping!* off something behind him, and the dead woman toppled to the deck with a heavy soft sound that was only partly water.

He didn't want to look at her, but he did.

She lay with her broken legs splayed open at unnatural angles, a gesture all the more obscene for the exposure of her breasts. What were once her breasts. They'd maybe suckled a child at some point, perhaps pleased a number of lovers, but most recently only fish had nuzzled there. If you were imaginative, it was where Death had laid his lingering kisses.

Terrence bent to pull the torn dress closed over them.

A plastic envelope, the kind designed to protect papers in a binder, was folded over and taped to her waist, Scotch tape looped around her body. The tape no longer adhered to her skin but it wrapped her like a belt and the swelling of her flesh had kept it there, something she was unlikely to have considered. Her suicide note was clearly visible inside.

He took it without thinking about what he was doing, shuddering at the feel of how her chilled skin moved under his fingers. It loosened in the water, which was why he always grabbed for clothing. Once, in wrestling one of the first bodies aboard by the hand and wrist, he had felt the skin shift under his grip, trying to come away like a glove.

This woman had written only a single page, but she had filled it. The top was little more than a blurry smudge of ink despite the plastic but the rest of it told of heartbreak and dependency and despair. Yet it was spotted with drawings of stars and hearts and had been signed off incongruously with a sun and a smiley face.

Terrence withdrew a notepad and pencil from inside his jacket and copied it down, drawings and all.

§

The note Bobby had left was written on the same paper as his poems and lay folded among them on the desk. Terrence hadn't noticed it for two days and even then he didn't recognize it for what it was. He had been looking for a note addressed to him, something explaining where Bobby had gone, why he hadn't called and wouldn't answer when Terrence tried. They'd been drifting apart, Bobby growing melancholy and Terrence trying to help but only making things worse. The first day he was gone, Terrence assumed he was in a moody sulk and staying with a friend, but the second day he became worried. Jill and Suzie had put a few calls around with no results. So Terrence looked for a note but found only pieces of Bobby's poetry, including *My Sad Captain. I used to think that obstacles to love were out of date. Much that is natural, to the will must yield, but I'll resist by embracing nothingness. I regret nothing.*

Only when he'd seen his name on the reverse did Terrence realize it was intended for him; the folded crease that was supposed to allow it to stand had failed in its duty, or Terrence himself had knocked it in his hasty search through the papers. Yet even when he realized it was for him he thought it was a break-up letter, a Dear John, thank you for fucking me but I'm leaving you. He didn't know it was a suicide note until an awful angry phone call from Bobby's father, who had identified the body. Terrence wasn't allowed to see it, nor was he invited to the funeral. He was never able to say goodbye.

My Sad Captain. I used to think that obstacles to love were out of date. Much that is natural, to the will must yield, but I'll resist by embracing nothingness. I regret nothing.

None of the words had been Bobby's, and in this new context they didn't even make much sense. Terrence had raged about it in a drunken fury to Jill and Suzie. All the fucking quoting and paraphrasing. The sad truth of it was, Bobby's poetic homage, his frequent tributes, were derivative and often misunderstood the original work. Terrence hated Bobby trying to write like someone else and Bobby's family hated him trying to live like someone else. "Bobby was only Bobby when he jumped," Terrence had said, back when he used to visit Jill and Suzie, before he realized how unfair those visits had become, how selfish. "Couldn't he just be Bobby? Couldn't they just let him fucking be Bobby?" And he had barked a harsh laugh because *fucking be Bobby* sounded fucking stupid, like an old rock 'n' roll number, and then he had sobbed. Jill had held him all the while, knowing about the churned waters of death and how there were no set tides, only a draining away that gurgled and spluttered and never really emptied.

There was no reason for it that anyone could fathom. Bobby never got on well with his family, his poetry didn't take off as much as he'd hoped, and his relationship with an older black man was under some strain (mostly because of those other factors) but none of this seemed enough, not when you knew Bobby. It wasn't enough to make him both the hurler and the hurled.

Temporary problems, Bobby. Temporary. Remember?

Terrence looked at the woman on his boat. Her reasons didn't seem all that different from Bobby's. It wasn't enough, not to Terrence. Hell, in that case he had plenty of reasons of his own.

He copied her note and replaced it. He would add his copy to the others he had collected. Soon he'd have enough to make a small book of them, *Words of the Dying*. Like that guy who made a film of them jumping to their deaths. Terrence had seen a part of it on YouTube, *The Bridge*, and it had been enough. He had been shocked and angered and compelled to watch, which Bobby said was the point. It was supposed to raise awareness, apparently, a grim visual proposal to build a suicide barrier. But such a precaution was deemed too expensive and too difficult, too much of a risk to the integrity of the bridge. Plus it would spoil the aesthetic, not to mention the view, and that would upset the tourists. "Not all of them are people 'who have come to go'," was how Bobby put it.

All the bridge needed was a net. There'd been one when it was being built, saving the lives of steelworkers who fell (the Halfway to Hell Club they called themselves) but there would never be a net now that it was complete. The only nets they found themselves in, other than whatever tangled one led them to jump in the first place, belonged to Terrence as he dredged their carcasses from the sea.

He wouldn't make a book, of course. They weren't his words to use, and the notes were private. They were the explanations and goodbyes he'd never had.

Terrence shook out a large blue section of tarp and draped it over the body, weighting it with coils of rope. She looked cocooned, ready to change into something else, though he had no idea what. Maybe something with more hope than she'd been allowed in this life.

The tarp moved. Terrence thought he'd imagined it. Thought his brain was still playing with the cocoon image. When the arm flopped out from beneath, banging hard against a rail then resting out over the water, he told himself a sudden move of the boat must have done it, one of the moves he was used to and hadn't noticed. But as he watched, her fingers curled until only one was left pointing. And she sat up.

There was a sequence of clicking sounds, a slow crackling as she rose in an effortless sit-up. She lurched to the right. Maybe to aid the pointing gesture, maybe because of the shape her spine was in. The sockets of her slackened face turned his way and he saw a darkness in them not very different to the one he saw each day in the mirror.

She opened her mouth and seawater came instead of a voice, draining from her skull in a slobbering splash against the tarpaulin, a brief loud sound in the quiet morning. A string of something dark was caught in her teeth. They came together with a sharp clack sound when her head lolled suddenly down to her chest, unsupported.

"I'm not going home yet, am I?" Terrence said.

The woman brought her arm in close and broken bone slid from the flesh of her elbow, disappearing back inside when she straightened the arm again to point.

"Alright. Okay. I'm going."

As if exhausted, the woman slumped back down, her head knocking hard on the deck. Her arm remained outstretched, moving like the needle of a compass as Terrence steered their course. He wondered if this time he had a suicide pact and he turned the boat around, feeling like the boatman on the river Styx as he steered into the mist creeping across the sea.

The Pacific is the largest body of water in the world. Its name means peace, but Terrence wondered how many had actually found any in its depths. How many would he have to fish from the water only to have them beckon him later to find more?

He had escaped the ebb and flow of it tides only once, and then not for long. He had gone to Aokigahara. There had been mist then, too, low and clinging, clutching the trunks of trees but torn to tatters by his moving feet. Before then, the closest he had been to Japan was the Japanese Tea Garden. He had been there with Bobby lots of times. When he went to Aokigahara, though, he went alone. Bobby was dead, and Terrence was seeing others like him. After the fourth, and the tests, and the fuss, he had gone to Japan to see if he saw them anywhere else; the Golden Gate Bridge was number one, but Aokigahara was the second most popular place in the world for suicide. It was a forest at the west base of Mount Fuji, also known as the Sea of Trees. Terrence had simply swapped one ocean of death for another.

There hadn't been much to see. The forest was famously absent of wildlife and the wind-blocking of the tall trees meant there was nothing more than shadows, an eerie quiet that had scared the crap out of him. Not like the sea which, even quiet, had an abundance of background noises. Terrence would never walk among those silent boughs again. There had been no sound, and no bodies. No rock-scraped corpse walked the woodland. Nothing dripped its blood from the branches, pointing with a tangle of intestines the path it had travelled down to get there. Considering *ubasute* was once practised in the woods of Aokigahara—the abandonment of the weak, the old, the infirm—Terrence had expected the forest to be a stumbling ground for aged Hansels and Gretels, frail with cold or starvation, looking for a way back to the community that had given them up. He saw none of this.

All he saw to tell him it was a popular suicide spot were the signs. Written in English and in Japanese, they urged people not to kill themselves, to seek help. They were probably no more effective than the help lines situated at points across San Francisco's bridge, the phones only there so people had someone to say goodbye to.

He stayed as long as he could before the city and its bridge called him home.

The mist that enveloped him was the outer edge of a full fog bank, but the sun would be up soon to burn it away into vaporous shreds. Besides, Terrence suspected he'd be going little further than the bridge he was under. The lady he'd retrieved was pointing along the length of its span, not beyond it, so he took the *Siren Cisco* north.

The bridge was the city's only route north. Before it, people had crossed to Marin County by boat, historical trivia Terrence found difficult to believe even though he'd seen the pictures. To him, the bridge had always been. It was a constant presence, reassuring in its solid construction and gaudy colour. To Terrence it was a symbol, albeit one he found difficult to define. A reminder of what could be achieved in life.

It was an altogether different symbol to those who jumped from it.

"From the golden gates to the pearly ones," Terrence muttered, trying to believe it. He didn't hold with the notion that suicides went to Hell, figuring it was exactly the place they thought they were escaping. But religious or not, those who jumped could only go straight down.

He looked out into the fog and saw nothing. Out there somewhere in nature's shroud was the famous Alcatraz, but Terrence knew that there were stronger prisons. He was in one. Laura, Matthew, Lee, Samantha, Jess, Dan, Stuart, Elisabeth, Catherine, Sun . . . they'd all been in one, escaping the only way they knew how: with a sudden, sharp spla—

—*sh!*

It came so suddenly on the tail of his thought that Terrence wondered if he'd conjured the sound. Less of a splash, more a crashing explosion of water—and to starboard a group of ever-expanding circles pushed outward. There was a sequence of smaller splashes as someone rose from the centre. Somewhere above was the screech of tires but it sounded to Terrence like his own internal scream, one he voiced by crying—

"Bobby!"

He knew it was stupid, that it couldn't be, but he called anyway. He'd have said the recently dead pointing him to new corpses was impossible, yet that's what they did, and he did as they told him so maybe this was his reward, Bobby brought back to him. A chance to save him.

Terrence surged forward, looking for the man to reappear, speeding to where he'd last seen him.

"I'm coming, Bobby!"

There, splashing, sucking up breath.

He cut the engine. "I'm coming!"

Oh Jesus, oh Bobby, why did you leave me? Why didn't you make me listen? I could have helped.

"Here!"

Terrence was leaning over so far he was nearly in the water himself. He was leaning too early as the boat drifted closer. Bobby was too far away, out of reach. His head was back, his long fringe a darkness over his face, mouth gaping, sucking up air with loud "huh-huh-huh" noises. One hand came out of the water occasionally and swept an arc that had him turning.

Terrence grabbed the boathook and knocked it to the deck in his haste. Picked it up, lunged it over the side, Bobby's hand coming down on the pole quite by chance. He clutched at it and Terrence pulled him in.

The water washed across the man's fringe, plastered it across his forehead, out of his face.

It wasn't Bobby.

Terrence growled, cheated, angry with himself for ever thinking such a thing. Of course it wasn't Bobby. He nearly wrenched the hook from the man's grasp. Nearly withdrew to lunge and spear him with it instead.

"Leemee."

Terrence was close enough to grab some sleeve. He released the boathook, let it sink into the bay.

"Come on, I'm here. Come on. Grab my arm."

He leaned back and heaved the man to the boat. The man gave a shrieking cry of pain, but Terrence was able to get his hands under the man's armpits. He heaved again, sickened at how easily his upper body moved as if separate to the limp legs that came up after. The man's chest went in instead of out, each ragged breath pushing it close to the shape it was supposed to be.

Twisting his own body around, Terrence leaned to bring the man up and over the rail. He struck the deck feet first with another shrill cry and Terrence saw the man had a length of bone sticking out from the bottom of his shoe, a jagged white shard pushing out from under the heel.

"You're going to be alright."

He stripped off his sweaters and draped them over the man. More of a boy, barely mid-twenties. Bobby's age. Bobby's build.

The man coughed up some of the Pacific. It dribbled down his cheeks in thin lines of bloody water. "Leave me."

"I'm going to get you to a hospital."

"Please."

Terrence saw the word on the man's lips but didn't hear it. It was too soft. He knelt closer and took the man's hand. It felt strange to Terrence, not because of how the wrist was angled but because it had been so long since he'd held hands with another man.

"Hurts."

"Yeah," said Terrence. "But you've got to fight it. Grit your teeth, come on."

"You," said the man, pausing to swallow a wheezy breath. "You don't understand."

He could no more understand than a net could hold water, but he realized then that he didn't need to. What needed to be understood was that he never would.

It wasn't Bobby, but it was. He said, "Let me go."

Terrence turned the boat and brought the engine to life with a throaty roar. His speed did not matter, for the man on the deck had already died, but even if Terrence had known he'd have leaned on the throttle all the same, speeding away from the bridge that haunted him.

Ahead, the lights of the city outlined the reasons he would never follow Bobby, or any of those he pulled from the bay. He didn't enjoy life, not anymore, but he clung to it as a drowning sailor might clutch at the wreckage of his ship. He'd clutch the wreckage and kick, toward, toward, and maybe sometimes he'd even scream for help, but he'd never let the dark waves take him.

He wanted to, but he didn't know how.

KNOCK-KNOCK

J-J looked at the door. He tried to speak but at first no sound came so he tried again and this time it came out but it was quiet. "Who's there?"

Instead of listening for an answer, J-J watched for movements where the shadows gathered in the corner of his room. He could make out the rectangle shapes of his posters, and the chair where he put his clothes, but near the desk, where the door opened, he thought he could see . . .

Something.

"Who's there?" he called again, louder. He never asked *what* was there. He didn't dare.

What should have been there, in that wasted corner of the room where the door opened (the sort of corner he never had in the old house) was a bin with a basketball hoop over it. And around that, maybe some loose balls of crumpled paper if he'd been having a bad day. He tried to remember if today had been a bad day and thought maybe it was. He'd sketched a few bumblebee cartoons his mother liked (she called them Buzzwords) and he'd tried to add a new character call—

There it was again. The knocking sound. On the door, on his bedroom door. On *his* side of the bedroom door. He was sure of it.

"Who's there?" he asked again, knowing in his heart that it was him. It was Dad.

"Joseph Jacobs, what's all that noise?"

That wasn't Dad, that was Mum. She didn't sound pleased, but she sounded closer the more she spoke which meant she was coming to his room instead of just shouting from hers. That was good. But she'd used both full names and that was usually bad, though not as bad as Joey.

Something in the corner, much taller than a rubbish bin, darkened for a moment. It bled its gloom into the other shadows of the room as the door opened.

"J-J?"

Mum stood in the light from the hall and her shadow stretched into the room with the others but that was okay because her shadow wasn't scary or even all that dark and anyway it was hers.

"Bad dream again, honey?"

J-J could only shake his head. He looked to the corner and so did she. She sighed. She opened the door wider to fill the room with light and came in. She sat on the bed, a reassuring weight that made the springs creak and a reassuring smell of cigarettes even though she'd quit and her hand took his and he could feel the reassuring oiliness of the moisturizer cream she put on before bed.

"The knocking sound?"

He nodded.

"What did we say about the knocking sound, honey?"

J-J filled his lungs and released the breath as a sigh that admitted he already knew she was right. "Just night noises as the house gets ready for bed." He would feel silly tomorrow, but that was tomorrow and right now he was still a bit scared.

"That's right. It's because this is a new place. The flat is settling down for bed, like you. It's just that you're not used to the sounds yet. Plus we have more neighbours and they make noise." She ruffled his hair, which was good because it felt good but bad because it meant she was about to go again. But then she said, "Knock-knock."

He smiled at her and replied, "Who's there?"

"Interrupting cow."

"*Mum . . .*"

"Interrupting cow," she insisted.

J-J slumped in pretend disappointment but he didn't really mind. It was an old one but a good one. He started his reply, knowing he'd never finish it.

"Interrupting c—"

"Moooo!"

They smiled at each other and there was something sad in it but that was only because of the old times in the old house.

"Knock-knock," she said again.

"Who's there?"

He was expecting the interrupting frog, the interrupting dog, maybe the interrupting duck.

"Interrupting starfish."

This was new. J-J sat up, intrigued, and began, "Interrupting starfi—"

Mum pushed her hand against his face, fingers spread wide *sort of* like a starfish, and muffled his laughter when it came. She pushed gently which was okay and pushed him so he was laying down and tickled him. He giggled and tried to push her hands away but he didn't try very hard. Eventually she stopped.

"Good one, huh?"

"Good one," he agreed, looking up at her from a tangle of bed sheets, one of the pillows half over his face.

"Good night. I'll leave the door open, alright?"

J-J nodded and felt a little embarrassed, but only a little. Then his mum kissed him on the forehead, her hair tickling his face so he had to wrinkle his nose, and she stood up. She straightened the bedding around him, said good night again, and went back to her own room.

J-J felt better, but he still waited for the knocking. He waited and waited and he fell asleep.

The knocking had first started about a year ago. He remembered because it was so close after his birthday, which was the first time Dad died, and now it was nearly his birthday again.

J-J had been sitting up in bed, decorating the cast on his arm with the new pens from Mrs. Davies next door. He had the curtains open so the streetlight came in. He was drawing a sequence of pictures, not knowing to draw boxes around them yet or to call it a comic strip, not knowing in another twenty years he'd be doing it for a living (with a series called Buzzwords). He was drawing a monkey trying to open a banana. His mother would keep the cast when it was taken off and sometimes, when he was older, and usually when he was a little drunk, Joseph Jacobs (never Joey) would look at it and see brown circles around a thick yellow arc and remember what it was meant to be. He'd called that monkey Chunky because of the ice cream he liked. He was drawing the third and final picture, the banana leaping out of its skin, when there was a knock-knock-knock! at the door. It made J-J feel like the banana but only because it was all of a sudden. Not because it was scary. Not yet.

"Yeah?" he said, thinking Mum would come in.

Knock. Knock.

"You can come in, I'm decent."

It was what Mum said sometimes, and sometimes it made her laugh when he said it.

From down the hall, from the front room, the TV suddenly went quiet and Mum called, "J-J? You ok?"

Knock. Knock. Knock. From right outside the room.

"Who's there?" he asked. He thought maybe Mrs. Davies or one of the other neighbours was staying over to keep Mum company. They'd started doing that since Dad died. But really he knew it wasn't Mrs. Davies or a neighbour which was why he asked it so quietly. He didn't really want an answer.

He was pushing so hard on the yellow pen that the felt tip disappeared into the plastic casing.

Knock.

. . .

. . .

Knock.

"Go away!"

The TV sound had crept back up but now J-J heard his Mum running down the hall and even though he knew it was her he screamed when the door burst open. She rushed in and scooped him up and held him in her lap, rocking back and forth and, "Shush, shush, shush little darling," she said, "Mummy's here."

J-J clutched at the pink fur of her dressing gown. "Someone was knocking on my door."

"Well, there's only me here, baby. Only me from now on, alright?"

He nodded against her.

"Alright?" she said again to check.

He nodded harder, but he wasn't sure.

"Hey, what are you drawing?"

So he told her about Chunky and the banana and she laughed and told him it was great, so J-J laughed too, and they talked about other drawings he would put on different parts of the cast. When they had filled it with imaginary pictures, J-J said, "Lucky it was my left arm, Mum, eh?"

She made a strange sound that was like a swallowed hiccup and sucked her lips into her mouth and stroked his fingers where they poked from the plaster. "You know he's not coming back, don't you honey? Not ever. He's gone now. I promise."

J-J looked at her and believed her because she was Mum.

"And soon your arm will be all better."

"And your nose," J-J said.

She stroked his cheek. Her nose was bigger than it usually was and she looked like she was wearing special make-up on her eyes but she wasn't. Older, Joseph would say that his Mum was a canvas Dad liked to paint on, but he didn't understand it that way yet.

"Yeah, and my nose. Might be wonky, though. Like Gonzo."

J-J laughed and she smiled, and she was right about his arm because it was fine after a while but she was wrong about her nose because that was fine too and not wonky at all.

She was also wrong about Dad and the knocking and the never coming back, not ever, because he came back again the very same night.

First he came back in J-J's dream.

J-J knew it was only a dream because Chunky was in it and a talking bee and sometimes weird things happened like he'd be outside but his bedroom furniture was there, or Mum would be at work at the pub and he was allowed in and she was working in her dressing gown and then when he went through a door he was suddenly in his room again.

Dad was sitting on the bed, turning the pages of J-J's sketchbook and looking at the pictures.

"What's all this shit?"

And now it wasn't much like a dream any more because it was real, this was something that had happened, and even though J-J wanted to change it, he couldn't. So he said exactly what he'd said last time when it was real.

"Pictures I drew. If you flick the pages fast they move."

"I know, Joey, I'm not a retard. Why are you drawing little girls in pink dresses?"

"She's a princess. She's gone to the tower to rescue the knight. If you flick it she climbs the—"

"I know to fucking flick it, Joey."

J-J backed away because Dad had said two bad words which meant he was being mean.

"Come here. Sit down." Dad patted the bed next to him and even though J-J knew what would happen and he didn't want to he went and sat down anyway because it was a dream. He could smell the oil on his dad's hands that was always there even when he washed, and he could smell the smell on his breath that made Mum angry because she smelled it all the time.

"The princess is supposed to be in the tower," Dad explained. "If you draw girls in pink dresses people will think you're gay. You're not gay, are you?"

J-J knew to say no because of the way Dad asked the question, but he didn't really know what the question was. Maybe if J-J showed him how the book worked Dad wouldn't mind so much.

"Look," J-J said, "If you flick it—" He reached for the sketchbook but Dad grabbed his arm like he really did the time when it was real and he pushed J-J away from the flick book and just like before he didn't let go when J-J fell and there was a cracking sound that hurt oh so much that J-J screamed and called for Mummy and still Dad wouldn't let go. He shook him instead and J-J screamed again because his arm moved different. The flick book fell to the floor and the dream was different now because the book was flicking all on its own and there was no tower or princess or anything, just a big brown door that opened and closed and opened and closed and from the pages came a knockknockknockkno—

J-J woke and scrambled a nest of bedding around himself.

The knocking was real. It was coming from his real door. There was no flick book but J-J had knocked the clock from his bedside table to the floor. The numbers on the floor glowed 03.46 and the 0 at the front meant it was early in the morning and not the afternoon. J-J didn't want to pick it up because he didn't want to reach outside the covers because the door was opening all on its own without the handle even moving which was impossible but it was still happening and maybe he was still dreaming. But he could feel how the cast on his arm itched and if he was dreaming he didn't think he'd feel that kind of thing.

The door swung inward and Dad was back like he'd only been on holiday but it must have been a bad holiday because he looked angry.

"Knock-knock."

J-J looked at the clock and saw it was 4.10 with an 0 in front which meant they had been telling knock-knock jokes for twenty minutes which was ages. He liked jokes and he liked the light on and he liked his Mum being there.

"Knock-knock," she said again, rapping her knuckles gently, always gently, on J-J's head to get his attention.

"Who's there?"

"A dwarf."

"A dwarf who?"

"A dwarf so short he can't reach the doorbell."

J-J laughed even though it wasn't funny but it was funny that she could keep making them up after all the ones she'd said already, even if some of them were really awful.

"Knock-knock."

"Who's there?"

"The talking rhino."

"The talking rhino who?"

"Hey, how many talking rhinos do you know?"

That one was really stupid but he loved it and because he loved it Mum kept going. She'd started with "Mummy" and the answer had been "Mummy who loves you" and she told that one a few times but there was also "boo who, why are you crying" and "toodle-who, what do you mean goodbye, I only just got here" and also "Smee" who was actually "smee again, the talking rhino." There was "lettuce in it's cold out here" and there were interrupting cows and pigs and dogs and cats and ducks and that first night was when the knock-knock jokes became what they did when J-J heard the knock-knock noise that scared him.

"Lettuce."

"Lettuce who?" J-J asked, even though he already knew it was cold outside.

"Lettuce go to bed now, you need some sleep. Ok?"

J-J nodded and Mum stroked his hair down flat at both sides and kissed his head. She stayed there until he was asleep and when she went she left the door wide open.

The next day, J-J was allowed to stay home from school because he was so tired. Mum phoned in to her other job and said she couldn't clean today and although J-J heard an angry voice on the phone Mum said it was all okay. She told him that Mrs. Davies might come round and it would be nice if she saw him using those new pens, so he sat in front of the TV drawing.

Mrs. Davies didn't come round but Mum's friend Jenny did, and she liked seeing J-J using the pens even if she wasn't the one who gave them to him. She always liked whatever J-J was doing, he could tell. She always smelled of flowers and she dressed nice and her hair was like someone from TV.

"Is that a rhino?" she said, tapping his cast where he was colouring.

"Yeah."

"What else are you going to draw?"

J-J shrugged.

"You heard anything lately?"

He looked at her and was about to ask how she knew but she was speaking to Mum now who stood smoking in the doorway. Mum must have told her about the knocking.

"No," Mum said.

"He won't bother you any more, I bet you."

J-J tried not to bother his mum ever, but he would try extra hard from now on.

Jenny started smoking too, standing up and moving away from J-J to do it. "He won't come back," she said.

J-J went back to his drawing, glad and happy and believing Jenny completely, and they left him to it.

J-J covered most of the cast that morning, drawing all the things he and Mum had talked about the night before. He left a space for Jenny to write something because that's what you were supposed to do and he gathered up a fistful of pens and went to see if she wanted to.

"And you said he was dead?"

"No, I said he'd gone away, but a *friend* at J-J's school said dead was what gone away meant."

Toby said that. His puppy had died before it was even a dog and *his* Mum said it had gone away, gone somewhere better, but Toby's Dad said it died, and that's what Toby told J-J. He said gone away and a better place and heaven were all words for died that made you feel better.

J-J watched Mum and Jenny drinking their coffee, waiting to hear what they'd say next. He knew he was probably being naughty but it was about Dad and sometimes adults said things different when they didn't think he was around. They didn't see him waiting with his pens.

Mum said, "It's better than the truth in a way. And he is dead, sort of. Dead to us, anyway." She stabbed out her cigarette. "Hope he fucking stays that way."

J-J gasped at the bad word and that was when they saw him.

"Will you write something?" he quickly asked Jenny, quickly, before he could be told off. Mum stood up and took the cups to the sink.

"Yeah, okay sweety. Come here."

She said what she was writing, which was get well soon, and she signed her name fancy and she put a kiss next to it and then she put a real one on his cheek that made him all shy. Mum and Jenny laughed in a nice way and he left them before they could remember he'd been listening to adult talk.

§

Knock. Knock. Knock.

J-J ignored it. He pulled the covers to his eyes and peered over the top. There was no one there. Mum said so.

Knock, *and* knock, *and* knock.

There was a small metal click because the door hadn't been closed properly and now it was opening. Opening. A wedge of light from the hall was growing on his floor. There was a shadow inside it.

J-J pulled the sheets over his head which made it worse because he didn't know what was happening or who was there, but now he couldn't pull the sheets down again because then he'd see what was happening and who was there and it would be . . .

Smee again, Joey. Daddy's back.

J-J shut his eyes as tight as he could get them. He was mostly scared when Dad had "been drinking" which was when he came in to say mean things about Mum. But J-J drank too, everybody did, you had to or you'd die (go away) and J-J never became mean or did things he shouldn't unless he was allowed a bit of coke which made him want to act out what he was drawing which might get him told off sometimes. But he was more scared of *this* Dad than the drinking Dad because this Dad should be gone away to a better place like heaven but not heaven because of the things he did.

The door creaked, a long sound that went up slowly, and then the soft bump against the desk corner stopped the door completely.

J-J could smell the Dad smell which was oil and sweat and where Mum worked and something else.

Why you hiding, Joey, you scared? You pussy?

J-J was not a scaredy cat usually, not unless the knocking came, but this time Dad was right.

Dad was stepping quietly around J-J's room. J-J could hear him. At one point there was the sound of the tin of pens on the desk like it had been knocked. J-J felt cold because his door was open and his radiator wasn't on any more but sometimes he felt more cold, a moving cold from head to toe or toe to head, depending which way Dad was going in J-J's room.

The door groaned slow as it moved again . . .

Gotta go, Joey, but I'll be back, don't worry. Leave the door open for me and I won't need to knock.

. . . and then there was the snick-click as the door closed and there was the muffled thump of the wood settling into its frame.

Even with the door closed again, J-J couldn't peek, couldn't come out from his sheets, because it might be a trick like his Dad sometimes played and he might still be in the room waiting to say boo and it would be like boo-who but not the funny kind because J-J was a scaredy pussy sometimes.

He fell asleep clutching the covers over his head and tucked into a ball but he didn't dream and that was good.

In the morning J-J asked his Mum about ghosts.

"Do I believe in them, is that what you mean?"

"No, are they really real?"

J-J knew that believing in something wasn't the same as it being really real because at school they'd learnt about God and in the playground Toby said Santa Claus was made up too just to make extra sure we could have Christmas.

"Some people think they're real. But they're just stories people make up to scare each other."

"Why do people scare each other?"

J-J was thinking of what Dad was like even before he died.

"For some people it's fun, if it's pretend." She stopped the washing up to look at him, her hands still in the sink. "Why are you asking about ghosts?"

J-J looked into his cereal, as if something he could say might be swimming around in his Cheerios.

"Is it the knocking?" She took her hands out of the sink and wiped them dry on a towel. Little drifts of washing up bubbles floated to the kitchen floor like what J-J used to think ghosts looked like. Mum pulled a chair around to sit near him at the table. "Is it the knocking, honey?" she asked again.

J-J nodded.

"And you think it's a ghost?"

"I heard you talking and you said you hoped he stayed dead which means maybe he won't."

"Oh honey." She took his hand in both of hers, the one that wasn't in plaster, and she held it and rubbed it and said, "Your Dad won't bother you again, okay? You have to trust me about that. He's not a ghost. He's gone away and he won't come back, he said so."

"How can he say so if he's not a ghost?"

He watched her decide to say something and then decide not to. Then the phone rang and she didn't have to say anything to him because she was saying hello on the phone instead.

She covered it with her hand and told him, "Get your shoes on for school," and then she carried on talking.

J-J went to his room. He pulled on his trainers and picked up his bag. He would show Toby his pictures today. He went to the desk for his sketchbook and grabbed it and realized it was open on the page where he'd drawn a bird learning to fly with a balloon. He hadn't drawn a door but there was one, a brown rectangle sticking up in the grass.

J-J's fingers felt stuck to the book like when you first take an ice-pop from the freezer, and they were a bit cold like that as well. He tore the page out because it was ruined and there were dotted lines to let you do that and behind it was his picture of a dog on skis but he was heading straight for an open door, a brown rectangle with a little circle handle.

All of his pictures had doors on them and then the blank pages after the pictures had doors on too.

"Joseph, come on, shoes."

J-J tried to say something but only made funny noises. He tried to show her the book but couldn't hold it still.

Mum said they needed some help and a few days later she took J-J to a special doctor.

J-J's Mum asked lots of questions about doors and Dad after what happened with the sketchbook and she told lots of knock-knock jokes and sometimes he slept in her room even though he was a big boy now. Dad used to say that sometimes but Mum said it different. The doctor asked him lots of questions about the knocking and if he had bad dreams and a different doctor asked about Dad and she asked some questions that made J-J shy but that was all they did and the knock-knock-knocking kept happening whatever he told them, so one day Mum said they'd move and then it stopped for a bit. They moved anyway just to make sure.

The new house was called a flat and it was smaller than the old house and the doors had to be held open with little rubber triangles or they closed on their own. Jenny still visited them sometimes and that was good, but Mrs. Davies never did and that was good too, really, because even though she was nice and gave him the pens on his last birthday she didn't *smell* very nice and sometimes she farted quietly and they didn't smell very nice either. They all had to pretend they didn't hear it or smell it because that was the polite thing to do.

The knocking didn't come for ages in the new house and J-J told himself that even when it did he would pretend he didn't hear it to be polite and not upset Mum.

It did come, though, just like he knew it would, and he couldn't ignore it even though he really wanted to.

It happened on the day of the phone call.

J-J heard the phone when he was in the bath on a Saturday and he heard Mum say hello and then all he heard was splashing as he began the diving competition, flipping toys into the air to see who could do more summer-salts before landing—ploop!—in the water. Spiderman was winning but that made sense because he was really gymnastic.

"—you fucking dare, I'll call the police!"

It was the bad word that made J-J stop playing and though he knew he shouldn't listen to others talking if they weren't talking to him he listened anyway. It was funny to hear because it was only one person, but not funny like a knock-knock joke.

"I don't care what she said, I don't want to see you and neither does J-J . . . I never said that . . . If that's what she thinks, she's got it wrong . . . So? So? What did you say to her? What did you say you'd *do*? Well she wouldn't just give it to you. She wouldn't give you this number without a fucking good reason."

J-J was sort of scared because Mum sounded really angry but a bit scared as well.

"What? No . . . No! Fuck off!"

She hung up the phone so hard J-J heard something break and then he heard something else break like when Dad was alive (it sounded like a breakfast bowl) and then there was the tatta-tat-tat-tat of his plastic cup bouncing around on the floor.

J-J held his nose and dunked under the water so he wouldn't hear anything else and he closed his eyes because of the soap.

When he came up again and opened his eyes, Mum was there with a towel. Her eyes looked like she'd got soap in them. She held the towel out to dry him which he usually liked but this time she did it too hard and it hurt a bit but he didn't say anything because she was speaking. She wouldn't stop speaking.

"... so we're not going to go to the park today, honey, because Mummy has to do some things and go to work later because Tricia called in sick which made me angry for a bit but I'm ok now, alright? I'm going to take you to Mrs. Davies and she'll look after you until I'm back—what's that?"

"Can Jenny look after me instead?"

Mum's mouth disappeared into a thin line and she breathed hard and she stared at him the same way she was breathing. She did it for so long he didn't know if she'd heard him.

"Can I go to—"

"No. You can't. Jenny's not our friend any more." She began rubbing him too hard again with the towel and he cried because he liked Jenny even though he was trying really hard not to.

"Oh, be *quiet* Joey!"

She covered her mouth with her hands as if to show him how, even though he was quiet already because she'd called him Joey.

"Honey, I'm sorry."

She picked up the towel and hugged him in it and that was good and now *she* was crying instead and he said it was alright, it was okay, which was what Mum always said to him and just like when Mum said it, it worked.

She wiped her eyes on his towel and said maybe they could go to the park later, but it would probably be tomorrow.

The next phone call J-J heard that day was at Mrs. Davies's house. It was weird going there because it was sort of like going home but not really because they went next door. One day there would be new people in the house where J-J used to live but Mrs. Davies said there wasn't anybody yet.

The phone call J-J heard was from Mum to Mrs. Davies and he knew straight away that it meant he'd be staying over which meant he'd be right next door to where he used to live where there was knocking.

"Yes dear, he's been an angel," Mrs. Davies was saying. "You just do what you have to do and pick him up whenever. We'll watch a film or something."

Mrs. Davies winked at J-J and he sort of smiled back even though he knew the film would be black and white.

"Yes, that's alright. I'll put him in the guest room or he can stay in with me."

J-J tried to hear his Mum's voice but Mrs. Davies played her TV really loud. Someone was getting excited about winning a fridge, which J-J thought was a silly prize to get excited about.

"That was your Mum on the phone," Mrs Davies said. She looked at the TV when she said it, as if she was telling the man concentrating there. "Charles Dickens," she said. "Do you want some chips?"

J-J had no idea why Mrs Davies called him a different name but he did want some chips so he said yes please.

When she went to the kitchen the man on the TV said Charles Dickens and everybody cheered and clapped including J-J because Mrs. Davies must be magic or something.

The room he was supposed to sleep in was the same size and shape as his old one next door but it had different furniture and smelled of the polish Mum used except all of the whole room smelled of it.

"When's Mum coming?" he asked, hoping Mrs. Davies wouldn't kiss him goodnight.

"Later, dear. When you're asleep," she said and she kissed him goodnight. Her lips were like the special rubber that can rub out pen.

"Did you like the film?" she asked as she was leaving, and then, "Do you want the lamp left on?" which was good because yes he did, please, and he didn't have to answer about the film which he didn't really like.

"Goodnight Joseph."

When she closed the door, J-J realized the lamp only really showed how dark the rest of the room was, but he tried to sleep anyway because that's when Mum would come to collect him.

He could hear the new people next door. Mrs. Davies said nobody had moved in yet but she must have been wrong. Someone was in the room that used to be his and he could hear them moving around, bumping into things. Knocking on the wall.

"Mrs. Davies . . ." J-J said, but he didn't say it loud enough. It sounded wrong asking for her when he wanted Mum but she—

Knock-knock.

J-J rolled away from the wall, coiling himself in a cocoon of bed sheets. At the foot of the bed he stared at where the noise had come from.

There was a darkness on the wall, like an upright puddle. It moved, and another knocking came from where it stopped.

It moved.

It stopped.

It knocked.

It moved again.

Right above the bed.

"Go away," J-J said. "Please go away."

The lamp died with a soft "tink," the bulb gone (away), and the room was dark as black and J-J tried to yell but only breathed out.

The knocking came again, muffled by the bricks of the wall at first, but getting louder as whatever was making the noise pushed through from next door, pushed through from somewhere else.

Knock.   Knock.   Knock-knock-knock.
KnocknocknocknocKNOCKNOCKN—

Interrupting cow, talking rhino, doctor, toodle, boo, lettuce—

Lettuce in, it's cold over here.

Dad stood in the wall near the bed, dark with something like oil that didn't smell the same and spread around him as a stain of shadows. His eyes were really really white in the dark and one looked at J-J properly but the other one stared off at a different angle. His hand was up where he'd been knocking and J-J could see Dad's fingers were curled in a knocking fist but two of them dangled loose in a weird way. Something that wasn't oil dripped from them and outside a car went past and its lights moved across the room so Dad seemed to move too and the drips from his hand made little red circles on the sheet because he was so close to the bed and that was how J-J knew the dark stuff on Dad was blood because he'd seen blood on his bed before. A puddle of it grew at Dad's feet and stretched darker than the dark. Dad stepped from the wall into the room and when he opened his mouth blood came out instead of sound. J-J heard him anyway.

Hello Joey, you little Mummy's boy. I was gone away somewhere else but now I'm back.

J-J tried to call out again and this time when he did it was loud like a scream—

You sound like a little girl.

—and Mum came running from her bedroom except it wasn't Mum it was Mrs. Davies and she wasn't quite running like Mum did. Dad stood with blood spilling down his chin and he pointed his bloody fist at J-J, at Joey, trying to point with the dangling finger.

The door opened fast and J-J screwed his eyes up closed so he wouldn't see what was there.

"Joseph?"

He opened his eyes to see Mrs. Davies.

Nothing else. No one else.

"Joseph, what's wrong?"

Knock-knock-knock.

Even though he was a big boy, J-J wet the bed. Mrs. Davies saw the spreading wet and said, "Oh," then looked down the hall behind her.

Knock-knock.

"Don't open it," J-J tried to say but he couldn't breathe properly and each word came out with a gulp of air between them.

"I'll be right back to clean you up," Mrs. Davies said. And she went away.

"No!"

J-J chased after her because he didn't want to be left on his own, but in the hall the knocking came again. It came loud from the front door.

KNOCK KNOCK KNOCK KNO—

"Okay!" Mrs. Davies cried.

The knocking stopped. She really was magic. But it didn't stop J-J from cringing when she reached out to open the door and in came—

Mum.

She pushed in quickly past Mrs. Davies. "Why didn't you answer the door?" She was wearing her long coat done all the way up, even though it wasn't raining and it was really hot in the house.

"Mummy!" J-J said, even though she was Mum now.

"Jesus, what's going on?" She picked him up and hugged him even though he was wet with wee. She took him through to the bathroom. "He wets himself and you don't bother cleaning him?"

Mum was angry at Mrs. Davies even though it wasn't her fault and Mrs. Davies looked scared even though she could make the knocking stop but J-J didn't care because Mum was here.

"He's only just done it," Mrs. Davies said, following Mum to the bathroom. "He had a nightmare, poor thing."

Mum set him down in the bath tub.

The bath had a shower hose attached to the taps and Mum turned it on without taking off his pyjamas and sprayed his bottoms with it. It was a bit cold and J-J backed away from it but she pulled him back in.

"The knocking noise again?"

He nodded. She pulled his bottoms down and helped him step out of them, but she did it quickly, like she was angry with him. She gave him the soap and he washed himself.

"I told you to stop worrying about that," she said, "Dad's gone, okay? You're safe now, forever and ever."

She was angry.

"I know," J-J said, "but he might come back."

Mum looked at Mrs. Davies. "Can you tell the taxi I'll just be a few minutes? It's waiting outside."

Mrs. Davies nodded and went.

"He won't come back," Mum said. She thrust a towel into his hands. "Not now. Not ever."

When they were home Mum started running a bath even though it was night and even though J-J was clean.

"You, bed," she said.

J-J went to his room and left the light on and waited under the covers for the final tuck. When he heard Mum crying he got up again to tell her it was okay, it was alright, even though she was trying to cry quietly so he wouldn't know.

She was leaning over the bath. Her long coat was on the floor and she didn't have her other clothes on either. They were in the bath, making the water pink as she rubbed a bar of soap over them.

"I bought you some paint," she said. She tried to wipe her eyes and pretend she wasn't crying. "I spilled them on myself so now I'm washing it out of my clothes, okay honey?" She sniffed. She was all snotty like she had a cold. "I got the yellow out, and the blue and the green, and now it's just the red left."

"It's okay, Mum. I don't need paint. I got my pens."

Most of the ones Mrs. Davies gave him had run out, but some hadn't. And anyway, he had coloured pencils.

"I want you to be happy," Mum said, twisting her clothes around and around. "You deserve all the bright colours in the world."

The knocking came one last time that night. J-J was in bed and tucked in safe but he wasn't sleeping. He heard the knocking far away down the hall. It was the front door. He looked at his clock but all it said was oh-oh, oh-oh, which must have meant it was a special time that wasn't late and wasn't early but it sounded like trouble if you said it out loud.

He heard the knock again and then Mum's voice, "Hello?"

She sounded like J-J did when he heard the knocking in his room and so he knew this was very bad, this was adult scary.

There was a voice from the other side of the door. J-J heard the shape of it but not the words. It must have been okay because Mum opened the door and they came inside. J-J knew it was they because the first voice he couldn't really hear was a man's and the next one was a lady's.

"We just have a few questions," she said. "It won't take long."

"Good," said Mum, "my little boy's asleep."

He wasn't, though.

They went into another room, the front room probably, and J-J could only hear the murmur of them talking. He heard Mum sometimes, though.

"No," he heard her say. It was loud but it was wet sounding too, like she was crying with her voice.

The other voices were a murmur again and J-J tossed back the quilt and got up. He put his Transformers slippers on so he was quiet and he went down the hall. He didn't sneak. He didn't tip-toe. But he held his breath so he could hear better and not be heard.

". . . not consistent with the accident," the man said, "and no fault could be found with the pit-lift. Looked like it had been lowered deliberately, and after he had sustained his injuries. Do you understand what I'm saying?"

J-J only heard his Mum cry.

"Should we be talking about this somewhere else?" the lady asked.

Mum must have said something because the man said, "What was that?"

"He was a monster," Mum said, and J-J started to cry because of how Mum was crying and because he thought she meant him and even when she said, "He was a bad man," and J-J wasn't a man, he still cried.

"Hello there."

The woman had come out from the front room and into the hall. She was smart like a man. She wore a jacket and trousers. She had long dark hair that was a bit silver and she smiled at him with her mouth but not her eyes.

"J-J?"

Mum came out too and she knelt down and hugged him, kissing his neck and his ear and his face.

"Mummy's got to go with these people for a while," she said.

"Can I come?"

"No honey, you can't come. I'll take you to . . . Jenny's. I'll take you to Jenny's, okay?"

J-J nodded because she wanted him to but nothing was okay at all, even going to Jenny's. He wanted the whole world to cry without really knowing why.

"I'll only be a little while," she said.

The man was in the hall as well now and he looked at the woman and she looked at him and J-J didn't like what he saw there at all because it was like they were saying Mum was wrong.

J-J looked very smart, everybody said so, but he didn't care about that. A nice man who Mum said was on her side gave him a pad and some pens but they were writing pens and not very good for drawing and J-J couldn't really concentrate anyway. He tried to listen to what was happening but there were lots of big words and some of it was very fast and no one really looked at each other when they spoke which made it hard to understand. Other people watched too, like it was a cinema.

J-J knew when it was finished because of Mum's face.

"Mum's going away," she said, just like he knew she would, "and—"

But J-J knew what going away really meant so he screamed "No!" at her and at everybody else in the room and he did it so loud that people started to get very upset, even the mean man with stupid white hair that wasn't even real.

"No honey, not there, not forever, just gone away for a little while. Somewhere else."

"Like Dad?"

"No, not like your dad."

"Can I come?"

Mum nodded, but what she said was, "You can visit."

Jenny looked after him and she took him to see Mum sometimes but he knew the woman they showed him wasn't really her. She was different, even though she looked like her. But she'd come back one day, he knew she would, everybody said so. It wouldn't be fair if Dad could come back but Mum never could.

J-J waited for her and he drew pictures. Sometimes he drew a talking bee, other times a rhino or a monkey, but most of all he drew *her*. He drew his Mum. And while he waited for her to come back he drew a frame around her like an open door. He waited for her every night, hoping to hear her knock-knock, and if it was her he wouldn't bother with "Who's there?" because he'd just say, "Come in!"

THE DEATH DRIVE OF RITA, NEE CARINA

Rita searched for roadkill on the nights she couldn't sleep. She would drive until she found a dead animal or became drowsy, whichever happened first. One-fifth of all road traffic accidents were caused by people falling asleep at the wheel, but Rita had never nodded off while driving. She didn't sleep much at all these days. Counting sheep only helped if they were broken shapes of bloody wool, and so far she'd never found such a thing. Instead she'd find an explosion of feathers that was once a bird, or a hedgehog spewing its own insides out, or a badger with its head twisted around on a bone-splintered neck. Once she'd found a fox that had been flattened by something so big that its body had separated into two pieces, one either side of a dirty orange-furred tire print smeared across the road.

There.

At first she thought it was a cat, but on a second pass she saw its ears had been torn from its skull by somebody's skidding wheels, and its once-fluffy tail was buried beneath a spaghetti pile of entrails. A rabbit. It must have been hit at least twice already, the second vehicle crushing the animal's midsection to flat skin and forcing out everything that had once been stored inside.

She parked her VW Golf, put on the hazards and clambered out using the passenger door because it was furthest from any traffic that might pass, even at such an early hour. She put on a high-vis vest and took a safety flare from the glove compartment, setting it one hundred paces from the car. She quickly spread an already split bin liner inside the boot, taking out the only other item stored there. It was a shovel.

She walked to where the rabbit lay and put the blade of the shovel between its body and the organs it had been forced to shit from itself. With a series of sideways scrapes she separated the insides from the outside then scooped them up and flung them to the roots of a nearby hedge, an offering to savage nature. The glow of her rear lights lent a hellish red glow to each of her actions, and every orange flash of the hazards added the suggestion of flames, casting Rita's face into regular repeated shadows. She didn't notice. Carefully, she slid the shovel under the furred body and peeled it from the road. The earless head lolled. Its hind limbs hung limp over the edge of the shovel. Flopsy rabbit, all right. But it was intact.

She walked quick mincing steps to the open boot, a grotesque egg-and-spoon race in which she was the only contender, and dropped the body inside. She wrapped it in the plastic and tied it. She wiped the shovel on roadside vegetation to remove the worst of the wet smears and wrapped the business end in another bin bag before laying it on the backseat.

She retrieved the flare, returned to her car, and drove home.

The garage had a workbench at one end. She reversed into the space, blipped the door closed, and got out as it lowered. Then she went to the boot and transferred the rabbit to the bench. Before anything else, though, she'd make a cup of cocoa. It was chilly, and there was no heating in the garage. The drink would warm her while she worked.

Rita lived alone. She hadn't always. But the kids' room was now a shrine and her husband's side of the bed had been cold for almost two years. It meant she didn't tidy up much. The kitchen was a clutter of cups and teaspoons—she only washed them when all had been used—but there was still the World's Best Mum mug which she always saved for last. She made her cocoa and took it back to the garage, stopping only to pull on some latex gloves.

The rabbit looked like a deflated toy, or a cuddly one with its stuffing torn out. Rita would fix that. She'd plump it back to life.

She selected something she thought was suitable from her shelves. It was too big, stretching the skin, so she created something smaller and forced it inside. When she had finished, scraping some of it out, forcing new contents in, the rabbit looked almost healthy. Almost. It was as close as she could get it, considering the missing ears.

Next, she stitched up the torn open end of the animal. Some of the tearing had been her, but not all of it. It was important that it looked as natural as possible. Not that anybody else would look as closely, or care as much, as she did.

Finally, she said her prayers.

When she was done, her cocoa was cold. It didn't matter; she was ready for bed now.

She hadn't done enough: she dreamed. She woke from its crowded fire to the emptiness of her cold room and knew what she had to do if she wanted proper rest.

She got up, and grabbed her keys.

Crouched behind an old dry stone wall, Rita tried not to think about where she was. She was cold, even with her coat and hood. Her knees were up to her chest, arms wrapped around the shins for warmth. She hoped it didn't rain. She was sheltered from the wind, but occasionally a gust was channelled down through the gravestones of the churchyard she sat in. Her car was parked some distance away, in a parallel country lane.

It was dark. The sky was cloudy and no stars shone. The moon was missing from the sky, an eye closed on what would happen. It was so dark that Rita didn't notice when her own eyes closed until she dreamed again.

She woke from the nightmare's *whoomph!* and its sudden heat to find herself cold and unrested in the churchyard once more. Names she hadn't spoken for a long time remained unvoiced in her throat but she saw them before her, chiselled in stone. Todd, Sian, Charlotte. She reached as if to trace the "forever sleep" of the inscription when the sweep of headlights threw her shadow long and far from the words.

A car was coming.

Rita stood and her knees popped. She crouched, and stood again; crouched and stood. Stretching like an athlete warming up.

The car was coming fast, relying on the lateness of the hour and the seclusion of the route to ensure a lack of oncoming vehicles. They clearly didn't know how dangerous this spot could be, knew nothing of its reputation. The full beam of its headlights cast shadows across the graves and soon it would be at the bend, slowing to turn and speeding again afterwards. Rita could hear music from its open window, something loud and heavy and repetitive, and she wondered if the driver was returning from a pub or party. One in six road deaths were the result of driving under the influence of alcohol or drugs. Alcohol slowed reaction speeds and removed the inhibitions that road safety depended on.

The car was here. It had turned. It was accelerating.

Rita stepped out into its path. She muttered her prayer standing still in the centre of the road, closing her eyes as the driver widened his.

She heard the loose stones of the rough road crunch under locked wheels and several struck her, but the car did not. She felt it pass, felt the rush of its motion-made wind, and then it was thumping over grass and tearing through hedge before slamming directly into one of the many trees lining the road. Rita opened her eyes with the gunshot report of its impact, saw the bonnet V around ancient oak and the windscreen shatter, heard the brief blast of horn as head met steering wheel before whip-lashing back against the seat.

Rita pulled her hood down from her face as she ran to the vehicle. She knew how frightening she looked, all facial scars and only sporadic hair. She peered in at the driver. A young man with a face of blood instead of features. His hand on the dashboard twitched in final spasms. Behind him, lying sprawled across the back seat, a young woman groaned but was still. Her eyes fluttered as if in a deep sleep.

Rita reached in and took the fluffy dice hanging from the rear-view mirror then ran away into the night. If the young woman passenger saw any of it she would only remember a monster.

Carina had only ever seen one car accident and it was the one she'd been in. Rita, the name she'd given herself afterwards, had seen fifteen more. There had been nothing accidental about any of them.

She tucked the rabbit into a blanket on the front seat beside her so she could get to it quickly. She had something she'd fashioned from a board and some nails stuffed inside. She'd wanted to use a four-pronged shape she'd made of twisted metal, something that would sit like a sharp pyramid inside the chest cavity, but in trying to insert it she'd discovered it was too large. The fur stretched around it unnaturally. So in the end she'd hammered a few four inch nails into a piece of wood half an inch thick and dressed it with rabbit skin. The nails were clustered enough that no single tip pressed the flesh into a tell-tale point. What she didn't want was for a do-gooder motorist to remove the corpse from the road and discover her contraption propped inside. Rita assumed she'd be all right; nobody would handle the animal with their hands anyway.

She dressed smart, as if going to work, in case she was stopped or caught or questioned or something and could look professional, trustworthy. She hadn't worked since the accident, she didn't need to, but she still had the clothes. She felt good this morning. Rested. Successful and with purpose, just as the clothes suggested.

"Come on, Flopsy. Let's hit the road."

Stupid expression. You didn't hit the road; the road hit you.

The engine started straight away; she kept the new Golf in good repair. She pulled out of the garage and headed for one of the main roads leading to the city. She'd missed rush hour, that ironically named period when cars barely moved, taking people to jobs that offered the same stunted progress. This was the *real* rush hour, now. The time when most were at work already except for those running late; the ones actually *able* to rush. The ones who wouldn't swerve for roadkill.

She drove a familiar stretch between roundabouts until the road was clear enough, then quickly deposited the nail board bunny near the middle of the road. There was enough green either side that it was a feasible spot for a rabbit, and she was far enough away from the main stretch to avoid CCTV. She got back in her car and drove it to somewhere she could park. Then she walked to a flyover bridge that offered a good view and waited.

§

The first time Rita deliberately caused a collision was three months after Motorway Day, one week after her release from hospital. She had taken her new name by then. Carina, wife and mother, no longer existed.

I will only exist in road traffic accidents, in RTAs. The road and I and traffic accidents. I am Rita.

It was perfect. She should have seen it sooner. But then her god worked in the same mysterious ways as everybody else's. Why would it let her survive and not others if not to tell her something, show her something? This is how I feed, it said. This is how I remind you I exist. Respect me. Fear me. Strap your belt across your chest, let bags of air cushion you with complacence, and I will still take what is owed. I shove engine blocks through steel and plastic to smash your husband's knees, folding him foetal, tearing his groin to ribboned ruins. I make children fly through broken glass to fall hard and fast, scraped bare, right down to bone. I shatter rear windscreens, shower children with cubes of glass, and while one of yours fumbles with the buckle in her lap I give her a motorcycle to tear the hair from her scalp in its spinning wheel, sear her face with hot engine metal. I ignite fuel with a *whoomph!* that is my war cry and you'll hear it in every dream with your daughter's scream as flesh roasts and drops from blackened bones, however briefly the fire burns. And you, held in place by belt and bag, will hear it all, smell it all, and know me.

And should you dare forget, I have marked you.

By the time Rita was in position, someone had already driven over the rabbit. The head was a flat smear and the impact had tossed the body onto its back. It wouldn't matter, there were nails both sides of the board. However, it was now more or less over the white lines, so unless someone was overtaking . . .

Rita waited.

In the early days after Motorway Day, Rita had considered dropping bricks from a spot like this. She'd wait for a car loaded with people and let it fall. The windscreen would smash and someone might be killed, but better would be a dramatic swerve into oncoming traffic, or a panicked spin, a skidded circle to face the rushing cars coming up behind. There'd be the squeal of tire rubber and cars would hit cars with the dull thump and crunch of metal, the soft smash of windscreen glass and the sound it made as it shushed and fell in chunks and scattered across the tarmac and maybe a car would even roll over and—

A slow Rover, 400 series, was approaching. An elderly man was driving. Rita could see him because of how low he sat in the seat, peering over the dashboard like Mr. Magoo. There was no danger of him hitting the bunny board, and he'd be a poor offering anyway, but behind, impatiently swerving out to check for oncoming, waiting to overtake, was someone in a Nissan Micra. Good enough car, sturdy, but just as vulnerable as any other at its wheels. Rita watched it coming, watched it coming, saw it swoop out into the other lane and pass under her. She turned to the other railing of the bridge and watched as the left back tire pulverized the roadkill into wet chunks and blew out simultaneously. The board pinned the flesh to the wheel for a moment then was tossed somewhere behind, car fishtailing left and right with a screech and *whumpwhumpwhump* of tattered rubber. Then a crunch as it struck another car, and the blast of a horn from somewhere Rita couldn't see because she'd closed her eyes. Her lips moved in muttered prayers as the wind blew her hair around her face.

She saw the new breeze as an acceptance of her gift, and the eventual cries from below—

"Somebody call an ambulance!"

"Hello? Can you hear me in there? Are you all right?"

"Call an ambulance!"

—confirmed it for her.

She ran for the stairs down, exhilarated and joyous.

When Rita had been Carina with a husband and two children, she had been an area manager for a mobile phone company. She would travel the county visiting the various stores where staff half her age sold the company product to customers half of theirs. She travelled a lot, in a company car. It was an Alfa Romeo, not the safest, not the worst, and it was red, which was statistically considered the most dangerous colour a car could be, after black, but looked good. The colour didn't have a bearing on what happened.

It happened on the motorway. Over 2000 people were killed on major roads every year. Many of the accidents occurring on motorways were due to changing lanes, with exits and entrances prime hotspots. None of that mattered in Rita's case.

She'd been on the phone while driving. In a recent survey, over 20% of drivers admitted to using their mobile phone while driving, and research showed it caused a 50% slower reaction time to any hazards on the road. It was impossible to establish how many accidents were caused by the use of mobile phones while in control of a vehicle, "control" being a laughable word in such context, due to a lack of available data. But that didn't matter, either, because Rita had been using a hands-free set, no more dangerous than singing along to your radio. In fact, she heard the sound of the collision up ahead before her husband did. He had been turned around in his seat talking to the children, trying to untwist Sian's seatbelt when the Vauxhall Astra three cars ahead turned into a sideways slide, and the Ford Fiesta two ahead flashed its brake lights and hit it and rose up onto its bonnet, and the car immediately in front of her, a Citroen Xantia, rear-ended it at the better part of fifty miles an hour.

Rita only had time to scream before their own car joined the pile up.

She dreamt it every night with only minor changes. She always woke at the same point, with the same hot stink in her nose and a scream upon her lips. She would wake and clutch damp sheets to herself and pat the left side of the bed, the passenger side, for Todd, but he was never there. Not any more.

The Nissan was creased sharply in on one side, one back tire flat and the other wheel folded under the vehicle entirely where the front of the old man's Rover was still buried. He was trapped inside, looking around and opening his mouth again and again as if surprised over and over at his situation. People were talking to him all at once, which probably didn't help, but no one could get him out yet.

The woman in the front car was clearly dead. A starburst of blood lined the driver's window, cracked where her head had struck, and her blonde hair was thick with it. You only knew she was blonde from the other half of her head, the half with the proper round shape.

A third car had hit the back of the old man, probably ploughing him into where he now sat. The bonnet was concertinaed and the front wing panel, the one Rita could see, had tried to copy the pattern. Steam hissed from beneath. The occupants had emerged unharmed, though a man shook violently at the verge as a woman comforted him.

"I've phoned an ambulance," Rita lied, in case anyone still hadn't done so.

One of the men roadside turned and nodded at her and then saw her face, her hair. Her hood had come down. Startled, he staggered back.

"Oh shit," said someone at the Rover. "Oh shit, oh shit."

The old man was clutching his left arm and his gaping mouth stayed open now, this time in pain. Sirens sounded in the distance but they'd be too late.

Rita wondered if a heart attack would count, if she would be credited for that. If not, she hoped one blonde woman in her early twenties would be a good enough follow up to last night's man at the churchyard.

She went back to her own car before the sirens could get much closer and before the road was closed. On the way she stopped to pick up a broken wing mirror from the Nissan. She tucked it inside her coat and hurried home.

§

Sian was five and Charlotte three when the god of road deaths took them. Todd had been thirty-nine. They were buried together at a funeral Rita couldn't attend. She'd been in hospital. She'd had several ceremonies of her own since then, though.

She flipped the kettle on to boil while she went to the children's room, a room that had become a shrine since Motorway Day. She took the broken wing mirror with her.

The door was white, panelled, with a rainbow arcing its way across the top section. Beneath it, in pink bubble writing, was each girl's name. Beneath that, written in marker, was Todd's. Beneath *his* name was a long list of others.

Rita went inside.

The beds were long gone, the shelves cleared of toys and trinkets. No posters adorned the walls. No dolls sat at window sills. This was not that sort of shrine.

"I offer you thanks for sparing me, and gratitude for preparing me, and I hope you will preserve me so I may serve you more," she said to the room.

The first time she'd offered such prayers she'd felt foolish, like she was only playing, but it hadn't taken long to realize her worship was true worship for there could be no other god, and after that it came much easier.

"I will add the names to the others when they are known to me," Rita said, "though you know them now, better than I ever shall."

There was nobody else in the room to hear her, but it was far from empty. Pushed up against the far wall was a bent and beaten shape of metals. An old engine bled its oil into the wooden floor, consecrating it, and attached to this dead heart were twists of exhaust and folded door panels. A buckled wedge of bonnet leant like a down-turned mouth, held in place by a length of bumper at its base upon which rested a row of jars like uneven teeth. Each jar was filled with broken windscreen glass, irregular shapes like uncut diamonds throwing back fractured light as Rita lit road flares on the bare floorboards. A couple of the jars held the broken plastic of shattered rear light covers; if the jars were teeth then these ones were bloody.

"I have another token," Rita said. "Something to give you strength in giving you shape."

She knelt and raised the broken mirror she'd taken from the day's wreck, then stood and set it in place. Above the bonnet mouth Rita had nailed two tires to the wall like eyes, hubcaps resting inside to create silvered pupils that shone in the flare light. The fluffy dice dangled from one of them like bright tears of thinned blood. Tears of joy. Rita had been surprised at their presence in the boy's car. A joke gift from parents, perhaps, on passing his test, or a gaudy pink piss-take from friends. Now they hung in Rita's shrine as a reminder of the chance people took every time they drove the roads.

"There shall be no swerving from the road I follow and the road I follow is yours. I make you another offering. Accept her blood and the wreck of her metal, accept her sacrifice, just as you accepted mine."

She put the wing mirror in one of the tire eye sockets and saw herself bisected in the broken glass. Her crooked nose. Her criss-crossed scars on the roadmap that was her new face. The bare scalp of burnt skin and the long wisps of hair that grew around it.

"I am yours," she said. Facing the mirror, it looked as though she addressed herself, so she turned away from her reflection and said it louder. She filled the room with her devotion.

"I am yours!"

She knelt to her road god effigy, sobbing thankful frightened prayers in a circle of road flares and traffic cones.

Before her, rising up the wall in a mass of murderous metal, her god watched.

S

Both incidents were on the news. Rita watched from the sofa, eyes half-closed with sleep, as a pretty presenter told her the man near the churchyard had been William Thomas. Police were appealing for witnesses, apparently. The woman's name, the one from the Nissan, had been Jennifer James. The old man, Mr. Magoo, was actually Peter Birch.

Rita would add their names to the shrine room door. She would write them like licence plates, W1LL14M 7H0M45 and J3NN1F3R J4M35. She wouldn't add the old man's name. She would do it before bed. After the rest of the news. After resting her eyes for a moment. Just for a moment . . .

She was on the motorway again but the crash had already happened, which was not unusual; it meant her god was happy with what she'd given. What was unusual was the lack of people; Rita was the only one in any of the wreckages. The airbag had burst and the steering column had smashed her chest. An arch of the steering wheel was embedded in her flesh and her blood ran into her lap. She pressed the button to release the seat belt, just as she did in every dream, just as she had on the day, and of course she was still trapped in the car.

Movement in her peripheral vision drew her eyes to the wing mirror. It was broken, like the one she'd retrieved this morning.

"Help us," Rita said, a bubble of blood popping on her lips.

"There is no us, not any more," said the woman, "just you." She crouched at where a window used to be. It was J3NN1F3R J4M35. "Hello."

"Hello."

"Strange place to keep a motorbike," said J3NN1F3R, peering into the back seat.

"It's my daughter's."

It wasn't, but Rita couldn't help saying so.

"Where's W1LL14M?" Rita asked.

J3NN1F3R smiled. "B1LL? Oh, he's around here somewhere. Nice trick with the fucking rabbit, by the way." J3NN1F3R sharply turned a wheel she no longer held, an invisible wheel, and slammed her head hard to one side against nothing but air, reliving the "accident" in perfect detail. Her skull flattened on one side so severely that her right eye split and oozed from the socket. Her blonde hair reddened in fresh dark streaks. "Any other day and I wouldn't have been on that road," she said.

"It wasn't any other day," said Rita.

"No."

"The road gets what the road wants."

"The road wants more," said J3NN1F3R. "It always wants more."

"And it wants you too," said W1LL14M, suddenly beside her. Where Todd should have been.

"It wants you too," said J3NN1F3R after, overlapping his words.

Which was where the motorcycle, as always, made its *whoomph!* and sudden heat engulfed her and Rita woke up.

The news was still on. Rita turned it off and watched the screen die. She went upstairs, wrote two more names on the door, and went to bed.

Rita pressed the accelerator firmly to the floor, enjoying the speed. Every pothole, every bounce, took the car out of her control for a moment, but she always managed to steer it back on course. It was late afternoon, and a wet one. Occasionally she'd speed through a lake-like puddle (the country roads were full of them) and a fantail of muddy water would arc to the side and behind. The tires would slip but they always found their grip again. Of course they did; her god protected her. Each life she gave it went towards preserving hers. She had removed traffic cones and flashing lights from construction work and skips. She had turned into oncoming traffic, dazzling with full beam headlights, laid barbed wire across muddy tracks. She had let air out of tires. She had once drugged coffee at a late night petrol station (but only once; it had been difficult) and she had stepped in front of speeding vehicles (hood down, face on show) time and time again. But as high as mortality rates were on the road, as easy as it was to have an accident, annual casualties were on the decrease, with recent years providing an all time statistical low. Car designs improved, the number of airbags increased, seat belts were compulsory, driving tests became harder; it was getting more difficult to die on British tarmac. Yet Rita's god was a bloodthirsty god, more bloodthirsty than anything Aztec or Viking, and so Rita made her offerings, contributing in her way in an attempt to readdress the balance. Her god, eager for more, would keep her safe.

The speedometer tipped eighty. She was racing away from something that didn't show in her rear view mirror, though occasionally it was there in her reflection. No, she was racing *towards* something, something new, a future with her god of crash. She was racing towards . . .

A Citroen. It was blue, like the one from Motorway Day. There was a child in the back, who turned to look out the window at Rita. She was saying something Rita couldn't hear. A sign beside the girl showed Bob the Builder proclaiming "Baby on board" but the girl was actually about three.

Rita slowed down, but not much. Staying close.

The driver, a woman, kept glancing in the rear view. She was speeding up even as the man beside her waved an arm out the window for Rita to pass. A family. In a blue Citroen. It was exactly what the road wanted. It would be fucking karma.

Car-mar.

The Citroen was flashing its brake lights. It would have to stop soon to give right of way; they were approaching a junction. But Rita continued tailgating the woman, pushing her into the sort of panic her god thrived upon. She'd be uttering curse words that Rita's god would take as hymns, an anxiety-heightened mantra that tenderised the meat and mind for the road god's pleasure.

The car turned into the other lane to let her pass. Rita turned with it. The Citroen swerved back into the correct lane but did not give way at the junction, couldn't give way, and Rita's god of roads and ruin delivered a Ford Fiesta because Rita was a perfect follower, she was car-ma, and all she needed now was a fucking Vauxhall Astra and a motorcycle. The Fiesta hit the Citroen and the Citroen spun and startled expressions of horror blurred past Rita.

Their vehicle clipped her rear bumper. Suddenly she was spinning with them in a tire-squealing tango. She tried to correct the spin, pumping the brakes, but the car jolted against something. Rita's head smacked the glass to her right, just like J3NN1F3R's had. The airbag filled the space around her but darkness engulfed her first.

Rita lay across the steering wheel but she wasn't on the country road. She was on the motorway. She peered over the ridges of her folded bonnet looking for Sian. A long thick line of blood, drawn from face and flesh, marked her path. It had connected Carina's car to Sian's corpse but Carina was Rita now so Sian wasn't there. The bloodline ended at nothing but ruin, the only body parts those of broken vehicles bent into new shapes.

Todd's seat beside her held the engine block, steam rising in lines where his blood had splashed. The motorcycle behind her, inside the car, thrummed and growled but Charlotte did not scream. Charlotte was not there. The growl diminished gradually until all Rita heard was the crunch of glass underfoot as someone approached. They knelt to look in at Rita. It was not J3NN1F3R or B1LL or any of the others. It was the fucking doctor.

"Hello Carina."

Rita pretended not to hear.

"I know you can hear me," he said, but he stroked his beard away from his mouth as if it may have muffled his words. "You're still hurting, aren't you."

"Actually, no," she said, and it was true. Rita was not in pain. It was a dream.

Doctor Hooper glanced down at his watch, then at the vehicle behind her, waiting to burn.

"You know what you're trying to do, don't you?"

Always the fucking questions, trying to force her to voice her thoughts. To force what was inside to come outside. But that would make her roadkill, so she said nothing. Instead, she waited impatiently for the *whoomph!*

"You're trying to die," Doctor Dipshit said. "An interpretation of your dreams suggests—"

Rita shook her head.

"The road always gets what the road wants," he said. He was reading from a pad he had never used during their sessions. "Well, the road wants you too."

And suddenly 5T4C3Y was there—"It wants you too"—and D4V1D—"It wants you too"—and C1ND1—"It wants you too"—and all of the others, H4RRY and K1M83RLY and GR3G0RY, all of them, even T0DD and S14N and CH4RL0TT3, each overlapping the last so Rita couldn't hear what they said after the first time.

"Well the road can't fucking have me!" Rita yelled.

Now the motorcycle would go up in flames—*whoomph!*—and hair and skin would crack, crackle, blister, burn, and she'd wake up, and—

Hooper was still there. They all were.

"The road wants you—" Hooper began.

"I know! Shit, I thought *I* was the one with the compulsion to repeat."

He had told her about that in the hope of getting her to talk about the "accident." He didn't understand her god, didn't understand her god had willed it, demanded it, for her ignorance. She didn't dream it every single fucking time because she grieved or missed her family or even because of any guilt but because it was a way of lessening her pain, according to the doctor. Talking about it, reliving it, was supposed to do the same, a coping strategy he'd said would turn passive suffering into active control. Well that was bullshit. She'd found her own way to control things.

"*I'm* not trying to die," Rita told him. "Carina wanted to die, and she did. *Rita* wants to force her pain onto others. *Rita* turns her 'destructive impulse'"—she made speech marks in the air—"onto others. *There's* my 'compulsion to repeat' you fucking Freud."

She'd meant to say fraud. It was almost funny.

"How many more?" he asked.

"At least one," she said, wishing she could make it H00P3R.

"One more for the road, huh?"

"Yeah, one more. For the road."

She knew what he would say next and this time she would let him, hoping for the fiery wakeup that would end it all.

"The road wants you to—"

And he told her. And once he'd explained what the road wanted her to do—

Whoomph!

§

Ahead, the Citroen was bent in half around a telephone pole. A man lay draped across a hole in the windscreen. The only sign of the Fiesta was a ragged hole in the low redbrick wall where it had plunged down an embankment. Rita checked the road behind her, switched on her hazard lights, and went to see.

The Fiesta had rolled all the way to the bottom. It was upside down.

Rita approached the Citroen at the telephone pole. "Is everybody hurt?"

She felt for a pulse at the man's neck. There was nothing. The blood that would have given him one was running into puddles at the roadside.

The woman driver lay head back, mouth open, as if sleeping. She wasn't sleeping. Her eyes were open. Both of them were red where the white should be. She had a curve across her brow that matched the shape of the steering wheel and something had cracked to leak pink-tinged fluid down her forehead. Blood trickled from her mouth like drool.

One of the passenger doors had been thrown open, wrenched from its hinges. There was no sign of the girl that should have been inside, just the usual clutter of a family car and . . . Something else. Something that surprised her.

She heard the sound of an approaching engine; someone was coming. But she was at a crossroads far more metaphorical than the one she could see before her. She knew what she was supposed to do, her internal satnav had told her, but she still didn't know if the doctor could be trusted.

The approaching engine was closer. It sounded like the growl of a motorcycle.

Rita reached in to the car quickly and took her souvenir before rushing back to where her own car was parked.

She drove away fast, rushing home with her offering.

§

"I have made my offerings and my offerings give you strength," Rita said, safe in the shrine room. She had to shout over the noise. "But it is not enough. It will never be enough. You have my worship, but it will never be enough.

"So you will have the worship of others."

She motioned to her latest construction, standing beside the blood-toothed smile of her god.

She had made it from a car boot lid with upright bars made of extendable head rests welded in place. Above it, radio antennas had been bent into criss-crossed shapes and hanging from those, turning gently on the mobile, were various air fresheners and dashboard toys and key rings. She'd made the crib's bedding from seat covers, but they itched the child that wailed inside. She would add its old name to the door, below those of its old family, and give the child something new. She would bring the baby on board to share her worship, nurse it with milk and spilled diesel, keep it safe.

And so she went to it, held it close, clutching at the scripture written in the scars of her skin, feeling the ridges of ragged flesh on her puckered chest where her breasts used to be.

The first of her god's new followers would suckle from her undying faith.

THE MAN WHO WAS

I stand upon a bank of sand in the middle of a sea that is entirely shore. I'm in the dark desert again, alone, and I know that I am dreaming not just because I'm in my pyjamas but because I've dreamt this many times before. My fists are clenched and grains of sand slip between my fingers, though I clench them tight. *Because* I clench them tight. Before me, the smoking ruins of tanks lay smouldering in the sand. It's night; I know they're smouldering because I can feel the heat, and smell the hot metal. It's a familiar scene. Not because of any experience I had there: I did not fight in the Gulf War, not for a single minute of its one hundred hours. It's familiar because of John.

The nearest wreckage is Iraqi. Almost all of the ruined vehicles are Iraqi. Still clutching the sand in my fists, I make my way to a turret that has become separated from the main body of the vehicle it once belonged to. Each ruined chassis is a dark footprint of war, walking away into the Arabian Desert only to stop suddenly, a route like an instructive dance map that starts and stops within itself, and the turrets protrude in bent and twisted shapes from the ground around them like dark growths. War flowers, budding. I know, because John told me, that the Americans called these tanks "pop-tops" due to the way they broke apart when hit, turrets flung clean into the air. They lie scattered before me, a field of blackened metal blossoms cast aside to wilt by some dancing warmonger giant.

I hear him call out from one of the wrecks. John. Man of my dreams, to make a cliché literal. His voice is deep and clear and familiar at first. Then it fills with pain. I try to go to him. I run. I know he's in one of the American vehicles, a Bradley, and I let go of the sand to run faster. As the last of the sand is taken by the wind, so his screaming stops.

And that's when I wake up.

Usually, that's when I wake up.

§

General John Smith; a name so plain, you'd think him made up.

I first saw him across a crowd of people at some charity event or dinner, the sort of occasion I usually hate to attend but find, as an occupational hazard, that I often must. It's my job to plan such events and I do it well; give me the internet and a phone and I can arrange anything. I can even mingle and make polite conversation and though I'm reluctant to talk much about myself, I can feign an interest in others. The General, though, aroused my full genuine interest, and did so immediately.

The event was black tie of course, and he cut a striking figure even amongst so many men dressed identically. *Because* of it, probably. He certainly wore his suit better than I mine. He stood at about six feet with the rigid bearing of a man who has served in the military, though his hair was much longer and glossier than military regulation probably allowed. Similarly, he had a very non-regulation beard. Neatly trimmed, lining his jaw in such a precise way as to emphasize the strength of it rather than hide any weakness of it, as many men with facial hair are inclined to do. When he smiled, which I saw him do frequently in his conversation, he flashed teeth that were movie-star straight and white, all the brighter for their appearance within his dark beard.

I fear my description doesn't reveal him accurately at all.

"I see you've noticed the General."

My companion took a sip from his champagne but the glass did little to hide his smile. He knew me better than most.

"The General?"

He'd said it like I was supposed to know who. I didn't. My companion had scored a point in the trivial game of gossip that thrives in such environments. I had guessed already, though, that the man I was drawn to had a military background. It was in his bearing, not only the straight way in which he held himself but in the confidence with which he moved between groups of people. He was not the host of the event but he commanded the crowd as if he was.

"General John Smith," my companion explained, and rolled his eyes either because I hadn't known or because the name sounded so phoney. Perhaps for both reasons. I didn't care; I was happy enough staring.

"You'll never guess how old he is," he added, admiring the man. "Served in the Gulf. Served after that, too, from what I've heard. Bloody hell, he looks good for it. Bet he's had some work done."

I disagreed, but kept my opinion to myself. Or maybe I simply hoped otherwise, seeing it as a vanity I hoped the man did not possess.

"Now he's set for politics."

"Swapping one battlefield for another?"

He smiled politely at my joke. "Ferocious man, by all accounts. In a good way, I mean." Here my companion widened his eyes at me. "Imagine."

I disguised my thoughts at that by turning to a passing waiter, swapping my empty glass for a full one.

"Women love him, of course," my companion went on, "on account of his tremendous bravery."

"His bravery?"

"Well, obviously not *only* on account of that. He's a man of calibre, if you'll excuse the military pun."

I excused it by ignoring it. "Did he see much of the war?" I asked. I knew little of the Gulf War except that it was brief.

"See much of it? You really haven't heard of General Smith?"

I admitted as much, caring little for the man's petty persistence in embarrassing me.

He pressed the advantage.

"Christ, really? Nothing of what he did in Kuwait?"

Again, I shook my head no.

"I tell you, to look at him is to become infatuated, but to hear something of his character? What he did in the desert? Doomed." He said this last theatrically, tapping my glass as if to toast the prospect. "To a life of love and longing."

We drank to that, and I surprised myself by doing so with enthusiasm.

"So what *did* happen out there?"

He raised an eyebrow, delighting in my ignorance. "Okay, quick version; he's the man who—"

But my companion had no time to explain, for the man who was the topic of our conversation was fast approaching.

The term statuesque is the staple of old fiction, terrible romances, but the proportions of him did indeed seem carved, solid; something the Greeks would marvel at and try to imitate in their art. His poise was perfect, his movements smooth as if choreographed.

"Gentlemen."

One word, and I felt something of the doom I'd been warned against. The General's voice was strong and clear, with the clipped assuredness of breeding but not too Ivy League. I found my own voice lacking, and so it fell to my friend to make the introductions.

"Good to meet you," the General said, shaking my hand. Holding it just a moment longer than necessary.

"Likewise," was all I could manage.

"And you organized all of this, did you?"

I nodded.

He released a breath as if it must have been an ordeal and said, "Bet that took some planning. We could have used someone like you in the Middle East." He smiled.

His smile was as dazzling close up as I had imagined when seeing it from afar, but it was his eyes that drew me. They were deep hazel and met your own gaze with such intensity it was difficult to not look away.

"By all accounts," I said, recovering enough to respond to his compliment, "it wasn't much of a party out there."

He laughed. I felt myself smile with the pleasure of having caused it and he clasped my upper arm, laughing still, and said, "It wasn't." I tensed, suddenly self-conscious about how my body might feel in the suit, but he released me quickly enough, with a friendly pat afterwards.

We talked for a short time about the party, though I barely heard the words. I was too focused on the musicality of his voice, the rise and fall of its timbre. It wasn't difficult to believe he'd once yelled orders but already he had the orator's skill he'd need in politics and I even wondered how he might sound singing. How his voice would sound when hushed into a whisper.

"This must feel like work," the General noted, "all this talk of the party."

I disagreed politely but he wasn't fooled, and so we talked of other things. It was some time before I noticed my previous companion had gone. I didn't care. The General was charming and well informed on a number of subjects, all of which he spoke of in a way that seemed to promise he could say more if only the two of you had a private moment elsewhere. His opinions felt like confidences and he heard my own with a seriousness that encouraged my honesty about a great many things. He seemed genuinely interested in anything and everything I had to say; if there was anything false about him, he was good at hiding it. He would do well in politics.

I tried to steer the conversation to his own exploits overseas, and he humoured the attempts with stories that held my attention while remaining modest. Indeed, his brave charge into enemy fire, his actions in the field, seemed all the more courageous for his reluctance to talk about them; he would always turn the conversation away again as soon as it was polite to do so. Where he became most particularly passionate was when talk turned to technology and advances in modern invention.

"It's wonderful, isn't it?" he concluded. "The things we can do today. The march of progress, the devices designed to make our lives easier. I mean, take our cell phones for example. Look at what they can do these days."

It was a wonderful way into exchanging details. Smoothly done, and innocent enough to avoid any potential embarrassment.

"I may need to plan a huge party some day," he said, filing my number away then looking around at all the guests mingling. I worried he was searching for a way out of our conversation, that I had kept him too long from other friends or obligations, but he was merely observing the size and nature of the group assembled. "Or perhaps not a party," he said, "maybe a military operation, eh Thompson?"

My name is not Thompson, but I didn't correct him. Indeed, I felt he'd made the error on purpose. Not as a slight, but as if to see how it would fit, or how I might respond to it. I tried to give him nothing outwardly, but he saw something that made him smile and that was how our conversation ended that first night.

Some nights I sleep through a thunder of gunfire, standing in a desert that is green and black, a foreign land of night-vision colours. A flare of white—bright, brief, dazzling—and the heavy concussion of a fired shell as dark shapes rush towards each other in the open plains. I call for John, but my voice is torn from me by a wind that carries the desert from one place to another; his name is taken from me in a gust of dust and sand. The air I breathe is full of it so I pull my pyjama shirt over my nose to filter the breaths I take. It does little to block the smell of burning metal, the stench of hot fires, or the acrid chemical odour of cannon blast. Later, when it is over, there will be the stench of roasting flesh, the lingering smell of fear and defeat. The victors will be suddenly gone and only a graveyard of machinery will remain behind. This is when the green light of goggles I do not wear disappears and I am alone in the night desert with torn vehicles and split lengths of track and huge discarded pop-top flowers. Black poppies in a field of sand. My fists are full of grains slipping between my fingers and I wait for John's voice to answer my call. When it comes I'll run to him. I will spread my hands open for speed, wind taking the sand from my palms, hurrying because his voice is so full of pain. So full.

I never manage to reach him.

§

Though John and I exchanged some messages after that first occasion of our meeting, it was some time before I saw him again, and even then it was a public and solemn affair. It was a memorial service, a formal event beginning at the grand cathedral for which our city is rather famous. I had arranged much of the event, was responsible for a couple of the speakers, and my presence was required to ensure it all went smoothly. Attending church is not a regular part of my life, except for such special functions, and I do not belong to an organized religion of any kind. I have my own relationship with God. The Reverend Drummond knows this, and accepts it, even if he doesn't fully understand my reasons and probably wouldn't accept them if he did. Still, we are friends, or close enough that I would often coordinate such ceremonies, especially if the city's wealthier residents were to attend and donations were to be encouraged.

As the Reverend spoke at length about the futility of war, a hushed voice beside me said, "I hear you set this up?"

I turned to see who addressed me though there was little need; she's worn the same perfume for all the years I've known her.

"Miss Arabella," I greeted her. Our little joke.

"*Mrs.*," she corrected as usual, waving her wedding ring at me as she always did. She had made a pass at me once and we'd agreed ever since to blame her marriage for her lack of success. Easier than to think my tastes would not extend to her, though she was boyish enough in build. There was still something of flirtation on her part whenever we spoke, as if she thought trying hard enough could one day "turn" me, but it was done in fun rather than frustration.

"Mrs.," I said. "Of course. And how is your husband?"

She waved the question away because neither of us really cared. "So tell me about the General," she said.

I was rather taken aback. The General and I had exchanged a few texts, a few phone calls, had even spoke via web-cam a few times (technology really is a wonderful thing) but I had not told anybody. My discretion is partly what makes me such a valued member of certain circles and plays no small part in the success of my business; I know who should receive invites to what and, more importantly, who should not, and I understood the subtleties of seating arrangements and the like. That Arabella should know something of my business with the General was almost as startling as my having no knowledge of him at all.

"Don't look so surprised," she said, "he's quite taken with you."

She laughed, for whatever surprise she had seen in me must have increased tenfold with such news.

"How sweet," she said, "you're blushing."

"What do you know about—"

The Reverend raised his voice over our whispered conversation and presented us with a look that was not lost on myself, Arabella, or indeed any of the people gathered close by. We spent the next few minutes in quiet and I used the time to wonder at this turn in events.

Conversations between the General and I had been long and interesting but often circled anything that might be construed as personal, an exercise in caution on his part that I was happy to entertain, enjoying as I do the thrill of the chase, the flirtatious hesitancy that precedes any new relationship worth having. I understood how any relationship we might have could compromise him, even in this apparently more tolerant day and age. He had only recently become a public figure, with an interest in political progress, not to mention a military background that would permit little by way of sexual scandal. I was surprised he may have mentioned any of our communications. It did not surprise me, though, that having done so, Arabella would hear of it. Oh, not from him, certainly, but she knew people who knew people.

"Such a handsome man," she said, whispering her opinion but not taking too much care as to how quietly. "Such a waste." Her tone left her exact meaning ambiguous as to which man she meant; flirtation, to her, was breath.

By this point I had neither confirmed nor denied any of her suspicions, save to redden in the face. But I saw it as a positive sign that he had mentioned me at all, and I enjoyed entertaining the idea of a romantic connection.

"I hear he served in the Gulf," I offered, steering the conversation away but keeping within the topic of her interest.

"Yes," she said. "Tanks."

"Saw a bit of action."

We received another glance from the Reverend who was still delivering a suitably sombre speech. It was rude of me to ignore it, disrespectful even, but I couldn't help pursuing this line of conversation. John was so reticent about the wars he'd served in.

"A *bit* of action," Arabella said, smiling with sarcasm, but seeing the tilt of my head and inquisitive frown she covered her mouth and widened her eyes and said, "Really? You don't know?"

"Don't know what?"

"Jesus," she said, though she knew full well where she was when she said it, at once appalled at the story she had and delighted that she could be the one to tell me. "Horrible. Tragic. The things that happened over there."

I nodded my agreement, perhaps hurrying her along quicker than was politely appropriate. "I tried Google but there was nothing."

"Well there wouldn't be," she said. Technology might have been bounding forward, but the internet had nothing on Arabella. "He was one of the ones who—"

"'Man hath but a short time to live!'" the Reverend announced with more fervour than the solemn occasion called for, our chatter not unnoticed. He maintained eye contact. "'He cometh up and is cut down like a flower.'"

I nodded at him, not in agreement but to acknowledge my fault and as a promise of quiet. I would ask Arabella about the General later.

Or, I decided, I would ask General John Smith himself. Man has a short time indeed, I thought, resolving to speak to him directly, honestly, and while I was being honest I would tell him how I felt. I would make the most of my life by offering to share some of it with him.

When the Reverend was finished, we filed out from our pews to a cenotaph in the churchyard where several servicemen made speeches about lost brothers in arms, remembering all who had sacrificed before them in wars we seemed to learn nothing from. The General was one of the speakers.

What a speech he made!

He was wearing full dress uniform and stood tall, proud, as he delivered a moving account of time spent on the battlefield, and of a more harrowing time spent with men in various military hospitals. He spoke eloquently, yet refrained from any poetics that might have added an unnecessary gloss to his words. At one point, speaking of lost friends, his voice, usually so strong and so clear, caught in his throat. He massaged the area for a moment, as if the fault lay in his larynx, and continued, not once referring to any prepared text. It seemed he had one, for he clutched a paper in one hand, but for most of the speech his hands were clasped behind his back. I admired the honesty with which he spoke and wondered if perhaps he had deviated from the prepared script. I could imagine something drafted by someone else, crafted to further the General's political aspirations while offering sentiment and condolences, just as I could imagine him ignoring it.

I kept a close eye on him as he spoke, and afterwards tried to find a moment to talk with him, but he was always in the company of others, mostly soldiers, and I did not want to mingle with a crowd so fully his own. What did I know of war? So I looked for Arabella to perhaps pick up from where we'd left off, a poor substitute for the General's company even as pleasant as she can be, but it appeared she'd already left. Many had, once the speeches were over; respects had been paid, and that was all that had been required.

The General noted my presence in the crowd, at least. He nodded to me, and smiled, though it was a smile somewhat lacking in its usual mirth. My nod in return was both a hello and a goodbye and I left him with his fellow servicemen.

It was as I settled into my car that I saw him finally snatch a moment to himself. He deposited what I had thought was his speech at the foot of the cenotaph and re-joined his friends as they were leaving. I watched them pile into a minibus I'd organized for the occasion, knowing it would take them to where a procession would move slowly through the park.

I sat in my vehicle for some moments, debating with myself. Eventually I pulled out into traffic and drove home.

That night I did not sleep. I lay awake, contemplating the events of the day, and the cruelties of war. I considered, too, the cruelties of love. I had a letter from John and I read it over and over, wishing it had been addressed to me. Just as I'm sure John wished he had given it to Thompson when he'd had the chance.

Several days passed before I spoke to the General again. It began with a text message, a polite enquiry as to my health and happiness, and proceeded to a web-cam conversation. I did not confess my feeling to him as I had planned because the distance between us felt too great when each of us was little more than a disembodied head on a fold-up screen. I longed to see more of him than this. But we exchanged some banter that finally crossed the line into undeniable flirtation and he spoke of arranging a meeting, something public but not too intimate. I told him of a coming performance I'd planned with the intention of garnering interest in a new acting company. The launch would offer just the right amount of excitement and frivolity together with the restraint of a public relations event.

"It won't be difficult to get you an invite," I told him.

"Not Shakespeare is it?" he asked.

"Er . . ."

He sighed, and we laughed. I told him there would be various acts to showcase individual talent, and a short play that presented the whole ensemble and he accepted the offer.

"'In visions of the dark night I have dreamed of joy departed'," he said.

"Is *that* Shakespeare?" I didn't think it was, but I was hardly Patrick Stewart.

On screen, John shrugged. The buffering made the action awkward, like something automated, and I realized how much I longed to see him in the flesh. The meeting we'd planned could not come soon enough, and I told him as much; the bravest of my flirtations. To my surprise and delight, he reciprocated.

Of course, the days until then passed slowly.

I was to meet John at the launch, which was taking place at a reputable hotel. I had reserved two of their function rooms together with the exclusive use of the bar, and I had invited all those who could benefit, or would benefit from, a theatrical association. For myself, I had taken the liberty of reserving a room. Partly it was to save me the bother of returning home the same evening, but it was a double room; the hotel was one that could be counted on for discretion, and I had my hopes.

He was late. For half an hour I was forced to mingle, smiling my pleasantries, which was when I met an old acquaintance I had once assisted with an art installation. I'd found him difficult company then, and he quickly proved he hadn't changed.

"Very modern, all this, isn't it," he said, "the actors mixing with the audience, all of that."

I agreed, but without the same expression of disdain. The performances were to occur amongst the guests rather than on a stage, an intimate and far more lively approach to theatre, I thought. It meant the people here were not all as they seemed, but apparently not everybody enjoyed the frisson of uncertainty.

"I could be chatting to some young thing only for her to suddenly take on some role," he complained. "She'd start bellowing poetry, or worse, and all my efforts would have been wasted."

I thought that any woman listening to him must already be an accomplished actress in order to feign interest, but I did not make the remark.

"Who are *you* with then?" he asked me. "Or do you have your sights set on someone here? Come on, who's your target?"

He was eagerly eying up the women. He did not know me well at all.

"I thought the General was to be here this evening," I said, answering his question indirectly but seeming, to him at least, to change the subject.

"Smith?"

I nodded, looking elsewhere as I sipped my drink. Acting the role of indifference.

"I hope so," my companion said. "Good man. Terrible what happened. Cruel lot over there, aren't they? Can't do this, can't do that. Hide their women under those God-awful sheets with eye slits. You see that film? You can't even fly a kite in those countries."

And so on. I tolerated as much as I could, hoping he might touch on something more personal about the General, but all I learned was how ignorant this man was, and how racist. He muddled countries throughout his soliloquy, or rather he lumped them all together as The Middle East or, honestly, "The Land of Tyrants and Terror."

"T and T," he said, "Tyrants and Terror. What they *deserve* is some TNT." He mumbled an explosion and mimed it with his hands before laughing at his own pathetic joke. When he saw I was not amused he at least had the good grace to adapt his topic.

"Soldiers coming back in boxes," he said, "or with bits missing, or just plain used up, you know? Used up and *messed* up." Here he twirled a finger around the side of his head, and though I was sure there was someone else I could say hello to, I decided to endure more in the hope of a snatch of gossip about General John Smith.

"Injured, was he?"

The man looked at me as if he'd forgotten I was there, or I'd startled him. "Who?" he said, downing what remained in his glass. "The General?"

I nodded.

At this, the man began to laugh. It was an absurd response to such a question, but my scowl only made him laugh harder. When he'd recovered, he said, "You serious?"

Which, of course, was when the show began.

The moment it began I realized how amateur it was and little time passed before I decided to leave, though in truth it wasn't as bad as that. I simply didn't want to admit to being stood up.

One of the performers, painted bronze to play Talos in some Greek story I barely followed, delivered his lines with enthusiasm if not skill. Created to protect his island, he pretended to throw food and drink at "invaders" who were merely bemused guests. I gave him a tight smile and continued past, though it meant shouldering a path quite forcefully through the other guests gathered to watch.

"Excuse me," I said, "pardon me. Coming through. Ex—"

My exit met the General's entrance and we faced each other, close in the crowd.

"I'm late," he said. "Sorry." Some of his confidence was gone. He stood a little less straight than previously and I realized he was nervous.

"That's okay," I said.

"I booked a room."

I was surprised by such a forward admission and at once thankful that a performance was taking place around us, distracting others from the one we were making a mess of. I laughed and blurted, "Me too."

We went to my room. I didn't know whether that was a gracious allowance on his part, or simply a willingness to be led in this, and I wondered if it was a first time for him. I took no delight in the idea. In fact, it rather worried me. Perhaps, though, with being a sudden public figure, it was merely the anxiety of being discovered. He was a man of many parts, military and political amongst others, but it only made managing his private life more awkward.

However, my fears of first time nerves were, I think, more accurate. I won't divulge the details of what happened in that hotel room, except to say that although I was pleased enough, I was allowed less physical contact with him than he with me. He dictated what little grappling there was and removed nothing of his clothing, though I longed to see the body I supposed was perfect underneath. Much of the pleasure came as a release of tension rather than anything as intimate as I'd hoped. And there was another problem.

"Who's Thompson?" I asked him afterwards. I was fastening my tie at the mirror but glanced at him in the reflection to gauge the honesty of his response.

John, already sitting ramrod straight on the edge of the bed, seemed to stiffen even more, but said nothing.

"You called me Thompson," I said.

"I did not."

I tugged the knot into place and straightened my collar.

"I *didn't*," he said again, standing this time.

I turned to face him. "Not just now. Earlier. The first time we met."

I stepped aside to pick up my jacket and left him facing his own reflection. When I turned back he was staring at himself with such an expression of regret that I felt terrible for my pettiness and pressed the matter no further, despite the letter I had found that day at the cemetery. The letter I had gone back for, and taken, and read, though it was no business of mine.

"People say I'm brave," John said. He scowled at his reflection. "They're wrong. I'm not brave." He turned away from the mirror and looked at me. "I spent the first half of my life doing as I was told, and all it did was ruin the second half."

"I'm sorry."

He grabbed his jacket from the bed, suddenly in a hurry. "I better go."

"No, John, wait. Please—"

"I'm going home." He tugged his jacket on, rather clumsy in his haste. I tried to stop him but I think I've remarked already on the man's build, his stature. He's built solid. When he barged past my outstretched arm there was little I could do. He was polite enough at the door to face me for a goodbye, but he said it in such a stern way that I knew it stood for more than just this evening.

I gave him a few minutes to make his exit before making my own.

Sitting in the car outside his place, I tried to clear my mind enough to go home and leave him be. He lived in a reputable part of the city, in a house far beyond my means, but admiring the property did little to distract me.

I'd fully intended to let our tryst be the brief encounter it seemed destined to be, but in moving through the lobby I bumped into the guest with whom I'd shared a few words earlier that evening. The performers were enjoying something of an interval, though mingling with the crowd it was difficult to tell, and many of the audience members were flitting between function rooms and the bar. I spoke a few hellos and a few goodbyes to some of them, including Mr. TNT.

"Ah," he said, "wonderful show." It was a different opinion to the one he'd begun the evening with, but then I knew how that felt. In his case I believe the way the actresses were dressed played a great part in his new view of things.

"I'm glad," I said, with a terse nod that should have bid him a good night, but he chose not to see it.

"Your friend's here," he said.

"My friend?"

"The General. At least, he *was*." The man glanced around. "I saw him."

"Thank you. I'll catch up with him some other time."

"Brave man." He slurped from his glass in a way that revealed it was only the last so far in a long line of many.

"So I've heard."

"Lives with one of *them*, you know."

"Excuse me?"

"Of course," he said, and I realized with a humourless laugh that *now* he thought I was bidding him goodnight.

So I made my way to the car, but all the way to it I wondered at his meaning. One of them? Lived with? And instead of driving home I found myself on the streets leading to John's side of town.

I waited and I watched.

Before long I saw John at a window, looking out into the street. He was focused on his thoughts rather than anything he saw and seemed to be on his own. He removed his jacket and began unbuttoning his shirt.

"Goodnight, John."

But as I was reaching to start the car I saw another man at the window. He was behind John, reaching around him to help him with his shirt buttons. I watched, and their two shapes merged as one undressed the other, and though they turned, then, from the window, and drew curtains closed behind them, it was very clear that this man was seeing more of John than I had been allowed.

I'm usually a calm and considered man, but the sight of them at the window combined with the evening's events sparked a sudden impulse in me that had me out of the car and striding to the house. I beat at the door rather than push at the bell and when it eventually opened I put my hand to it and pushed it open further, forcing my way past the startled man who asked what it was I wanted. He was dusky-skinned, Middle-Eastern, and his English was heavily accented. Clear enough, though, for me to know he was demanding I leave. I ignored him, save to spare a disdainful glance, and made my way up the stairs calling for John.

The man pursued me up the stairs.

"John!" I cried, more upset than I had supposed, less angry than I had intended.

"Please," called the man behind me, "he is not decent."

"No, he's not," I threw back.

The man pursued me but I was quicker.

"Let him get himself together," the man tried.

It was too late. I was in the room.

"Where is he?" I demanded of the man who followed me inside. I gave him no chance to answer but instead picked up the heap of clothes that had been discarded onto a chair. I had intended to sling them at the man, jealous and already embarrassed but unable to stop. The clothes were heavy. I'd picked something else up with them.

The bundle shifted in my arms and a face peered at me from the crumpled clothes. I let out a cry of alarm and horror at what I held and cast it aside. Something of the face had been John's. But not much of it.

The other man cried out as well, though his was one of concern as he rushed forward to catch what I had thrown. He was too late; a groan that was all John—had I not heard it only an hour ago?—issued from the floor. The face I had briefly seen contorted momentarily in pain. Then it rolled with the tumble of garments and heavier items.

The other man knelt by the bundle and rummaged amongst it, casting foul looks my way as he righted the pile into something . . . squat. It smiled a grin that was all lips and blackness, no teeth, and said my name with a harsh rasp of breath.

The Middle-Eastern man hushed him. "Quiet, Mr. Smith. Wait a moment. Let me help you."

I backed towards the wall with both hands covering my mouth, a child disturbed by a nightmare, but the nightmare I saw took a more certain shape before me at the hands of this foreign man.

What I saw was a torso, a very stunted one, with a face that peered from a shirt that had gathered around it in the chaos of my tantrum. The Middle-Eastern man pulled this down and John's head emerged from the collar. It was stripped of hair, all pink skin on scalp and jaw. One eye was missing. He had a nose but it had slipped to reveal the cavity behind. John spoke too quietly for me to hear, but the man with him nodded, absently but efficiently fixing the nose before going to a nearby dresser. In a moment he was settling a wig in place and then pressing something into the vacant socket of John's eye. Then he put his fingers into John's mouth, prised it open, and inserted something not unlike a denture plate, only with more substance. It gave John's face a more defined chin which settled left and right with a series of clicks as John worked his jaw.

"Better," he said. His voice still had something of a croak but the other massaged the throat and suddenly John was coughing. There was a resounding thrum for a moment, and then when next he spoke he had the same strong, clear voice I knew.

"Not much to look at, am I?" he said, and laughed. It wasn't a pleasant sound.

I could only shake my head, dismissing what I saw rather than agreeing.

"This good man here is Hakim."

The good Hakim was inserting something into John's trouser leg, turning it once, twice, three times, and then fussing with the cuff so it settled over a foot that was entirely shoe. He repeated the procedure with the other side, screwing apparatus into place and then leaning John up into a standing position. He kept his arms around John's waist and looked around the floor. I could see the piece he wanted but could only point.

"There," said John for me. "Go on, I'll be all right."

His companion stepped away from him and John took an experimental step without him, finding his balance. His shirt sleeves hung empty by his sides and I wondered, if he fell, could I find the strength to catch him?

"My Bradley took a hit in '91," he said.

I nodded, and tried to keep eye contact.

"It's a tank, not a person. I thought I'd better explain, in case you became jealous."

The foolishness I'd feel for my behaviour would not come until later. Right then I stared with wonder that was, I'm ashamed to say, something like horror. My gaze was drawn to this or that part of his body, and the places where his body used to be. Now Hakim was attaching another prosthetic, an arm, connecting valves and screwing slim cables into place. He went about his business like a tailor who had known Smith's custom for years. Perhaps he had.

"The Gulf War?" I managed.

"Sort of. Part of that, anyway. The Hundred Hour War they call it, as if it was a play. But it was very real."

The story he told had the sound of practice about it, though I can't imagine who he may have told it to. Perhaps, judging from how his friend nodded at intervals, it was part of the dressing process. His . . . assembly.

"The Iraqis had these God-awful tanks Hussein had bought from the Soviet Union. Piece of shit hand-me-down heaps that were slow and inaccurate and popped their tops when they took a hit. Literally fell to pieces." He countered something in my expression with, "Ha! Like I can talk." It was too bitter to be part of any rehearsed speech, and his companion slowed in what he was doing at John's other sleeve.

"You can leave us, Hakim."

"Your hands, sir."

John looked at his blunt wrists then put them in his pockets, dismissing his assistant with, "Problem solved."

When the man was gone, I tried to explain my presence but John cut me off before I could get any further than his name.

"We waited in the night through a heavy storm. Middle of the fucking desert and it was raining. Wind howling, battering us with wet sand. That's a sound you don't forget in a hurry. Sounds like the night is hissing laughter at you. Maybe it was. Maybe it knew what was coming."

It was a sound I couldn't imagine at the time, but I've dreamt it many nights since.

"They came at us, and we expected that, but there were more of them than anticipated. I was forced to take evasive action, breaking out of formation, cutting ahead at the right flank as the Iraqi numbers tripled right before our eyes."

Here he touched the eye I'd seen Hakim insert.

"I have seen such terrible things," he said. His stump of a wrist pressed against the pupil, an accident that shifted it slightly in the socket so that he seemed to stare beyond my right shoulder with one eye when he added, "I've done such terrible things."

"It was war," I said, rather pointlessly. He ignored the comment, as he had every right to. He was still there.

"Round after round," he said. "Twenty-five cal slamming into hard packed sand. Blasting the desert and tossing tanks into torn shreds of metal."

John closed his eyes at the memory. I was selfishly thankful to be rid of that skewed gaze.

Eventually he spoke again. His voice was soft. "We wiped them out." When he opened his eyes the crooked one had somehow righted itself. He met my gaze with a fierce stare, but his anger was clearly aimed at someone or something other than me. "*Of course* we wiped them out. We were better armed, better equipped. I mean, isn't technology wonderful?"

He lifted the stumps of his wrists to me before realizing his hands were elsewhere. He compensated by rubbing appallingly at his crotch. "They think of everything!"

I was disgusted, and then ashamed of my disgust, and then I didn't have to think of it because he continued his story. The one I had so wanted to hear until I was hearing it.

"Like I said, we were out of position. Sand was flying, bursts of metal flying in the night. Explosions rocked us, but we targeted tank after tank.

"One of them was ours."

He wiped at one of his eyes—the one that worked—and was silent for so long that I thought he'd finished. Before I could say anything, something that would no doubt make it worse even as I tried to make it better, he said, "Friendly fire. That's what they call it."

"John, you don't need to—"

"Yes I do."

He moved to where I'd seen him at the window. The curtains were drawn but he stared anyway.

"Thompson was the name of one of the men in the tank we hit."

"I'm sorry."

"He died."

Thompson was more than an accidental casualty. I knew, because I had read the letter John had left at the cenotaph. John could not have known, but he knew that I understood. Thompson was the line in the sand neither of us would cross, but we both knew he was there.

"I can't remember who fired first, but it doesn't matter. It doesn't change what happened."

John cleared his throat, a sound most of us make when overcome with emotion but in his case it sounded like a mechanical necessity. I imagined him gargling lubricant to allow his strong smooth speech and I hated myself for it.

"We've got laser-guided sensors that can identify vehicles by their heat signatures. We've got satellite pictures. We've got fucking night vision for Christ's sake. But it makes no difference if your men are tired. And we were tired. Hundreds of hours of combat experience and simulations, but no amount of training can counter sleep deprivation. Took a while for them to learn from it, too, because twelve years later you've got Operation Iraqi fucking Freedom and tanks are veering off course and—"

By this point I was finally able to go to him.

"Now I don't even *want* to sleep," he said.

I put my arm around his shoulders and tried not to think about how hard they felt. The strength I had admired in him earlier had become something . . . else, and I'm loath to describe my feelings to you because of how I would seem. I did my best, let me leave it at that, and he must've taken some comfort from it because he settled against me. I put a hand to his hair to stroke it, remembered it was not his, and stopped.

He said something I didn't hear.

"Pardon?"

"It was hell. Fire. Metal. Shells exploding. I was burning in hell, just as I knew I would. You know, our suits can withstand temperatures of two thousand degrees. Two *thousand*."

"You're alive," was all I could think to say. "And you're a good man."

At this he nudged me aside.

"A man?" He laughed a hard sound. "A man? Look at me; I left most of myself over there. I'm not a man. I'm barely anything." And then he looked at *me*, an up and down that remembered how I looked beneath my clothes, how I felt, and he said again, "I'm not a man."

At first I thought he simply meant by comparison, a comment of self-pity, but the way he reddened afterwards told me he regretted the words and I realized he'd meant something else. He was not a man, not a real one, not because of what had happened to him years ago on the battlefield but because of what had happened only recently. His embarrassment, or his anger—whatever it was that made his skin flush—highlighted the parts of him that were still human. There wasn't much.

"Goodnight, John."

He at least had the decency to call out, to try to stop me from leaving. But he called the wrong name. He called the man he'd have preferred beside him.

He called the man I'd have liked to have been.

I have not seen General John Smith since that evening, though I keep up with his progress in the papers and the gossip keeps me informed as to his private life. At least, it speculates. I doubt anybody knows much about him really. Brave man, I hear. Terrible business.

Some of that I can agree with.

I may not have seen him since then, but I hear him almost every night. I dream of a desert I have never been to, thunder-blasted beneath an ashen sky and a cool horned moon, and I see machines destroyed by what they carry. Metal corpses litter the sands, empty shells that smoulder with a fading heat, and it's John's voice I hear calling from them, screaming out his pain between echoes of artillery as I squeeze my fists around handfuls of sand. Sometimes he gives it a name, this pain. It's not mine. Even so, I run to find him and the sand falls away quicker than in any hourglass. Time runs out, and all the cannons erupt my way, belching flame, raging with fires that roast those caught inside, and I'm hit with thousands upon thousands of letters. A barrage of folded envelopes bearing the same name in his neat cursive script. And I'm buried beneath them feeling a deep pain of my own.

Sometimes, when I wake, it's like the nightmare has just begun and all I had worth keeping, all that was real, I left behind in my dream. These are the days when my hands seem filled with sand, slipping through my fingers however I try to hold it. These are the days when I cannot pull myself together, dwelling instead on all that was said and unsaid. Dreams within dreams. Things that were, and things that could have been. I think of John, a haunted man in pieces, and I think of the range of friendly fire.

Even awake, I hear his voice, calling from a broken machine.

SHARK! SHARK!

We'll begin right away with the title.

"Shark! Shark!"

We're on a beach in the summer. I could tell you about how beautiful and clean the stretch of sand is, and how the sea is calm and bright and blue beneath a sky that's just the same, but you won't care about that now, not when someone's calling, "Shark!" The cry comes from a blonde woman in a bikini, her hands cupped around her mouth, looking around the crowd. "Shark!"

But it's not what you think. She's a director, one of *two* directors actually, calling for the shark man. The shark man is just some guy, no one for you to worry about. Here he comes, with a big ol' fin on a board, making his way through the crowd of extras. He'll be swimming with that above him in a minute and not only is that the only part he'll play in the film but it's the only part he plays in this story.

That's a lot of onlys, I know. Forget them. Look at the directors instead. They're a husband and wife team. The wife looks Scandinavian but isn't. You've seen her already. She's the blonde in the bikini, of course, making it look good even in her late thirties, body streamlined and supple. Not your typical director attire, perhaps, but this is California (although, for the sake of the film it's Palm Beach, Florida). Anyway, bikini or not, her baseball cap has "director" printed on it, only without the inverted commas. The husband's the big man with the curled greying hair and the scraggly beard. Nothing neat and Spielbergy for him, oh no. This guy could be a lumberjack. But he's not, he's British, in his forties, and he's a director. His cap says so, just like hers, but he never wears it, just lets it rest on the canvas seat that also has "director" printed on it (without the quotation marks).

"I want you to swim out to the raft and just circle it a coupla times, 'k?"

The shark man nods at her while looking at her breasts, thinking that because she wears sunglasses she can't see him looking when actually that only works when it's the other way around. He's stupid. He won't go far, not even in movies.

"Jesus," she says as shark man heads for the sea.

Her husband says, "Will I do?"

She swats at his butt, what he would call his arse, because they still have that kind of relationship. Even on set they are very firmly husband and wife.

"Seriously, what is it?" He's looking at her breasts, but that's okay because he's her husband and anyway, they're good breasts.

"Shark guy was doing what you're doing right now."

"Well, they're good breasts."

"Thanks."

"Real, too. And so much in this business isn't."

"You're so deep."

"Deep as the ocean, baby." He flashes her a smile that's bright in his beard and it's the same smile he caught her with all those years ago, although the beard is different now. More grey. She smiles back and he sees this as encouragement, as men trying to be funny often do, and so he continues. "The people in this country of yours aren't used to seeing anything real. Except Coca-Cola, of course. That's the real thing. You gotta cut him some slack."

"Can I just cut him?"

"Sorry."

The two of them look out to sea where extras hold their position in the shallows.

"You think if we use that Coke line in the movie it will count as product placement?"

"Can you see him yet?"

The wife has one hand up to shield her eyes from the sun, even though she's wearing sunglasses. The light on the water dazzle-flashes her as it moves with breeze and tide.

"There he is."

"Swimming?"

"Yep. Unless it's a real shark."

The wife, who deserves a name really so let's call her Sheila (although she's not Australian, just like she's not Scandinavian), cups her hands around her mouth and shouts, "Action!"

Bobby, that's her husband, says the same thing into a handheld radio and they are filming, baby. Making movies.

The film began as a conversation in a bar about *Jaws*. (The film they're making doesn't actually begin that way. It begins with a water-skier discovering a body. She hits it, in fact, and there's a tumbling splash and then she surfaces and it's floating right at her in the wake of the boat and that scene alone will probably get them an R rating but we don't care about that.) The film doesn't begin with a conversation in a bar about *Jaws*, but the *making* of the film begins that way. The idea, which turned into a script, which eventually became casting and all the rest of it, *that* began in a bar with a conversation about *Jaws*.

Glad that's clear.

"Seriously," Sheila said, "has there ever been a decent shark movie since?"

"Can there be? I mean, it's kinda difficult to top. Even the man himself couldn't do it, no matter how many times he tried."

"Be fair, he didn't do the sequels."

Her husband supports that statement as a good point by raising his glass and toasting it. He's drinking something that's red and orange and yellow, a sunset in a glass, and it has some fruit stuck on the rim. Little details like that are important. Not to the story so much, but the general sense of atmosphere. Exotic, sunny, fun. You're meant to like this guy, this couple, and if you've ever been on holiday with a lover and had drinks at a bar near a beach then you'll know the feeling I'm going for here.

"I want to make something scary that isn't all dark and stormy with vampires in it. Something scary in the sunshine."

"Good title."

"Thanks."

Bobby uses both hands in a gesture that's meant to represent words appearing on a screen or the bottom of a promotional poster. "Sunny Florida—it's a scary place." He smiles his smile at her and drinks again. See? He smiles a lot. He's likeable. "Actually, this whole country scares the shit out of me."

"Yeah, well, it's warmer."

"True, and I do like a warmer climate. But I still feel like a fish out of water here. Get it? Fish out of—"

"I'm serious. That movie scared the shit out of me when I was a kid."

"Yeah, when you were a kid. Now it's a rubber shark and a head rolling out of a wrecked boat."

"It's got good shots, good story."

"Good music."

"Good quotable lines."

"Good monologue." Bobby rolls his sleeve and points to a tattoo scar that isn't there and slurs, "'That's the USS Indianapolis'."

"Exactly. *And* it's scary."

"Which is what you want."

This time she toasts *his* point because it's accurate. She's drinking something in a classic martini glass to suggest she's cooler, not as frivolous, but still a drinker and therefore fun, like you and me maybe.

"So, scary summer film. With a shark."

She frowns and nods and says after a moment's thought, "Yeah, I'm thinking so."

"Okay."

"I like sharks."

"I know you do, baby." He smiles, and drinks.

"But we're not just throwing a load of pretty teenagers into the water to kill them off one by one."

"Heavens, no." He signals for a couple more drinks with one of those friendly gestures that says they come here often, theirs is a good marriage, and to prove it he takes her hand in his other one without even thinking about it.

"Although we'll have to have a significant number of deaths."

"Of course."

"And none of that false alarm scream crap either. None of that oh-my-God-it's-a-shark-but-no-it's-not-it's-my-boyfriend-messing-about-underwater crap. In fact, I want the *boy*friend screaming, fuck the girlfriend."

"Fuck the girlfriend?"

She gives him the look that couples have for each other when one of them is being silly at the wrong time.

"Because that's a different film entirely," he says anyway.

"It needs to be something different."

"Unless you mean he's screaming 'fuck the girlfriend'. Is that what you mean?"

The look has evolved into a look with raised eyebrows.

"A mutation maybe?" he says to compensate. "Genetic experiment?"

She wrinkles her nose at that.

"A feeding group brought close to the beach thanks to climate change."

"Too many, keep it simple."

"One big giant shark then."

"No, something *different*."

He raises his hands to the heavens in mock exasperation and then suggests "Vampire shark?"

"Keeping it real, remember."

"When so much in this business isn't."

"Exactly."

"*Open Water* tried to keep it real. And that sucked."

They both toast to that point, tipping their drinks back together.

Right, back to the movie business.

The good-looking man, slouched on a towel, reading from a sheet of paper clutched in one hand while a finger on his other hand follows the words, is an up-and-coming movie star. He moves his mouth when he reads, but to be fair to him he might be practising pronunciation or delivery or something else actors do. His name is immediately forgettable for now until you've seen it lots of times on posters and movie credits, something like Tom, Brad or Colin (but if you're thinking of another Tom, Brad or Colin currently working in the movie business then stop because he's younger and more surfer-dude type, and I only used those names in a Tom, Dick or Harry kind of way). Phil. That's his name. Probably Philip if he wants to be taken seriously, and he desperately does want to be taken seriously, although he never will be.

"Who's that?"

She only means to glance over to see who Bobby means but she lingers a little because although their marriage is good, the man on the towel reading his lines is a damn fine-looking specimen of a man. "That's Phil."

"I mean, who is he in the film? I don't remember any surfer-types that actually have lines."

"He's our Dreyfus."

"Hardly."

"He's our shark expert. You know, our way of telling the audience things they need to know about sharks so they can be properly scared."

"Who isn't scared of sharks?"

She shrugs.

"Stop staring at him."

"But he's a damn fine-looking specimen of a man."

"Bit too good-looking for a shark expert, isn't he?"

"What, they're all ugly?"

He shrugs. "Anyway, sharks are on Discovery Channel all the time. People know it all already. And they've seen that movie. You know, that other one about a shark." He clicks his fingers, feigning memory loss.

"I think I'll change into my bikini."

"Don't you dare, or I'll change into one too."

"Gross."

"Gross is cutting open a shark and seeing everything spill out, like a fish head and a licence plate. Is the beautiful Phil going to do that, too?"

Sheila frowns at Bobby.

"You know, the autopsy scene? He pulls all that crap out of—"

"We're not just ripping off *Jaws*."

Bobby knows he's gone too far because they really aren't just ripping off *Jaws* and she's sensitive about that.

"Phil is actually Bodie," Sheila explains. (I know Bodie is a bit like Bobby but I'm trusting you won't get confused. It's also a bit like body, which might give you some idea of his role in this movie, and this story for that matter.)

"Okay," says Bobby (*not* Bodie) as he remembers the script.

"He was a surfer once until a narrow escape from a . . . tiger shark? Bull? Not sure. Anyway, he doesn't surf anymore but he's been obsessed with sharks ever since." She peers over the top of her sunglasses at her husband. "Maybe he watches Discovery Channel."

Bobby holds up both hands and backs away with that smile we've seen a few times already although this time it seems a little strained. And if this was a movie instead of a story, the bunch of girls in bikinis that come running in now would do it as part of the same shot, appearing behind him and running past with shrieks of laughter, giving us a smooth transition from him to them. They frolic in the shallows which is just about the only time you can ever use the word frolic (unless Sheila and Bobby were making a film about lambs in the spring, which they aren't). Bobby turns his head to watch them run by so when they splash each other and scoop up handfuls of water to throw, the view we have of them is his view.

"Hey!"

Sheila's voice brings us back to the director couple and she stabs at Bobby's eyes with forked fingers. He closes them and covers them with his hands and turns away before she can get him, not that she really would have.

"Good," she says, "stay like that."

"But they're damn fine-looking specimens."

"Shush."

He peers at her from between his fingers, probably smiling but we can't see that because of how his hands are up. What he sees is Sheila watching the girls kick water at each other and turn away shrieking. It's a sound she'll segue into a scream when they actually put it in the movie but for now they're getting too wet for a rehearsal.

"Girls, no nipples until we're rolling! Stay dry up there please!"

Sheila looks at Bobby and shrugs. "Gotta have something for the trailer."

"True. True."

"I figure we'll get a view inland from the jetty crane," she makes a sweeping gesture with her arms, "get them all frolicking with the store in shot behind them."

The store she means is a actually a set. They've already filmed the inside shots at the studio, two couples buying supplies for a doomed fishing trip.

"Funny word," says Bobby, "frolicking."

"We'll get that 'live bait' sign across the top of the shot, girls underneath."

"Subtle."

"After that, we'll kill them all."

Bobby claps his hands together and rubs them with maniacal glee. He's allowed to rub them with maniacal glee because this is a horror story about a horror film and I may never get the chance to use the expression again.

Alright, rewind again. Flashback.

"The shark's gotta be more than just a shark," says Sheila.

"Like I said, vampire shark."

"Asylum have done that already, surely."

"You're thinking octoshark."

"Really?"

He shrugs, and drinks.

We're in the bar again. Same bar, same drinks, because it's the same conversation. I only ended it where I ended it before so you didn't get too bored reading the same scene and so I could end with that little dig at *Open Water*. It did suck, though.

"I mean it has to be a symbol, or a metaphor or something."

"Why? Isn't a thousand years of evolution into the perfect killing machine scary enough?"

"Scary, yeah, of course. I mean it's practically just muscle and teeth. But it needs to be something more if we aren't going straight to Blu-Ray."

"Careful. Did you ever read *Jaws*?"

"Read it?"

"Yeah, the book. Quaint little things made of paper. People sometimes make movies out of them."

"Funny."

"The paper makes it easier to cut bits out."

"I know it's a book. I'm just surprised you do."

"Right."

"Peter Benchley."

"Now you're just showing off. Alright, Benchley, whatever. Anyway, there was a metaphor in there that was *pretty fucking* lame."

In case you haven't read it, don't worry, because Sheila can't remember and Bobby has to explain.

"Out in the water you've got a lone shark, preying on the people of Amity, right? Is it still Amity in the book?"

"You're the expert."

"And on land, you've got a money lender bleeding the people dry. A *loan* shark. As in L, O, A, N."

"Really?"

"Really. As in really terrible."

They've got into the habit of toasting a good point, so Sheila does so here. "Well we should have something deeper than money anyway."

"Sex."

"I'm serious."

"Me too."

"I'd rather talk about the movie." She waggles her eyebrows like I'm told Groucho Marx does, or did, to show she's joking.

Bobby feigns disappointment by sticking out his lower lip, just going along with her joke because he loves her, then adds, "Big prehistoric phallic symbol of a shark."

She considers it, but, "I'd prefer vagina dentata."

"Why not both? Can it be both?"

"Oh *I* don't know."

Both of them slump in their seats, defeated for a moment. Thinking for a moment.

Bobby complains, "Why can't a monster just be a monster?" Then he blows bubbles into his drink with a straw.

It's a good point to end on for the moment, so let's go back, or rather forward . . .

S

. . . to the movie. The movie stars, more precisely. They aren't being filmed right now but they are acting. Not too much emphasis on the acting, what they're doing is mostly natural, but they *are* acting a little bit.

We're with Phil and an actress called Brenda who we saw earlier splashing in the waves with her shrieking girly friends. Brenda was being Cassy then. They're not in role here, though. Phil is being Phil and Brenda Brenda and they're fucking each other in a crummy chalet room. They're still acting a bit though because each wants the other to think they're good at fucking, and each wants the other one to think that they think *they* are good at fucking, mainly so they can keep fucking on a regular basis for a while. For at least as long as it takes to make the film anyway.

They are both naked. It's all very well lit. Phil is sitting on the bed and Brenda has straddled him, bouncing in his lap at a speed that must be bringing him close, or her close, whoever—the main thing is, we're joining them at a critical moment. She's bouncing, ponytail hair whipping around behind her, with one arm draped around Phil's neck and the other groping at his pectoral muscles which is fair because one of his hands is on her chest too, holding one breast then the other as if trying to stop them bouncing too much. His other hand is at the small of her back so she doesn't fall off the bed, or more importantly so she doesn't fall off of him. She is making a lot of noise because she wants him to think he's good and she wants him to like how much she likes it so they can keep doing this for a while, and before this movie she did some others she's not so proud of so she knows how to make those noises pretty good. Phil is giving her an occasional "oh yeah" so she knows it's working.

You get the picture. Young, damn fine-looking specimens enjoying the fact that they are young damn fine-looking specimens.

They near climax, and it's bound to have happened perfectly together if not for this interruption. The door to the room bursts open suddenly with the same shocking force their orgasm might have had, had it been allowed, but instead we're going to have a climax of a different sort because, let's face it, there hasn't been any blood yet and a horror film tends to need some. Not always, some of the best ones don't have any, but this is the movie business, albeit the budget movie business, and in the budget horror movie business blood is something they can always afford to use. Besides, they're having sex, so death is sure to follow. It's still the rules, even if *Scream* told you that already.

Brenda turns, surprised, and for a moment her breasts are free of Phil's hand so we get a tantalizing glimpse of both of them together. Phil gives a manly, "What the hell are you doing here?" which tells us whoever has come in is someone he knows but if it were a film they would not be in shot. As it's a story I can even have the intruder speak and you still won't know who it is.

"No wonder there's been no chemistry."

And Brenda screams, and so does Phil.

You must have a good idea who it might have been; there aren't many characters to choose from. Unless it's someone new but that wouldn't be fair at this point, would it? Bit like cheating. So let me just say you're right, and move on with the story.

Bobby and Sheila are watching Phil and Brenda on a monitor. Nothing kinky—it's footage from earlier in the week, not the sex scene from the motel. The sex you just read hasn't actually happened yet, this is another flashback.

Phil is being Bodie and Brenda is being Cassy and they are sitting on the raft we saw right at the beginning. Cassy is laying on her back, sunning herself, in a tiny white bikini because white is pure and virginal (though Brenda isn't) and she is going to be one of the survivors (though Brenda isn't). Phil is sitting next to her, glistening because he's just been in the water and because the reflected light gives his torso more muscle definition. If all had gone well, this would have been the poster shot for the movie, with an added fin circling the raft.

"You know, there was a shark attack here last year," says Phil who is Bodie to Brenda who is Cassy.

She sits up, but not entirely. Just enough that we can see she has a flat stomach and perfect breasts. She is propped up on her forearms and elbows, which pushes her chest out more. She knew to do this without direction because of the films she's made before.

"You're kidding."

Bodie (you know it's really Phil pretending to be Bodie so I'll stop saying so) he shakes his head without looking at Cassy. "They like the warm climate." He's looking out to sea.

"Bodie, are you trying to scare me?"

"No."

"Because there are other ways to keep me on this raft, you know."

("You see," says Sheila, pointing back and forth between the characters on the screen, "there's supposed to be some chemistry here. Some sexual tension. We've got nothing.")

Bodie glances at Cassy and she smiles a dazzling smile that is nearly as white as her pure virginal bikini and he says, "It's true." It's a deliberately ambiguous reply because it's true that there are other ways to keep her on the raft, but also it's true that there was a shark attack here, the audience has already seen it in the film. We're meant to wonder if we'll see another one in a minute, or if we'll get the kissing and groping Cassy seems to be hinting at. Either way the audience would be happy, most likely. What they get instead, though, is back story and shark info.

"They'll eat anything, you know. Turtles, tin cans. Surfers."

("But probably not your meatloaf," says Bobby and Sheila slaps his arm without looking at him, looking only at the screen. "This is shite," she says. It's a Britishism she likes.)

Cassy sits up fully now, and the close up is of their faces together. It's going to be one of *those* moments, where lead characters get closer emotionally as well as physically. The movement also tells the audience this is going to be important information.

"They've got these jagged teeth, triangle teeth, and not just the one row. There are lots of teeth. They shed them and replace them all the time. And when it comes at you, its jaw drops open all the way down, like, ninety degrees, and all you can see is teeth and darkness."

Cassy puts her hand on Bodie's arm, squeezes his bicep.

"You know, when it's got you, a shark will just roll, left and right. Waving its pectoral fins. The water resistance keeps you from moving much but the shark can move, and its teeth cut back and forth like a chainsaw."

"Oh, Bodie . . ."

He looks at her then, pulled out of his memory, and gives her a weak smile. Then they kiss. Then they lay back. They kiss again. Cassy's hand is on Bodie's thigh. As she caresses him, his shorts rise up and we can see the beginning of a bite scar there.

("This is meant to be tentative," says Sheila. "They're kissing for the first time, she's kissing for the first time *ever* actually, but here . . ." and because they're married and they finish each other's sentences sometimes, Bobby says, "Here she looks like a college slut." "Yeah," says Sheila, "She might as well just go right for his cock.")

As they lie kissing, a fin rises up out of the water briefly, passes, and is gone.

Sheila hits the pause button so all there is on screen is dark water.

"And that was take a hundred or whatever."

"I thought they were messing it up on purpose. Get a little more kissy-kissy." Bobby gropes an imaginary woman in front of him.

"They're killing my movie."

"Our movie, baby."

"We'll have to re-shoot it."

Except they can't, because Phil and Brenda, who are the Bodie and Cassy they need for the scene, for the rest of the film in fact, will be dead soon.

But then you already knew that.

The chalet door is open and the bed sheets are tangled and there is blood everywhere. There's blood everywhere because there isn't a body to hold it all anymore, not exactly. Both bodies are here, but they're in pieces. Blood has soaked the bed, the floor, and it splashes up the walls in long lines. There's even an arc of it across the ceiling.

The man standing in the doorway is wearing a blazer, despite the heat, but no tie. His shirt is a grubby white because he's a good guy but not too squeaky clean. He is looking over the scene calmly, hands in his pockets. He's clearly a cop, even though he's not in uniform and there's no gun visible or anything. He just is, and you can tell just by looking.

"Sir? You can't be in here."

A patrolman stands near. He reaches for the man, then reaches for his gun when the other man reaches inside his blazer.

"Steady," says the man in the blazer we know is a cop. He produces a flip-fold ID. He shows it upside down, realizes, and turns it the right way. A little detail. It keeps us with the photo and the police badge for a moment. See, he's a cop.

"Sorry sir."

"New?"

"Two weeks, sir."

In any other story, that would mark him as a dead-man-to-be. Not this one. He's not in the story anymore, except for his arm in a moment, and the arm is still attached to his body when that happens.

The detective steps further into the room and looks around so we can see again the bloody horror of it all. So much blood. And chunks. Occasionally there's a piece you might recognize, like an elbow or a few toes still connected.

"Let us through," comes Sheila's voice from outside.

"Ma'am," says someone else, "stop." Our two-week-old patrolman.

The man who is a detective glances behind at the noise briefly, then squats down and tilts his head to look under the bed. It means the doorway is free behind him to frame a good shot of Sheila and Bobby together as they stand on the threshold, held back by the arm of the patrolman. Sheila brings her hand up to her mouth, either to stifle a scream or hold back vomit. Bobby says, "Bloody hell."

"Bloody," says the cop, reaching under the bed with a pen. "You got that right."

"What happened?"

Bobby's question is a stupid question in the general sense, but in the specific actually quite interesting.

The cop brings something out from under the bed using his pen. It is triangular and jagged.

"If I didn't know any better," says the cop, "I'd say it was a shark attack."

It's too early to say so, of course, but it saves writing a post-mortem scene. Besides, this is the CSI generation. He should have figured out the whole case by now.

§

"What are we going to do now? We can't just re-cast both of them."

"Just one, then."

Sheila thinks about it. The day of filming has been cancelled, so they're sitting on set in the sun. The set they're sitting on is the raft because it keeps people from coming over and asking them questions. They can see everybody else, the crew, the cops, the reporters, back on the beach.

"He said shark attack."

"Yeah."

"On land. Interesting."

"Yeah. Shame we're not making a film about making a film about a shark attack, it could have been a good scene."

"Original."

Bobby dips his foot into the water, likes the temperature, and puts both feet in. Sheila is lying back, propped up on her elbows. Her bikini is black and oily looking because it's wet. She is thinking about how to fix the film but Bobby is thinking about her bikini and how he'd like to take it off but figures that might be a bit weird after what just happened. And anyway, they'd have an audience. Not you, so much, but the people on the beach. Sheila and Bobby don't know about you, this isn't *that* kind of story.

"The scene where Bodie looks out to sea with his arm around his surfboard."

"What about it?"

"Well, instead of having him turn around and walk back inland, another failed attempt to get back surfing, we could just cut it with him looking. We could put that in *after* the raft scene instead, which we already have—"

"Without chemistry."

"Without chemistry. And then that can be his last scene. Looking out to sea, surfboard in the sand beside him, arm around it like a lover."

"There was more chemistry between him and the surfboard."

"We don't see him again, but we do see the surfboard. It washes up on the beach—"

"—with a big bite out of it."

"Exactly."

"Emotional."

"Yeah. He finally kisses Cassy, having told his story, gets some closure of sorts, and that's it."

"Meanwhile, Cassy the virgin never-kissed-anyone feels like it's her fault."

"Yeah."

"Except we don't have a Cassy anymore. And too many shots with her and Bodie together to simply re-shoot."

Bobby kicks his feet in the water. He's not worried about how a shark can detect minute disturbances in the water with its lateral line sensory system. He knows about it, he just isn't worried about it. Neither is Sheila. She drapes one hand into the cool water as she thinks about how they can fix their movie.

"Bobby? Sheila?"

The voice comes from the radio Bobby has clipped to his shorts. They didn't swim out—they came in a small motorboat.

"Ignore him."

"It's Tony," Bobby explains. "You know how he gets." He unclips the radio and says, "Yeah, Tony, Bobby."

"We got a dwarf here wants to speak to you."

"Did you say dwarf?"

"Midget, then. Vertically challenged. Whatever. Says he was in *Jaws*. Says he's come to see you."

"Shit," says Sheila, "I totally forgot about him."

"Dwarf?" says Bobby again, this time to Sheila.

"Little person, for the cage scenes with the real shark. To make it look bigger."

"Oh."

She makes a gimme-gimme gesture for the radio and he hands it over.

"Hi Tony, Sheila. We'll come get him."

"Roger that."

Sheila sighs. "At least out here nobody *else* will bother us."

Bobby puts his hand on his wife's knee and tries his smile. It nearly works. "We'll get through this."

There's another burst from the radio.

"Bobby? Sheila?"

"Tony, yeah, what?"

"There's someone here to see you."

"A dwarf, yeah, we know, keep your panties on. We're coming to get him."

"No, not him. A cop. Says it's important."

Bobby looks at Sheila who says, "Fuck it, bring him out here too."

Bobby looks at their tiny outboard and says, "We're gonna need a bigger—"

"Don't. Don't say it."

§

The cop wants to talk to Bobby and Sheila about some film footage. Not theirs, though.

"You got somewhere I can play this?" he says to them as they pull their boat up onto the sand. He shows them a video cassette.

"Not here," says Bobby, "we use digital."

"What is it?" asks Sheila.

"I'd rather just show you," he says. "Let you clear something up for me."

So far, so Columbo.

Sheila shrugs. "There's a player in the warehouse set."

"Warehouse?" The cop looks around but there's no warehouse here.

"Warehouse *set*," Sheila says. She points at the bait shop they'd used earlier. "It's different inside."

So they head over. Tony approaches with a small guy you only know as the dwarf or midget or vertically challenged man from *Jaws*.

"Later, Tony," says Bobby. "Something needs clearing up first."

Bobby doesn't sound like Columbo when he says it. He sounds more like the Godfather or something.

Inside, the set is empty. There's no shooting today. The warehouse is all old-looking boards and crates. In the middle of the room, though, is a large fish tank. As in the tank is large, but also as in it could hold a large fish. Both definitions apply. Anyway, beside this is the video player and a small TV and a few plastic chairs.

"What's all this?" He's a cop. He's naturally curious.

"We got a guy with a baby shark in these scenes. He's filming it, studying it. Feeding it. Lets us show the audience how a shark feeds in close up detail that won't bring the rating up or get us censored. It's also why people keep getting killed, the parents have come for it and are terrorizing the beach."

"Parents, huh."

"Yeah, there's two. Only you'll never see both together. One will get killed and you'll think it's safe and then wham, here's the other one. It's like our twist."

The cop peers in. "Where's the shark?"

Bobby and Sheila exchange a glance.

"We don't have one."

"It'll be rubber or CGI or papier-mâché or something," Bobby explains.

"But it'll look real enough."

"Oh."

"So what's the tape?"

The cop, let's call him Travis, pops the tape into the machine and says, "You tell me."

There's no need for anyone to tell him anything, it's clear immediately what it is. It's security footage of the parking lot of the chalet motel where many of the actors are staying. It doesn't play continuous footage but a sequence of stills taken at intervals. And here. Comes. A car. Parking. In the next shot the door is suddenly open. And heeeere's—

Bobby.

"You went to the motel?"

Bobby looks at Sheila who is frowning. She even takes a step back away from him.

"Yeah," Bobby says. He says it somewhat reluctantly. Then again to the cop. Travis. "Yeah. I did."

"Why?"

"I just wanted to talk to her." Bobby says this to Sheila. Her arms are crossed and her frown has deepened.

"She wasn't alone, though, was she," says Travis.

"No."

"One of the other guests heard an argument."

"That's right. I wasn't, *we* wasn't, we *weren't*, happy with one of their scenes. I told them so."

"And then what?"

"Not what *you* think."

"And what do I think?"

"That the next thing I did was kill them."

"Actually, no. If I thought that, we'd be doing this downtown, as they say in the movies. The only screams I got from this neighbour are the 'get the fuck out' kind, and look." He points at the screen and Bobby's car is. One shot. At a time. Leaving the lot. Too soon for him to have done much of anything.

"Oh."

"So?"

"Well, the next thing was Cassy quit."

"You mean Brenda?"

"Yeah. She said she didn't like having a pervert director and could earn more doing other films."

"Weird," says Sheila.

"Why's that?" asks Travis.

Sheila looks at him and says, "Well I've seen her other films."

Travis looks like he wants to ask something, then doesn't, then does, but this time it's probably different to what he wanted to ask. He's a cop. He can figure out the films Brenda used to make for himself. "Then what happened?" is what he says to Bobby.

"Bodie quit too. Phil. Moral support I think. I left them to it, figuring they'd cool down and change their minds in the morning."

"Is that all?" Sheila says.

"Yes."

So she says it again to Travis. "Is that all?" and gestures to the empty parking lot on the screen to emphasize her point.

"Not quite. Hold on."

They wait.

"I'd fast forward only I'd probably miss it and then we'd have to rewind again and it's easier if—here we go."

And here it is. Another. Car. Parking.

Sheila's.

Sheila shows Bobby her palms and says, "I just wanted to talk to him."

"Wasn't there though, was he," says Bobby.

"No."

"Because he was with Cass—with *Brenda*."

"Well I know that *now*, yeah."

Travis, the cop, feels he should ask another question or two because he is, after all, the cop. "The question I have for you both is this . . ."

Both of them wait a moment.

"Any ideas who'd want them dead?"

§

Alright, nearly finished.

You hear that? Of course you don't. You'll have to imagine it. Imagine a soundtrack that sounds a bit like *Jaws* even though it's trying really hard not to. An underwater moving shot along the ocean bed, coming up to where the sun dapples the surface of the water, glinting and sparkling. Cut into this brightness with the sleek dark body not of a shark but the underside of a boat. No mini motorboat this time but a proper big vessel. Not too big, as you'll see as we come up out of the water, just big enough for a small crew and a shark cage and a dwarf. Okay, so the dwarf doesn't need much room, but he's there too so I need to mention him. The dwarf is Manny and he's definitely a dwarf and not a midget. He's not the guy they used in *Jaws* by the way, he just says he is to get more work. No one ever checks.

"Okay, okay, this will do."

Bobby has to shout it because he's at the front of the boat looking in the water.

"You sure? We're not very far out." This comes from the boat owner, Smith. He knows the front of the boat is really called the bow but he's not writing this story. He's dressed as if he's going to be in the movie; woollen sweater, tatty at the seams, a baseball cap with anchor insignia, shorts stained with fish-gut, sandals. He's not in the movie. He's not even in the story for much longer, and he certainly doesn't have any more dialogue.

"He's sure," says Sheila. "He has a good sense for these things." She gives the thumb-to-finger okay signal to her husband up front as Smithy kills the engine.

"I feel ridiculous."

Manny is fidgeting with what looks to be breasts but is actually a stuffed sports bra he has on underneath his wetsuit. Some of the crew laugh again. They've laughed at him a lot.

"You're Cassy," Sheila reminds him, "troubled teenager, anxious to face the shark that took the man you loved."

"I'm Cassy. Right."

"Well, from a distance."

Sheila thinks that for the close ups they'll get one of the girls to wear the mask and be all wide-eyed with fright. She figures she may even have the girl spit out the respirator in panic so her underwater screams and the released oxygen give them a lot of bubbles to obscure things. And they'll tear the suit in such a way that as she swims away she's pretty much naked flesh and breasts so no one will notice the body double.

"You sure you wanna do this?" Bobby asks.

"Yeah, no problem," says Manny, which is a bit embarrassing because Bobby was talking to Sheila. "Oh."

"Yeah, we don't have much choice but to kill her off now, do we?" she says.

Neither of them pay much heed to the fact she has been killed once already, for real. This is showbiz.

"I hear your girl got herself murdered," says Manny. He's stepping into the cage now, breasts and all. It's a specially adapted cage, smaller than the usual.

"Sort of," Bobby admits. He has come down to help.

"Shark attack," says Sheila.

"Huh?" is as much as Manny can protest because Sheila calls to the winch guy and Manny-Cassy is hauled up into the air and over the side of the boat. He would like to call, "Wait!" and get some more details about the shark attack but he's already being lowered and he needs to breathe so he puts the respirator in his mouth instead and disappears into the deep blue sea.

"Dinner is served."

"Roll cameras."

Bobby announces, "Time to chum the waters," and returns to the front of the boat where a couple of tubs wait for him. Each is filled with fish heads and tails and guts in a soup of blood and scales. Bobby has a trowel in his hand and he shovels the stuff into the water. It's sloppy splashy work, and smelly too. Look as one scoop of blood and chunks is slung over the side: *sploosh!* And another scoop that looks already chewed: *sploop!* And this one, red-wet and blood-slick, is an open flip-fold ID with a police badge and picture we know better upside down and without all the blood . . . .

Splash!

So what happened to the cop?

Well, you know what happened. He's dead. But what actually

happened, what are the details?

He wanted to talk to Bobby and Sheila, remember? He wanted to talk to them about some film footage. And after that he asked if they had any idea who might have killed them. (Of course they did, but they weren't going to say so.) Well after *that* he said he wanted to shut them down.

"The thing is, it could be any one of your cast or your crew, and if it isn't we're still gonna need to talk to all of them. It'll take a while."

Bobby stands. "Out of the question, chum."

Travis looks at Sheila with raised eyebrows. She shrugs and says, "He's British," by way of explanation.

"Your two main characters are dead, how are you still filming anyway?"

"They *were* the main characters. Now they're bit parts."

Sheila stands beside her husband. "We evolve."

"And evolution never stops."

"Well, this movie does." Travis stands up too. He ejects the video cassette. "For a little while, anyway. Sorry."

"If we stop filming the movie will die."

"Like a shark, huh?"

"This movie is our baby."

Travis looks from one to the other. He wants to touch his gun, just for the reassurance, but he doesn't because that would be silly because this man is a British film director and this one's a woman in a bikini, and anyway he has the video tape in his gun hand.

"What's going on here?"

"A ruthless business," says Sheila.

"Cutthroat, really," Bobby agrees.

"It'll chew you up and spit you out if you're not careful."

Finally beginning to see the significance of their comments, Travis glances at the cassette tape in his hand.

"We went back later," Sheila explains. "Together. Parked down the street."

Travis swaps hands with the tape and goes for his gun but Bobby is already smiling at him and there are *a lot* of teeth in that smile. A lot.

"What *are* you?"

Bobby's mouth is open. It has expanded for all the teeth, so many teeth, too many teeth. They snap together as he tries to speak.

"Shust a monshter."

"What?" Travis asks Sheila. It's a pretty big question that could simply be an abbreviated repeat of what are you, or what is he, or it could be what shall I do, or maybe it's all he can manage of a good plain what the fuck.

Sheila chooses to think of it as what did he say and answers accordingly.

"He's trying to say, 'just a monster.'"

It shouldn't be a surprise to you, there were plenty of clues. I mean, I mentioned his teeth a lot, and his smile. Plus there was that "fish out of water" line near the beginning, and that "warmer climate" reference. A few others. And shame on you if you thought it was the shark man from the beginning, the one with the fake fin, because I told you he wasn't in it again.

There's a tearing sound as Bobby's fin, a very real fin, splits the fabric of his shirt. But like I said, you shouldn't be surprised.

Travis, the cop, the symbol of law and order in a world that's just gone all messed-up otherworldly, *is* surprised. He's not used to this. He's used to the butler did it, or a jealous mistress. So faced with a man with an elongating head, a greying head, a head with an open maw of teeth and receding beard, Travis can only stand paralyzed. He thinks it has to be a special effect or something, and he has a goofy smile on his face when he looks at Sheila to say, "Alright, joke's over."

But Sheila says, "You know what scares me most about *Jaws*?"

Travis can only shake his head, but it might be in disbelief rather than as an answer.

"It's that such a magnificent creature was stopped by an everyday seaside cop." Her eyes are fully black now, as oily dark as her swimsuit. "The joke's not over until you smile, you sonofabitch." She shows him how. Then her own mouth stretches and opens, opens, as it fills with teeth, lots of teeth, so many many teeth.

It shouldn't be a surprise to you, there were plenty of clues. I mean, there's the twist in their own film, for one thing, with the two sharks and their baby and all. And look at the title; it's not just Shark! is it, it's "Shark! Shark!" (I was going to go with "Somewhere, Beyond the Scene" but a pun sets the wrong tone, don't you think? Like this is a funny story or something, and not serious horror.)

Travis can only watch, gun useless in one hand and video tape in the other, as the husband and wife step closer. They'll eat anything, even a cop, especially if it threatens their movie.

Sheila's jaw is hanging right down to her chest now, impossibly large and open, and Bobby's is the same. If this were a film then one of them would come right at you, quick, an extreme close up down the throat as the jaws close and the screen goes suddenly black.

Imagine that in 3D.

Back on the boat, Bobby is still scooping a bloody swill of chum into the sea. Evidence, really, but some genuine fish chum too.

"How's the little guy doing?" Sheila asks her crew. The camera crew, not the boat crew.

While everyone's attention is on the cross-dressing dwarf, Bobby scoops a handful of bloody guts from the barrel and tucks it quickly into his mouth.

"How we doing up there?" Sheila shouts to him.

He wipes his mouth clean and scoops the next lot overboard like he's supposed to.

"Getting hungry," he says, thinking maybe she saw him.

"As soon as we've got some shots of our fishy friends we'll break for lunch."

She shouts it to everyone but Bobby knows better: she saw him for sure.

He turns to the ocean, shovelling chum and eager for the promised break, calling, "Shark! Shark!"

- Fin -

Roll credits. (Rock music optional.)

BLOODCLOTH

Tanya drew circles in the dust on the floor while she waited for her father to come home from the caves. She drew a smile in one of them, intending to make a face, but it didn't look right so she made it another circle within the circle. She looped them together with another one, turning a half circle herself when the floorboards nearest her knees were full. She was humming something half-remembered but didn't know until Mother called for her to be quiet. So she was.

She could hear Mother's breathing now, long and slow, and it made her think of Grandma, which made her look at the curtain hanging in front of her. She didn't like the curtain because of what it did to Grandma, but she liked to sit by it for the same reason. Mother hated it. She hated it because of Grandma, but for lots of other things as well. And she was scared of it. Tanya would understand when she was older but she wasn't sure she wanted to.

The curtain was pale at the moment, except for a fading pink near the middle where Father had wiped his hands. It was still creased and bunched a little in that area, but mostly it hung straight and heavy, its faint meaty smell barely noticeable. Folds of its flesh piled upon themselves on the floor at the corner, the rail still crooked because Father was too used to it now to make fixing it a priority. There were two dead flies in the creases there, their bodies dried husks, legs curled in tight. Tanya wondered if there were any entombed within the folds, if they would disintegrate into flakes and add their dust to the rest of it on the floor.

"Hummingbird?"

Tanya stopped humming again but asked, "Yes Ma?" in case there was more. She heard her mother shift in bed, the creak of the wood.

"What time is it?"

Tanya stood and brushed her skirts clean. She went over to the mantle and checked the clock there. It didn't tick, it only tocked, offering a moment of quiet remembrance for each missing sound between. Tanya would sometimes get a big tick at the schoolhouse if her work was right but Father said just because the clock didn't have any didn't make it wrong. Mother had smiled, but to Tanya it always sounded like something was missing, when she noticed it at all. Usually it tocked like she hummed; without knowing and barely heard. When she noticed it, though, she noticed it all the time.

"It's nearly six."

"Your father will be home soon."

Tanya sat again and resumed her circles, moving dust round and round with her finger as the clock tocked quietly. Tocked. And tocked.

"Yes Ma."

The curtain shivered but Tanya ignored it, pretended not to see, because she knew why it moved and what it waited for.

Tanya set the table without knowing what dinner would be, laying out bowls on top of plates and lining up spoons next to forks next to knives. She put the two candles they had in the middle and put a cushion on one chair in case Mother joined them in the kitchen. She was trying to plump it into a shape it had given up long ago when she heard the gate catch on the gravel path with a sudden sharp crunch, and then the rusty groan it only made when closing.

"Dad's home."

He was late, the tocking clock close to half past seven.

But it wasn't Father. It was another man from the caves, a man called Gerald who had a bushy beard but no hair on his head.

"Hello Tanya, is your mother home?"

He must have known she was. Everybody knew she was bedridden. Only for a little while, but everybody knew.

"Who is it?" Mother called from her room.

"It's Gerald, ma'am. Your husband, he's . . . Well, he's working late." Gerald was calling the information from the door because Tanya hadn't invited him in yet. "Asked me to bring you some dinner."

"Come in. I'll be with you in a few minutes."

Gerald came in, giving Tanya a smile with a bottle of pop drink. She didn't have pop drink often so it was very easy to smile back.

"No, don't get yourself up. It's just a bit of stewing beef and a few vegetables. I'll put it on the table."

Which he did. It was more than a few vegetables, and the stew-beef was wrapped in a lot of paper so there was probably more than a bit of that, too. Tanya thought it was a nice lie, though.

She twisted the lid off her bottle with it near her face so the hiss-fizz of it would wet her cheek and tickle.

Gerald went to the doorway where Mother's room was. "It's simple enough for the little one to cook," he said. "You rest up some more."

Mother said something in reply but Tanya didn't hear it because she was swallowing. She took too much and had to burp quietly afterwards. She hid it in her hand.

"No, I'll show her how. Don't you worry. Can I get you something to drink?"

He didn't go into the room. Maybe to be polite, maybe because of the sick smell.

"Here," said Tanya. She went in because she was used to the sick smell now. She held up the pop drink. There was most of it left still.

Her mother was lying on top of the sheets and Tanya couldn't help but think of the flies on the curtain though she didn't mean to. Her mother smiled because she didn't know about the flies or Tanya's thoughts and said, "No, dear, you drink it."

"It's delicious, you'll like it," Tanya promised, words her mother and father had used on her plenty of times, even though sometimes it wasn't true.

"It tickles my nose too much," Mother said. But she licked her lips and Tanya thought maybe it was another nice lie that adults do sometimes. "Go and help Gerald in the kitchen." Then louder, to Gerald, "Would you like to stay for supper?"

Gerald was stroking his beard like he was far away, looking over at the curtain in the front room. Tanya wondered when Father would be home, and wondered if the curtain wondered.

"Ma wants to know if you'd like to stay for supper." She took another sip of drink. A little one, to make it last longer.

"That's very kind," he said. He said it twice, the second time so Mother could hear as well, adding, "I've got to get on back to the caves."

He crouched so he was nearly Tanya's height, though he was so big he could never be so small, and asked, "Do you want to learn how to cook a grown-up dinner?"

Tanya thought that was even better than a pop drink because she only knew how to make sandwiches (without cutting them because knives were Dangerous) so she nodded hard enough to put her hair in her eyes, which made Gerald laugh.

When he was finished laughing the house sounded more sad.

Gerald told her to wash her hands first, then showed her how to fill the pan with enough water to cover the meat. There was a lot of it. Some of it was stringy but he said it didn't matter because of how it would cook. He showed her how to cut the vegetables and said to use them all even though there was a lot because they wouldn't keep but in the stew they would. He showed her how to use the knife properly and safely and said big chunks were better but Tanya knew that was because it was safer. When Father cooked he cut things really small.

"It will take a while to cook properly. When it starts to bubble, turn it down so it just bubbles a little bit, and stir it once in a while." He showed her how. "And then just wait until your mother says it's ready. She'll know when. If you get hungry waiting, eat some of the carrot pieces we saved, remember? I always save a couple to nibble on."

Tanya decided she loved Gerald a little bit.

He came down next to her again, squatting so they were nearly the same height but never quite. "You know, your father works hard so you both have food and this house and so you don't have to pay tribute too often. You know that, don't you?"

Tanya nodded. She tipped the pop bottle up for the last of it but the last of it was gone.

"And he will always try to keep things that way, all right? Even if things look bad, he'll try and make it good like it was."

She nodded again, giving up on the bottle but deciding to keep it. She'd put a flower in it for Mother's dinner tray.

Gerald stood and ruffled her hair.

"Good," he said. "That's good."

He wiped his hands on his trousers after, even though her hair wasn't dirty, and then he did something unexpected. He walked quickly over to where the curtain hung and put his hands to it. He didn't wrap them up in the middle like Father did, bunching it up around his hands like he was drying them, but placed them palm-flat against the flesh and let it feed. It was such a surprise that Tanya watched even though she never liked to. She watched the red spread from his fingertips, saw the lines become pink as they stretched out from his hands, only to deepen to crimson as he waited, and waited. Waited. With a final grunt, he withdrew his hands and stepped back. The curtain where he'd touched it was so dark it was black. Father never gave it *that* much.

"Right," he said. His face was still dirty from the caves but it was white, too, around the dirt. Pale, like the curtain used to be. "You watch that stew now."

Tanya nodded and he left, calling a polite goodbye to Mother but Mother was asleep again.

"Bye Gerald," Tanya said for her, but the door was already closing. She heard the gravel beneath his boots as he walked away and watched his black handprints fade to dark brown and then maroon, deep red to mauve to a fading pink. The colours of dying, that's what Mother called them. Briefly, it had been the auburn colour of her hair.

Tanya watched until there was no longer any trace of tribute, by which time the stew was ready.

Tanya first learnt about the curtain at the schoolhouse. She never used to want to go to school, she wanted to work in the Drapery when she was older like Mother, and like Grandma used to before she got sick. Grandma told her stories about it, which was like being at school half the time anyway. Grandma told her about Grandpa too, who was a brave man and fought in a war but didn't come back. He wasn't killed, he just didn't come back. Father said that meant he wasn't brave at all but Mother said there was always another way of looking at it and he probably had his reasons, which is what Grandma said as well. There were lots of photos of him in an album Grandma kept, a big book which was almost as cracked and leathery as Grandma.

"This is him when we first met," Grandma pointed out. Tanya was sitting on the bed with her, drinking tea because Grandma said she could. She didn't like it much but she pretended to.

"He's younger than Father."

"He was then, yes. And that's me."

Grandma looked just like Mother, and people said Tanya looked just like Mother too, so that meant she'd look just like Grandma one day.

"You're very pretty," Tanya said, which was true but sounded like boasting.

"I was a bit. Not now. I'm cleverer now, though, and that's important."

Which was how they started talking about the schoolhouse where Mother and Father wanted her to go. Tanya didn't want to because she knew it would be expensive and Father already paid a lot to the cloth. He was the only one who could, except Tanya, and they wouldn't let her.

"I don't want to go," she said again to Grandma, but of course Grandma persuaded her it was for the best.

They had a curtain at the schoolhouse bigger than the one in Tanya's house. It was mostly for the teachers but sometimes, on special days, the children had to touch it too. The curtains were a part of their lives long before they knew what they were, just like tables and chairs and the sky.

When Tanya went to Koji's house once she saw their bloodcloth wasn't a curtain; it was shaped and positioned like a flag. When Mr. Aibagawa touched it he used his head instead of his hands, bowing so the top of his head met the bloodcloth. When he stepped away it looked like the flag of where they came from, Koji explained. Mr. Aibagawa never touched it long enough for it to go black and dark, just red, but he made up for that by doing it often. Every day, Koji said. And one day Koji would be allowed to do it too. Tanya used to be jealous of that, once. Mr. Aibagawa was always pale. So was Mrs. Aibagawa, but she used makeup to look that way.

Mrs. Tucker at the schoolhouse said some people were so rich or famous or respected that instead of a red carpet they were welcomed to places by a sodden bloodcloth laid at their feet so soaked that they could walk barefoot without paying tribute. Tanya didn't know if she believed that or not, but she believed most of what Mrs. Tucker taught her. She liked history lessons best because they sounded made up but weren't. That was when she first learnt about the bloodcloth curtains, but it was Koji who told her about ubasute.

"Hummingbird, what's wrong?"

They were in the bedroom, bowls of stew in their laps. Tanya was looking at her Mother, watching her eat.

"I was thinking of Grandma."

Mother pulled the blankets down and sat up straighter. She looked a lot like Grandma now, especially in bed, but not much when she sat up and shook her head so her hair hung back.

"I'll be all right," Mother said.

Tanya nodded.

"This is delicious stew," Mother said. "Is there much left?"

"Gerald said enough for three days if we filled up with bread as well."

Mother nodded and spooned herself another mouthful. Her hand trembled a little bit and she spilled some but it landed back in the bowl.

"Gerald touched the curtain before he left," Tanya said.

The spoon stopped partway to Mother's mouth, which she opened prematurely and then closed again. When she opened it the second time she managed to speak.

"How?"

Tanya told her about him putting both hands flat on it until it went dark, leaving his prints like waving bruises.

"He gave it a lot. Was it because Father's late?"

Mother began to cry.

There had been an accident at the caves. Father had been standing near one of the mangles when the chain that turned it buckled and snapped. The roller dropped and fat folds of bloodcloth spewed from the line behind like a thickened tongue, spilling and spilling into itself without the heavy press of the machine to flatten and shape it. Father had reached out to push the roller back in place and his arm had been engulfed in unprocessed flesh, wrapped in heavy bloodcloth that was getting heavier as it drained his limb. There had been no pain, he said, but he screamed and screamed because of what it might do and some of the other men managed to stop the machines and pull his arm out for him, digging through the layers of bloodcloth like it was laundry.

His arm was mottled yellow, like an old bruise. It had already withered to limp flesh and narrow bone. The rest of him was white, like moonlight.

"I wanted to see how bad it was," Father explained, "so I stayed in one of the bunkhouses for a while. I was hoping . . ." He shrugged instead of finishing.

They were sitting around the table. There was more stew cooking, reheating Tanya's and Mother's abandoned meals, but Tanya doubted she would ever eat stew again. The smell would always make her think of Mother crying, and Father's hitching breath as he tried not to.

"I wanted to see if it would . . . plump up." He raised his arm from the table as if they might not know what he was talking about. He did it too quickly, not yet used to the lightness of it. "I'm lucky I can still use it, I suppose."

He had avoided coming home until he knew more, but after Tanya said about Gerald and the curtain, Mother guessed something bad had happened. She made Tanya go and get Gerald again and then she made Gerald tell her what happened.

"You can lift it," Mother said. "You can't use it."

"No," Father agreed. "It's dried up."

It was quiet between them for a long moment.

"The arteries might open up again," he said. "Veins might redirect. If not, they'll have to amp—"

"Will you be able to work?"

Mother had asked Gerald the same thing but he didn't know.

Neither did Father.

Tanya was silent and still. She knew if she made any noise or moved they'd remember she was there and send her to her room. This was adult talk and normally they'd have a conversation like this in their own room, where she could still hear but where they didn't know she could still hear. Tanya was crying without fully understanding why, but she was doing it quietly.

Father's arm looked dead. It looked like the stringy meat Gerald had brought them, but with less colour.

"They didn't cut the cloth," he said. "No damage, no debt." He tried to smile for that at least, but it was weak.

Suddenly Mother struck out at Father, which was something Tanya had never seen and it made her shriek in surprise. Mother was sick and frail, so it wasn't much, but Father flinched from her as if it burned, and then she hit him again, and again, but she was sobbing by then and Father was gathering her in with his good arm and holding her close and she cried against him instead of hitting. She hugged him and hugged him.

"It's all right," he hushed, whispering into her hair. He beckoned Tanya over with a tilt of his head and hugged her too. "It'll be all right. We'll be all right."

The arm that held Tanya was dead and heavy on her shoulders, and his words were heavy in her heart because they didn't sound true.

§

"That's a lie," Tanya said, but Koji shrugged like he didn't care if she believed him or not.

"That's what they did when Mr. Olderstein stopped working. He said he wanted them to do it when he couldn't teach no more because if he couldn't teach anymore he couldn't do much else either. They did it in assembly, wrapped him up in the schoolcloth so the classes wouldn't have to tribute for a while. It was before you were here."

"Yeah, maybe," Tanya allowed, unable to prove otherwise, "but Mrs. Gowan is a woman. Women can't tribute."

"*Old* women can, just like little girls. It's the ones in between that can't. I dunno why."

Tanya thought she might know why because Mother had told her about the special blood that made you a woman. She didn't tell Koji, though. He would think it was gross.

Mrs. Gowan worked in the Drapery where most women worked, although she was a supervisor instead of one of the cutters or pressers because she was old. Grandma said she sometimes did cut and press, though, if they needed people to. She'd put on special gloves. She worked a lot because her son was what Mother called special but the kids at the schoolhouse called stupid and slow and other mean names because he was a grown man but acted like a baby. When Mrs. Gowan took on the sickness she wasn't able to do much anymore. Tanya always thought they moved away but Koji was saying she let them wrap her up in the curtain. They lay it on her like a bed sheet, he said. She did it for her son, Koji said, but couldn't explain more than that. Koji's dad said it was very noble, which was a word Tanya liked when Grandma explained it.

Tanya's father said it was stupid and that it should have been the son who was curtained to help the mother because he couldn't do anything and after her tribute what would he do? "Probably got wrapped up anyway," he said. "I reckon that's what the hospitals do all the time."

Father did not like the hospitals. Not many people did.

When Tanya asked Mother about it Mother asked a lot of questions, sometimes more than once, and was angry with the Aibagawas for a while.

It was Grandma who explained what noble was and why Mrs. Gowan did it.

Later that year, Grandma did the same thing herself.

§

After dinner, Tanya was told to go out and play, but not outside the fence. Mother and Father had a lot to talk about. They must have forgotten how late it was, probably because there'd been two dinners, but Tanya kept quiet because she wasn't usually allowed out at night.

She put on her jumper, one that Grandma had knitted. It had a lamb on it and the fluff of its fleece stuck out from the front. Tanya liked to pull it into shapes like hair styles. She went out the front but would go around back to hear what they said.

It was dark, and the town was quiet. At the front of the house the path twisted its way up into the mountains where the caves were. The mountains were big jagged triangles and you could only tell they were there because of where they cut into the sky, hiding the stars. A few of the other houses on the path had their lights on and Tanya watched shadows behind the curtains as people moved around inside. Window curtains that you could see through. She went around the side of the house, jumping down quietly from the porch and running through the tall weeds, slowing down when she saw the light spilling from the kitchen onto the back garden steps. If she sat on one of the low ones she could hear them without being seen from the window; the garden was very steep.

". . . livestock allowance," Father was saying. Tanya hoped they were finally going to get a goat.

"We've been turned down every year we've applied."

"Yeah, well, things are different now aren't they."

Father sounded angry and it made Tanya want to cry again. The lights of the town below blurred because her eyes were wet, but she didn't cry.

"Alan said he'll appeal about the accident, have the blood count as our—"

"Come on, it'll go to the town kitty if it counts at all."

Father had nothing to say to that.

"I could teach her at home," Mother continued. "As long as I'm sick, I should do something useful."

"We're not pulling her out of school."

"I can—"

"No."

This time a tear did fall but Tanya wiped it quick as if it were never there. She didn't want to stop school, but she would if Mother said so.

"Look," said Father, and his voice was softer, "I know you could teach her, but for how long each day before you had to rest? And it's not just about the lessons, it's about the other children. She needs to make friends and all of that."

"Then let's move and she can make new friends. Not all towns have this stupid fucking tribute law."

The idea of moving made Tanya gasp and the bad word made Tanya gasp again straight afterwards. The light she was sitting in suddenly had a shadow in it and she nearly gasped another time because of its weird arm but she realized it was Father even before he opened the back door. She hopped off the step quickly to run back to the front but she slipped and fell, hitting her knee on the stony ground and tumbling someway down the path so it scraped the skin of her shins. Then Father was there, kneeling next to her and hushing her tears.

"It's all right," he said. "It'll be all right."

This time Tanya believed him.

Even after she'd been sent to bed Tanya lay awake for a long time. She kept pressing her knee which felt bigger than usual and squishy. It hurt a little bit but not too much, and the strange feel of it was interesting. It felt like the curtain did sometimes when it was full. Farther down from her knee her shin pulsed with a dull throb. She could ignore that though because she was still trying to hear Mother and Father talking. She tried, but she couldn't make the sounds into proper words. When she closed her eyes to hear better, she fell asleep.

She dreamt of Grandma, calling her name from the front room, but every time Tanya went to see, she wasn't there.

It was nearly afternoon when Tanya woke up, which was all right because there was no school. She got up and winced because the sheet was stuck to her leg for a moment. She had a thin scab over her scrape and her knee was a dark colour but it only hurt if she touched it. It made her remember Father's arm and she went to see if it was better.

The bed in his room was empty. She went to Mother's room but hers was empty, too. It still smelled of the sick smell but the window was open and the bed was sort of made.

"Ma?"

Mother was in the kitchen. She was trying to make bread but she wasn't pushing the dough very hard. "Breakfast? There's some oats left."

Tanya shook her head.

"Your father's gone in to work today."

"What about his arm?"

"Yes, well, he's going to see if there's a different job he can do if he can't do his usual one."

"Is it better?"

"No, I doubt he'll get a better job, not now."

"I meant, is his arm better?"

"Of course it's not better."

Tanya was worried. Mother was moving the dough around but she wasn't doing much except pushing flour onto the floor.

"I can help," Tanya said. She went to the sink to wash her hands because she'd been playing with her new scab.

"I can do it, *I'm* not a cripple." Then she leant over the dough and her shoulders began to shake. "Sorry, hummingbird," she said. Her voice sounded watery. "Sorry."

Tanya said it was all right.

"Why don't you go and play for a while?"

But Tanya didn't want to play, not with other children anyway. Not today. She went to the living room and looked to see if her circles were still there in the dust. They were, though a couple had been scuffed a bit by Father's boots. The flies were still there too, and at first she thought there were more but it was a scattering of loose pebbles from the path outside where she fell. Next to them was the handkerchief Father had used on her shin. She gathered the little stones up into her palm, leaving tiny dots wherever her fingertips touched the cloth. She could have used the handkerchief but she wanted to feel the cool clamminess of the curtain, to see if it felt different.

She couldn't tell.

Some people didn't like to touch it at all and they would "let their blood," Mother said. When Tanya said that sounded unfinished Mother said it would never be finished, so Tanya still didn't know what they let their blood do. It gave people scars, though.

She spent the afternoon waiting for her father to return, putting tiny pebbles into each circle she'd drawn, and picking carefully at the scab on her leg. It was still too fresh but she could lift it at the edges if she was gentle. Eventually, after some careful patient picking, she had only the fresh pinkness of new skin on her shin and the thin scab in her hand.

She dropped it where the curtain gathered on the floor. It was bleached white in moments.

"What are you doing?"

Mother stood in the doorway. She had flour on her dressing gown and on her cheeks.

"Nothing," said Tanya, but Mother came over anyway to see. By then the scab had crumbled to something a bit like flour and then even that was gone and they were looking at the "nothing" Tanya had said.

"You shouldn't play so close to it," said Mother.

"Why?"

Mother didn't reply. She just stared at the curtain, looking like she had a hundred questions of her own. Or was carefully considering an answer to a different question altogether.

When Father returned he had a slip of paper that said he couldn't work in the caves.

"They've shut it down."

Mother was lying on her side because it made breathing easier, but she turned and sat up. "All of it?"

"Just the system where it happened. Officially it's because of maintenance, but really they're worried the taste has hungered it. They didn't cut the cloth so now they need to let it settle, starve a little, work the other caves so it doesn't think . . . well, whatever it thinks. Then they'll declare the machines safe again."

"Can you work one of the others?"

Father sat on the bed and reached out to take her hand. He reached with his bad arm out of habit but Mother pulled away at first. Then she apologized and held it and Tanya wondered if she should be watching. She was in the doorway, standing on tiptoes and then lowering herself; tiptoes up, and then back down. It was easy if you held the door frame but trickier if you didn't.

"There's not much going. Now that they've closed one cave they've had to reassign men enough as it is, and some are out of work until it's open again."

"But you—"

"I was the man responsible. It's fair."

"It's *not* fair." Mother raised his arm by the wrist and shook it so his hand flapped.

"Stop it, Marjorie."

"You've got this and nothing else and a child to feed and put through school."

"Stop it!"

She dropped his arm and he pulled it away from her.

"You still want to move? Fine, where will we go? Look at what happens at the other places; the loss of livestock and sometimes worse. *Often* worse. The lotteries, or a whole town enveloped just because—"

"I don't think that happens."

She said it to the covers and even Tanya could tell Mother didn't mean it.

"We all pay our bit and it stays away and we do all right. The accident's ours. The blood I lost has been reassigned to us. We'll be all right for a while. I'll find something."

Mother closed her eyes. "I need to get better, Henry. That's all."

"Yes." He stroked her forehead. He used his good hand. "Get better." Mother smiled and looked at him, took up his other hand in her own again.

It was a moment so intimate and tender that Tanya stepped away quietly from the room.

"Why isn't *your* mother sick?"

Koji shrugged, but he had an answer. "She had an operation after I was born."

"What kind of operation?"

He shrugged again, and this time there was no answer except, "I don't know. But she could pay tribute now, if she wanted. Father won't let her though."

Tanya wondered if the sickness and the bloodcloth in the mountains was linked. Mother said it was. She said it couldn't take their blood so it took something else in a different way. "Blood, sweat, tears, and spirit," she'd said. She had been trying to explain what happened to Grandma and Tanya wondered how she didn't cry because *she* couldn't stop.

Tanya remembered it very well. She'd come home from school and the first thing she'd noticed was the curtain in the front room was gone. The wall behind it was a cleaner dark colour than the rest of the wood and for a moment it looked like a door. Next she noticed Father's work things on the kitchen table, which meant he was home early. She went rushing in to her parents' room, for they'd shared a bed back then, calling for them, wanting to ask about Father being home and the missing curtain but also wanting to tell them about school and not knowing what order to do it in. They weren't there, but coming out she heard hurried voices, sharp like an argument but not angry, coming from Grandma's room, and then Father was coming out.

"Hey, little darling."

He tried to close the door behind him but she screamed for "Grandma!" because she'd already seen inside. It startled Father enough that she was able to get past his legs and into the room.

Mother was sitting beside the bed, her eyes red and puffy from crying. Grandma must have been in the bed like always but Tanya couldn't see her because the curtain was laid across it. She could tell where she lay, though, because the bloodcloth was a dark crimson colour clinging to the shape of her body like wet linen. Tanya could see the shape of Grandma's head, the tiny slope of her nose, the pillow rise of her breasts. She could see each arm, the hands little spheres where Grandma had clenched them into fists. Her legs together made her seem like a mermaid, especially because of how her feet pointed up and out to make a triangle of curtain cloth.

"Hummingbird . . ."

Tanya thought it was Grandma speaking at first and yelped but the cloth at her mouth had not sank, she hadn't opened it, she—

"She can't breathe!" Tanya cried. "Ma, she can't breathe, get it off!"

Father had held her shoulders, tried to turn her around and out of the room, but Mother said no and that was when she explained. She told Tanya it was Grandma's decision, and she tried to explain about ubasute, which was a word Tanya had forgotten, but Tanya didn't really listen. And she couldn't look at Grandma either. She stared at the curtain pole that had been leant in the corner on the room, and one of the gloves Father was supposed to wear at work on the floor beside it, as Mother talked quietly. She said Grandma would always be with them, but Tanya didn't want her always in the curtain, and Mother brushed at her hair and rubbed her back to make her feel better. It didn't help because Mother was still wearing the other glove.

"Hey, Tanya." Koji pulled her hair to get her attention.

She rubbed her eyes and hoped he didn't think the tears were there because he'd yanked her ponytail. "What?"

"Drummond said that all girls have their own red curtains and that they bleed for a whole week every single month. Is that true?"

Tanya could see Drummond and his friends having a spitting competition against the schoolhouse wall. The other children were running around each other, calling and laughing and playing games while she and Koji sat on the bench eating their lunch.

"I think so," Tanya said. "I don't really know."

"Do you have to cut yourself? Where does it come from?"

Koji took a bite of his sandwich. Tanya decided not to tell him and shrugged instead.

"A whole week?" he said around a mouthful of bread. "How come you don't die?"

Tanya didn't know that, either. And anyway, thinking of Grandma and how sick Mother was, she sort of thought that they did.

Tanya went to bed that night thinking of the conversation she'd had with Koji and hearing her parents argue quietly in the room next door. It made for a troubled sleep.

She dreamt that she went to the caves, which was how she knew she was dreaming because girls weren't allowed. She was wearing her father's overalls, the long legs folded under her feet and wedged in the boots like thick socks. The safety helmet on her head was too big; when she looked up at the mountains she was walking to, it fell back and she had to hold it on, and when she looked back down at the path she walked upon it fell forward and covered her eyes. She had Father's long gloves clenched in one hand and kept trying to put them on, but they were always too big or, strangely, too small, and every time she tried she said, "Damn things don't fit right," even though she knew not to say damn. She would throw them to the side of the path but after a few steps towards the caves they'd be in her hands again and she'd try them on again and all the time the caves weren't getting closer at all.

Pulling yet another glove onto her right hand she felt it fill with cold water but when it spilled over her cuffs she saw it was actually blood and she grunted her disgust, pulling the glove off quick and dropping it to the gravel path which was more like the one in her back garden than the road leading to the caves. Blood continued to spill from the glove, and it began to rise up out of the ground, emerging from beneath the small stones like a bath was filling up underneath. Her shin was bleeding again, but instead of running down her leg it looked like it was running up from the ground and into her scraped graze.

"Get away!" Mother screamed, "don't play so close to it!" But when Tanya looked up, letting the helmet fall off her head this time, she saw not her mother but all the men from the caves running downhill towards her. "Get away!" they all yelled together with Mother's voice. Some even made giant gestures with their arms, sweeping them forward to show her which way to run which was down, down, the same way as them, away from the caves, down.

Behind them, spilling from caves which were suddenly close, was wave upon wave of thick curtain flesh, bloodcloth unravelling from the mountain darkness like a huge fat tongue. It folded upon itself and pushed its way downhill, knocking down trees at the roadside and engulfing those too slow to outrun it.

Tanya turned and ran, not to flee the horror but to warn her parents, but somehow the curtain had overtaken her and she was running on top of it, terrified of falling over. It sank and squelched under her feet, blood spitting up like puddle splashes, the meaty smell as thick as the flesh it came from. Ahead of her, the mass of it washed up against the buildings below in giant fleshy waves. It poured into open windows and knocked down doors, filling houses with its hungry cloth that wasn't cloth, was never cloth, demanding its payment with a voice nobody could hear but everybody listened to which meant they couldn't hear her screaming, "No! No! No!" The only person who knew she was screaming was Tanya, and it woke her up.

Even awake, in her bed, in her room, the fear still gripped her, as tight as the cloth that was all over her like it was on Grandma, clutching at her legs, wrapped around her arms, and she fell from bed trying to get away from it.

Father came in and struck a light, Mother's calls of concern behind him in the dark house, and Tanya saw the curtain she struggled with was only her own bedding. The sheets were soaked with her sweat and her tears, but not with her blood.

§

Tanya blew the dust on the floor, bored of the circles she saw there. She rubbed them away with her hands. The wooden boards under her palms were worn smooth with age and use, and yet she felt a stab of pain; one of the edges had been scuffed rough and now she had a splinter in the pad of her finger. She pulled it out easily and waited for the blood to rise, wondering if she should give it to the curtain. She was never scared of her own blood like some children were. "Blood is a sign of living," Father said.

He won't bleed right, not anymore.

Tanya looked up because it sounded like Grandma but of course Grandma wasn't there. The curtain shivered in a breeze. The back door was open to let some air in for Mother but Tanya couldn't feel any.

He'll not be able to work, not a good job. And you know what will happen then.

The blood had come without her seeing. A small drop of it on her fingertip, a perfect half sphere rising from her skin. A tiny ruby.

The curtain brushed at the floor, tipping fly carcasses from its folds

You could . . .

Tanya popped her finger into her mouth and, watching the curtain, sucked her own blood away.

The curtain was still. Tanya thought about what Grandma did and thought if *she* did it, yanked the curtain down and let it fall on her, then Father wouldn't need to worry about work until he got better, and Mother might even get better too and everything could go back to normal. Except it wouldn't be normal because Tanya wouldn't be here, she'd be with Grandma, and that bit would be all right but not being stuck in the curtain. She wondered what it would feel like, letting it take her blood, all of it, and she wondered what it would feel like to let her blood, let it do whatever it did when you gave yourself scars.

It will feel noble.

Tanya stood and went to the kitchen where she couldn't see the curtain anymore and couldn't hear it use Grandma's voice. She would ignore the curtain's call. There were dirty dishes still from when she made the stew and she thought she would wash them for Mother. That was what she meant to do.

Instead, she took up the knife she'd cut the vegetables with. She took it to the front room.

She still felt no breeze, yet the curtain, heavy as it was, shuddered. Tanya sat where it bunched in the corner, where the crooked pole dropped too much of it to the floor so that it gathered. She took up a length of it and felt immediately the pull of it in her hands. Was this how it felt when Father paid? Was this how it felt when his arm was swamped within its meaty crease? She felt warmth, like she'd plunged her hands into heated mittens, but none of it came from the cloth. Her hands were blushing, and wherever the cloth clutched her it fattened pink, red—and her hands were numbing. She had to be quick.

She held the knife to the curtain edge and pulled it across. The flesh parted easily, easier than she had expected. Like slicing a mushroom. One moment, and suddenly Tanya had a long corner length of bloodcloth in her lap. It curled where it had been cut and it bled a little before it could close. But it wasn't the curtain's blood really: it was hers.

Her hands tingled as if she'd been leaning on them too long, the tickly prickle of pins and needles. There was no blood on them. On the wall it rose in peaks, her blood rising like fire from the curtain's new wound. She wouldn't touch it again. This time she would bring her arm down in a long hard swing, dragging the blade through the cloth-flesh until she had split it down the middle. She would make it bleed. She would make it give back all that it had—

Mother's scream was so shrill, so loud, so close, that at first Tanya thought it had come from the curtain. It had burst the still air of the room at the precise moment she struck and she thought she'd stabbed Mother, that Mother was behind the curtain. But Mother was not behind the curtain, she was beside it, as sudden as her scream had been, and she wrenched the knife from Tanya's hand and pushed her back to the floor with surprising strength for one so sick.

"What are you doing? Don't!"

Tanya landed hard on her behind, teeth coming together on her tongue. She covered her mouth against the pain with both hands. The long slit in the curtain gaped at her as if surprised. There was nothing inside it, and nothing behind but wall.

"What are you doing?"

Tanya couldn't answer. She couldn't say anything, her mouth hurt so much. She wasn't even sure Mother had asked the question this time because she didn't wait for an answer. She pressed the parted bloodcloth together quickly, kneading it with more vigour than she had the bread, smoothing it over with her palms. It took nothing from her, of course, but it took the shape she forced it into. She retrieved the bloated slug-length of its severed piece and pushed it to open flesh, rubbing it into a new seam just as she had countless times at the Drapery, because the cut was fresh. It held. And it healed.

She turned to Tanya. Her breath was wheezing. She was wide-eyed, and Tanya saw the fear there turn to anger, but before she could take the full force of any reprimand, Mother's expression changed again. It softened. A glance down at something that had caught her eye caused her to return Tanya's pained look with one Tanya had never seen before. For an absurd moment it was like she had a sister instead of a mother and only the quiet tocking of the clock separated them.

"Oh, baby."

Tanya looked to her lap and saw the skirt of her dress was stained with blood. Not much, just a little where it bunched between her legs.

"It's mine," she said. Something she'd made the curtain give back. It made her want to smile, but she didn't because Mother was kneeling down next to her like Gerald had tried to do and she put her hand to Tanya's cheek and then to the side of her head, tucking a curl behind her ear.

"Yes, it's yours. Just a bit earlier than expected, that's all."

She began stroking Tanya's hair back.

"I heard Grandma."

"Hmm?"

Mother was smiling. She was breathing easier, too.

"In the curtain."

"Never mind the curtain," Mother said. "Not now."

The curtain was quiet. It made smiling back easier, especially when Tanya saw that, despite Mother's efforts, it now had some scars of its own.

THE TILT

"*Ça y est, Carcassonne,*" the bus driver told them. "You are here."

"Really? Already?" Nicky pulled the single iPod headphone from her ear and yanked the other away from Luke. He grabbed at it but she was already winding up the wires. "We're here," she told him.

He leaned to look out of a window across the aisle. Tourists were moving in groups, staring up at the towers or down at ice creams bought from a nearby van, colourful and incongruous against the medieval backdrop of stone walls and battlements. "That's the citadel."

"Yeah, we're here. Carcassonne."

The driver was still turned around in his seat, pointing. He'd promised to tell them when they'd arrived at the hotel. He was pointing to the huge gate and crenellated walls of the citadel.

"We're staying at the Best Western," Luke told the driver.

The driver pointed again, nodding. "*Oui.*"

"In there?"

But the driver was checking traffic, waiting to join it again.

Nicky shrugged at Luke and said, "Cool." They grabbed their bags from overhead and stepped off the coach. "*Merci.*"

"Are we actually staying in the Old Town?" Luke asked.

"Must be."

"Maybe we're round the back of it or something."

"Well what did they say at the travel place?"

"Charming hotel close to the castle," Luke said. "Something like that. But this isn't close, this is inside. I bet he dropped us at the wrong place."

"Stop being a whiny bitch. Let's just have a look."

The bus pulled away and already Luke had shifted his attention to something new. "I'm looking," he said, "I'm looking."

He was looking at a young man photographing the gates.

"Tell him *you've* got a nice opening he can look at," Nicky said, and

Luke laughed. She slapped his arm. "Just don't make me a fag-hag the whole weekend."

"Don't worry, we'll find you a nice French girl."

"Ooh la la." She hooked her arm through his and they crossed over into Carcassonne's citadel. "Wow, look at this place," Nicky said.

They were in a wide open space between two huge walls.

"What's this, the bailey or something? The moat?"

"Moat? The water would be flooding through the gates, you idiot. We're in the Lists, with a capital L. The Upper List, actually. Runs all round the town."

Nicky was always the one who read the travel guides. She'd learnt all about Carcassonne on the plane while Luke eyed up an air steward.

"You've got one big outer wall for protection, and all this space for troops, but if the attackers got in you could retreat into the town."

"Behind another big bastard wall."

"Exactly."

Tourists were taking pictures and admiring the architecture. Kids were running around, kicking up dust where horses used to. Above them, other tourists were walking the battlements, looking out over the river or down into the town itself.

"Wanna walk around them?" Nicky asked.

"Let's find our hotel first."

They approached another gate—"Those are the Narbonne Towers," Nicky told him—and into the town itself.

Nicky gasped and gripped his arm. "OhmyGod it's *gorgeous* here."

Luke had expected ruins, but Carcassonne was a proper town. Its narrow cobbled streets were filled with souvenir shops and food stalls and antique dealers and all sorts. In the summer the place was probably packed, but they were able to walk freely, visiting off season. Though cold enough for jackets, the sky was a bright blue and surprisingly clear for October.

"Wow, look!"

Nicky left Luke for a crêpe stand, impressing him with her fluent French. She laughed at something the man said as he spread a thick coating of Nutella over her pancake before folding it. "You want one?"

Luke shook his head. "No thanks."

She took an exaggerated bite, adding extravagant sound effects.

"Very lady-like."

She showed him her chewed food and Luke turned away, laughing.

"I don't *want* to be a lady," she said, words thick with masticated pancake batter. She pointed at the buildings around them. "You know, in the old days, all of this would have been blacksmiths and carpentry shops and fruit stalls, stuff like that."

"Fascinating."

"Hey, come on. I love all this stuff."

He smiled. "Yeah, I know. That's why I brought you. All the history and French and pancakes and everything."

"It was cheap, wasn't it."

"You know me so well."

She nodded. "All our lives."

It wasn't true but it felt like it. Nicky had once added that it felt like all their lives *plural*, as in all their past ones, and Luke reminded her of that now by calling her a hippy. She laughed, linked arms with him again, and together they worked their way deeper into the town.

Their hotel really was inside the citadel.

"This," said Nicky, "is fucking, awesome."

The Best Western Hôtel Le Donjon was sort of cute, if you liked that kind of thing: stone walls for the ground floor, yellow rendering for the ivy-clad walls above to set off pretty blue shutters. "Not bad."

"Everything's right on our doorstep."

"Is it Donjon as in dungeon?"

"Why," Nicky asked, "did you want to bring me somewhere kinky?"

"Honey, you're not my type."

"Good looking, intelligent, fun?"

"The female form," Luke said, and shivered. "Ergh. Horrible."

"I've got a great arse."

"Yeah, but nothing in front to play with." He demonstrated with a well known hand gesture.

Nicky slapped the gesture away and took a photo of the hotel.

"Donjon mustard?" Luke said. "It would go with the colour scheme."

"You mean *Dijon* mustard. Donjon is French for keep, I think."

"Oh. That's slightly disappointing actually."

The interior was spacious and cool, with a subtle scattering of *objets d'art*, an attractive man on the desk, a lounge area—

"Fuck me, that's a proper suit of armour!"

Nicky was talking with the receptionist but she smiled at Luke and said, "Yeah, you did good. Classy."

"Remember Di Caprio in *Romeo and Juliet*? Orlando in *Kingdom of Heaven*?" He stroked the armour.

Luke was pretty sure that everything Nicky said to the reception guy afterwards was French for I'm sorry about my friend, he's a bit of a dick sometimes, but the man gave Luke a smile that might have been more than polite and he gave Nicky a key card. She waved it at Luke.

"Room 3."

"*Trois!*" Luke said.

"Stop showing off."

The man directed them around the corner with an elaborate gesture and Nicky led the way.

"I know a lot of French," Luke said.

"Whatever."

"*Baguette*," he said.

"*Très bien.*"

He exaggerated an accent for, "*Déjeuner . . . Déjà vu . . .*"

"Here we are." She swiped the card and turned a red light green.

"*Déjeuner.*"

"You said that already."

"*Déjà vu!*"

"Very witty." She pushed the door open and they went inside.

It was a modest size, with two windows providing a lot of light. There was a mini-fridge, tea making stuff, all the usual. And a double bed.

"You did tell them twin, didn't you?" Nicky asked.

"Of course I did."

"This doesn't look like a twin." She went to the window.

"I'll see if we can swap."

But Nicky beckoned him over, "Look."

Their view was tiled roofs, the top of a distant rampart, and one of the round towers. A light breeze buffeted a flag on its blue-grey pinnacle. Behind it all stretched green hills and French farmland.

"I don't want to swap," she said.

Luke shook his head. "No way."

"Don't butt-fuck me in the night."

"Don't sit on my face. I wouldn't know what to do."

"Most men don't, that's why I switched."

They dumped their bags, opened some drawers and cupboards,

checked the bathroom, and then jumped up and down with squealing giddy glee.

"We're in France!" Nicky said.

"Yeah, baby!"

"Let's go look around."

It didn't take long to look around Carcassonne. There were only a dozen or so streets within its walls, and all of them led back to a square where several cafes and restaurants competed with each other for business. It was a friendly competition though, with staff standing in doorways and waving to each other across the expanse of tables as they waited to see where new arrivals chose to sit.

"Oh look, here we are again," Luke said, "back at the square."

"This way."

Nicky led him down a cobbled street he was sure they'd used twice already, but this time it took them to a shop declaring *chocolat, nougat,* and *fabrication artisanale*, whatever that meant.

"Okay, it's official, this place is amazing," Nicky announced. She stepped up to the window for a proper look at the display. Huge slabs of chocolate were stacked atop each other, bricks of nougat in the space between them, and long strings of marshmallow in various colours draped the whole lot wherever there was room, filling gaps like fluffy mortar.

"You gonna buy something then?" Luke asked.

"I'm just going to salivate against the glass for a bit." But she went inside.

Luke waited. If he had his bearings, at the end of this street they'd come back to the big church, the basilica of someone or some such.

"How much of this do you think you could get in your mouth?" Nicky asked, returning with a heavy-looking paper bag in one hand, and offering a long thick string of something foamy and pink in the other.

He took it from her and held it in both hands before his mouth. Nicky snatched it back. "Please, I don't want to know."

They dawdled, Nicky taking pictures and pointing out sights that were mostly cute old buildings. And then, sure enough . . .

"The Basilica of St. Nazaire," Nicky announced, always the tour guide.

"Next!"

"Heathen."

"Have you read the bit in the Bible about how being gay is like laying with a beast of the field?"

"Have *you*?"

Luke held his hands up in surrender and Nicky mimicked him for a truce.

"You said we'd explore the streets first and *then* visit places," Luke said.

"I think we've done the streets."

"I think we've done the streets twice."

"Let's do the walls," she suggested, "or the Lists."

"The castle."

"*La grand Châtelet*, actually."

"Potato, pot*ar*to."

Nicky broke off a wedge of chocolate. "Let's have a drink and decide."

"*Drink* drink, or coffee drink?"

"Drink drink."

"Brilliant. Let's go."

The street looped into a new one taking them back the way they'd come. They took their time, passing chocolate back and forth.

"When do we start talking about it?" Nicky asked eventually.

Luke was surprised it had taken her so long. "Talk about what?"

"Fair enough."

"When we're having that *drink* drink," he said.

Nicky nodded.

"How about you? Things with Chris still okay?"

"Tina. Or *Christ*ina. She hates Chris."

"*She* hates it, or you hate it?"

"Both."

"Are you ever Nick?"

Nicky glared at him, but the effect was somewhat ruined by the size of the chocolate piece she was trying to cram into her mouth. She took it out to say, "You ever Lou?"

"Come on, which one's the bitch?" Luke said.

She answered his earlier question instead, once she'd chewed her chocolate down to size. "We're good, thanks. Might not be when I get back, though. First break in months and I go away with . . ." she paused for impact, "A *man*."

"Thanks."

"Well, a male."

"I know she doesn't like me much, but she could have come, you know."

"Nah. This is about you."

"Phew. Yeah, it is. I was just being polite."

"She understands. She won't be pissed, not really. Maybe jealous when I tell her about the gorgeous French girls . . ."

"How long have—"

"Seven months and fourteen days." She looked at her watch. "And eleven, twelve, hours depending on the time difference."

Luke laughed. "But who's counting?"

"I bloody am."

"Why do you always have to have such serious long term things?"

"Why do you have to always have to have wham-bam-thank-you-mans?"

Luke winced. "*Touché*."

"Shit, sorry."

He shrugged. "Maybe I should take a leaf out of your book."

"What, switch to women?"

He cocked his head at her.

"Did you want things with Steve to be serious?"

Luke shrugged again. "*C'est la vie*."

"There you go again, showing off with the French."

They'd arrived back at the square, and without discussing it they took seats outside a place serving alcohol.

"So talk."

He told her about Steve, and about the others, and about what Steve had said at the end.

"*Too* gay?" Nicky asked. They were on their second beer.

"That's what *I* said, right? What, my hair? My clothes? My Kylie collection?"

Nicky laughed, then said seriously, "Kylie's gorgeous."

Luke nodded the fact, it was a given. "He wanted someone more mature."

"As in older, or just, you know, behaviour?"

"I think he meant settled. Not sleeping around, trying to prove something. Which I don't."

"Of course you don't."

"Not any more."

Nicky nodded, but with her eyebrows raised.

"Oh, fuck off," he told her, "get me another drink."

"Okay, but just one more here. I want to get changed if we're going to do this properly."

Luke reminded her that part of the reason for coming to Carcassonne was because it was quiet, no clubs and no gay scene, but she waved that away. "We'll make the most of it."

Luke smiled, grateful she'd come with him all the way to France.

"You know, sometimes I wish you were a man."

Nicky grinned. "Yeah, me too."

"Ha! I knew it! *Tina's* the bitch."

When their drinks arrived, Nicky raised hers and toasted, "*Too* gay."

Luke raised his middle finger and they drank, smiling at each other.

It was dark in the Lists, and Luke couldn't find Nicky. He staggered to a set of stairs leading to the outer ramparts thinking he'd climb them for a better view.

"Nicky!"

His voice echoed off the walls and came back to him.

"Fuck," he mumbled, crawling up the steps on all fours in case he fell, "I'm wankered."

He reached the top and stood up and the world tilted. Luke tilted with it, taking a few steps sideways to keep his balance, reeling to one of the battlements. He leant against it, barely realizing how lucky he'd been not to have stumbled through one of the gaps and all the way down.

"Nicky!"

This time her name went out across the darkened countryside and down to the New Town before coming back to him diminished.

"What a bitch," he muttered, though he didn't really mean it. He looked at the inner walls of Carcassonne and remembered Nicky telling him they lit up at night. These, though, were dark. Still, there was enough light from the moon and stars to see. A breeze tried to ruffle Luke's hair despite the generous handful of gel. It had more luck with the banners though, long triangular pennants fluttering at each of the towers.

There was a figure at the top of one of those towers, watching him.

"Nicky?"

The figure pointed and Luke turned to look.

He heard it before he saw it. Heard the hooves on stone, slow and unhurried; clop, clop-clop, clop. Then, from an archway set in the lower wall of a tower, emerged a mighty steed, dark as night. Upon it sat a figure in full armour, plates of blackened steel atop a glinting suit of chain. Coming out from the arch, the knight raised a lance.

"Holy shit, I've time travelled."

The horse raised its legs high with each step in a way Luke had seen at horseshows. Fancy. Tourists must have loved it. The knight, though, was motionless. Silent.

"I'm a bit lost," Luke called, starting down the stairs. "I'm trying to find someone. Do you speak English? *Parlez-vous* English?"

The knight tugged the reins and the horse turned a tight circle on the spot.

"Wait! Can you show me the way to the hotel?"

Luke ran down the rest of the steps, leaping the last few more by accident than intent and stumbled.

The knight had already reached the far end of the List, disappearing around the corner to follow the double walls of the town. Luke would be lost in-between.

"Wait!"

Before he could try to catch the knight, the ground beneath Luke tilted. He staggered again, bent over, and was sick. It splashed out of him, thin and white, until only dribbled lines of vomit connected his mouth to the dirty ground. He pinched them away from his lips and shook the residue from his fingers.

Knight and steed turned to face him.

"Sorry," Luke said.

The horse snorted and stamped its feet but did nothing else, not yet. Then the knight tipped the lance and kicked at the horse's flanks.

They sped at Luke.

"Oh shit. Oh no, oh shit, oh *fuck*!"

Luke turned and ran. Or rather he tried to run, but the ground sloped up too steeply or down too suddenly and he careened from one wall to the other, all the time hearing the hooves coming closer, closer, close, until they were right behind him.

Luke fell and rolled and raised his hands, "Please!"

But the knight was gone.

Luke was on the floor of the hotel room, tangled in bed sheets. Nicky peered over the mattress at him. She was holding her head as she tried to open her eyes. She rubbed them, trying to make sense of what she saw, but only succeeded in smudging what was left of her makeup.

"What the fuck, Luke."

Luke lay sprawled, panting. He could taste vomit with each breath.

"You been sick?"

"I'm not sure."

Nicky groaned and rolled onto her back. "Come back to bed," she said.

But Luke only looked around the room, already forgetting if he was searching for something or hiding from it, and wondering why it scared him so much.

§

Nicky emerged from a cloud of steam that came out of the bathroom with her. She was wearing a white towel and bunching her hair dry in another. "All yours," she said.

Luke winced and pulled a pillow down over his head. He was curled in the foetal position, squinting against the light coming in through the slats of the shutters.

"Come on, you'll feel better."

"Did you spike my drinks last night?"

"Only with vodka. Come on, lots to do." She threw the damp towel she'd been using for her hair at him. He pulled it from his face to see she'd dropped the other one and was standing at the wardrobe naked.

"I think I'm going to be sick," he said.

"Well thanks a lot. I'll put some clothes on then."

Luke ran from the bed, leaning with an imagined tilt of the floor. He knelt at the toilet and heaved but nothing came. There was something inside him he needed to get out but couldn't. He cradled his head in his arms, leaning on the seat, breathing in the remaining steam from the shower. The mirror was fogged. The floor tiles were wet. In the corner, under the sink, was the underwear Nicky had slept in. She came back in to pick it up as Luke heaved a second time.

"Seriously, you okay?" She squatted next to him and stroked his hair with her free hand.

"I feel a bit queer," Luke said, managing a weak smile.

"Only a bit? Let's get you some breakfast then, babe. Nice big sausage?"

Luke laughed as much as he was able. Everything was going to be all right.

§

Their first full day in the citadel of Carcassonne felt like a history lesson to Luke, but he didn't mind. It was good to see Nicky so animated, and she probably thought she was helping take his mind off Steve. Which she was. And he liked Carcassonne. He'd always wanted to come, and now that he was here it felt . . . right. Nicky added to that.

"You know, there were Romans here, then Visi-goths or Vi-sigoths or however you pronounce it, then Saracens, then the Christians came and turfed out the Muslims . . . and now there's us lot."

Nicky pointed her guide book at the other tourists walking the same walls. Various nationalities and cultures and religions had invaded the town, this time together. They were walking the wall of the western side where the citadel benefited from the natural defences of the river and a very steep slope.

"That river down there is the Aude."

"Yeah, you've said."

"I was reading—"

Luke interrupted with a groan. Nicky shoved him—"Wanker"—and he stumbled to the edge, regaining his balance before he could fall.

"Wow," he said. "*Déjà vu.*"

"What, you've been called a wanker before? I'm not surprised. Anyway, I was *reading* . . ." She looked at Luke but he didn't fill her pause with any comment, so she went on. ". . . about Lady Carcas. She was awesome. There was a siege, right, and it went on for ages and they were all starving and it was only her left, pretty much. She set dummies up at the battlements and went around firing arrows all day from different positions, you know, making out like there were all these men?"

"Did it work? Pretending there were all these men?"

"Wait, this is the best bit. She was starving but she fed her last pig the last of her grain, stuffed it full, and then chucked it off the wall and its stomach split—"

"Gross!"

"—and all the grain spilled out and the attackers, who'd been trying to starve them out, remember, thought, 'oh fuck, they've got tonnes of food' and left."

"Really? It says, 'oh fuck, they've got tonnes of food' in your book?"

"I'm paraphrasing. So the attackers left, but she felt bad for winning with a ruse so called out for them to come back. And one of them said, this *is* in the book, 'Sire, *Carcas te sonne*,' which means Carcas is calling you."

"Did they go to her?"

"What? I dunno. But that's where the name comes from, see? *Carcas te sonne*. Carcassonne."

Luke clapped. "Brilliant. They should make a movie."

After the walls, they looked around the shops. They found a shop selling medieval costumes, which was pretty cool but expensive. "Shame," Nicky said, "I'd have looked good as a buxom serving wench."

Luke agreed, but said, "Too clichéd, even for me," when Nicky held a leather vest against his chest.

"This?" She held up a knight's helm, moving its visor like a mouth to say, "Go on, try me."

"No." Luke shoved it away before she could get it to his head.

Nicky lost her hold briefly but the shopkeeper was there to take it from her before she could drop it, unleashing a torrent of fast French and then, "No touch!"

Nicky apologized and frowned at Luke. He apologized as well, aiming his at Nicky. She shook her head and pretended to look at other items.

"Look," Luke said, "I like a nice big helmet as much as the next man, but I've just done my hair."

Nicky laughed, forgiving him immediately. "Bet you've said *that* before."

"Come on."

They left the shop, to the owner's obvious relief, and browsed nearby for postcards. Nicky plucked one from the display and held it up for him. "You should send this to Steve." It showed a line of knights in armour and tutus and made a joke about the can-can. "Write on the back, 'Too gay for you?' or 'Wish you were queer' or something."

Luke laughed, took it from her, and bought it.

"You won't send it," Nicky said.

"I might surprise you."

She looked at him and wrinkled her nose. "Nah."

They continued their wandering. They found a well in the street but looking down saw only darkness. They took pictures of each other sitting on its wall.

"Oh look," said Nicky, lowering the camera and pointing, "you *did* bring me somewhere kinky."

The building proudly declared itself a museum of torture. It even had a set of oversized stocks outside for photographs. Nicky held up the camera.

"Okay, but only if you do it too."

Luke put his head and hands into the holes and exaggerated a sad face. But when Nicky went to take the picture another tourist offered so she could pose beside him.

"Thank you," she said, "*Merci.*" She examined the picture as Luke freed himself and laughed at what she saw. "Brilliant. That's a keeper."

Luke peered over her shoulder. "Nice. One for the mantelpiece."

"You know, in the old days you could be left in that thing all night. A friend would have to stay with you to make sure nobody took advantage when the crowds were gone."

"Someone to watch your arse?"

Nicky laughed. "Yeah, although with women it wasn't so much the arse, exactly. You could get knocked up by someone and never know the father."

"That's not just the old days."

Nicky smiled and pocketed the camera. "So," she said, "we gonna do it?"

"Jesus, look at this one."

"Stop calling me Jesus," Luke said, but he went over to the exhibit. "Fuck *me.*"

"Or not, as the case may be."

They were looking at a chastity belt, a rusted band of metal that fastened around the woman's waist and cupped her genitals. Instead of blocking access, though, this one had an opening in the crotch with triangles of metal teeth pointing inward.

"That," said Luke, "would hurt."

"Yeah, think of her poor girlfriend's tongue."

They proceeded along the various displays. Mannequins were presented suffering an assortment of tortures, bound to a rack or bent over a wooden block to expose parts of themselves for further pain. Sometimes only the devices were shown, genuine apparatus from the ancient look of them. They saw metal cages and wooden wheels, a gallows, a guillotine. Some of these were outside in a small courtyard, a line of rope leading you around the display and then back inside where a woman in a white gown, torn just enough to expose a plastic breast, was contorted in a permanent ecstasy of pain. False fires licked their way up her skin.

"Witch?" Luke asked.

"Or a heretic."

Luke ignored the signs prohibiting contact and tried to cover the model's breast.

"The Inquisition was based in the castle here," Nicky explained.

"What a lovely town."

"Yeah, thanks for bringing me."

"Did you know," said Luke, eager to have a go with the trivia, "they burnt gay men along with witches? They made the flames hot enough to send her to hell, apparently. That's where we get the term faggots from. As in firewood."

"You just made that up."

He shrugged. "Actually, I don't know where I heard that, so you might be right."

The next torture was presented as an illustration framed on the wall.

"Oh, my, God."

It was another wooden stake, and another woman, but this time she was on the stake instead of tied to it. Her legs had been forced open by lengths of rope and the stake tip disappeared inside her. Large metal weights were attached to her hands and feet, pulling her down.

"What did she do to deserve that?" Luke asked.

"Probably nothing."

They were moving quicker now, eager to finish but still drawn to each piece.

"Look."

Nicky pointed to another illustration. This time it was a man. He, too, had his legs drawn apart by lengths of rope but he was suspended upside down.

"Doesn't look half as bad," Luke said.

She pointed to the long rusty saw on the wall beside it. There was also a postcard of text. "Read this."

Luke's eyes widened as he did so. "Bloody hell. They put it between his arse cheeks and—"

"—they cut him in half."

Luke was still reading, hand over his mouth.

"Because he was homosexual," Nicky said for him.

Luke touched the points of the saw. It was longer than he was tall. A man either end would drag it back and forth, down through the victim.

"Shall I lighten the mood with a joke about a 'saw' arse?" Nicky said.

Luke looked again at the picture. A crowd had gathered to watch the man's suffering.

"Let's get a drink," he said.

"*Drink* drink?"

"Definitely."

§

They drank at a little place nearby that had a view of the castle. Luke traced lines up and down the condensation on his glass.

"What's wrong?"

"Everything in that place."

"Hey, don't take it so personally."

"How can I not?"

Nicky leaned over and took his hand, partly to stop him playing with the moisture on his glass. "I love you, Luke, but you can be a bit of a dick."

"What?"

"You don't have to be so gay *all* the time."

He pulled his hand from hers. "But I *am* gay."

"Ssh."

"Why? I'm bent. Queer. Totally homo."

"Keep your fucking voice down."

"Embarrassed?"

"Of the scene, not your sexuality. Jesus, this is exactly what I mean. I'm gay too, remember?"

He settled back into his chair and crossed his arms. "Say it loud, say it proud."

She sighed. "Let me put it differently. I'm Nicky. I'm twenty-one. I'm a woman. I work in a shop. I used to smoke and occasionally I still do. I love my younger brother but my older one pisses me off. I enjoy history, travel, and music I can dance to. And I'm gay. All different parts of who I am."

"So?"

"So you're gay. You like Kylie, and you're gay, and you're funny, and gay, and bitchy, and gay, and you've got more shoes than I do, and you're gay, and you like musicals and Baz Luhrmann movies and, oh, by the way, you're gay. You get so defensive about it, putting it right out front all the time. Like it's the only thing defining you. Plus the Kylie thing? Musicals? Come *on*. It's like you've got a 'how to be gay' guidebook. And it's wrong, by the way."

Luke left a moment of silence, then said, "Wow."

"Sorry."

"You sound like Steve."

"Don't be stupid, Steve has a squeaky voice."

Luke laughed, but she'd startled it out of him. It made him angrier. "You don't understand."

Nicky sighed and took a drink. "Look, let's drink this and go in the castle, eh?"

"Nah, you go." Luke got up suddenly, the metal legs of his chair scraping on the cobblestones. "I'm going to walk around a bit."

"Walk in the castle with me."

But he was already gone, ducking into the first side street that took him away from her and what she was saying.

The colours of early evening settled over the citadel, the last of the light lingering somewhere beyond the walls. Carcassonne was a pretty city by day but in the evening it was beautiful. Luke, though, barely noticed. He couldn't find Nicky. He imagined she was walking different streets, looking for him while he was looking for her. He imagined her on the *same* street looking, unable to see him. It was unsettling.

He turned up the collar of his coat and looked down to fasten the buttons. A chill had descended with the evening, bringing with it a fine rain that Luke hadn't noticed. It seemed to hang in the air without falling. Maybe that was why the town was suddenly empty, the weather driving everyone indoors.

No, not everyone: at the end of the narrow street sat a knight on horseback.

As if waiting to be seen, the horse snorted and stamped one hoof. Breath plumed from its nostrils. The fading light shone from the knight's armour and lance.

Luke felt the world tilt beneath him as the knight kicked, spurring the horse forward in a sudden charge. He fell to his knees, turning as the knight came for him, lance lowering. Lowering.

"Fuck *me*."

He scrambled on his hands and knees, moving awkwardly on all fours until his momentum lifted him into a run. Behind him came the stamping of hooves on cobblestones.

Luke fled through the streets.

He called for help but the streets were empty. Dark figures looked down from the perimeter walls, though, so he called to them.

They only watched.

Luke ran.

He sprinted on ground that was rising, a gradual incline where the walls narrowed and swallowed him into shadows. On one of the towers a set of sails turned, part of an improbable windmill. Figures moved and looked down from the battlements either side of it. One of them dropped something at Luke. He dodged it, barely, and a rock ruptured into pieces beside him.

"Don't," Luke said.

The knight was right behind him, the horse's breath hot on his neck. "No."

Another rock came down, and another, stones splitting all around him, spitting sharp shards at his ankles. The figures were hooded and when they bowed to look down on Luke the stones fell from where their heads should have been, faces falling at him in the dark. Broken pieces stared up from the ground, solid masks that would fit no face. Luke stumbled over one that looked a lot like his own. It sent him sprawling.

The knight was upon him, horse stamping, thundering, lance aimed low. Luke only had time to turn around again. Not to get up. Not to run.

The lance speared him from behind and came out through his chest in a rush of blood. He felt it puncture his heart, felt his heart torn to pieces, and saw these dragged out of his body in bloody chunks that dropped into the hands he cupped to catch them.

Luke clutched his chest and struggled upright in bed, pressing his back to the headboard. A figure stood in the shadows of the room, briefly silhouetted by a light behind then merging with the darkness as the door closed. Luke tried to cry out but only managed a soft noise.

"It's me," Nicky said.

He heard her stumble into the room, heard her shoes come off, and by then he could almost see her.

Luke was breathing hard. He checked his hands. They were clean and empty.

"You okay, Luke?"

He said nothing, just watched as she slipped off her jacket.

"You going to be sick?"

"No."

"Good." She stripped off the rest of her clothes, giggling a little with the clumsy drunken effort of it, and came to bed wearing only her knickers.

"I've been looking for you," Luke said.

"I've been having a drink with a lovely man called Pierre. Or a lovely man I called Pierre." She turned away from him and pulled up the covers.

Luke looked again into his hands. There was nothing there, though his chest still hurt. It felt ruined and empty.

"I'm still a bit pissed," Nicky said.

Luke didn't know if she was pissed drunk or pissed angry. "I've been looking for you," he said again.

"I'm right here. Go back to sleep. You can apologize in the morning."

They both apologized over breakfast, but Luke didn't want it to develop into a rehash of the discussion that had led them to argue in the first place so he suggested visiting the castle. "You can play tour guide."

"Okay. But you're paying."

"Fair enough," he said, though he wasn't sure it was. He'd merely been defending himself yesterday, hadn't he? She was the one that attacked him. Still, he was happy to put it behind them.

It had rained in the night and the streets were wet and puddled. Water dripped from guttering and hanging plants. It was a little cold, but to Luke it felt like everything had been washed clean. A fresh start to the end of their short break.

The castle had been wonderfully restored and Luke said so. As they queued for tickets he peered into the moat they'd have to cross. It held only the water of the recent rain. "Not sure that's much of a deterrent."

"You're the expert on defence mechanisms." She smiled to show she was joking. "*Deux, s'il vous plaît.*"

"So this was the last line of defence? Seems a bit much to have all these big walls, a citadel town, and then a *castle* inside as well."

"It was partly in case Carcassonne turned on itself, somewhere for the rulers to hide from those they governed. And you'll like this: it was also where young men were sent to have their 'bad conduct' punished."

"Bad conduct?"

She shrugged. "Could be anything. Here we are. The fortified heart of the city."

They were in a magnificent courtyard where a single huge tree dominated. Above, wooden balconies ("hoardings," Nicky said) followed the upper level around, and towers pointed their pinnacles to the sky. Luke held Nicky's umbrella while she took more photos and told him again of Lady Carcas and the pig. He didn't mind. He loved how it brought her to life, seeing her differently and understanding something of what she'd said yesterday; there was much more to her than her sexuality.

"Beautiful, eh?" The wind tossed her hair and the sun was shining. She shielded her eyes and looked over the river and the surrounding fields.

"Definitely."

"Come on, I want to show you something."

"You've shown me lots already."

She took his hand.

"What's this way?"

"A museum."

"Oh joy."

But he let himself be dragged. He wasn't really bored, and Nicky was doing a wonderful job of distracting him. Until . . .

"These are funerary heads. Look at them all."

She showed him faces carved from marble. As preserved as they were, each was damaged in some minor way; a nose missing, a section of forehead cracked, chin's broken. Luke shivered.

"Someone walk over your grave?"

"*Déjà vu,*" he said. "Again."

"Spooky."

Luke didn't know if her comment was a reply to him or a reaction to the tomb lid she was pointing at. It leant upright against the wall, a knight in repose clutching a sword to his chest. The stone sarcophagus beside it was empty. Luke didn't like that either.

Nicky handed him the camera, "Take my picture," and posed. "Wait." She took the umbrella from him, held it point down like a sword. "Okay, take it."

Afterwards, he handed the camera back quickly before a foolish part of him could check the picture for ghosts.

§

Nicky made him scroll through the camera as they tucked into a hearty lunch. She had *moules frites*, while Luke had a burger that was barely cooked.

"It's how they like it here," Nicky explained, slurping another mussel from its shell.

"You do that so well."

"Practice."

Luke left most of his, though, picking at the bread and pinching chips from Nicky's plate. "Not a big fan of raw meat," he said.

"Not what I heard."

He smiled, taking them through each photo because he had a hand free and she had juice all over hers. He glanced away when they reached the knight's tomb, though Nicky declared it a keeper. They deleted some and picked out others worth framing.

"That one, definitely," Nicky said.

Luke, imprisoned in the stocks, stared forlornly at Nicky beside him who posed with her arms crossed.

"Whatever turns you on," Luke said. "Oh look, the Lists again."

Nicky licked juice from her fingers, ready to take the camera back.

"Where's the tower with the windmill?" Luke asked.

"What?"

"The windmill. One of the towers had a windmill on it, didn't it?"

"Er, *yeah*. A hundred *years* ago. The Moulin du Midi tower. You been reading my book?"

Luke sped through the pictures. "It's not here. I thought—"

He stopped. He'd gone too far back and found a picture of himself with Steve. He stared at it.

Nicky took the camera. "Stop torturing yourself."

"I miss him."

"No you don't. You just want to."

It was true. He did want to. It would be so much easier. He was sick of visiting the same bars and clubs, meeting the same men with different faces. He was sick of pretending. He wanted to love someone, and for them to love him back for who he was.

"Hey," Nicky said before he could become sullen or melancholy, "let's make the most of our last night, yeah?" She raised her glass.

Luke lifted his. "No more fighting."

"The past's the past," Nicky said, clinking drinks. "Here's to new beginnings."

§

"I won't run anymore," Luke said.

The knight he faced came forward slowly, lance held vertical. Its point was stopped with something slick and dark, and lines ran down from it in glistening stains. The horse walked a circle around Luke, legs coming up high as if it was eager to trample him beneath its hooves.

"I know who you are," Luke said, turning with them.

Behind them the sails of the Moulin du Midi windmill stopped.

"You're me," Luke said.

The knight yanked hard on the reins and the horse reared, immediately huge and threatening. It gave a shrill cry, kicking its forelegs before settling again.

Luke held his arms out wide, exposing his chest. "Come on, then."

The clatter of the lance was loud against the stones and the knight dismounted with equal sudden speed. Luke took a step in retreat but the knight came no further, only mimicked Luke's open arms. The two faced each other as if to embrace, the knight an armoured reflection of Luke.

"You're who I want to be . . ." Luke said.

The knight's breastplate fell away and the chainmail beneath began dropping in pieces, cascading like small silver coins.

"Or who I need to defeat . . ."

Gauntlets, rambraces, rerebraces, greaves—it all came off.

"Or something like that, anyway."

As the last of the chainmail links fell, hands that were bare and pale removed the helmet, dropping it to the cobblestones to look at Luke with eyes that had seen him a thousand times. Eyes that were not his, nor any other man's.

"Stop torturing yourself, Luke."

She stood naked in the moonlight, her arms open to him, and the world Luke had made for himself didn't so much tilt as lurch violently upside down.

§

Luke and Nicky were tangled together beneath covers that clung like drunken breath. Luke was curled around Nicky, spooning her, eyes closed against the tilting and spinning of the hotel room, trying not to wake up. He cupped one of her breasts and kissed the back of her neck.

Nicky said something soft and sleepy and fidgeted against him. He began pulling at her knickers.

"Luke?"

He was hard against her. He pushed closer, tried to—

"Luke!"

She shoved him off and rolled away, fast, gathering the sheets around her. "What the *fuck*?" She stared at Luke with a wide-eyed expression he tried to block with raised hands.

"Nicky, I'm not—I just wanted—"

He ran from the room instead, and then the hotel, chased by more than Nicky's angry screams.

§

They had gathered in the street, each of them robed and with a hooded face of stone. They bowed as he ran past, stone heads falling from their cowls, and they bowed in lines ahead of him, too. Each face that fell was that of a past lover. The one he stumbled on was Steve's and it sent him sprawling into the castle courtyard. A saddled gelding stamped its hooves around him and men watched from the walls and hoardings.

"I'm not like that!" he yelled at them.

The knight drew her steed away, though she lowered her lance to point accusations at Luke. She said something in French he didn't understand.

"No," he said anyway, "I'll prove it. I'll show you."

He snatched at the tip of the lance and drove it deep into the soft meat of his belly. He opened himself up for her, dragging the lance point through his flesh. A torrent of semen spilled from his stomach, evidence of every lover he had ever consumed, and he cupped his hands full of it. "Look! Look!" But the thick pool in his palms slipped between his fingers and he saw it was not the proof he thought it was but wet grain. He cast it at the horse's feet and it reared with a shrill sound like laughter.

Luke knelt, penitent, and the gash above his groin gaped open like bloody lips. He waited for the hooves to fall on him but the knight turned her steed. She eased it through the gathering crowd, her back to Luke, and the hooded men closed ranks around her, keeping her distant. Keeping her away from Luke.

"Come back!" he called, only for one of the hooded men to step close and strike him with a stick. He struck so violently, and so often, that his hood fell down and Luke saw no partner from his past this time, only himself, ferocious in his fury. He raised his arms to ward off the blows and eventually his attacker stopped, dropping the weapon with a grunt of disgust. Luke picked it up. The wood was veined, carved into a shape that repulsed him, and he tried to return it but it went limp in his hands to become a warm wet length of rope, or something like it.

The others surrounded him, lowering their hoods so that the cloth gathered around their necks in wrinkled folds from which their heads protruded, red-faced and swollen with rage. They snatched the rope from Luke's hands and it seemed to unravel from inside him.

Luke lay back and let them take it all, let them yank it free and tie each of his ankles. When they slung the other ends over the branches of the courtyard's tree he cried, "See? See? Look at me!"

Nicky was a mighty figure among the men, high on her horse with a clear view looking down on Luke. She raised her visor to watch as he was hoisted into the air.

The world turned upside down but still he yelled. "See? This is what I am!"

Two of the men had a large saw. They lowered it into position between Luke's legs, against his flesh.

"This is me!" Luke cried against its biting. "This is *me*!"

But the knight, on her horse, tilted her head and saw him differently. Saw him divided in two.

BONES OF CROW

Maggie tapped her cigarette twice on the pack before putting the filter to her mouth, an affectation she'd picked up years ago when she first started smoking. She'd seen it in a movie; it packed the tobacco tighter or something. Whatever the reason, it was as much a part of her habit now as sneaking up to the roof to enjoy it. Her lighter was a cheap throwaway but it did the job. She cupped the flame, brought it to her cigarette, and sucked in the day's first glorious breath of nicotine. Pocketing the lighter, she took the cigarette from her lips and exhaled the smoke with a sigh.

The block of flats she lived in was fifteen floors high with a view of urban sprawl and a sky that was early morning grey. Not that she came up for the view. She did like the air, though, away from the traffic and the fast food smells. Up here, the only pollution was of her own making, clinging to her clothes and making her father tut and grumble. "Your health," he'd say, meaning his. He'd say it the same way he said, "There's no need, I'll do it" and "You should get out and find a husband." He didn't mean it.

The roof had a low wall running around it. It wasn't the greatest safety precaution, coming up only as far as Maggie's thighs, but she supposed it stopped someone simply stepping off the edge. If you wanted to do that you at least had to make some effort. In her younger years she'd considered it, but only in the absent way she supposed most teenagers did. Now her suicide of choice came one drag at a time. With every breath she died a little.

There were two small buildings on the roof. One housed the stairwell. The other was some kind of storage facility, its door chained shut. Maybe there was a generator in there or tools or something. Otherwise the roof was nothing but scattered puddles and low walls.

Maggie went to the wall and glanced down at the people on their way to work. Or, more likely, on their way to look for work. Once upon a time she'd wanted that too, hoping to make something of herself like her sisters, but with her father's pension and disability benefit, and the benefits they were claiming for her, there was little need. It used to bother her how rarely she went out but the television showed her all that she was missing and it wasn't much. And as for marriage, children . . . well, there was still time. In theory. Until then there was always plenty to do around the flat. Cleaning. Cooking. Plus she had her smoking.

Maggie turned from the street and leant back against the wall in a sort of half sit, half lean, posture. She braced herself with hands either side, smoke curling up from the cigarette between her fingers, and looked out across the roof. The opposite wall blocked her view of the city so all she saw was grey sky but she knew that beyond it was the park, a grand term for what was little more than a pathetic triangle of grass with a solitary climbing frame and a circle of asphalt where the roundabout used to be. It had been taken away because kids were using the wheels of their mopeds to turn it faster than it was designed for. A girl had been flung from it, flying briefly before cracking her head open. Maggie remembered seeing it on the local news. The family petitioned the council to get rid of what they called a "death trap," though their daughter hadn't died and it had been her own fault anyway.

She smoked her cigarette down then checked her watch, knowing the time she'd see. Time to wake father. Time for his breakfast and time for his pills. Time for hers. A final drag and she twisted out what was left on the bricks behind her, dropping the butt into a pile gathered in the corner between roof and wall.

"Okay."

She pushed herself away from the wall and hoped the momentum would help carry her to the door, to the stairs, and back down to the flat.

Maggie's father had developed chronic obstructive pulmonary disease almost immediately after Maggie's mother left him. In his more romantic moments he claimed it was because he couldn't breathe without her, but of course it was because he'd smoked most of his life. Now his puffs came from an oxygen canister. His lungs were weak and his natural defence mechanisms were so reduced that he required various medications to fight infections. Maggie looked after him though. She'd effectively raised her two sisters as well but they'd flown the nest as soon as they were able. She didn't hate them for that. She tried not to hate them for that. Just as she didn't hate her father for needing her so much.

Maggie lit one cigarette from another, stubbing one out and drawing breath from the next. The view from the roof hadn't changed much since morning. It was still overcast, low cloud giving the late afternoon a premature evening light. Instead of time flying, though, it seemed to barely pass at all.

Day in, day out, her routine was the same. Her father couldn't perform even the simplest of tasks without suffering a shortness of breath, but really all he needed was her company. Someone to watch television with. It was as much her duty as checking his oxygen and feeding him his pills. He had a plastic organizer for his medication which Maggie sorted for him because he couldn't get the lids off the bottles. All he had to do was tip the day's cocktail into his palm and then into his mouth and drink a glass of water, but when the time came he either spilled the pills onto the floor or made such a pathetic attempt to hook them from the container that inevitably Maggie would end up feeding them to him one by one. Pop one in his mouth, raise the water, tip it to swallow, and repeat, wiping away what spilled between repetitions.

Maggie sighed, glanced at her watch, and took another pull on her cigarette. Today he'd coughed one of the pills back up. It had slipped down his chin on a thin line of saliva. He'd wiped his mouth but the pill fell into the fibres of his dressing gown.

"I've got it, Dad." She plucked it from his sleeve, pressed it between his lips, and helped him with the water.

"You're a good girl. Why haven't you been snapped up yet?"

Maggie stared across the roof as if she might find the answer in the grey sky, the bricks and stone. She thought of all she could do to improve her life. It didn't take long. She took in a lungful of smoke and examined the burning end of her cigarette, tapping away its ash. There was less of it left than she'd thought.

She flicked the butt away across the roof, a tiny flare for no one to see. It sparked as it bounced and skittered out of sight behind the small storage building. Whatever was in there she didn't much care, but she did worry there might be litter behind it. Newspapers or magazines, somehow dry, or a puddle of something flammable.

She pushed herself away from the wall to check, surprised at her own recklessness; she always crushed them out, the wall black-spotted with proof. She must've been more frustrated with her father today than she thought. Or with herself. She was due on soon. Maybe that was it.

The cigarette smouldered where it lay. She squashed it out beneath her shoe and saw she'd been right to check. There *was* litter, a whole load of it, gathered in the narrow channel between storage building and the outer wall. Except litter seemed too accidental a term for it.

"What the hell?"

A lot of it was newspaper and magazine pages, polystyrene food cartons, plastic carrier bags, but there were other kinds of street debris too. An old traffic cone, a *For Sale* sign, even a scaffold pole leaning at an angle across it all, resting on the wall. The rubbish had been shaped into something like bedding and Maggie's first thought was of a homeless person, but then a homeless person who could get into the building would probably tuck up under the stairs somewhere, or in the foyer by the post boxes. There were clothes, though. Mismatched items, some with pegs on them, all of it grubby with bird shit and roof filth. A torn duvet cover was draped over something bulky in the middle of it all. Maggie dragged it aside.

There were eggs underneath.

"What the *hell*?"

There were four of them, four of the biggest eggs Maggie had ever seen. They had to be fake. *Had* to be. Each was knee high, about the same size as a barrel for a water cooler. Each was the colour of cement and speckled with dark freckles. She squatted beside them, pressing the back of her hand to her nose and holding her breath against the moist sour odour, the musky wet straw smell of a pet shop. She reached for one of the eggs but withdrew suddenly because she'd read somewhere that touching an unhatched egg meant it would be abandoned. The bird would—

Bird?

Maggie laughed and reached out again. Touched it. And again she snatched her hand back.

It was warm. And something inside had . . . moved. A vibration of life beneath her skin.

Maggie stood and dug the cigarettes from her pocket, double-tapped one, and popped it in her mouth. She sparked a flame, lit it, puffed a hurried breath, and said for a third time, "What the hell?"

Darker clouds were gathering, and the small light fixed to the outside of the storage building blinked to life prematurely, tricked into thinking it was night. A storm was coming. Maggie could feel it in the sky.

She smoked her third cigarette staring at the eggs. They shone like small speckled moons beneath the light. If it hadn't started raining she probably would have smoked her packet empty watching them, wondering what on earth could have put them there.

Maggie was awake at first light, despite having stayed up late. She smoked the day's first cigarette out of her bedroom window, enjoying the cool air, and thought about going to the roof earlier than usual. She'd Googled different types of eggs, and she'd browsed various images, but found nothing useful. The largest eggs nowadays came from the ostrich, but they were only a pathetic six inches high. Not even close. The great elephant bird of Madagascar had laid eggs that were a foot or so high but they were extinct now.

Maggie smiled. Egg-stinct. Eggs-stinked. She blew smoke into the morning air.

Anyway, the eggs on the roof were twice the size of the Madagascan ones. Even the largest dinosaur egg she could find online wasn't much bigger than the elephant bird's.

Outside, the city was slowly coming to life. An Asian man was pulling at the metal blind of a newsagents, rattling it up, and a street sweeper was doing his or her best to tidy the city. Someone was walking a dog that kept trying to squat, yanking the lead before it could foul the pavement. A jogger, favouring the empty streets over the tiny nearby park, was running a course that would end in the same place it began.

In the park, someone was standing on the climbing frame. The climbing frame was two upright ladders with another leaning at an angle, and connecting all three was a horizontal section of bars to swing across. The figure was balancing in the middle of this, standing on the bars rather than hanging below them. Too big to be a child. Maggie was several storeys up, and a good distance away, but she still had the distinct impression that whoever was down there was staring straight at her.

"Hello," she said quietly, bringing her cigarette up for another breath, giving a little wave.

The figure shuffled sideways a few steps. Maggie supposed they had to go sideways because of the climbing frame, but wouldn't they want to see where they were stepping? Once it had shuffled to its new position, the figure opened up a long coat, black with black beneath, and Maggie wondered if she was looking at a flasher down there, or some other kind of pervert.

"Goodbye."

She scraped her cigarette out on the bricks of her window sill and brought the stub inside, pulling the window closed. She levered it shut and went to make a coffee. Maybe the person down there knew about the eggs. Maybe they'd put them there, and was waiting to see how Maggie would react. Maybe it was some sort of elaborate joke.

She readied a cup for her father, though he wouldn't be up for some time yet, and she put his morning pills on a saucer. She spooned coffee granules into her own cup and took her own pills waiting for the kettle to boil. Tiny ovoids in her mouth, sitting on her tongue. She thought about the eggs on the roof. She thought about keeping one, bringing it down to the flat stuffed under her jacket, "Oh, I'm pregnant, Dad, didn't you know?" Like he'd ever believe her. Like she could ever compete with Julie or Jess. Like she would ever have kids. She spat the pills into the sink and washed them away. It didn't matter. Looking after Dad was more than enough.

She took her coffee up to the roof.

In the early hours of the morning, the air on the roof smelled different. There was a coolness to it, a fresh promise that today was new and anything could happen. She liked the quiet, too. Few cars, no TVs in the flats below, workmen yet to arrive at the site opposite, filling the world with their radio and banter. She didn't pause to enjoy the air or the peace, though. She went straight to the space behind the storage building, half expecting to find only a clutter of litter, but the nest was still there. The eggs were still there. She raised her cup to them, "Good morning," and took a sip. It was very hot but good and the smell of it did something to dispel the rotten odour of the nest. "Sleep well?"

She wondered how long they'd been there before she'd found them. Some eggs, she knew from her research, were actually fossils never to hatch. What were these? One had been warm yesterday, hadn't it? She crouched to touch it, the same one as before, and yes, there it was. An internal heat. Or maybe a residual warmth. She gave it an experimental tap and though it didn't yield beneath her knuckles she could tell that it might, with enough pressure.

There were no feathers in the nest. That was unusual, wasn't it?

Because four giant eggs was completely normal.

She took another sip of coffee and put the cup on the wall before pressing both hands to the egg. She caressed it, marvelled at how smooth it was, just like a real egg. With one hand either side she attempted to lift it. It was heavy, and something inside fidgeted, a confined squirm that made Maggie snatch her hands back. She wiped them on her jeans as she stood then took up her cup again, glancing out to the park.

That same figure was still on the climbing frame. It hunched suddenly as she watched, and with the action came a shrill scream that broke into a sequence of aborted noises. Then it dropped from its perch and its coat opened, opened, opened far too wide either side and flapped, flapped, because it wasn't a coat at all; with two hard beats of its wings the thing was aloft.

Maggie fumbled the cup she'd hardly taken hold of and it spilled, dropped, smashed, "Shit!" She glanced down as she stepped away from it and when she looked up again the sky was clear. She peered over the wall and saw nothing coming. Still, she left the broken pieces of her cup where they lay. She headed for the stairs, not running but certainly hurrying. Dad would be wanting his morning cuppa and she had to take her pills.

She didn't look up and she didn't look back.

She was supposed to be watching an old movie with her father but her mind wasn't on the plot. At least she didn't have to follow any conversation though; he was wearing the full breathing mask today rather than the nostril tubes. It fitted around his nose and mouth and it prevented him from talking. He had to look his question at her when she got up during the adverts.

"Toilet," Maggie said. She checked his oxygen, adjusting it on her way out. "Cuppa tea, Dad?"

He nodded, returning to the black and white world of the TV.

Maggie had a packet of cigarettes hidden in a box of tampons in the bathroom. She grabbed them and flicked the kettle on in the kitchen before letting herself out into the corridor. She closed the door quietly and lit the cigarette early; she needed the nicotine *before* getting to the roof this time. She was confident there wouldn't be enough smoke to set off the alarms. Confident, too, that they probably didn't work anyway.

It had been a few days since her last visit to the roof. Since then she'd enjoyed her cigarettes in the bathroom, extractor fan on, her hand and face at the tiny open window because she was too worried about what she might see from her own. The one in the bathroom had glass that was opaque even though they were so high up, and more importantly it didn't face the park. She'd had nightmares about the park, dreams in which the thing she'd seen there had flown right at her, crashing into her bedroom in an explosion of glass and brick only to drag her out screaming, both of them screaming, and then she was falling until she was suddenly awake. One night she'd woken from this to find her father shuffling in the hallway. He'd opened his dressing gown and released a flock of dark birds at her and she'd woken a second time, smothered beneath her blankets. She was ready to check the roof again now if only because it might put an end to the dreams.

At the door to outside, cigarette somehow half gone already, Maggie paused. She listened. Nothing. She opened the door.

As soon as it was open she heard shrieking, an endless series of short, sharp, stuttered cries, *shrie-shrie-shrie-shrie-shrie*, and she knew what had happened.

The eggs had hatched.

Cigarette in her mouth, Maggie put both hands to her ears as she nudged the door wider. The things weren't loud, exactly, but shrill and constant, overlapping. *Me! Me! Me! Me! Me!*

She stepped out onto the roof with her eyes to the sky. She checked the park. A woman with a pram was walking through, that was all.

Eventually Maggie was able to look away and lower her hands, wincing at the din but knowing she'd get used to it. She could get used to anything. She dropped her cigarette, stepped it out, and approached the nest, careful to keep her distance. She only wanted to see them.

They were ugly little things. A shuffling mass of black, puffy with erratic plumage, they held their beaks up to *shriek-shriek-shriek!* at the sky. Pale grey eyelids clenched closed against what little sun there was, they beat at each other blindly with stubby wings as they fidgeted into new positions.

When a dark shape blurred into her peripheral vision Maggie screamed and crouched and covered her head with her arms. The thing dropped from a high position behind her, landing at the nest. It settled on the scaffold pole as Maggie scurried backwards towards the stairs in a crab position, hands and shoes slipping on the wet roof.

The bird was huge, even hunched over. As tall as her but more broad. Wings the size of ironing boards folded against its body. It was entirely black, so black that it gleamed, and the one glassy eye Maggie could see was so dark it absorbed all other colours. A hole's shadow, dark as ink not written. In its beak, in its terrible split black beak, it held a giant snail.

The young in the nest jumped, jumped, knocked against each other, and beat their stumpy wings. They snapped at the air and set up a discordant chorus of shrill calling so intense it forced Maggie to stop fleeing just so she could cover her ears again. She still heard the crack, though, when the mother slammed its catch down against the roof wall. *Crack! Crack-crack!* A couple of those, then the bird held its catch on the wall, talons spread to grip it steady. The beak came down. Hard, quick, darting stabs. *Crack! Crack-crack-crack!* And Maggie realized at last that what she saw was not a snail. Of *course* it wasn't a snail.

"Oh, Christ."

Its beak withdrew from the motorcycle helmet with a string of something red and meaty. It tossed this to its nest. As the young fought over the flesh it pecked again at the hole it had made in the visor, scooping more from inside, nodding to throw more strips to its children. Maggie saw blood spill from the opening, a single thick line of it running down the helmet to drip into the nest where the three snapped at thrown morsels until the helmet was dropped for them to peck at. They rammed their beaks into whatever gap they could find, nudging and shrieking at each other in between.

Beyond them, visible now as they fed themselves, was the last egg. The one she'd touched had not hatched.

The young were quickly done. They craned their necks upwards, tipped their heads back, and held their beaks open for short pauses between squawks. The mother dipped to each in turn, opening its beak in theirs to regurgitate a previous meal. Perhaps the rest of the motorcyclist. Perhaps something else. Maggie tried not to think of the woman she'd seen in the park. The one with the pram.

"Oh fucking *Christ.*"

The bird looked up. It turned its head one way then the other, locking one dark eye at a time on Maggie. It shuffled sideways on its perch, as she'd seen it do on the climbing frame, then arched its body forwards with its beak open wide. A long bloody tongue uncurled from inside with a scream of vowels, accompanied by the spreading of wings. They unfolded like vast blankets.

Maggie scrambled in retreat until she felt the closed door press against her back. She slapped around for the handle.

The bird's long call became a sharp sequence of noises like nails being wrenched from wood. It flapped its wings, leapt, and swooped at her.

Maggie yanked herself to her feet and the door open at the same time. She rolled around the frame, slammed the door shut behind her. Holding it closed, she braced herself for an impact that never came. When the automatic light in the stairwell finally registered her existence, it blinked and flickered a rhythm as quick as her breathing.

Another cry resounded off the walls, deafening in the confined space of the stairwell.

Maggie shoved herself away from the door and took the stairs down two at a time, chased by a long dark echo.

Maggie's father had died while she was on the roof. All those years she'd spent with him and she hadn't been there when it happened. It didn't seem fair.

At the cremation, people gave Maggie their condolences and platitudes, spoke of a tough man she didn't recognize, spoke of mods and rockers but never explained how her father fit in. The man they knew had died long ago. The man in the photographs her sisters provided for the wake—Dad on his motorbike, Dad with his wife and girls—was a stranger to Maggie. The man she knew wore a faded grey dressing gown and had died with his eyes bulging and his hands twisted into claws that couldn't get the mask from his face, couldn't turn the oxygen dial. He'd wet himself, too. The small living room had been ripe with his odour.

Maggie spent the funeral thinking about a group of crows. Everyone in black. She thought of her father's bulging eyes, his clawed hands, his stink, and found it hard to say she loved him. She let her sisters say it for her and thought of crows.

There had been few things to do afterwards. He only had a small selection of mismatched clothes to sort through. He'd left her with little more than his ashes. She had seen her sisters through their grief, but they didn't stay long. They invited her to stay with them for a while, but they said it the same way Dad said a lot of things he didn't mean. Within a fortnight of his passing, the house was finally empty and Maggie could do whatever she wanted. Hell, she could even smoke.

She went to the roof.

She tried to light a cigarette but her hands were shaking too much. She had to hold one with the other to keep the flame steady enough, puffing out quick breaths of relief before releasing a slower drag that calmed her. It would be her last one.

A chill breeze carried her smoke away and swept her hair into tangles. She zipped up her jacket to the sounds of them all screeching, hacking out their staccatos, calling her to their nest.

They were even uglier close up. The beaks seemed too wide for their feather-fluffed faces, and the eyes bulged beneath closed grey lids. Their squat heads were ruffled with a scruff of down that extended to the wattle of their throats. They were all elbows and claws, it seemed, feathers dark like tar, wafting their stench around as they *shrie-shrie-shrie-shrie-shrieked!*

Maggie dropped what was left of her cigarette and twisted her heel on it. "Stop it," she said.

At the sound of her voice they became louder, scrabbling at the debris of their nest as they shoved each other, straining their heads and necks for their next meal.

"*Stop* it," Maggie said, "stop it, stop it, *stop it!*"

She grabbed the nearest one under the foreshortened stubs of its arms or wings or whatever the hell they were and barely registered the weight of it. She scooped it up and cast it skyward, over the edge of the roof. It hung there for a moment, turning with the force of the throw, and faced her. It rawked and beat at the air, caught in the pause between up and down, flailing with limbs barely feathered. It had never seen another fly, not yet, but that didn't matter. Seeing it done didn't mean you could do it yourself.

Gravity snatched it away.

Maggie grabbed the next—it was warm in her hands, wriggling—and she turned on the spot to throw it harder, further. "Fly!" she said, and watched it drop.

The crash of the first one landing was followed by the wailing repetition of a car alarm. She didn't hear the second one.

Maggie put her hands on the third sibling, pinning its wings, and raised it to chest height. It snapped at her breasts and her head so she held it straight-armed and turned her face away from its beak. She walked it to the wall and let it go.

"There," she said, facing the remaining egg. "Just us." She stepped into the nest with all its filth. She crouched, put her palms on the egg, and caressed the smooth coolness of its shell. Nothing pulsed inside. Nothing moved. It was cold. It may as well have been stone for all the life it had. She tapped at it with her knuckles, "Hey!" then knocked her fist against it, "Wake up!" She held it by the top and rocked it to and fro, pulling the base free from a caked mound of bird shit. The broken pieces of her coffee mug lay nearby. She retrieved a section that was mostly handle, dirtied with smears of black and white, and tossed it aside. Another fragment, cleaner, was a sharp triangle of ceramic. It fit snug in her hand.

She drove it down hard against the egg.

The egg cracked. Another hit, and a network of fissures flattened the crown. The cup shard broke its way inside. She pulled it out and threw it away, hooked her fingers into the egg, and pulled at the shell. It came away easily, a viscous fluid spilling over her hands and into her lap, releasing a stench as thick as the albumen or yolk or whatever it was that coated her, a bloody sepia slime that stank like snotty menses.

There was a dead bird inside.

It lay against a concave wall of shell as if sleeping, head burrowed into its partially feathered chest. Maggie cupped the beak under one hand and gently raised the face. It was mostly pink puckered skin, slick with fluid, a patch of feathers wet against its head. Its eyes were wide black domes without lids, sightless pupils dark as blindness. Dark like oil. Dark like tar. Maggie saw herself reflected there, distorted.

"Poor thing."

She unzipped her jacket, took it off, and lay it on the ground. She slipped both hands into the remains of the egg and gently withdrew the bird from inside. It was much lighter than the others, all loose bone, sagging skin, and limp feathers. Its talons had been tucked beneath its body but now they dangled, flaccid grey-ringed toes curled with the weight of hard claws. Maggie lay the creature on her jacket and folded both halves over it, tucked in the top and bottom, made a neat parcel of what she'd found.

"You'll be okay now."

She took the cigarettes from the pocket of her jeans, withdrew the lighter, and lay them on top of the jacketed bird before settling herself into the nest. She fidgeted, clearing a space amongst the papers and food boxes. Flies buzzed at the motorcycle helmet but she kicked it away and the dark cloud dispersed after it, reforming once it had stopped rolling. Her backside slid on a cushion of thick droppings, and she put her hand down into something bloody, but she no longer cared about things like that.

She waited.

She didn't have to wait long. The car alarm was still repeating, but over that came the *whump!* . . . *whump!* . . . *whump!* of beating wings. Maggie looked up and, yes, there it was, swooping down at her, bigger than before, diving with urgent speed and the scream of an eagle in descent, talons outstretched.

Maggie tipped her head back. She closed her eyes.

The claws did not come. She was buffeted by a wing-made wind, but not struck. She felt the nest-litter stir as the dark bird hovered, smelt the damp feathers beating near her face. She heard the scrape of metal on bricks and knew that it had settled upon its scaffold roost.

Maggie opened her mouth.

The bird screamed for her and thrust its beak in hard. The suddenness of it surprised her but her cry was strangled before it could become sound. She squeezed her eyes closed tighter and grabbed at the scruff of its feathers, all spiny and coarse and thick as starless night, impossible to wrench free no matter how hard she pulled in pain. And still the beak came, filling her throat, stretching her lips around it so that the corners of her mouth split. A mass of feathers smothered her as the point of its beak rooted deeper until finally it found what it wanted. Maggie opened her eyes then. Something inside was wrenched free and her eyes were suddenly wide, hands falling limp to her sides as she gagged around whatever it was that came up her throat, thick and moist and ravelling out of her. She convulsed, gasped, retched. With a flick of its head the bird tossed it aside and Maggie saw twin black sacks fold open like tiny wings before they fell away. When the bird's beak entered her a second time, rummaging, she barely felt it. The third time she felt even less, saw all that was black and bloody coming out of her—black heart, black feathers—and was only dimly aware that the jacket beside her stirred. With her arms by her side, fists clenched, she leaned back as the dark bird emptied her, twitching like the jacket as the big bird broke her bones and scooped her hollow, scattering her insides like ashes to be borne on the wind.

When all that remained of her was a vacant sack of skin and clothes, Maggie collapsed in upon herself, mouth open as if hungry for all she had lost.

Her jacket burst open with a sudden flurry of fledgling energy, and a long shrill cry that might have been pain, might have been joy.

PINS AND NEEDLES

"Prick."

James plunged his hands deep into the pockets of his coat as if he'd stepped aside voluntarily instead of being pushed from the queue. Others shouldered past him, knocking him with bags, and he had to duck quickly, sidestepping, when an elderly lady lowered her umbrella as she clambered onto the bus.

"You coming on, mate?" the driver called out to him.

James shook his head—the bus was too crowded—and the doors closed with a stuttered cough. With a tired exhalation of exhaust the vehicle merged slowly with the rest of the traffic, leaving James behind at the bus shelter.

"Prick!" he said again, louder this time. An elderly man seating himself on the narrow beam of a bench looked up with a scowl then busied himself rearranging the shopping in his carrier bags.

James pulled up the hood of his grubby anorak and zipped it so the matted fur of its trim hid all but his eyes and forehead. He headed out into the drizzle. He'd walk to the cinema now that his bus journey had been ruined.

With his hands in his pockets the coat was pulled down tight. He could feel the reassuring bulge of what was stowed in the inside pocket as it pressed against his chest. Squashed ball of Blu-Tack. Curled tube of superglue. Folded card sleeve of sewing needles, thread long since discarded. Small plastic box of drawing pins. He'd used a few so his walk was accompanied by a metallic *ch-ch-ch* as they shook, a quiet echo of each step that only James could hear. The hobby knife with its retractable blade took up the most room. He kept it in the packaging in case he was ever stopped by a policeman. "I just bought it," would be his excuse. "I make models." He knew he looked the sort.

The cinema was one of the last of the flea-pit varieties, somehow managing to stay open despite the nearby multi-screen haven with its wall of pick-n-mix and staff who looked too young to see half the films they screened. James would have preferred the multi-screen but he was banned, and though he could sometimes get in anyway—there was always someone new taking tickets—he didn't want to risk another disappointment today.

"One, please."

The machine in front of the woman ejected his ticket and sliced it neatly, only for the man a few paces away to tear it in half before gesturing James inside. He picked up some popcorn first. Stale, salted, the only kind on offer. It didn't matter. He wouldn't eat it.

The screen was still dark and a soft music played, soundtrack scores rendered banal by popularity. There were a half dozen people seated already. Two couples sat together near the back. One person sat near the front looking up at the black screen, waiting for its light and pictures. Another sat near the aisle as if eager to leave immediately should the film be bad. James thought it probably would be. Reel Films only showed arty films or foreign films. Or arty foreign films.

He took a seat in the middle of a row near the back. People liked this sort of position, he knew. He just hoped the shitty weather was enough to lure more people inside.

Not yet, though.

He put his popcorn on the floor and unzipped his coat. The plastic blister of the knife packaging was only gummed down lightly to the cardboard, a job he'd done himself before coming out, and he carefully peeled it away to release the knife. He used it to make small incisions in the fabric of two seats to the left. Next he pulled two small balls of Blu-Tack from the fistful in his pocket and pushed these into the openings he'd made, squashing them down against the base of the seat. Finally, with the speed of practice and the assurance—even in the dark—of familiarity, he pressed two of the longer needles into the Blu-Tack. Then he shuffled along as if he didn't like his original seat and repeated the process.

His work done, he got up and moved a few rows back, first taking care to spill popcorn over the seats in front and behind.

He settled down and waited for the show.

James left the cinema smiling. It had been better than he'd dared hope, and afterwards the film hadn't been too bad either. The French girl in it had been beautiful and naked a lot. The young woman with the kids wouldn't have liked that, had she stayed, even if there wasn't any sex. So really, James had saved her some embarrassment, and this way she probably got a refund too, which she wouldn't have done if she'd left because of a French girl's tits and pert perfect bottom.

James was still smiling when he arrived home. The rusty front gate screeched his arrival and next door's cat fled from beneath the hedgerow. James had once turned a foam ball into a sea urchin for that cat but the results had not been satisfying.

"I'm home," James said, closing the door behind him. Nobody lived with him anymore but he liked to say it anyway. He took the things from his pocket and lay them out on the kitchen table, hung his coat on the back of a chair. He took a Coke from the fridge and sat down to check his new model. The boosters were dry. He'd assemble the weapon deck tonight and apply the transfers to the main body of the craft while the glue set.

First he went to the bathroom, turning on the stereo as he went. No need to put the CD in, he'd been listening to it this morning. He pissed to the gradual sound of track one, flushed as Ziggy Stardust told him about ground control and Major Tom, and by the time he was assembling sections of spacecraft he was singing.

It had been a good day.

The woman with kids had come into the cinema after the trailers and adverts, just as James was beginning to despair that anyone else would come in at all. Judging from how soaked they were, the rain had worsened. The woman was hushing the kids forward having won a temporary quiet with sweets and soft drink.

"Not there, Sam, look at all the popcorn. Your dress. What will your mother say? Come on. No, Kevin, here. Come on you two, sit down."

James had waited with held breath as the three of them moved sideways past the aisle seats to those further in. As the woman helped the boy out of his coat the girl sat down, only to stand again with a shriek.

The woman hissed a sharp "Ssh!" and, best of all, grabbed the girl's arm and pulled her back down into her seat. "Sit. Down."

The girl screamed a second time and leapt up, spilling her drink over the woman James assumed to be a babysitter. Kevin, at the same time, sat down only to be catapulted up with a cry. Launched like a rocket.

James grinned and popped the tab of his Coke. It spat and foamed but he sucked it up quick and burped quietly. He put the can down away from his work.

REM sang of a man on the moon. It wasn't one of his favourites. If he wasn't busy he'd usually skip it, and "To The Moon and Back" by Savage Garden. They didn't feel right. Dad probably put them on for a joke but after five years the novelty wore off. "Loving the Alien" was okay, even with no aliens in it. David Bowie was good, or Ziggy Stardust as he was really called.

The plasma cannon had to be held firmly to dry and James blew on it so the hole for the laser turret didn't seal over with excess glue. He looked at the map on the living room wall while he waited, wondering where his father was now. He'd stuck flags in where he thought seemed likely, enjoying the way the pins slid easily into the corkboard behind. The corkboard had been the only good idea his mother ever had, apart from running away.

"Look at all those holes," she'd said, having pulled his poster down to redecorate. He'd looked and seen his own constellations in the paintwork. This one was Father's Journey, and this one over here could be Father's Smile. There, Father Waiting. Dad didn't sound right.

"Well? What do you have to say about that?" his mother demanded.

"Cool," said James, and she smacked him around the head.

"You're lucky they're small enough the paint will fill them."

He didn't feel lucky. He rubbed his head and sulked.

"Aren't you too old for all this space stuff now?" she asked. If she knew why he had the star charts she pretended to have forgotten. "You'll get picked on at big school, you know."

"I don't care."

"You don't care." She looked at the poster in her hands, the swirls of stars and the coloured gases of the universe, and for a moment James must have inherited the mind-reading power only mothers had because he suddenly knew she meant to screw it up and throw it away.

"No!"

"Alright," she said, "okay, you don't care. Fine." She'd dropped the map onto his bed, paper slightly crumpled but at least away from the bin. "You better take all of those down, too," she said, pointing to where his models dangled from the ceiling. "Heaven forbid I get paint on the captain's solar ship, or whatever."

It pissed James off when she did that. He'd sulk until tea time now. She knew it wasn't a solar ship.

"You're just like your father," she muttered as she left and suddenly there was no need to sulk anymore.

James had taken down his rockets and spaceships grinning.

At work, James tapped at a keyboard at a small desk nestled between two other men tapping at keyboards at a small desk. Occasionally the phone would ring and one of them would answer it with the practised, "Good morning, IT department," and then one of them would go and fix an easy problem one of the muggles elsewhere in the company was experiencing.

"Computers are the future," James' father had told him, and James believed it, he really did. He just wished the future would hurry up and get here so he could play an important part in it.

In the meantime, he coloured a drawing pin with permanent marker. The ink would wipe off the metal with each back and forth of the pen if you weren't careful but James knew to use single strokes and to let them dry before applying another on top, darkening the brass to black. At the end of his shift he pocketed the pin and took it with him when he left, sure to put it in the right pocket—the other had a hole in it and pins could end up in the coat lining.

There was a multi-storey car park near the building where he worked. He went to the lift and rode it up a few floors, applying glue to the back of the pin just before the doors opened and admitted people heading down. He stepped out as they came in and, once the lift had begun its descent, pressed the base of the pin to the call button, holding it there till it was secure. Then he hid himself between a couple of cars and waited, fumbling as if for keys whenever anyone passed.

The quiet growl of cars climbing in slow spirals rumbled somewhere below him. Engines thickened the air with the smell of petrol, exhaust, and warm rubber as tires turned tight circles, squealing at each ramp. The lift came and went but that was okay.

Eventually, a sleek vehicle parked on the same floor as James and a man in a rush hurried past. At the lift he jabbed the button. It jabbed him back. The man swore his pain so loud it echoed back and forth amongst the concrete columns. James emerged from where he'd watched and approached as the man peered closely at the lift controls.

"You feeling okay?" James asked.

"Some bastard's stuck a pin there," the man said, pointing. A small bead of blood marked the pad of his finger.

"You feel alright?"

"Yeah, it was just a pin. Fuckers." He wiped his finger on a handkerchief. He knocked the pin away with his briefcase but James didn't mind, it had done its job. He stood on it when the man wasn't looking and enjoyed the reminder of its *tap tap tap* as he walked home.

When James was five his father left to be a rocket man. James couldn't go with him because of his medication, but when he was better he'd be able to go into space.

"Live long and fuck yourself," his mother had shouted at the door, making a hand gesture that didn't belong with the proper saying but seemed to suit hers. She said it as if she was angry, though daddy must have been saving the world or exploring the universe for the benefit of mankind or something. She'd even used the f-word, aiming it at the front door, but if she was angry with dad why not aim it at the sky? Adults were confusing. But his daddy was a rocket man and James couldn't wait to tell his friends at school.

Sitting on the bus, James remembered those days with a mix of pride and perplexity. Even as he'd grown up his mother had remained a mystery. Occasionally she would pass news of his father on to him. He was always away at strange sounding places. Slough. The Witterings. Newport. The last he imagined as a space station rather than a planet, huge and bright and busy with vessels from various systems and federations. It pleased him to learn, eventually, that these places were named after real places on Earth not far away from where they lived.

One day his father sent him a CD.

"Something useless from your father," his mother had said, throwing it to him like a toy. He hadn't been able to play it—they didn't have a CD player yet—but he had admired the way it caught the light in rainbow lines across its shiny surface as he turned the curve of it this way and that. He liked the words that came with it, written on a folded piece of paper. His mother passed this to him only after checking its contents herself. "Spaceman," Babylon Zoo. "Space Dog," Tori Amos. "Space

Oddity," David Bowie (Ziggy Stardust). Strange names, alien names. He wondered what a Babylon Zoo looked like, what animals you'd find there—a space dog, maybe. Best of all, he liked the last track listing. It was another David one, "Hallo Spaceboy," which he liked to imagine was his dad's way of saying hi. Later, "Rocket Man Elton" by someone simply named John would become his favourite, but not until he could play the album. Even now, knowing the correct title and artist, James liked to think of it that way. Rocket Man Elton, burning out his fuse up there.

He skipped the tracks on his iPod until he heard the piano of the intro and settled back into the seat to watch the streets flash by beyond the window. The rain had stopped but drops still streaked the glass, speeding down in diagonal lines that were nearly horizontal as the bus accelerated the last stretch of main road.

It was almost empty, the bus. James' stop was one of the last and they were nearly there. Even though he wouldn't be around to see it, he pushed one of his needles base down into the fabric of the cushioned seat beside him. No need for Blu-Tack because the foam was firm and would hold it upright until someone sat and was speared.

They stopped and a woman got on. The bus started before she could sit down and she took a few quick steps forward, catching the rail.

James pressed the button for his stop.

"Is anyone sitting here," the woman asked, indicating the seat beside James. Clearly nobody was sitting there, but he understood the question.

"Go ahead," he said. He held his breath.

She was pretty. A little large to be beautiful, maybe, but lovely eyes that sparkled and an easy smile. She was wearing the uniform of a dental nurse. Well, a nurse of some sort. It was the sticker saying "I'm a brave girl" with a grinning tooth beneath it that suggested the dentist part. Maybe she was a normal nurse who'd just been to the dentist for a—

"Fuck! Ow!"

She stood up quick, hand clasped to her buttocks. The bus shuddered to a stop and she staggered forward with the motion, catching at a pole to steady herself.

"You alright, love?" the driver called.

She held the needle in her hand. She must have pulled it from the seat when she stood, its point buried in her flesh.

"There was a needle on my seat," she said, dropping it in the bin for used tickets. And then, amazingly, she laughed.

"You feeling okay?" James asked.

She laughed again. "Well, that woke me up," she said. "How embarrassing."

The driver suggested a tetanus shot and asked if she wanted him to record it for health and safety reasons, pulling a clipboard out from somewhere near his seat. "Wasn't a syringe or nothin' was it?"

"Didn't look like it," she said, rubbing where it had stuck her. "Just a sewing needle. Nothing on it but my arse."

"What's your name, Miss?"

"Angela," she said. He began writing it down. "Oh, don't bother, I'm alright."

A car beeped behind them and the bus driver made a gesture out the window for it to pass. They re-joined the traffic behind it.

"If you don't mind, I'll sit here," Angela said, sitting down across the aisle from James.

James realized he was staring and wondered if he'd been doing it the whole time, if she suspected it was him, or if she thought he was just another gormless weirdo that rode public transport.

"This is me," he said, getting up.

She smiled her goodbye. He smiled back. Earlier, after her scream of pain, she had laughed. Laughed!

"Thank you," James said, stepping down from the bus.

He watched as Angela put earphones in and wondered what music she liked to listen to. As the bus moved away, James wondered if she liked David Bowie.

§

There was a starman waiting in the sky, James knew. Track five. Ziggy Stardust had a lot of good songs. To think, this magnificent collection of music had simply hung on a thread from his ceiling when he was a kid. Like a flying saucer, suspended with the small fleet of spaceships that flew there.

Now, years later, the CD was down and all of his ceilings were an armada of spacecraft. In a matter of an hour or two there'd be another one to join the ranks.

He carefully applied another coat of paint to the tail section. He started with the tail section because the tail section needed to dry first so he could put the transfers on.

"Shit."

He dipped a tissue into the water jar and wiped the mistake he'd made on the ship's escape pod. The escape pod had to be gunmetal silver, not sunburst.

He couldn't stop thinking of Angela. Every time he managed to get into the Zen of painting, there she was, leaping from her seat as if into orbit. He saw again the way her hand clapped the right cheek of her behind, the way she turned to try and look as she withdrew the slender sliver from herself. Sometimes, even though he was sitting behind her when this happened, he saw the way her breasts must have bounced under her dental tabard. Beautiful large soft planets of flesh.

"Shit!"

He'd done it again. This time the line of paint swept right across the escape pod and down to the droid bay. He wiped it clean again and washed the brushes, setting them upon a dishcloth to dry. There was no point trying to finish it tonight.

He grabbed a bottle of beer, a box of pins, and a roll of sticky tape and took them into the living room. He'd watch an episode of series 4 and make what he called pinstripes, pushing drawing pins through strips of sticky tape so he could fix them under banisters and door handles at a later date. Mindless work. If he imagined Angela in first officer uniform or fighting off the amorous advances of the charismatic captain, it wouldn't be a bother.

He'd made his first pinstripe at school, when he was nine. After the day of the fight.

"Those boys are so much bigger than you, James. Boys, plural. You don't fight, James, look at you."

"They said—"

"They said what?"

They said his dad was not an astronaut. They said there was no such thing as spaceships, even though they'd watched one take off on TV in science class. No Martians, even though there was a face on Mars that someone must have made.

"Nothing."

"This isn't nothing." She'd shown him the tear in his school trousers. "This isn't nothing." She showed him the note from his teacher immediately afterwards. "When you do things like this, it hurts me, James. Alright? It hurts me. And then I have to hurt you, so you'll learn."

He'd hurt Bobby and Tom and Justin the next day even more. He'd stuck a strip of pins to a ruler and slapped each of them with it until their hands and faces bled.

He had to move schools after that.

"I should send you to your father," his mother had said, as if it were a threat.

"Yes!"

"Oh, you think you'd like that, do you? Think *he'd* like that? Then why hasn't he come for you already? Why doesn't he visit us more often, hmm?"

"He thinks he'll blow our minds!" James yelled.

His mum had laughed, recognizing the lyric. Not a nice laugh, like Angela's.

"The only blown mind is his. Go to your room."

His mum didn't understand punishments. His room was the best place she could send him.

She didn't let him eat any dinner that night but he had three packets of Space Raider crisps hidden under his bed and plenty of books. "Food for thought," the librarian had said, and winked as if he knew the same secrets Ray Bradbury and Robert Heinlein did.

James set about reading so he'd be ready when his dad came, stopping only when his mum came in to give him his medicine shot.

"All better," she said, part of the routine, rubbing at where she'd injected him. Then she remembered she was angry with him, remembered he was like his father, remembered she didn't like him at all, and with the knowing power of all mothers she reached under his pillow for the book hidden there and confiscated it for the rest of the night.

Angela got on the bus at the same stop as before. She was wearing the uniform again but not the sticker. She said hello.

"Any pins?"

At first James was so startled by the question he almost said yes, reaching to his pocket as if to offer her one like a piece of gum or cigarette. He caught himself and made a show of sweeping the seat instead, pushing down on the cushion. "Nope."

He'd thought about it. All of last night he'd thought about it, Angela jumping up with a cry in all sorts of different uniforms and then nothing at all until finally he'd had to masturbate just to be able to go to sleep. He'd been thinking about it on the journey home, too, but finally decided he'd rather sit next to her this time. Besides, it would be too suspicious if he did it again so soon.

She sat beside him. Her perfume was something sharp and citrusy.

"I think you fixed my computer once," she said.

He looked at her but couldn't remember ever doing any such thing.

"Council office," she added.

"Yeah, I worked there for a bit."

"Me too. You came down to show me why I couldn't enter data like everybody else."

She laughed. It was wonderful.

James could only look at her.

"Number lock," she said. "So embarrassing."

"Oh."

"Not as bad as yesterday."

"How's your bum?" he asked.

She slapped his arm. "Cheeky." Then she laughed again; "Cheeky!" she realized.

James laughed too, though he wouldn't understand the pun until later. She'd hit his arm. He was thinking about that.

"So, do you want to take me and my bum for a drink?"

It would have taken James weeks to ask, and he would never have dared put it that way.

"Yes," he said immediately.

"Want to get off?"

He didn't know what to say. That was a bit forward, wasn't it? Were you supposed to plan these things ahead?

Angela pointed at the open bus door. "This is your stop, isn't it?"

The bus driver was turned around in his seat.

James leapt up as if he'd sat on one of his own contraptions.

"Tomorrow?" Angela called after him.

"Yeah," he called. "Tomorrow."

On the way home he stuck drawing pins under the door handles of people's cars. With the pinstripes already prepared, it was a quick operation. If he walked slow enough in the morning he would see it affect approximately three people on their way to work. Most of them had stopped checking now.

She got on the bus wearing a skirt and jacket instead of her work clothes.

"So where you taking me?"

He took her to a pub in town rather than one of the locals near where he lived. He was no longer allowed in the pubs near where he lived because of an incident with some darts.

They drank—white wine for her, cider for him (James loved how the Irish barman pronounced pint)—and they talked. It was easy. Easier than he thought. Later they ate—a burger with chunky chips for her, a kebab skewer with fries for him—and they talked some more, sitting closer. He held back about his dad, not sure he trusted her enough yet. She liked films starring Ethan Hawke, who she said looked a bit like him, and she liked musicals, which she said she couldn't help, and she liked books by Anita Shreve for the same reasons she liked musicals.

"What books do you like?"

He told her. She laughed when he said he liked Dick but this time he got the joke and laughed with her.

"Favourite book?" she asked, dipping a chip in mayo.

His favourite book was one he liked because of the cover. Not the best reason to love a book, perhaps, but with its gleaming rocket standing mighty and slender on the surface of some barely there planet it was impossible for him not to love it. The rocket was silver, shining in the light of two suns, coming to a point that dazzled with reflected light.

"I like *Fahrenheit 451*," he said instead. He wasn't lying, but it wasn't his favourite, even though The Hound in it was pretty good.

"Talking of which, is it just me or is it hot in here?" Angela took off her jacket, revealing a low top that tucked in under her arms to leave her shoulders as bare as the upper curves of her breasts.

"Yeah, you look hot," James dared and she laughed, hitting his arm in the way that said cheeky like on the bus.

"Let's go back to my place, then," she said. Her eyes were a little wide with alcohol but not so much she didn't know what she was offering, or to who.

James wanted to prick himself to test he was awake. "Alright then," he said, before she could change her mind.

"Just pop to the ladies' before I burst."

While she was gone, James paid for their dinner and pocketed the skewer. Then he walked her home.

"It happens to lots of men with a new partner," she said, hastily adding, "I read it."

James lay beside her, breathing heavy. His penis was shrinking, wet with his finish and her sex.

"As long as you enjoyed it," Angela said, turning to face him. Her breasts were still heaving with her own breaths, nipples still hard with arousal. "Besides, you can always give me another go later."

He did. It lasted longer the second time but he was still the only one to climax, firing his come into her like tiny rockets.

"You're my universe," he said to her, drowsy.

"Aww," she said, "sweet."

On the way home James stabbed a dog with the skewer. It yelped and ran off. It took the skewer with it, sticking from its flank, but that didn't matter. It had yelped.

§

They met up again mid-week. At first it had been strange, seeing her on the bus, but she acted normal and they fixed a date for a second drink. They drank less (her idea), and on the way home he told her about the stars.

"That one's Polaris. The North Star, but really it's three. It's about 430 light years away."

"How far is that?" Angela was holding his arm and leaning close as they walked.

"About two thousand five hundred trillion miles." He rounded down, though he knew the answer was 2,522,249,280,000,000 miles. Ish.

"Wow."

"And those, that bunch near it, see them? That's Ursa Major. Like a big saucepan?" He drew it with his finger, connecting the dots.

"Oh yeah, I see it!"

They stopped walking and looked at the stars.

"Pin pricks in the sky," James said. His voice was soft, wistful.

"I've got an idea," said Angela. She took his hand and led him to a taxi rank near the station.

"Greendown Hill," she said.

The view below was of the city, its lights bright and fuzzy and too orderly. But above, the sky was a huge dark blanket and the stars winked and twinkled within it. James pointed out all the ones he could name, and the constellations, and together they made up new ones of their own. When the burger van had closed, and the boy racers had sped back to their homes, Angela took James by the hand and led him to an area sheltered from the road by a copse of trees.

"What are you doing?" he asked her, but it was clear enough. She was unfastening his belt, pulling down his trousers. Made a joke about his "pocket rocket" that delighted him.

"We better use one of these this time," she said, taking a condom from her purse.

James wondered if she was more health-conscious sober or if it was to reduce his sensitivity. She opened the packet and reached to put it on.

"I'll do it," he said. He sat on the grass and turned his body, self conscious. When he turned back, she had taken her knickers off from under her dress. She sank down upon him, warm and wet, and controlled the movements.

"Do you like this?" she asked.

Behind her was nothing but the night sky and its glitter of starlight. Angela slipped the straps of her dress down, pulled it lower to ride him topless.

"Oh yeah," said James. He liked it. And then, "Yeah," and then "Yes!"

James thought about her all day at work, every day, for the next week. He craved her, needed to see her again, looked forward to every bus journey.

So of course, the days passed slowly.

He thought about all the things he'd tell her. If they were going to be together, she needed to know about his dad. His mum, too, he supposed, but mainly it was his dad he wanted to talk about. He was the interesting one, and James knew he could trust Angela with that sort of information. As long as it didn't seem he was showing off.

First, he'd find out if she liked David Bowie. Partly because he'd made a copy of his CD for her and a lot of it was Bowie. Mainly, though, because it would lead into the serious conversation, a link via "Life On Mars" or "Starman." Then he'd tell her about his dad, up in space.

"Hey James? Earth to James?"

It was Daniel. He was holding the phone so his hand was over the mouthpiece. James hadn't even heard it ring.

"Want to go fix an internet connection in HR? Or you busy?" He nodded at James' monitor. He had opened one of his spam messages for once and now its embarrassment was filling his screen.

"I'm blocking this site," James explained.

"Whatever, mate. You want this call?"

It was just the two of them in the office. If James took care of the call, Daniel could check his internet history. If he stayed, Daniel would tell the girls in Human Resources what he'd been looking at. He'd get a reputation, at least a few sniggers when he was nearby. He'd get a nickname, "Two Minute Man" or "Needle Dick," whenever he wasn't around.

"You take it," James said. He didn't care about the HR girls.

When Daniel was gone James slid needle tips between some of the letters on his own keyboard, then he went. He left a note saying he was sick in case anybody cared.

He didn't go home, though. He went to the dentist he knew was near the bus stop Angela used.

"Is Angela working?" he asked the receptionist.

"She's up with—Hey, you can't go up there."

James went up the stairs and opened the surgery door to find her laughing at something said before he came in. The dentist was sticking a needle into someone's mouth.

"James!"

The patient grunted with pain and the dentist withdrew quickly with an apology.

"Get out of here!" he yelled at James.

There was no need. James was already running.

"James! Wait!"

He pulled up his hood and held the button on his volume control until The Prodigy raced through his ears at a furiously loud pace.

Angela chased after him, came around in front and held his arms before he could step past her.

"James," her mouth said. He heard only that he should find another place, or race—he could never tell—and then The Prodigy promised to take his brain to another dimension.

Angela tugged the cord rising out of his pocket and the plugs fell from his ears. The music sounded tinny and chaotic, like a sequence processed by computer. Which it was, really.

"I wanted to talk to you," James explained.

"I'm working."

"Sorry."

"You can't just come and see me at work. In my break, maybe, but not when I'm actually working. Why aren't *you* at work?"

Because Daniel's a prick.

James shrugged. "I wanted to talk to you," he said again.

People were looking at them. James noticed and Angela noticed.

"We'll talk tonight, okay?" she said. "At The Buzz?"

The Buzz was the pub where they'd had their second date. James didn't like it much, it was very busy, but it had a good name. Named after Buzz Aldrin probably. James had made a joke about atmosphere he'd had to explain.

"Okay," he said. "I want to tell you something."

She smiled at him but it wasn't at full brightness. He'd upset her, coming to work.

"Yeah. I want to tell you something, too," she said. "I'll see you tonight."

⚲

When James was twelve he was caught burying knitting needles point-up in the park. They stuck from the ground where kids would land if they jumped from the swings. The policeman had been shrewd enough to check the rest of the area and found some of James' pinstripes stuck down across the tops of the monkey bars.

"Why do you do this? Why do you have to find new ways to hurt me, James?"

Because it's the only way to make you feel something. Because sometimes the hurt is good, it helps, and eventually you can get used to the bad part, the pain, if everything's all better afterwards. Just a quick pain, a nip, just a bit of a sting, that's all. Then gone. All better.

That was how James wanted to answer her but he didn't have the right words to say it, not in the right order.

If James didn't make someone feel something it was like they were asleep and couldn't notice him. A point in the right direction and they noticed him, they woke up to everything around them, and the yelp, the leap, the sharp words or jabbing finger, gave James a tingling feeling, like *he* was waking up, like—

"Pins and needles."

James said it aloud, surprised he'd almost forgotten them. He went back inside and retrieved his things, checked himself in the mirror once again, and headed for The Buzz.

Angela stared at him through the silence, waiting for his response. She drank too much wine while he tried to make words.

"I don't understand," James said.

"It's not you. I just don't think I'm ready for a relationship yet."

"I love you."

"James . . ."

"So it was just a physical thing, then."

"I don't think that was really working either."

James stared into his cider. "You don't feel anything?"

"I feel awful. But we can still be friends, can't we?"

He hadn't told her about his father, the rocket man, up in space. He hadn't given her the CD he'd made, the one that his father sent even before CDs were invented and even his mum admitted they didn't have a CD player yet and she usually lied about dad because she didn't like him much any more.

"She didn't try hard enough," James said.

"Who?"

"You didn't try hard enough to feel something, but I can help you. I didn't feel much either after my dad went away, and then my mum went too and it was like I was numb but then I met you and I started to feel things again, properly. Like the tingling feeling you get when you've rested on your arm or foot too long and then the blood comes back. Weird at first, then nice, and then you're whole."

"James—" Angela started, then burst into tears. James reeled back as if jabbed. Angela gathered her handbag, wiped her eyes, and ran out of the pub.

It took James over two hours to get home. He walked the entire way, a slow shuffling step with his eyes on the ground even though the night was clear and there were stars and stars and stars. His hands were in his pockets and in each fist he held a handful of pins which he squeezed sometimes when the pain was too hard.

When he arrived home, the phone was ringing. His hands had been clenched so tight it hurt to open them and he had to shake the drawing pins from his skin before he could answer.

"Hello?"

"James? Is that you?"

"Angela?"

"Did you mean it? What you said in the pub, all those things?"

She sounded drunk.

"Of course I did. My dad—"

"Because I get so lonely too, sometimes, you know? And I did want it to work with us, I did. I'm not usually easy. I did try to feel something. I'm not cold or mean or anything."

"I know you're not."

"I know I just said I'm not easy, and I have been drinking a little bit because I felt so bad after seeing you—"

She felt.

"—but will you come over?"

"Yes."

"Come over and we'll try one more time. Do you understand what I mean? Come and show me that you care for me, I need to feel it."

She made a noise that was part laugh and part sob and to James it was the best sound he had ever heard.

"Did that make sense?" she asked. She sniffed.

"Yes."

"So you'll come over? Just for tonight?"

"Yes."

Angela was wearing a thick dressing gown instead of the trousers and top from earlier, but she was still drinking wine. Her hair was wet and he could hear the bath emptying somewhere else in the house.

"I made you a CD," said James. "It's a copy of the one my dad made. I used to think Rocket Man Elton was his message to me, an explanation and apology, but sometimes I wonder if mum was right and—"

She took the CD and put it down without looking at it. Put it down near the stereo but didn't put it *in* the stereo. "James, let's not talk about that now. Do you mind? Can we just go to bed and lie there, together? I still need to think about things."

He nodded and she took him to her bedroom where the quilt was fresh and clean and turned down. She shrugged off her dressing gown to reveal she was naked beneath, but there was no show in it. She slid into bed and pulled the covers over skin that was still pink and warm from her bath.

"Come on, James."

He stripped down to his shorts and got in beside her.

"Turn the lamp off? The switch is just behind the—Yeah."

With the lamp off, James saw she'd bought some of those glow-in-the-dark stars you could get in toy shops. They were stuck on her ceiling in make-believe constellations, imaginary galaxies, though one cluster sort of resembled—

"Ursa Major," she said, pointing. Her arm was a darker shadow in the gloom.

"I can't believe you have these," James said.

"I bought them after our moment on the hill."

"Oh."

"I was going to take them down after seeing you tonight, depending how things went."

Her hand searched for his penis under the covers. Found it.

"Shall we try again?"

James wondered if she meant try the sex again, or try the relationship again, and realized the latter depended on the former. He tried to focus on the stars. His mother had bought him glow stars many years ago.

"Put your hand here," she said.

He did.

When her breathing became heavy he could smell the wine she had been drinking.

"Now," she said eventually, gasping between kisses, pulling him, urging him inside.

"I need to put something on."

"Don't bother, I'm on the pill."

"I need to."

He got up, opened the bedroom door.

"Where are you going?"

"It's in my coat," he said, glancing back. The sheets had become tangled at Angela's waist, exposing her breasts. The indoor stars cast a green glow over her skin and James could barely control himself. This had to work.

He grabbed what he needed from his coat and put it on. He used a generous amount of glue. He put the CD on while waiting for the glue to dry. A bit of mood music.

"I can't wait long," she called over the intro, and the sounds she made around her words added truth to them.

He went to her with a new eagerness, one he knew he could control, and was pleased to hear her gasp when the light from the hall behind him put his body in silhouette. His shadow stretched out on the floor before him, mighty and slender between his legs and better than anything he'd seen on the internet. His pocket rocket.

The sound Angela made was one like the laughing sob she'd made on the phone.

"James?"

"You'll feel me this time," he said. "The Earth will move."

The capsule tip was heavier than he'd anticipated and the model bobbed with his steps. Angela backed away from him, gathering the sheets around her body.

"What the fuck is that?"

"The Saturn Five," he said. "Completely to scale." He'd caught some skin between the two main halves of the model but the pain was only slight.

He leapt onto the bed as if launched by the first of her screams and he tried to joke with, "Thrusters ready, prepare for launch," as he grabbed at her thrashing body, tried to tell himself no, Houston, there was not a problem.

In the front room, Elton John sang about how lonely it was out in space, but James had found a way to make it all better.

He waited for the chorus.

GATOR MOON

The body looked bigger by moonlight. A six-foot wedge of tarpaulin wrapped top middle and bottom with electrical tape, it sat in the flatbed of the truck looking bulkier than it had before. Maybe because now they had to move it. Had to bury it.

Nate and Boyce stared at it a while. The moon was red in the sky, a bloody eye looking with them and not caring what it saw.

"Alligator moon," Nate said, seeing it.

Boyce stared.

"Yo, Bo."

"It look bigger to you?"

"Some. It's the tarp." He looked up at the sky again. "We got us a blood moon up there."

"Seems right fitting."

"Heads or tails?"

Bo laughed. When Bo laughed he'd suck in two or three breaths and then he'd spit. "You call it."

"Heads," Nate said, but he grabbed the nearest end. He dragged it out as Bo wiped his palms on his pants and sidestepped left and right before taking some of the weight in the middle. Nate fed more of it to him and got both hands under his end of the body.

"Fuckin heavier, too," said Bo. "How far we takin it?"

It was a humid night. Sticky. Nothing new for South Louisiana but nothing you got used to either.

"Just a little ways."

They were parked by a cane field. They trampled their way into it with their burden. It sagged between them for a while and a few metres in Boyce dropped his end. Rather than pick it up, he grabbed the middle and helped drag it.

"Here?"

"Bit more."

They found a gap between rows of crops that was deep enough in the field that no one would see them from the road. The truck, yeah, but not Nate and Bo, not unless they stopped to look for them. They dropped the body and exhaled together with a huff. Boyce put his hands to his back when he straightened and grimaced at the moon. Nate paced a few steps back and forth. "Get the shovel," he said.

"It's your shovel," Bo told him, "you get it," but he did as he was told anyway.

Nate squatted amongst the sugar cane, rested his arms on his thighs, and hung his head. He was tired. He'd been tired for days.

"Why you care so much about this nigger anyways?" said Bo, returning with the shovel on his shoulder and the six-pack in his other hand. The shovel he shrugged off with little care, but the beers he put to the ground carefully. He unhooked one and slung it to Nate, then popped the tab on one for himself.

"Saw his wife in the store," Nate said. "Saw his boy, too."

Bo guzzled beer then nodded as if the answer was good enough. He bunched up the top of his grubby t-shirt and wiped his mouth with it.

Nate put his can of beer down unopened and picked up the shovel. "I'll dig for a spell," he said.

Bo nodded.

Nate's flannel shirt was soon damp, new sweat mingling with old, but once you got a rhythm going it was easy enough. In the distance, a deeper darkness of rain cloud waited in the sky.

"You ever fuck one?"

Nate paused, leaning on the shovel, and wiped his brow.

"Hey, Nate. You ever fucked a nigger?"

"Woman of colour."

Bo snorted a laugh. "Sure. Whatever. Or a man of colour, if you're liking that these days."

Nate tugged the shovel free and got back to tossing dirt.

"I've done Mexican, if that counts," Bo said. He crumpled the can he'd emptied, tossed it, and pulled another from the pack. "Ain't never done no knee-grow though."

Bo thought on that a while as Nate heaved soil to one side. When he stopped to open up the last few buttons of his shirt, Bo handed him a beer and Nate swapped it for the shovel. Bo looked at it for a moment, shrugged, then hopped down into the shallow trench. Nate stepped out.

The beer was warm. He rubbed the can across his brow but there was no moisture to be had. He only wiped his own sweat around.

"You know, niggers in the old days did this with a hog," Bo said, turning the soil. "Buried it in the field and made the moon go red with its blood or some bullshit."

"It's dust in the air makes the moon red."

"Dust. Yeah. So?" He shook some spilled soil from the cuff of his pants. "Still red."

"And they didn't bury the hog, just its blood. To make their crops grow. Make the cane bigger."

"Hog's still dead ain't it?" He looked at Nate. "Would've been easier to bury a hog."

Nate needed to walk around a bit, roll his shoulders, so he stepped over the body to pace a line of cane. But mid-stride, the body bucked beneath him. It flopped up in a violent spasm that tore some of the tarp.

Nate yelled and staggered as it scissored again, stumbling as it writhed on the ground, and fell onto his back beside it. In the shallow grave, Bo pushed the shovel away from himself and flattened up against the opposite bank of soil with a cry of, "Jesus fuck!"

Nate grabbed the handle of the shovel from where he lay and brought it up and over in a long arc overhead. It came down hard and the body was struck motionless for a moment. He got to his feet while it was stunned and hit it again. Finally he stepped the blade of the shovel down, tearing the tarp open and cutting into flesh. A line of blood spurted, dark and hot on Nate's bare chest. He brought the blade down once more, driving it down with both hands, and then everything was still.

"Careful," Bo said, stepping forward, looking into the tarp.

Nate grabbed a full can of beer and threw it at him. It caught him directly in the face and he fell back, clutching his mouth and nose. "Fuck!" he said at Nate, then clutched his face again. The can lay fizzing at his feet, a geyser of beer soaking his legs.

"You ain't dead, are ya? Just clipped you is all."

"All right," Bo said, checking his hand for blood, touching his face, and checking again. "Okay. All right. I get it."

"What did you fucking shoot it with, a cap gun?"

"I said all right, I get it." Bo bent for the beer and put the hissing can to his mouth. He took a few gulps, then broke the tab open to drain it properly.

Nate used the shovel to turn folds of the split tarp. Inside lay the body of an alligator. It looked dead, but it might not have been. He'd opened a gash in the yellow hide of its underbelly and there was a hole above one of the eyes from where Bo had supposedly shot it.

"Tough sonofabitch," Bo said, looking. "Didn't wanna die, did it?"

"Would you?" He rolled the gator to the shallow ditch they'd made. "This is good," he said. "Yeah. This is better. We get its blood now, too. As it dies."

"I think it's dead, Nate."

"Yeah, you said that before."

Bo climbed up out of the ground and Nate rolled the body in. The hole was just about deep enough but it wasn't the right length.

"Help me get this off."

Nate pulled at the tarp and Bo unfolded a knife to cut at the electrical tape. Most of the gator lay in the ground between them. When the tarp was off, Nate began scraping the soil away from beneath its tail so it would fit, shovelling the soil into the gaps around the rest of its body.

Bo said, "I'm only doing this because you asked."

"Yeah, I know. Sorry about your face."

"That's not what I meant. Why are *you* doing it?"

"They deserve some help a little bit. They got a shitty crop and no old man to work it."

"Yeah, you saw them sad at the store, I know. Whatever. Got yourself an attack of good Samaritan, that's fine. That's your business. But you don't believe this shit."

"*They* do."

The soil he dug away he tossed further down the trench.

"You can't know that," said Bo. "Just because they're niggers? Shit, plenty of em got the church now, Nate."

"Yeah, so?"

"I'm just saying, slave days is over, for better or worse, and it don't matter none even if you're right and they *do* believe it. Burying a gator to bump their crops won't work if they don't know you gone done it in the first place."

Nate trod the tail down into the hole he'd opened up and used the shovel to drag loose soil over it. "You don't need to know something's happened to know it's done something."

Bo threw his empty can into the grave. "That don't even make sense."

"You spike a girl's drink, she don't know does she?"

Bo grinned. "Not if you done it right."

"Gets horny, don't she?"

Bo didn't answer. He didn't need to. It didn't matter none to Nate if he understood or not anyways.

"You think it was racial?" Bo said eventually. "Paper said it was. You think it was?"

"Bo, stop bullshitting me, you can't read."

Bo sucked in his laugh a couple of times and spat. "They said he was beaten up good. His lady say anything in the store?"

"She weren't talking much about it."

"Figures. You think they'll sell this place? It's just her and the boy. I'd sell it."

"Would you buy it?"

"Hell no."

"Think anyone else will?"

"That why you've gone all Christian? This ain't you, Nate. Helping thy neighbour. Burying a gator in her crops." Bo clapped his hands on his knees. "That's it, ain't it? You want to bury *your* gator in *her* crops." He laughed, spat, laughed some more.

"Pass me that there beer."

"Sure. No, wait, hang on. I'll shut up."

Nate walked over the fresh ground a couple of times.

"They won't know what you done," Bo said.

"What?"

A wind whispered through the cane. It was a warm wind, not light with the smell of the Gulf but heavy with the smell of swamp.

Bo lifted his hands in surrender against what he saw in his friend's face. "I ain't going on about it no more." He pointed at where a long line of earth rose up between rows of sugarcane. "I just mean they won't know. You can barely see it any."

Nate nodded but trod it down some more. "He wore a coin," he said, "around his ankle. To keep away the *gris gris* or something." He looked at Bo. "You know. Bad luck."

"Didn't work then, did it."

"Weren't wearing it that night. His lady dropped it into the grave with his coffin." Nate smoothed over the turned soil with the flat of the shovel blade. "They believe in *all* of it. Like I said."

"You was at the *funeral*?"

"Joe Witter was. He told me."

"Must be true, then." Bo watched Nate fuss a while longer with the grave. "What coin was it?"

"I dunno. A dime?"

"Hm. And where's the nigger buried?"

Nate looked at him. "Shady Acre. Why?"

Bo took the shovel and raised it to make his point. "A dime's a dime."

Nate shoved him, but he smiled. "You're a real sonofabitch, you know?"

"Daddy always said so."

"You don't want no dead man's dime, Bo. That's bad luck too." He picked up the remaining beers and the tarp.

"Did they put a stone on his grave?"

"Seriously, Bo."

"No, not a headstone, just a regular stone. On the dirt. Something big and heavy. Witters say anything about that?"

"No."

"No, what? No, they didn't, or no Witters didn't say?"

"Why?"

"It's supposed to keep the spirit from wandering."

"They probably did, then. Unless they *want* him to wander. Maybe he's in this here field right now, *wondering* why you're yabbering on when we're done."

They made their way back though the canebrake to the truck. Bo tossed the shovel in back and slammed the tailgate shut. Nate tossed the tarp in with it and gave the beers to Bo who took them up front with him. They both looked at the sky before getting in the cab. The moon was a full dull red and watching them still but then a cloud swept by and the bloody eye closed.

"Gonna be fierce tonight," Nate said, looking at the clouds come in. The wind had picked up suddenly, or maybe they just hadn't felt it in the field. It shook the cane around them.

"Yeah," said Bo. "Reckon you're right."

Nate nodded. "Reckon it's due."

Nate dropped Bo off on his way home. For Nate, home was back off a track most people only took by mistake. Even so, you wouldn't never see the house unless you were looking for it, and even then you'd get nothing but a brief glimpse between cypresses and leaning oaks draped with hanging moss. A line of chain with a stolen stop sign used to block the entrance to the drive up, and that maybe caught the eye of a passing driver once or twice, but Nate was out of the habit of hooking it back in place and now it lay in the dirt. He drove over it, bumped his way into dips and over stumps, and croaked the handbrake outside a one-storey trying real hard to be none.

"Home sweet home."

The white paint had been gray the whole time Nate owned it, had cracked and flaked and blistered off the wood entirely in most places. Lichen greened the guttering and the roof sagged in the middle. The porch leaned forwards and sagged in the middle too, as if in sympathy. One corner rested on cinder blocks. A window by the front door was missing a pane of glass. Nate had replaced it with a flap of cardboard torn from a box. He didn't remember how it got broke in the first place.

He killed the lights, grabbed the crushed can Bo had left on the seat, and stepped out of the truck. He threw the can in the direction of an old oil drum but didn't listen to hear if it went in. The oil drum was ventilated with rust holes and peppered with rifle shot and he used it for burning garbage. Beer cans thrown from the porch lay around it in crushed and folded shapes like tiny corpses.

The yard was knee-high with weeds, the dirt packed down only where he drove in and drove out and where the tread of his boots walked a path to the porch. He used to cut the grass and weeds but the mower busted when he ran over the metal nozzle of a hosepipe. Coils of cut rubber pipe were still out there somewhere, a snake hiding in the grass. The mower was rusting behind the house, which was where he dumped anything small enough to carry that couldn't be burned. There was a watermelon patch back there somewhere underneath it all, too, someone told him once. Big stuff, like the corroding frame of a swing set, he left where they'd always been. The jagged necks of beer bottles hung from cords tied to its horizontal bar, smashed glass beneath testament to Nate's skill with a rifle, pockmarked trees behind testament to the opposite. The swing seat dangled on one chain. It had belonged to whoever lived in the place before and Nate had kept it for his own boy, but the kid didn't get brought for visits no more than three or four times. He'd be near the nigger boy's age now anyways. Probably driving. Probably playing football or baseball and sticking his fingers in girls. Nate wasn't missing nothing. He'd done it all himself and still remembered.

The porch creaked where it dipped under his weight and the screen door whined open. With the *reep-reep-reep* of the frogs, such sounds were his only welcome home. He let the door bang shut behind him and went through to the kitchen. He left the lights off, letting the bulb in the fridge scare away the dark for a moment. The door rattled and tinkled when he opened it because all he had in it was bottled beer. He took one, popped its lid, and guzzled it by fridgelight. He took off his shirt, soaked a corner of it with beer, neverminding how much of it spilled on the floor, and used it to wipe the dried blood from his chest. He threw the shirt aside, shut the fridge, and took down a vest from where it hung on the sink. He pulled it on as he sat at the table.

Nate stared into the dark neck of his beer bottle in the gloom of the kitchen and thought about the man he'd killed two days ago. Lawrence. Lawrence LeBlanc. Nate used to think the name was funny for a nigger. A man of colour. He didn't think it was funny no more. The paper conjectured it was a racial attack but it weren't nothing but an accident. Stupid nigger was walking at night with no light, how was Nate supposed to see him? When he did see him, the man was a sudden face at the windshield, a shape coming at him hard and fast in the dark, and then he rolled away into the night again. His feet kicked up behind him like he'd been yanked on a chain.

Nate tipped the beer to his mouth and grabbed a crumpled pack of smokes from the table. The lighter needed a few tries but he got it to work. He threw it aside with his first puff and settled back into the hard chair. The smoke did little to hide the smell of rank water that sat beneath the house. A pipe had broke, and he'd fixed it, but the damage was already done.

"Why'd you go out so late?" Nate said to his beer.

He'd heard from someone that Lawrence had been looking for gators, and it seemed likely enough. The road was a single track out by the bayou. It was a shitty road with flooded woods either side, trees swollen or sinking dead into the water. It wasn't a place to park your truck in the middle of the night and go walking, especially when the truck's blue, and especially when your skin is as black as the night you walk in. Nate came up fast on the nigger's truck, turning around it with barely a dick's width to spare, and he'd been looking at it as he passed, wondering at it being there, and then—WHAM!—he had a nigger on his windshield.

Nate tapped ash into a saucepan at the centre of the table. It was crusty with some long ago meal and filled now with twisted cigarette butts.

The nigger had twitched something fierce. Nate got out, checked his truck, and the man was casting shadows in the headlights from where he was propped against a twisted cypress. His eyes were open, one rolled white, and his legs were kicking. His head was flat on top, caved in at the crown, and Nate thought he was probably brain damaged. He knew a woman once who had a kid that was retarded and it weren't no fun for anyone. He grabbed the shovel from his truck and used it till the man was still.

"Should have dragged you to the water," Nate said. He was staring at all the dead cigarette ends he measured his life by. He chased another swallow of beer with smoke, exhaling it with, "Should have let the damn gators finish you. Walkin in the middle of the night with a wife and kid home. Hunting for some damn mojo to solve all your problems. *Fuck.*"

He threw his beer and it exploded against the wall in a shower of glass and froth.

Nate sighed. He stubbed his cigarette out on the table and dropped it into the pot. He ran his hands through hair that was longer at the back than on top and greasy with sweat.

"Jesus Christ, who am I even talking to?"

He clasped his hands behind his head and bowed to the table, resting on his elbows. He thought about calling Molly, wondered what she'd say after all this time. He figured a talk with her could go one of two ways. She'd either listen to him and then ask what it was he wanted and he wouldn't know, or she'd remind him that Louisiana was made up of all the shit and sediment that got washed down river and tell him he weren't no different. So he thought about driving back to Bo's and talking to him about it. But Bo weren't the kind you told things to. Shit, he'd sort of tried when he said about seeing them in the store, but that line of talk went nowhere. "You ever fuck a nigger?" Bo had said. Yeah, Nate thought, I gone fucked a whole family of them.

When she'd come into the store that day Nate thought she'd come for him. She held herself straight, and though she was head to toe in black she made it look good. Serene. She wasn't there for him, though, and she ignored everyone else looking at her, too. She went right to the counter where Lemmy was tallying up groceries.

"I'm right sorry for your loss," Nate told her as she moved by. He'd wanted to say more but didn't know how. She gave him a curt nod. The boy, though. The boy gave him something different. That sonofabitch stared right into him. Couldn't be no more than sixteen but he met eyes with Nate and stared his apology dead. Nate couldn't breathe with that look on him, felt like he was drowning in the hot air of the store, and then someone else muttered condolences and the moment broke. It weren't a scene, not really, but it might have been if the boy hadn't quit staring. Nate had felt something underneath it, a mosquito drone buzzing under the quiet, the kind of noise you didn't really hear but knew was there.

Nate stood in line, waiting to pay for his beer, and the widow asked about her tab. Old man Lemmy wrote it down on a piece of paper on account of how quiet the store was. Whatever he wrote, she only gave that curt nod again and said she'd settle it as soon as she was able. Said she might sell the place, and her boy looked around as if daring anyone to say how difficult that would be.

The kitchen lit up with the sudden sweep of headlights outside and was dark again just as quickly as whoever it was turned around. Nate waited to hear them drive away again, but the engine only idled.

"You're too late, Bo," he said, getting up. He'd talked it through in his head enough already. He didn't want to say none of it out loud, not now. He'd have another beer or two with him, if that's what he was offering, but that was all. A man weren't a man unless he had a secret to take to the grave.

§

The truck next to his in the drive was blue. It had turned around to leave but hadn't yet. The engine was grumbling quietly. The tailgate was down and the flatbed was empty but Nate couldn't see anybody through the window of the cab. It wasn't Bo's truck. It was the one Nate had seen on the single track through the bayou. It was the nigger's truck. Lawrence's truck.

Nate pushed the screen door open but went no further than the threshold. "What you want?" He held the door open with one hand, patted at the wall beside him for the porch light. It was quiet out there. Even the frogs had stopped their reeping. There was only the engine of the truck, Lawrence's truck, and nevermind that Lawrence was dead.

But a man hunting gators would take his boy, wouldn't he? Of course he would.

"You're Lawrence's boy, ain't you?" Nate called into the dark. "What you want?"

He found the switch and flipped it but there was no light. He looked up to see if the bulb had been broken but it was still there. Maybe it had been loosened.

Nate's rifle was still racked in the truck.

"Look, I'm real sorry about what happened to your daddy, but you got no right being here."

He was damned if he was going to let some kid spook him. He stepped out onto the porch, let the door slap shut behind him, and heard the boards creak in their familiar way underfoot. Then he heard something else. A shuffle. He looked to his right and saw nothing. But when he looked down he saw the long dark shape of an alligator on his porch.

"That's about right."

He went for his truck as the gator attacked. It didn't do no more than clip him, but it hit his shin hard and he fell down the steps and sprawled on the ground. He pulled up handfuls of grass getting to his feet, managed a few steps more, then tangled his feet in an old coil of hosepipe and fell again. He struck his chin hard and stunned himself some. So he rolled onto his back, ready to kick.

Nate saw the weeds part at his feet, saw the side-winding shape of the alligator, and then the sky flared. The lightning kept itself within the clouds, but the sudden bright pulse and flicker of it revealed the gator in a quick sequence of images. It lunged, its mouth open, and sank its teeth into Nate's thigh. Then the two of them were thrashing in the grass and thundering dark. Nate grabbed its head, trying to stop it from twisting and tearing chunks from his leg. His other leg kicked in uncontrollable spasms. He rolled when the animal rolled, prehistoric muscle tumbling under him and over him, the alligator trying to drown him on dry land because it was instinct, habit, and you couldn't change things that were part of yourself.

They knocked the oil drum over. Nate swept his arm through the trash. He found a burnt broken length of guitar neck and stabbed at the animal's scaled head but the wood split and crumbled in his hand with the first hit. The gator released him, only to strike higher, clamping down on Nate's hands. Nate roared. He kicked at its belly. He pushed up at the tapered end of its snout, pushed down, felt the teeth moving in his palms but pushed anyway, trying to prise the jaws open. It released him only by tearing meat from the bone, wrenching a chunk of flesh away with some of Nate's fingers. It snapped its head back and gulped them down. Nate screamed his agony to the sky.

He was answered by another rumble of thunder, deep and heavy. The gator came in again. Nate pushed at its head with ruined hands. He raked limp fingers over the horny scutes and ridges of its body as it settled its weight onto him again. He tried to find something he could grip enough to turn it away from him. He found a leg that was scrambling as frantically as he was as the animal tried to claw a path up his flesh. He wrenched at this, yelling with the pain it caused him, but a hard twist and suddenly it was off of him. Nate felt something break away in his grip and clutched it in his fist. The thrashing of the animal's heavy tail hit him once, twice, and then it was passing him.

Nate lay panting when he knew he should be rolling, getting up, running. He just couldn't. He held his weak fist up to the light to see a leather cord. Dangling from it was a coin, wet with his blood. He recognized it. It was a dead man's dime. Throwing it aside, he twisted onto his stomach with the same motion and tried to push himself up from the ground. He couldn't. He lay in weeds awash with red from the truck's rear lights, staring at the blood on his hands.

The clouds pulsed and thunder grumbled. It sounded to Nate like the throaty sound of an alligator, and it felt like something coming from himself, something that wouldn't be still until it was broken. Or maybe it was just the engine noise of the truck pulling away as Nate bled into the ground.

He dragged himself across a circle blackened from ancient oil drum fires and red with rust and found within it the bloody coin he had torn from the gator's body. It lay heads up to the sky.

Nate turned himself over to do the same as a full red moon came out from the clouds.

"What are you looking at?"

Its only answer was to slip away again behind black clouds.

"Sorry," Nate said. It didn't matter none, but he said it anyway. "I'm sorry."

Something came at him hard and fast in the dark.

It would never let go.

WHERE THE SALMON RUN

The Kamchatka track is rough, throwing them up, slamming them down, and Sergei turns to Ana to ask, "Did you miss this?" Pines and firs pass the windows in green blurs that fill the truck with a fresh wet scent.

Ana smiles. "Yes."

Kamchatka does not have good roads. Less than two hundred miles of them, in fact, in an area bigger than many American states. Access is easier via helicopter, but Ana is thankful that Sergei collected her in his Land Rover. It's shaking as if it might fall to pieces (and considering how it is held together with wire and rust that's a good possibility) but still she's thankful; the way it pitches her about is a physical reminder that Kamchatka remains a wild place. She tries to tell Sergei some of this but a particularly violent bump has her teeth clacking together so she abandons the sentence and holds on, one hand on the dashboard and the other on her stomach. He won't understand anyway. He's never known anywhere but here.

Thrusting from the eastern edge of Russia, Kamchatka enters the cold Pacific Ocean at an angle as if to shy away from America. To Ana, Kamchatka's shape is its network of rivers and the way the land rises and falls under her feet (or a vehicle's wheels) but the in-flight magazine had reduced it to an outline of block colour. She remembers its more rugged coastlines, its vast lakes, mountains that are snow-topped even in summer. She remembers its frequent rain, the lack of permafrost, the good natural drainage, its separation from the mainland rivers, everything that makes it ideal for the salmon. There are some, even now, who think Kamchatka so perfect for salmon that it must have been designed by the great god Khantai himself. Even the magazine map, which showed nothing of this, outlined Kamchatka in such a way that it *looked* like a salmon, at least to Ana; the south-west of the peninsula is its head, fattening into a plump body spined with mountains and jagged at the edges where the sea has battered it before tapering into a tail forever fastened to Russia no matter how it might long to swim away. Perhaps Ana saw a salmon because she feels like one herself, coming home.

Sergei glances at her and smiles. He hasn't changed much over the years. His hair is still tightly cropped, still a curly mat of brown, but there's some grey in his stubble now and he has a few more crinkles around his eyes when he smiles.

"What?" he asks.

"Is that the same jumper?"

Sergei laughs and Ana laughs with him, knowing his answer. Of course it's the same jumper. Yuliya made it for him and he wears it more than any other. Loops of wool have been tugged out of shape, the sleeves are tatty and frayed, and in one place it has been repaired, sewn together with wool brighter than the rest, but Ana recognizes it because of the way he has to wear the neck rolled, an unintentional design that he insists to Yuliya keeps him warm.

"How is she?"

"Good. Big and round and healthy."

"She's pregnant?"

Sergei laughs, looking away from the road to share it with her. "We have two children now, but no more," he says. "She tells me the extra weight keeps her warm."

As the road bounces them up and down, shakes them left and right, Sergei tells Ana about his children. Irena, two, and little Sergei, nearly catching up. Ana notes the way he says everything through a smile and sees how he's gained those new wrinkles at the corners of his eyes.

She rubs her stomach, thinking of how happiness shapes the body. How it wears lines into the skin gradually, like a river. Scars, on the other hand, are quick to leave their mark.

For a few minutes the only noise is the loud growl of the engine, the *tink!* and *ping!* of loose stones thrown up against the vehicle as it speeds too fast over a poor track.

"He's not with anyone," Sergei says eventually.

"Who?"

She tries to smile. Sergei does a better job.

"He had someone, but not any more. She went back to Petropavlovsk."

"Navy?"

"Engineer."

Ana has no right to ask, but she does. "What was she like?"

Sergei slows the truck a little so he can prolong eye contact. "She wasn't you."

Kamchatka is a wild place of eagles, wolves, and bears, but for Ana it was always about the fish. *Oncorhynchus.* Specifically, salmon. They have a tough life, salmon, especially those from the Malki hatchery. Released as fry, small enough to hold in the palm of your hand, they have to traverse more than a hundred miles of river to reach the sea. From the narrow channel of the Bystraya, through the Central Range, they descend into the largest river in western Kamchatka—the Bolshaya—and into the Sea of Okhotsk, all the while avoiding predators. Before entering the sea they smolt, transforming themselves in order to survive salt water, and once they have adjusted they leave the estuary to grow large and strong in the ocean. Then they repeat the entire dangerous journey in reverse. Guided by magnetic senses and polarized light and smell, they head back to where their journey began, ascending the rivers to spawn and then die. Birth and death. Death and birth. These are Ana's thoughts as Sergei guides them through the boreal greenery of Kamchatka, the wild place that calls to her heart.

"This isn't the way," Ana says.

"Ahhh. You remember."

"Of course."

"We are going to the Kol."

The Kol River, like the Bolshaya, also drains to the west, but there are no hatcheries and far fewer roads, especially alongside the rivers. It's part of the Kol-Kekhta Regional Salmon Reserve, an excellent habitat home to six species of salmon: chinook, sockeye, chum, coho, masu, pink; they all come back to the Kol.

"There are so many fish here," Sergei says, "you can barely see the water."

"They're protected."

Sergei merely glances at her, but she thinks she sees something of his smile again.

The natural challenges salmon have to face makes their lives difficult enough, but there are other factors to consider too in a post-Soviet Russia. Over-fishing is one of them. There are quotas, of course, but there's also a great deal of corruption that allows companies to ignore them. It's so common it even has its own term, *perelov*, salmon shipped off to China, Japan, and South Korea in greater quantities than is legal. And of course, there is all the poaching.

Aleksandr had told her he was a fisherman. He hadn't really lied. Ana had been hiking one of the Bystraya tributaries and found him standing up to his waist in the water, waders pulled high, straps crossing his broad chest. His jumper was sodden as if he had taken a fall, but the woollen cap he wore was still dry. With rubber gloves up to his elbows, he was scooping fish straight from the water with his hands and tossing them to the bank where several others glistened.

"Hungry?" she asked.

It startled him, but after a quick look around he nodded and said, "You?"

And so their first dinner had been on a cold riverbank, fish split across an open fire. Afterwards, Aleks put the salmon's heart and its bones back in the river. "So the salmon will return," he told her. She didn't know if he meant the one they'd eaten or if it was a superstitious ritual to ensure the salmon would run again next year.

"My name is Aleksandr."

"Anastasia."

"Like the princess."

That was how they met.

Sergei slows the Land Rover, looking left and right at foliage close enough to scrape the doors. It reminds Ana of the first time she'd seen him, steering a johnboat through a narrow channel as he helped Aleks gather salmon.

"That day I met you," Ana says, "you asked if Khantai had sent me."

"Yes."

"I thought you meant for Aleksandr, but you meant for the fish."

"I did then. I don't now."

"What does Aleks think?"

Sergei shrugs. "I know he's happy you've come home."

"How do you know that? Did he say anything?"

"No. That's how I know."

Sergei turns from what little road there is and takes them into a narrow space between the trees. "Now we walk."

Of all Kamchatka's exported fish, one hundred and twenty million pounds of it is illegal. It's big business. The eggs are particularly sought after; caviar fetches a high price and is very easy to preserve, to hide, to transport. Ana learnt all about it in her first weeks at the hatchery. A team of inspectors had even showed her a stash of stored eggs they were watching, waiting to capture those who came to pick it up. The confiscated eggs were always burnt.

"A small team can work very fast and take many eggs," one of the inspectors had told her. His name was Kirill Krechetov. He helped protect the interests of places like Malki hatchery. "Five tonnes?" he estimated. "Yes, five tonnes in one season I think. With fifteen or so crews working during any one season, that makes . . . seventy-five tonnes? I think so. My math is not so good." He smiled, flirting with her, the naïve girl from the hatchery, but Ana was more interested in what he was saying. In less than a year she'd be working for the Wild Fishes and Biodiversity Foundation.

"What happens to the fish?" she'd asked.

Kirill made a tossing gesture. "Tonnes of fish, wasted."

Ana nodded, imagining the rivers empty. She saw how it would happen, fewer and fewer fish returning each year to spawn.

Kirill put an arm around her. "You come and work with me," he said. "We will make a great team and wipe out poaching forever!" When he released her he shook his head and said, "But we are not well paid. The poachers? They earn ten times as much as they would fishing legally." He shrugged. "We are outnumbered."

They didn't earn *that* much, Ana had thought, thinking of Aleks. The second time she'd met him he'd been with Sergei, Moisey, and Pyotr. They'd been fishing quite openly, though it was a rather secluded spot. Sergei was towing a net across the river then guiding it back downstream, directed by Aleksandr, herding the salmon with Moisey and Pyotr. They'd worked quickly, grabbing fish as they flopped and leapt, tossing them by their tails into another boat which would take them to a waiting truck. Ana watched them take a thousand pounds or so of fish in half an hour. Only when she met the wives, Yuliya, Nadya, Rebekka, did she learn the men were poachers. The wives had assumed Ana already knew, and maybe she had. It made little difference. She was already in love with Aleks. Had fallen in love with him over that first riverside supper.

My name is Aleksandr.

Anastasia.

Like the princess.

She even helped the men gather their catch that first time. *Oncorhynchus tshawytscha*, chinook, the king salmon. Fat, with purple dorsal markings from their time in the sea. To Ana these had looked like deep bruises, a testament to their struggle.

Jumping down from one boat and moving to the next, Sergei asked, "Is this her?" and Aleksandr nodded. Ana was pleased he'd spoken of her.

Sergei had smiled then. "Did Khantai send you?"

"Maybe," she said, smiling at Aleksandr.

Aleksandr looked at her and smiled briefly. Then the fish wriggling in his hands managed to twist away from him, a flash of silver in the air, folding one way and then the other before escaping into the netted river. He would get it again, or someone else would.

Across the Pacific, American salmon runs had been depleted not only by over-fishing but because of development, logging affecting drainage patterns, new dams and other constructions reducing or polluting the habitat. This is something they worry about less in Kamchatka, but there are still plans for precious pipelines and new mines, both of which bring their own dangers; not just potential spills and poisonings but roads. More roads make the rivers more accessible to everyone, including poachers.

Not that a lack of road is deterring Sergei right now; Ana watches his machete flash left and right as he cuts down shelomainik, nettles, tall grasses, ferns. She has to watch her step—the terrain is sometimes rocky, sometimes wet—but with Sergei cutting the path it's easy to keep up, even with her pack. She can tell they're nearing the river because of the white-flowered meadowsweet, and occasionally she thinks she hears the engine of a johnboat.

"It's beautiful here," she says. "I've missed this."

"Yes," Sergei says between strikes of the blade. As he stamps down a tangle of foliage he says, "Yuliya has a proverb for you."

Ana smiles. "Of course she does."

"I was supposed to tell you as soon as I picked you up, but here is better."

Ana can see glimpses of river ahead. Sergei quickens his pace, waiting until they have emerged from the forest before delivering Yuliya's message.

"*V gostyakh khorosho, a doma luchshe,*" he says.

Visiting is good, but home is better.

They're standing at one of the Kol's tributaries. The water is in no hurry except where it bubbles and froths around some rocks. It's muddy, and the sky's grey, but still it's beautiful. "There's no place like home," Ana agrees. She puts her hands to her stomach. She isn't showing but that doesn't matter; she can't see any salmon in the river either but she knows they're there.

Sergei points to where the river splits around an angle of forested island. "There." He starts away but glances back at her and sees her hands. The way she cradles herself.

Ana strokes circles over her stomach. "Do you think it was Khantai this time?"

Sergei goes back to her and gathers her in for a careful hug, awkward around her backpack. "It is always Khantai," he says. "How—"

"Not long."

It's easier than explaining.

Sergei holds her at arm's length and looks at her stomach. She caresses it again, this time self-conscious.

"Congratulations?"

Ana nods, then shrugs.

"And the American man?"

She shrugs again. "Still in America."

Sergei holds her face. His hands are rough but his touch is gentle. "I'm sure Yuliya will have another proverb for you," he says. It's his way of apologizing for having nothing himself. Then he takes his hands away and points down river. "Ready?"

"I think so."

She fidgets her pack into a more comfortable position and follows Sergei with all that she carries.

Ana can hear singing. It's an old song, calling the fish and dedicating them to Khantai. She smiles.

"They're singing for you," Sergei says.

Ana wonders how the men will greet her. "This is a reserve," she says. "The fish here are protected." Not that she's here on any official business.

"People still poach."

She wonders how Khantai would feel about that, then answers her own question. "It's all connected," she says quietly.

Sergei glances at her but doesn't ask.

Tom had been the one to explain the connections. The American man. He worked for the Wild Salmon Center, and the WSC was partnered with Ana's foundation. He'd come to Kamchatka as part of an exchange project in support of the Kol-Kehta Regional Experimental Salmon Reserve. Partly it was to warn them of what could happen if Russia followed America's example, and partly it was to learn from them, to benefit from some of the same precautions the WFBF were putting in place. They were especially interested in the ambitious project that would see five more areas added to the reserve—the Kolpakova, Krutogorova, and Utkholok area, plus the Opala and Zhupanova rivers. "It could work," Tom had said. His Russian was clumsy, but the attempt was admirable. He was the only one of the Americans who could speak any at all without a translator.

"English is okay," Ana told him. "My mother taught me. She'd always wanted to see your country."

Tom smiled, his gratitude obvious. "You'd have the world's biggest salmon reserve and maybe we could do something like it back home." He smiled again. "Anything you can do, we can do better."

His enthusiasm had been exciting, his passion inspiring. At the time, Ana had been balancing a relationship with Aleks with her job protecting the fish. Tom made it clear how important her job actually was. "It's all connected," he'd said.

Their team had been out on the Ozernaya River, checking the numbers of sockeye. Ana thought it was an ugly fish with its long head and hooked nose. The way its upper jaw overhangs the lower gives it a permanent expression of stupidity, an imbecilic menace. They were spawning, scales mottled red as if they'd swum through an ocean of blood to get this far, scouring themselves against the current as if trying to wash it off in cleaner water.

"You mean the rivers?" Ana asked.

"Well, yeah, *they're* connected. I do mean that. Rivers join rivers, and there's the aquifer underneath it all, but I mean it's *all* connected. An entire ecosystem. Look." He scooped a fallen leaf from the water they stood in. "See? Leaves fall and provide food." He held it to her.

Hungry?

"Nutrients," he said. "The insects feed, and the fish feed." He pointed to a leaning tree and said, "Entire trees fall, and they provide shelter for the fish. And the fish, they swim upstream. They mate," he gave her a thumbs up while waggling his eyebrows and Ana laughed. "Then they die." He turned his thumbs down and exaggerated a sad face. "But their bodies decay and release nitrogen and whatever phosphorus they've picked up at sea and they replenish the nutrients in the water. They stop it all simply washing away downstream forever because *they come back and—*"

Ana held up her hand to stop him; she knew all this. But Tom asked, "Too fast?"

"A little." But she liked being reminded, and hearing her own previous passions expressed back to her in another language made it all clearer somehow.

"They come back," Tom said. "And life comes with them."

"And if we lose the salmon . . ."

"You lose everything else. Yeah. That's pretty much it." He sighed and added, "All gone," in Russian, dropping the leaf he'd been toying with into the river.

Ana watched the current carry it away.

"Well, we better pray to Khantai then," she said, turning her attention from the river to smile.

Tom frowned. Ana didn't know if all Americans were so expressive or just Tom. Everything he felt was on his face to see. "Khantai?"

She nodded. "A river god."

Tom pretended to look for Khantai in the water moving around them. He thought it some quaint superstition—that was clear on his face too—but he wanted to humour her because he liked her and he wanted Ana to like him as well. She thought maybe she did.

Did Khantai send you?

"Before the others came, before immigrants made their home here, the people of Kamchatka had great respect for the salmon. The Itelmen especially. They made the fish a part of their culture, their religion. You know the Itelmen?"

Tom shook his head no.

"The first men, the early men. And women. They worshipped Khantai, who was half fish, half human, and they gave him thanks for the salmon. Made offerings of their catches to feed their god."

It was everything Aleksandr had told her that first night by the river. When he'd cooked for her the fish others had worshipped. When they'd thought themselves the only people in the whole world.

"Do they still believe?" Tom asked.

Ana thought of Aleks. After their first meal he had placed a salmon heart with its bones back in the river. It meant the fish would return. "Some do," she said to Tom.

The river flowed around them. Ana felt fish swimming between her legs, hurrying towards breeding and dying.

"So they still exist? The Itelmen?"

They did. Mostly in Kovran on the west coast, their wooden idols worshipped only during special festivals now.

"A lot has changed since the Soviet era," Ana explained.

"I bet."

"Stalin's enemies of the state, Gorbachev's *perestroika*, privatization; none of it left much for the people." She looked at him and waved her own rant away. "Sorry."

Tom shrugged. "No wonder they become poachers."

Again, Ana thought of Aleksandr.

"*Altynnogo vora veshayut, a poltinnovo chestvuyut,*" she said.

Tom waited for her to explain.

"*Altynnogo vora veshayut, a poltinnovo chestvuyut,*" she said again. One hangs the thief who stole three kopecks but honours the one who stole fifty. She didn't tell him this, though. She just said, "It's all connected."

"Come on, we're nearly there," Sergei says.

Ana picks up her pace. "Doesn't it worry you? Poaching in protected waters?"

Sergei smiles. "It worries me in a different way now."

"Because of Yuliya. Because of your children."

"Yes. But not the way you think." He stops for a moment and steps aside to point. "Look."

Ana had expected a simple camp, a hastily constructed lean-to with a johnboat dragged close to the trees so it couldn't be seen from the air. She'd expected Moisey and Pyotr, opening up salmon stomachs at this time of year and scraping them empty of eggs, bright orange roe glistening like tiny wet gems. But that is not what she sees.

There are several shelters—semi-permanent constructions—and an array of tents. There's a johnboat, blatant beside the riverbank, and a tank-tracked vehicle as well. The men gathered around it are wearing camouflage trousers and thick jackets with furred hats. They're still singing, not only for the pleasure of the sound but for the rhythm to help them work, unloading equipment, putting up more shelters.

"What's going on?"

Instead of answering her, Sergei takes up the song, startling her. His voice is loud and deep and he marches to the rhythm, glancing back at her and beckoning her to hurry. "It's dinner time."

Ana inhales the aroma of seared fish and the warm curling smell of wood smoke.

One of the men stands back from whatever task he had been busy with and Ana knows immediately from the way he holds himself tall and strong that it's Aleks. She takes another deep breath, this time for courage, and follows Sergei to the camp.

Aleksandr has changed less than Sergei. Physically, anyway. His hair is still dark, his body straight, thick with layers of flannel and wool. He doesn't smile at her, but that's not unlike him either.

"Anastasia," he says.

Like the princess.

Ana smiles. Her hands are on her stomach but in the pockets of her jacket.

"She returns," Aleks adds. He looks like he might say something else, perhaps "to me," perhaps "at last," perhaps even both, but he closes his mouth on it and offers her a plate instead. "Hungry?" If he remembers the significance of the question it doesn't show.

Ana takes the plate. "Thank you."

Some of the other men look at her with interest. She's a new face, that's all.

"Where's Moisey?" she asks. "And Pyotr?"

"They don't work with us anymore."

"What's going on?" She's looking around at the camp, the tank-tracked vehicle, the rusted oil drums set up as tables. On the tops of these and leaning against them are rifles.

Aleksandr sees what she sees. "Poaching has become more dangerous," he explains, cutting a potato with the side of his fork and bringing it to his mouth.

"You have rifles."

"We're authorized to use them. But we don't, if we can help it."

"Authorized?"

Aleksandr exchanges a glance with Sergei. "You haven't told her."

Sergei smiles and shrugs. "I thought you could."

"Told me what?"

Sergei spears fish and potato but before he eats it he laughs, and because Aleksandr is still silent he says, "*Grom ne gryanet, muzhik ne perekrestitsya.*"

A man won't cross himself until thunder strikes.

"We don't poach any more," Aleksandr says. He speaks to his plate, pushing potato around in the juices of his fish.

Ana smiles. She nods and puts a forkful of hot food into her mouth. It's delicious.

"Good," she says. "This is good."

As she eats she wonders about the thunder that has changed his mind and hopes that it was her.

As Ana is the only woman in the group she's given a shelter to herself. It's unnecessary but she appreciates it; it means she has a surprisingly large sagging canvas bed that sits off the ground on an iron frame. Roped timbers and boughs that still have their bark form the walls, each draped with dark tarpaulin and natural foliage. One "wall" is only wire, open to the camp, but she's able to hang blankets on it for privacy.

She lies fully clothed in her sleeping bag under several other blankets, her arms wrapped around her stomach, shivering. It will take her a while to adapt again to Russia's weather. She thinks of the little one she knows is inside her. Adapting. Russia will make her strong. This time it will be different. It doesn't matter what the doctors said, the doctors are wrong. That whole country had been wrong. None of it would have ever happened if she'd stayed in Russia. She thinks of how many times she's woken with an ache in her breasts, her nightshirt wet with the smell of her own milk, and tries *not* to think of such things.

The roof of her shelter is mostly branches but a sheet of corrugated iron rests directly above her bed. Rust has eaten holes into the metal and she catches glimpses of stars when the dark clouds shift. They're clear and bright. She thinks of how they had looked reflected in Kurilskoye Lake. Aleks had taken her all that way to show her the bears.

"I've seen a bear," she'd told him, gently mocking his poor excuse to get her away but appreciating the effort. She'd always wanted to see the lake. She may have even said as much, which was all the more reason to appreciate his effort.

"You've seen a bear," Aleks repeated.

"Yes."

"I'm going to show you lots of bears."

And he had. Brown bears were usually solitary animals but at Kurilskoye Lake Ana had seen groups of them clawing fish from the water.

"The salmon brings them together," Aleksandr said. She'd thought it deliberately romantic but then he handed her some flares, saying, "In case they get too close." She still has them somewhere, like treasured love letters.

"Have you really come back?"

Ana raises herself onto her elbows and looks at Aleks, backlit in the doorway by the dying embers of the fire outside. He's little more than a silhouette, speaking as if in a dream, but if he's sleepwalking then he's doing it fully dressed, boots on, hat pulled down against the cold.

"I don't know," Ana says.

Aleksandr steps into the shelter. He comes up to her bed and puts a hand to her hair. She'd let it grow while in America but before returning she'd cut it back to the length Aleks remembers.

"It feels like you have," Aleks says.

Ana turns back the blankets. "Hungry?"

Aleks pulls at the zipper of her sleeping bag for his answer and joins her.

"Are you all right?" Aleks asks afterwards. There's enough light from the moon and stars that Ana can see the way his skin glistens with sweat. He can probably still taste the salt of hers on his lips. It had felt more like coming home than anything else, but . . .

"Ana?"

"I don't know." She doesn't know anything any more. "I'm pregnant," she says.

Aleksandr laughs. He does it as quietly as they'd made love. "You can't know that already," he says, smiling. He strokes her hair and meets her eyes and she sees in his face more than she had ever seen before, things that make her wish she'd never left. Then she sees his realization. His hurt. His anger. He rolls away from her, as much as he is able.

"Aleks—"

"We'll sleep," he says. "Talk in the morning."

Ana doubts both, but with Aleks beside her the first comes easily.

She wakes from a bad dream. She immediately knows where she is, and she knows Aleksandr is gone before the grey morning light can show her, but the residue of her nightmare is still strong with her so she tosses the blankets aside, yanks the sleeping bag open without fumbling for the zip, and checks between her legs. In her dream she had birthed a warm gush of ruby-red eggs, thousands and thousands of them. The tide of roe had flooded her sleeping bag until it was full and somehow she had drowned in it. Awake, she fears the dream was an interpretation of a miscarriage.

Her hands are wet at her thighs, and sticky, but not with blood, and not with eggs. Some of Aleks is still with her. Inside her, swimming to a place they can never reach.

Ana's relief is only momentary: she remembers more of the dream. This time she pulls at the jumper she'd put on in the sleepy hours. She tugs it up to her chest, exposing her belly, but sees nothing of the scales she'd dreamt were there. No gleaming silver. No red flush. Only the scar.

Physically it's healing well; a long river of pink puckering her skin, tiny dots either side where the stitches had been. But even as it heals she feels her baby girl growing behind it. The baby they had taken from her, cut from a womb she couldn't push her from. They had taken her body, her tiny body (small enough to fit in the palm of your hand) but Ana didn't need expensive American scans to know that her little girl is still there, and she doesn't need anyone to believe her either. "They come back," she'd told Tom, reminding him of his own words, but when he'd said it he'd only meant the fish. "*She's* come back."

Ana strokes her scar. "We're home now," she tells her stomach. "The mother country."

She settles back into bed thinking of her dream and thinking of Khantai. He'd spoken to her, but she doesn't understand his message.

As she dresses, Ana is struck by the quiet. The early morning is almost silent. She hears men moving around, occasionally exchanging a word or two, but mostly all she hears is the river.

Outside, some of the men are dismantling the tents and setting equipment beside the boat and tank-tracked vehicle. One man is making breakfast, which smells like burnt porridge. Another, dressed only in his long-legged underwear, exercises with a dumbbell made of engine parts set at either end of a metal bar. He smiles good morning and strikes a foolish pose and Ana smiles, though she finds it difficult.

Aleks is standing at one of the rusted drums. He barely looks at her when she approaches but he says, "Good morning, Anastasia." He's dismantling his rifle, setting the pieces on the corroded barrel top.

"He seems to be struggling," Ana says, nodding to the man with his engine weights.

Aleks shrugs. "He's managing."

Ana takes a deep breath of crisp morning air, rich with the aroma of hot oats and trees and soil, and underneath it all . . . the river. "Smells good."

"Porridge. Unless you want fish heads?"

"Why would I want—"

But she remembers. During a conversation about the Itelmen he'd told her how they fermented fish heads in a barrel. The heads were rich in vitamins and were used to clear out the stomach. Ana can't tell if he's thinking of her health, or the baby that will eventually make her stomach swell.

"You sound like him now," Aleks says.

"Who?"

"You have an accent. A different accent. And sometimes you use English words." He glances at her, daring her to ask when. She remembers when.

"I'm the same woman."

Aleks says nothing. The only expression on his face is one of concentration as he cleans his rifle, pushing a dirty rag into the barrel.

"I'm still Ana."

"So you'll leave again?"

Ana returns his own stoic expression but he doesn't see, only hears her silence.

"Will he come back for you?"

"Will you care? Will you do anything this time?"

Aleks busies himself reassembling his rifle.

"Aleks, please. Do you need to do that?"

He levers the bolt action back and tests the firing mechanism. "Yes." He looks at her. "We treat poachers differently now."

Among the rest of the group, Aleksandr is all business. He explains to Ana how the Bolshaya has become even easier to get to since the new pipeline. The pipeline takes gas to Petropavlovsk and crosses many rivers, even the protected Kol. The roads that came with it means the rivers are easily plundered. In recent years, resources had been increased to put a stop to poaching but it only means the poachers have become more desperate.

"Some of them even come here, to protected land. Not poor men, doing what they need to, but organized criminals. And so . . ." Aleksandr hefts the rifle slung over his shoulder to make his point.

We treat poachers differently now.

Ana looks away, only to see the tracked vehicle belch fumes as it grumbles into life, engine warming as the men prepare to move out.

"It gets stuck," Sergei tells her, leaning close and speaking quietly. "We won't go with that group."

The team is dividing. Ana is to go with Aleks and Sergei and two others. She had been introduced to them as an employee of the American WSC rather than the Russian WFBF and she had nodded, though she works for neither organization now. She has returned for more personal reasons.

Ana says, "This cannot pay as much."

Aleksandr glances up from loading the johnboat, grunts as he hefts another canvas bag. "*Ne v dengah schastye.*"

She had said the same thing to him many times, trying to persuade him to stop poaching. Money is not the key to happiness. "So what is?"

He stops stowing the equipment and looks upriver. Downriver. Finally he looks at her. "I don't know anymore," he says. "Do you?"

Ana thinks she does but says nothing. She bends to grab one of the crates but Sergei takes it from her before she can lift it. He casts a look at her stomach and she puts a hand over it, feeling only the coolness of her waterproof jacket and the soft padding of layered clothing beneath. She doesn't need to feel anything else.

"What was it like?" Sergei asks. "You know, over in the great United States?" He probably only means to give her something to do, but she wishes he hadn't brought it up. Aleksandr, though, acts like he hasn't heard. He takes the offered boxes and bags, puts them down, takes more, all without looking at her.

"It was very different," she says.

"Better?"

Instead of answering with a yes or no, Ana explains that most of her work had involved touring hatcheries to ensure they were limiting their numbers. The salmon produced in hatcheries were competing with the wild salmon and the wild salmon were losing out to the more predatory and aggressive hatchery-reared fish.

"There are lots of fish, but not the right kind."

"Poachers?" Sergei asks.

"Some. Not like here."

"Dull," says Sergei.

He's joking, but it's true. "Yes," she says. Some of the salmon in her district had even been landlocked, stuck in lakes and reservoirs. They were safe, secure, but they were prisoners.

Aleks starts the boat. "Come on," he says, "let's go."

"Where are we going?" Ana asks.

Sergei points. "Upriver."

"Like the salmon."

Aleks gives her a single nod, "Yes," and then they're moving.

Ana looks behind and watches their wake, thinking of how wide it spreads from a single point. She wonders how it affects the fish.

Many people romanticize the salmon's journey, their noble efforts against the current, their determination in the face of adversity, but to Ana their struggle is tragic. They face so many challenges both in leaving the place of their birth and in returning to it, particularly *these* salmon, Pacific salmon, which survive several perils only to breed once and then die. It's difficult to appreciate the miracle of birth, Ana thinks, considering the cruel swift finality of death that follows. She thinks of her own little one, the way she had slipped from her body all bloody and silent and tiny, unable to even breathe, drowning in the air. Put her back, she had told them. She isn't ready. But they had taken her anyway.

"Ana?"

She looks away from the river to see Sergei, frowning. She smiles, or tries to, then turns from him before he can ask anything more.

There are two other men with them in the boat and they stand talking, sharing a cigarette. They had been introduced to her only by surname, Osipov and Zaporotsky, and she can no longer remember which is which. Both have the same lean build and angular faces. Had she not known their surnames she would suppose them brothers.

One of them notices her looking and asks, "Why are you here?"

Because it will be different this time, Ana thinks.

The other soldier laughs and slaps his friend across the head. "This is Yuri Osipov and he has no manners."

"We don't see many women on the river, even from the foundation," Osipov explains.

Zaporotsky apologizes. "We're glad you're here."

Ana looks at Aleksandr. He's focusing on the river, navigating their slow course with more concentration than is necessary.

"Ana once caught a notorious poacher single-handed," Sergei says. He puts his hand on her shoulder and winks at her. "Nobody else had ever managed it."

"What happened?" Osipov asks, reaching for his turn with the cigarette.

Ana says, "I let him go," then, "He got away."

"Well, which is it?"

"Enough talk," Aleks says.

For a few moments the thrum of the outboard is the only sound, but Ana answers anyway. "I don't know," she says to Osipov. "Perhaps both."

Sergei inhales from his cigarette. "Doesn't matter now," he says, and uses the release of his smoke to signal an end to that conversation. "These are military men," he explains to Ana. One of them, Osipov, salutes her. "They are more interested in poachers than fish."

Ana nods.

"Did you know," Sergei says to the soldiers, "salmon change their colour? They start silver in the freshwater, but when circumstances force them to, they adapt."

Ana can tell that Aleks is listening, though he only stares ahead. She thinks Sergei's analogy is clumsy but the soldiers won't know.

"They adapt?"

"They have to. They lose the silver, become darker. Stronger, too."

Aleks nods. Ana doubts anyone else notices.

"And when they are ready to spawn, they come home," Sergei finishes. Ana flushes with embarrassment, or maybe shame, but Sergei only nods. "And they become a deep red colour," he adds, smiling.

"A proper Russian fish," says Osipov.

"A Soviet fish," Aleks says. "A thing of the past."

"They are not gone yet," says Sergei. He points to where a short run of rapids feeds into the river, water frothing over rocks, and all but Aleks turn to see salmon leaping, throwing themselves without mercy against the current. Their bodies arc and flap and twist, bright and beautiful, but they make little progress. Another evolutionary test.

"We need to protect them," Sergei says, "right, *comrade*?"

The soldiers laugh and Ana smiles. She had missed Sergei.

"Aleksandr?" Sergei says.

Aleks says, "Yes," but it sounds like a question.

Zaporotsky crushes his cigarette out against the side of the boat and sees something in the water. "Look."

A salmon passes them downriver. Floating. It's been folded open, though plenty of its meat remains. Another passes them, and another, and Aleks slows the boat to look himself. There are so many. Silver ghosts, turning, vanishing, passing beneath them. One bumps against the boat and flattens into a cubist perspective that shows Ana both sides of the fish at once. It stares at her for a moment with two dead eyes before rolling over to show its open vacant belly and sinking, gone before the water can close the wound.

Aleks kills the engine and steers the boat to the riverbank. It's suddenly very quiet.

"Ana? Are you all right?"

She wants to clutch her stomach but she's too afraid of what she might not feel.

"I'll be fine," she says, and wonders if it will ever be true.

The poachers are easy to find. There's only two of them, but Aleks is cautious. He signals for Osipov and Zaporotsky to take flanking positions and as they circle the camp, fast and quiet, he whispers for Ana to, "Wait."

Ana nods. She has no authority here, and no rifle even had she wanted one. She does have a baby. She does. That's all the reason she needs to wait.

Sergei puts a cigarette in his mouth but does not light it.

The two men are manoeuvring a couple of plastic drums, rolling them in tight upright circles towards a tree that leans out over the river almost horizontally, an easy marker to find later. The site has been cleared, meadowsweet cut and trampled flat where tents might have been, though now only two large backpacks and a prepared campfire occupy the space. Ana can see no weapons but that doesn't mean the men aren't armed. Both are large and muscular. One has short brown hair and a dark beard that does not grow well. The other wears a furred hat with flaps over his ears. It looks new. There is no sign of a boat. Maybe it's hidden further upriver.

Aleks nods at Sergei and stands from cover. "My name is Aleksandr Khalilov," he announces, approaching. Sergei follows.

The poachers stop and look up, clearly startled. They look at Aleks, then at Sergei, and back to Aleks. Aleks has his rifle in front of him but only holds it with one hand against his body to stop it swinging on its strap. With the other he gestures, "This is Sergei Sakharovskaya."

Sergei takes the cigarette from his mouth and says hello as Aleksandr explains their roles as officials. Sergei pats his pockets for a lighter. His rifle is across his back.

The other two men say nothing. The man with the hat is still bent over one of the barrels to move it. His companion is standing straight by his, hands at his sides.

"Who are you?" Aleks asks. "What are you doing here?"

Again, neither of the men say anything, though this time they exchange a glance. The man with the barrel begins to straighten up.

Sergei lights his cigarette and exhales smoke around it in his mouth. Ana realizes this is a signal they've used before because Osipov and Zaporotsky step out from the trees. They hold their rifles ready but pointed low.

Aleks identifies them as part of his team. "Now you know who we are. Who are you? What are you doing here?"

The man with the poor beard says, "We're camping." He points at the backpacks but none of the men look.

"Camping," says Aleks.

The other man stands away from the barrel he'd been moving and looks back and forth between his companion and Aleks.

Aleks turns his attention to him. "What's in the barrel?"

The man says nothing.

Aleks points with the hand that had held his rifle still and it sways out from his body. Ana knows that none of his gestures are without purpose; the weapon is noted by both men. "What's in the barrel?"

"We are camping," the bearded man says again. The beard shades his chin so that the rest of his narrow face seems to hang over it. He looks like a sockeye salmon.

"Not fishing?" Sergei says.

The man shakes his head. "There's a fine, isn't there?" He looks at his friend then says to Sergei, "Do you want us to pay a fine?"

Sergei looks at Aleks. It's a bribe, Ana realizes. She wonders how often they accept it.

"Why doesn't he speak?" Aleks asks. He's still looking at the man bent over his plastic barrel.

"He doesn't understand. He's not from here. He's a . . . tourist."

The ban against tourism in Kamchatka had been relaxed a little but not much. Kamchatka isn't exactly a holiday destination. The man with the hat seems to understand the word tourist, though. He tries to repeat it but his Russian is clumsy. "*Turistichesky.*"

This time when Aleks points to the barrel he uses his rifle to do it, holding the weapon with both hands. "Open it."

The man looks to his friend. The bearded poacher shakes his head.

Aleks raises his weapon so that it points at the man. "Open it."

The man raises his hands instead and backs away as Aleks takes quick strides towards the barrel. But he ignores the barrel and pursues the retreating man instead.

"*Turistichesky!*" the man says, and, "*Turistichesky! Turistichesky!*" He stumbles against one of the packs and puts his hands down suddenly to steady himself. The men yell at him to put them up again. Zaporotsky has his rifle at eye-level to aim. The man raises his hands as commanded but loses his balance and falls.

His companion uses the distraction to draw a blade from his belt.

"Knife!" Ana cries, giving up her hiding place. "Knife!"

The poacher holds his weapon pointing at Sergei. A quick thrust and it will be in his stomach, slicing him open. Sergei tells the man to drop it. The man hesitates for a moment but then does as he is told and as quick as that it's over. Sergei offers him a cigarette. The man reaches for it with a hand that trembles.

Ana exhales. It's loud. She holds her stomach with both hands, thinking of knives.

"Don't look at her," Aleks says. He still has his gun on the kneeling man.

"*Turis—*"

"Don't look at her!"

Aleks shakes the strap of his rifle from his shoulder and reverses the weapon to strike the man. The blow knocks the man's head back and puts him on his behind. It splits his eyebrow and a line of blood runs from somewhere under his hat. He tries to wipe it away or hold himself but before he can reach Aleks strikes him again. Ana stifles a cry with both hands. The man falls back, bloody now at the nose and mouth.

"Aleks!"

Sergei catches Ana's arm before she can get any closer. He holds her back but says nothing.

Aleks lowers his rifle and paces a circle back and forth around the man. He strikes out once more when the man sits up but this time only uses the flat of his hand to knock his hat away.

"I'll open it," says the bearded man. "Please, I'll open it."

Osipov and Zaporotsky go to the barrel. Aleks nods and they prise away the lid.

"It's just eggs," the bearded poacher tells them.

One of the soldiers confirms it, tilting the barrel so Aleks can see.

"Take it to the fire," he says.

When the fire's lit Aleks is the first to scoop a double handful of bright orange roe into the flames. The man on his knees groans, touching the wound at his brow. Aleks looks at Ana as he throws in the next wet handful, rubbing his hands over the flames, wiping eggs from his palms and fingers to sizzle and spit in the fire while Ana tries not to cry.

While Aleks and the others busy themselves with the poachers, Ana makes her way to the river. She tries not to think of the fire still burning behind her. There had been little warmth there.

"Others will come," Aleks had said, looking at how the smoke from the fire sent a dark river skyward. An easy signal to follow. "They'll come back for what they think is still here."

Ana wonders if he'll be ready when they do and then she wades into the river.

The cold forces her to take quick shallow breaths but she removes her jacket, letting it float open downriver. Next come the layers of wool before they can become too difficult. She walks until the press of the river is against her breasts, river parting around her body but trying to take her with it. Then, immersed in the river's icy grip, she raises her shirt and exposes her stomach to the current.

Within her, something stirs.

Ana stands with her legs apart for balance, snatching sharp gasps against the cold. Her stomach is numb but there's enough feeling in her fingers to find the ridge of her scar.

It leaps beneath her hands. It curls and it opens, flesh parting in an easy unseaming of skin she barely feels as the weight of all she's carried shifts into the running river. An unravelling, followed by a sudden tautness in whatever imagined cord binds it to her, a last sharp tug as it resists its freedom. Then it's gone, swept away with the current.

Empty, Ana holds herself open to the promise of the river and lets it fill her, lets it swell inside to take its own shape.

And from somewhere far away she hears Khantai, calling.

INDIAN GIVER

Every man carries his share of ghosts, but there are those who listen to them more than others. That was Grady's opinion, anyways. And most of those listenin' didn't much like what they heard; that was his opinion, too. So he wasn't surprised to see Tom stumblin' across the darkening yard towards him. If he was surprised at all it was only that it had taken the man so long.

The taming of the wild west was something Grady never saw—he was a proper lieutenant, not a glorified book-keep or ledger-maker (though there were plenty of those)—but even so, all he saw of the west was tired and worn down. Land *and* people. Native people, mostly, but Tom carried the same look himself right now. He had something in his hand that was supposed to be Tennessee whiskey but probably wasn't. It would taste right, though. And they'd drink it down just fine. A tale of woe was best punctuated with whiskey.

Seeing Tom made him think of that Philly boy, of course. Stick a city man out here and it gets to him sometimes, that was true, but Grady wasn't so sure that was the thinking this time. Still, those ruminations were likely to get him morose and melancholy when he was drinking, and it looked like he was going to be, so he tried to think of other things.

Tom saw Grady was sitting on the porch and stopped. He hitched his belt up, touched his hat. "Evenin'."

"Evenin', Tom. Been a while. Where you been?"

"The pen."

"You're spending a lot of time there these days, I hear. Keeping company with our noble savages."

Savages. All Grady saw was farming folk with darker skin and longer hair, wearing expressions pressed on them by hard work. The white man had taken their animals and taken their land and they weren't about to give it back any time soon.

"Noble savages," Tom said, nodding. "Don't see much noble civilized, do we?"

Grady looked Tom over. The last of the light was leaking from the sky but he could see enough in the dusk to know Tom was in a bad way, and drunk with it.

"Got somethin' to talk about," Tom said, showing Grady the bottle he held.

Grady nodded. He got up from his chair with a creak he pretended was the wood and went in for the cups.

"Alright," said Grady, sitting back in his accustomed chair. There was another beside it, and a small table. They had the whole stretch of planks to themselves. The men inside were sleeping. Grady, though, liked to stay out late, watch the stars.

"It's one of those stories that needs tellin' because it's heavy," Tom said. "Tellin' it makes it easier to carry."

Grady heard a lot of stories like that. Carried a few, too.

"Alright."

He poured them both drinks.

Tom had a story to tell, but he kept quiet a while. That was fine by Grady. He watched the stars do nothing in the sky, and listened to the quiet sounds of men snoring and shifting in their beds behind him. Occasionally a breeze carried the smell of wood smoke and bacon grease from across the yard.

"North wall's goin' be extended," Tom said eventually.

"What for?"

Tom shrugged. "Colonel wants to."

Grady could have asked "what for" again, but didn't like to waste breath he could whistle with.

Tom tipped his cup and took all that was in it, refilling as he swallowed. Grady offered his own cup for more. He didn't want Tom's nerves to soak up all the whiskey. "Slow down, Tom. It's been a while since you and me shared a drink."

Tom acknowledged that with a nod and poured. "Did a round up couple of weeks back," he said. "Mountain flush out."

Grady nodded. Drank. "That a fact?" He knew it was, but this was how it had to start.

"Went into the hills." Tom counted them off on his fingers; "Me. Henry. Cody. Packard. James."

Grady nodded. Five was about right.

"You wanna talk to me about James, Tom?"

"It got messy up there, sir. But I fixed it now."

Tom was paler than the half moon above them, dark rings like smudged soot under his eyes. Tom hadn't been sleeping well, that was how Grady reckoned it. He had questions, but he waited. He'd done his fair share of round ups. Companies went into the mountains looking for Injuns hiding out or just plain missed. There were a lot of them out there still, holed up in caves or just living so remote they were easy to miss first time round, even second and third. Course, the more Injuns they rounded up and persuaded west was best, the more they learnt where others were. Families wanted to go west together. These people had been tribal once and bonds were still strong.

"It was a small place tucked away in the crags," Tom said, "screen of trees round it. Vegetable patch. Chickens. There was a well out front with a low wall."

Tom paused to drink but really he was remembering. He wasn't on the porch with Grady no more. He was somewhere in the mountains.

"The man, he's big. Goliath big. Huge. And he's wearing all this fur that makes him seem bigger. Hair's long and all untied,"—Tom gestured with his hands— "down over his face. You seen 'em like that? Real wild looking, but with that look they all got, the one that says he knows they're beat and never had no hope otherwise."

Grady said, "Stamped down like trodden ground."

"Yeah, that's it. That's how he looked. I gave my speech, just like always. Had my ledger, took a record of what they were leaving, told 'em they'd be reimbursed and paid a relocation fee just for going where the land was better anyways."

Grady nodded, but he had his doubts about that last bit. To his mind it was like taking off someone's feet then giving them a pair of boots. Even if they *were* given land, Grady reckoned it wouldn't be long before someone took it back again.

"He wasn't really listenin'," Tom said, "but he started gatherin' things from the yard. Like he'd been expectin' us a while. Two young'ns—"

Tom's voice caught in his throat. He put his cup down and said something to the floor Grady preferred to hear in church.

"A girl and a boy, both dirty 'n' scraped a bit but smiling. They came out to see." He stared at his empty hands as if wondering where his drink had gone.

"The others, they was all in the saddle, same as always. Cody, he had a smoke. James and Packard were talking about Philadelphia. They talked so much about a place they both lived in, I don't know how they managed to say anythin' new. They knew each other all but Biblical." He tried to smile at that but it didn't work. "Then Henry happened."

"Henry?"

"He did what was usual for him. We'd give 'em time to pack and Henry'd use that time to ride round 'n' round their house. Said it put the hurryin' on but really he did it 'cause he liked to rub people wrong. Henry can shoot, salute, 'n' spit a little, but that's about it, so he makes the most of a job like this."

Grady knew the type and said so, but Tom wasn't listening.

"Second time Henry comes round from back he's got a woman followin' him. She's all dressed in deerskin and bird shit, got a cloth tied around her waist held full of eggs. Her hair's long 'n' braided 'n' gathered up a bunch at the back. I remember that 'cause she was shoutin' Injun at him an' shakin' her head and the braids were fallin' loose. Henry just laughed, spurrin' his horse a few steps to turn a circle so as he could laugh back at her face."

"What did she do?" Grady asked, pouring them another drink.

"She threw an egg at him." Tom laughed, but it was a harsh sound. "Got him, too." He slapped his right hand against his left shoulder to show where.

Grady paused, cup hovering at his lips. He knew how a story with a bored young soldier and an angry Injun woman could end after something like that. And Tom had said it was messy. James said the same thing by doing what he did, tasting his own gun and putting a stain of himself on the walls of his bunkhouse.

"What did he do?" Grady asked. "Henry, I mean."

"He crapped in their well."

Tom looked out into the stockade, though there was nothing to see out there but cabins and they was only dark shapes in the gloom. He swallowed his drink down.

"He crapped in their well," Grady said. "Well, sure."

"He did that a lot. If they pissed him off some, or they took too long packin', he'd crap. Got so I wondered if he held back for the occasion. Usually he'd crap front of the house, in the doorway or some place. No reason for it when it's a home they're leavin' anyway, but he knows they don't wanna see that as they leave. It's spittin' in a man's wound. Even Injun knows that."

Grady agreed.

"Henry's got broken egg shell runnin' down his chest, and a face that's fiery fierce. He's dismountin' in a hurry 'n' so am I but my damn boot tangles in the stirrup. Henry's stridin' at this woman, hand on his pistol, and she's ready to throw another one, yellin' at him 'n' all us, and I'm thinkin', shit, my money's on Henry."

Tom was talking in the present sense of things, Grady realized—they were getting to it now.

"I'm too far away to stop anythin', but the big fella, he steps out from the house 'n' grabs his woman's wrist from behind, bursts the egg in her hand. Then he scoops the rest from her apron 'n' lets *them* break as well. He's calm, though. Sayin' soft things to her. Henry calms down too, but not enough to let things be. Not Henry. He strides over to the well they have out front, drops his britches, and takes a crap perched over the edge."

As far as bad stories went, this wasn't one to lose much sleep over, Grady thought. Which only meant it weren't finished yet.

"Henry finds it funny every time he does it, so he's laughin' even as he's droppin' his dirt. James and Packard, they're laughin' too. They've not been out with Henry before so it's new to them, and James is as fresh as tit milk, but even so I reckon they was just easin' down after the tension. Cody don't say nothin', of course."

Grady knew Cody. Everybody did. Cody was likely the oldest in Tom's group and should've been in charge, but for reasons no one talked about he *wasn't* in charge. Those reasons were him leadin' out after Willy Wilson and none but himself coming back. Wilson was a bad man with a greased holster and a fondness for other folk's horses. Just one man, but Cody couldn't put him down clean. That was a long time ago, but people remembered a thing like that.

"Cody keeps out of it," Tom said. "By now the young'ns have come back out because of all the yellin' an' cussin'. The girl's filled a cookin' pot with things to carry out 'n' she hugs it to her stomach, watchin' her mamma stride over to Henry. He's still squatting and straining and she shoves him! Sonofabitch damn near falls in! He makes a wild grab 'n' gets some of the wall 'n' some of her deerskin, and likely he lets another load loose, too, without thinking 'bout it, but then he's laughin'. It's the nervous kind a man has when he's been scared. We all know it, and he knows we know it. So he slaps her across the face."

Grady shifted but couldn't get ready for it. This would be the messy bit.

"Sounded like a bear trap going off," Tom said.

Right now. Blood, most likely.

"Henry's pullin' his pants up, yankin' his belt, but that woman comes right back to push him again, you believe that? He keeps her off with a shove of his own 'n' puts his hand to the grip of his pistol after. I didn't like that, didn't like any of it, but I'm still dancing around with one foot tangled up.

"The big man, all fur 'n' muscle 'n' hangin' hair, he comes over and I think he'll be like before, you know, calm her down some. He puts his basket down and he looks like he's makin' to restrain his squaw cause he puts a hand on her chest to keep her back and he puts another out for Henry. Like he's keepin' them separate. But he shoves Henry hard. Henry backs up a few steps and the well gets him behind the knees and over he goes, topples right in. Gone."

Grady couldn't swallow his drink for a moment. When he did, it choked a single cough from him. Tom didn't notice.

"We don't hear nothin' at first when he falls. He's surprised like us, most likely, and don't scream or nothin'. There's just a sound that's thud and splash.

"We all start yellin'. My foot's finally free but I'm hoppin' round a minute. James dismounts with that flashy kick he has 'n' runs over, Packard right there with him. Cody just turns a tight circle on the spot 'n' says, 'Hey'. Just that. 'Hey.'.

"The Injun fella, though, he ignores everythin' but his wife. Holds her face real gentle with both his big hands, checkin' her. Her cheek's already swellin' and her eye's closin' up. He grunts 'n' kisses her forehead.

"By then James is there with his gun at the Injun's face but looking at the well. He glances down, then back at the Injun, then down the well again. He calls, "Henry!" but if there's a reply we don't hear it. Maybe because I'm shouting at everyone to shut up and calm the hell down.

"James yells, 'Henry, you down there? I can't see nothin' but dark' and I think, of course he's down there. Packard's yellin' for Henry as well. He's got his gun on the woman. The only people makin' noise is us.

Even the young'ns standin' there are quiet, though the girl's got some tears."

Tom stopped and took a ragged breath. He grabbed for the bottle of whiskey but knocked it down. Grady scooped it up quick before anything could spill.

"Only thing that tastes right," Tom said.

Grady agreed. When he thought about it later he realized they weren't talking about it the same way.

"James and Packard got nothin' from the well. Injun fella looks down at James like there's no gun between them. I'm reachin' for 'em, thinkin' I don't know what, when for no reason I can gather other than he's nervous or somethin', James shoots the Injun square in the face."

Grady wasn't surprised, and yet . . . well, he'd hoped different.

Tom nodded as if agreeing with something and wiped at his neck. "A splash of somethin' made a thick noise on my coat and it was on my neck and in my hair. And we're all just starin'. The only noise comes from Cody. This time he's sayin' 'Hold on, hold on' like he needs a minute.

"The Injun, he turns back to his squaw with a hole where his eye used to be, a flap of cheek hangin' down all blistered. He don't seem to know it. Where he's stood, James gets the full effect of that face and whatever he sees up close is enough to make him scared. And James, he lashes out at times like that. So that's what he does."

Grady said, "Christ." Muttered it to clasped hands as he listened, like a prayer.

"Now the wife's screamin'. Forever, seems like. James is beatin' her man who's on his knees now, only still up because of the way James is holdin' 'im, hittin' 'im, scared at what he's done 'n' what he's doin' 'n' but doin' it anyway. Packard's yellin' at the woman to quiet, just quiet, for God's sake quiet."

"And you?"

"Had my gun on James." He looked shamed to say so. "Didn't know 'til I was puttin' it away."

Grady was struck by a memory of Tom: four of them fumbling for a gun at Kathy's, Tom the only one with wits enough to draw clear and clean. There'd been a stupid fight over cards—cards!—and Tom took turns aiming at each of those dumb enough to think a game worth killing over. Drinks were exchanged instead of bullets and Tom got something extra from Kathy, on the house. He'd remind him of that later, when this hellish business was done. Try to put a smile where there was nothing but woe.

"James steps back, blood to the elbow, and the Injun falls down. I can't say *face* down no more on account he's not got one. The woman rips at her own hair. Two whole handfuls come away. She throws it down 'n' jumps on James before any of us can see. She's still screamin' or screamin' again, I'm not sure any more.

"Packard's quicker than me. He gets her round the neck but he can't get her more than a pace back 'n' forth. She's fightin', clawin' his face like a banshee."

Harpy, Grady wanted to say. That would be the usual comparison. But screamin' 'n' all, he supposed banshee would do.

"Packard says, 'Get them damn kids away,' so that's what I do. Took 'em into the trees. They don't resist none. They're confused 'n' cryin', both of 'em, cryin'. I'm sayin' things but I don't know what or if they even understand me but I keep sayin' it anyways. I do that for a long time."

Tom nodded to himself, tracing his thumb back and forth over the rim of his cup. Stayed that way a while.

"What happened while you were gone?" Grady needed an answer but he didn't much want one.

Tom shrugged. "Don't know. Don't *want* to know. All three were bloody when they came back for me and it weren't their blood. Theirs had drained away, making them proper pale-faces." He snorted. It weren't nothing like a laugh but was probably meant to be.

"We said we wouldn't tell. Not ever. But here I am, tellin' it to you."

Grady nodded. He'd heard plenty of bad stories. Probably would for the rest of his days. This one, though, weren't done.

"What about the children?"

"Brought them back here to the holdin' pen."

Something about that didn't sit right, though. It was like wearing a new gun belt—it fit 'n' all, and it held your guns, but until you broke it in it felt all wrong.

Tom picked up on some of that. "I put them with an old squaw who had more blankets than friends. She was happy to take them. Very happy. She didn't ask about parents."

Better, thought Grady. You're breakin' it in some. But that's still not all of it.

Grady eased back into his chair, the old wood bending and creaking around him. "You want me to report this?"

Tom shook his head.

"I could go to Frazier instead of—"

"No."

"Well shit, Tom, what did you go 'n' tell me a story like that for? I have to do *something*."

Murder was murder, be it full-blood, half-blood, Chinaman, whatever. And two murders was two murders, and three was three, which was what it sounded like.

Tom looked away from the empty yard and met Grady's eyes for the first time in a long while. "I ain't done yet."

It didn't seem like he was going to be, neither, for a little while. Grady waited. He listened to the night. Heard its music and thought of dead men.

"We got back," Tom said, "and when we did we swore our secret and went to our bunks. We sold Henry's horse 'n' gear over the river, told people he'd gone to town after a week in the peaks. None of us spent the money." That seemed important to Tom, so Grady nodded.

"That night I dreamt of where Henry *really* went. Saw him fall. Saw the Injun lose his face. Cody 'n' James 'n' Packard dreamt the same but they didn't tell me nothin'."

"You'll have dreams like that a while now," Grady warned him. He had plenty like it himself.

"Every night," Tom agreed. "And worse."

"Worse?"

"The water. It's got blood in it."

Grady said nothing. He looked down into his cup.

"It's true," Tom said. "I can't have nothin' but milk or liquor else I taste it in there."

"What about the others? What about Cody?"

"I can't say because Cody's gone. I'll get to that. James 'n' Packard, *they* taste it." He remembered James. "*Tasted* it. And we *see* them, too."

"See who?"

Tom gave Grady a sideways look and took another drink.

"See who, Tom? Say it loud. Hear how damn foolish it sounds."

"At the window sometimes, in the yard. Once," Tom said in a quick whisper, "Packard woke to see the woman lookin' down at him where he slept. She was standin' on his bed. Her feet left muddy prints on his mattress."

"Y'all talked about this?"

Tom nodded. "Cody gathered us up. Said he was seein' the big man all over the stockade. Said he was going mad, wanted to let us know he was ridin' out before he ruined it for the rest of us 'n' said somethin'. Said he'd let folk down before and it near killed him and he weren't doin' it again. Packard, he saw the squaw. James didn't give details but he said he saw both."

"And *you* see them?"

"Behind every person I speak to. Standin' there. Lookin' at me."

Grady checked around himself, slowly.

"You see them now, Tom?"

Tom turned away and stared out into the darkness of the stockade.

"No. I fixed it."

"Well that's good, Tom. That's good." Grady offered him something to smoke but Tom waved it away so Grady didn't have one either.

"We went back to the place in the mountains. The four of us, drinkin' whiskey for days because we couldn't brew coffee without it havin' the coppery taste of blood, no matter how strong we made it. When we got there it looked just as it did first time. Broken egg shells. Chickens scratchin' around out back. Things were piled up and still there; tools 'n' cookin' gear and the like.

"It took a while to get courage enough to look down the well. When we did it was for nothin' cause we couldn't see. James suggested lowerin' a light, but 'What's the point?' I said. We was there to give the dead proper burial. Mighta been only me willin' to say it, but no one argued. So we rigged a harness 'n' down I went. It was my group and it was my idea and it was me who let things go so bad."

Grady hadn't been there so he couldn't argue, but he thought Tom was probably taking more responsibility than was his. Sounded like there was plenty to go round.

"It stank in that well. You work a ranch or serve as long as we have and you get to know what death smells like, but this was different. This was bad; rank 'n' wet and . . . bad. Like . . . Well, I don't know what like. It was a rough well. A shelf of rock down there, too hard to shift, made a ledge next to what looked like a puddle but wasn't. It was much deeper."

He made a shape of it in the air with the drink he held.

"Henry was on this ledge, which explained the thud we'd heard. The other two, the Injuns, were at the watery bottom. They'd been weighted down, so I had to get wet to make sure they were there. I was worried they'd got out, see. And so were the others; Cody, anyways, cause he called, 'They there?', real anxious. Like they might not be.

"I said they were there and then I saw Henry's fingers. They were bloody, and his nails were broken. I held the light up a bit 'n saw where he'd tried to claw his way out. And God Almighty, his son and all the rest of it, that shook me. I looked up at the others, three faces lookin' down at me like I was in my own grave, and that shook me too, so I got the hell out.

"I said nothin' about Henry. I didn't tell them he only had a broken leg 'n a head wound like you'd get in a brawl. Didn't tell them he prob'ly starved down there."

Tom faced Grady. "Do you think if he'd known those two Injuns were down there with him he still would've starved?"

Grady was given plenty of time to answer the question but he chose not to. He wasn't so sure Henry starved, not in that short time. Not with a belt and boots to eat.

"We got them all up 'n' buried, anyhow. If the others saw Henry in pretty good shape, none of 'em said nothin'. We made simple graves, read a bit of God's word, and came back here."

§

"Here," Grady echoed, doing away with the cups and passing the bottle. Tom kept it at his mouth for three swallows. He coughed a couple of times, handed it back.

"Quite some story," Grady admitted, taking a pull of his own.

Tom held up his hand. "A bit more. Let me tell it all."

"All right."

Grady was leaning forward in his chair, bottle hanging between his knees. He was looking at Tom who was looking at the past. His features were drawn and weary, his voice heavy.

"I saw the Injuns again as soon as we got back. Saw them playing with their children. All I could do was open my mouth 'n' point. Cody, James, Packard, they all said they saw nothin', 'n' when I looked back they were right. Cody, though, he was lyin'. Saw 'em a few times after, too. Now he's gone. Told someone in his bunkhouse he was off to the same place as Henry. They thought he meant town. I reckon he was bein' more phil'sophical than that."

"What do the others reckon?"

"Well James shot himself, didn't he."

Grady straightened up. He *knew* that, everyone knew that, and he'd been waiting for it near on an hour now, but he still dropped the whiskey and to hell with it, let it spill. "Shit."

"Yeah." Tom mimed a grim suicide, shot his face with his fingers. "Looked that way, anyway."

"Packard?"

"Locked in his cabin. Right now, even as we sit here. Got furniture at the door 'n' boards on his windows. Won't come out. I told him I'd fixed it. He said if that was true, how come he's lookin' at the biggest scariest fuckin' Injun he's ever seen? Says the two of them are sittin' with him, waitin'."

"Waiting for what?"

Tom shrugged, like he was worn out. "Maybe it takes time. The fixin'. Maybe they're waiting for what I gave 'em."

Tom had told most of his story to the boards at their feet, but now he looked Grady in the eyes for what he had to say.

"I figured it out, see. They're a family lot, these Injuns. You've seen it, sir. Not one of them wants to go west without the rest of 'em."

An idea was fighting through the whiskey. "Oh Tom, what did you do?"

"I went to the old lady and said the parents wanted their kids back." Tom was openly weeping now. "She didn't like that, not once I'd given them her. They were already close, you see. A *new* family. You know how they are."

"Tom . . ."

"I took them from her and I took them to the mountains. Took'm home. Gave them back. We never should have taken them in the first place. None of them. We shouldn't be takin' *any* of them. They were here first. We should give it all back."

"Tom—"

"I made it quick, sir. And I buried them right next to their parents."

He sobbed a while after that and Grady let him. When he fell into a fitful sleep in the chair on his porch, Grady let him do that, too.

In the morning, when Tom woke, Grady asked him to tell the story again. He had Frazier with him.

Frazier was old but an imposing figure, neatly groomed but in a way that said he didn't give a rat's ass if he got dirty. He shrugged his shoulders in a casual gesture that put his coat over the star on his chest, doing his best to be friendly. His moustache was grey-through and thick. It softened his words a little. "It's all right, son. You can tell me."

Tom looked at Grady. Grady looked back. Tom nodded. "Let's do it somewhere else," he said to Frazier, getting up. "This man's heard enough."

I have, Grady thought. And ain't no one can take it back.

Frazier put a hand to his hat, nodded with the gesture, and moved aside so Tom could step down from the porch.

"He's been drinkin' nothin' but whiskey for days," Grady said, "so give him time to straighten his story out. It's got some mighty strange kinks in it."

"Will do, Father."

Frazier was the only one still called Grady that. He took off his hat and ran his hand through his hair. It wasn't quite yet the same colour as his moustache, not entirely, so he grew it long. He put his hat back on and with another nod, this time for Grady, he followed Tom down across the yard.

Grady watched them leave. Frazier's horse was drinking from a trough in the yard and something about that drew Tom's attention.

Then it all went to hell.

Tom screamed and he backed away so fast he fell. He scrambled back to his feet quick but still stumbled some. Frazier's horse reared up, stamping its forelegs in the air, whinnying loud and shrill. Frazier had both his guns drawn but he was pointing them at the trough. Whatever he saw there was enough to stagger *him*, too.

Tom shouted at the water, "I gave 'em back! I'm sorry, y'hear? I gave 'em back!"

What happened next depends on who tells it, but Grady saw it like Tom leapt at the trough. Just dived right in and thrashed about in the water until he drowned. Some say he was pushed in, others that he was yanked forward, but pushed or pulled, nobody could say by who. A few suggested Frazier did it and it made his reputation more fierce than he was used to for a while. Grady, though, he'd seen Frazier at the trough and when that man's hands were in the water he was trying to pull Tom out, not hold him under. Couldn't do it, though. And Grady wouldn't ever say what he saw holding on to Tom to stop him.

Occasionally, when the whiskey was in him, Frazier would add more to the story, but it was a story Grady didn't much like to hear. There's no giving a story back when it's told, so if talk ever went to Tom or James or what Packard did to himself shut up in his cabin, Grady took his old bones elsewhere. He had ghosts enough of his own without adding more.

A MOTHER'S BLOOD

"Life swarms with innocent monsters."

Charles Baudelaire

The child smiles and so she smiles and later she will hate herself for it but right now all that matters is that smile, so she lays out the sticker book and puts on the cartoon and returns to her work, which is in itself work for the child. She stuffs the rest of the load into the machine, turns the dial that tells it to wash stains from clothing that's getting all too expensive as it becomes too small all too quickly; "I'm a little monster" says one tiny top, bright and fierce, while others host familiar faces that push the price up, announcing, "The force is strong with this one," "To infinity, and beyond." As the machine gurgles full and begins the first of its hesitant turns, the start of its cycle, to be followed by another cycle, and another, round and round, so the child in the next room gurgles its pleasure at the screen as friends it has never met, flat and two dimensional (however much they claim otherwise), lead him into song. She tries not to hear it even as she mouths the words.

She's tired. She's so very tired. While the child can run from one activity to the next, bounce to every new demand and call its commands with vital enthusiasm, she can only respond with weary obedience, too exhausted to do much more than offer an occasional feeble reprimand. She feels drained. That's what it does. It sucks the life out of her, suckling first her milk and then everything else; her energy, her essence, and every single dream of what she could have been. They drain you of you and make you them, an extension of what they need, what they want, and they make you like it with that tyrant smile.

Out here, a room apart, the smell of soured laundry still stuck in her nose, she is able to hate the child. With a little distance she can despise the demands and resent the restraint it puts upon her life. She can seethe with jealousy at the life it leads while hers drains away, bleached and thin and unable to sustain her. She mutters her complaints where nobody else can hear, picking up the detritus of domesticity as she carries the washing basket back to the bathroom, her words a familiar incantation and her actions the repetitive ones of a ritual that does nothing to keep her safe.

She returns the basket, ready to fill again, and goes to her room to get dressed. She ignores what she sees in the mirror, turning away from reflections the child will never have, the saddening sight of stretch-marks and scars, unsightly lines she carries beneath her clothes as battle wounds that tell of victory and defeat together; she expelled the child but now she's tied to it by umbilical bonds of obligation.

She won't shower—she's not going anywhere.

The clothes she hides herself in were new before the child was born but now hang as limp and as dull as she has become. Her face is a plain face that wears no makeup, only wears down, and her clothes are the grey of many washes because the child has bled her of colour, taken it for its own, scattered it around the flat in the form of bright toys and garish cardboard books with enough colour spare to spill from pencils and paints and crayons. And if she risks the room where it rests, where no prison crib could ever hold it, if she dares to enter its lair, where bedding is bunched into a nest of hoarded treasures, then she will see all the colour that her life lacks painted on the walls, contained in the posters and the cuddly toys that are stuffed full in a way she will never be again. Its name is on everything; loud blasts of primary colour on its door, stickers on its toys, labels in its clothes, and it's written in her flesh as well, a stretch-marked ownership she feels in the extra weight she still carries around her hips, in the new looseness she has below, and in the hanging shapes above that are her empty breasts where it once suckled, bruised, and bit.

She makes the bed. Later she will lie in it, but not yet.

"Turn it *down*, please," she calls, bending to retrieve a smiling car, a plastic snake, a green-muscled giant. "Don't make me angry."

But it will make her angry without trying, without listening, just by being, and it will feed from that as well, take it away with that tyrant smile or surpass it with anger of its own, shrill and sharp and shinier than hers. She is enthralled to this child in the living room, the only one who can use it for that purpose, the child who doesn't watch the television but will cry if she turns it off and so she listens, again, to the celebrities pretending to be animals, the animals pretending to be humans, and thinks all the time of how much like an animal she is herself, part of a species that produces parasitic soul-sucking progeny.

She goes to the kitchen and puts milk that's no longer hers back in the fridge, cereal back in the cupboard, a bowl in the sink. She'll swill it clean of soggy circles later, so many sodden rings that none could have possibly been eaten, and on the table is the proof in the shape of a clean spoon and the torn plastic wrapping of whatever "free" gift had been inside the box. It needs food, it needs love, it needs attention, but most of all it wants to play, and it can, because she gives it food, gives it love, gives it attention.

From the other room, bubbling laughter like a series of hiccups sends a thrill coursing through her blood, carrying with it a forced desire to do whatever it wants if only she can hear it again, or see that smile, and be around for the next adorable antic.

She has to get away. The bathroom, where there's relief to be had in a shut door and the chance to sit down.

She gathers a handful of loo roll and gives the toilet seat the necessary wipe, tosses the tissue, pulls down her clothes, and sits. She inspects her underwear for blood, although she's already done so in dressing, because she longs for her next period, yearns for the relief it will offer in what it tells her she's not. And then there will be the opportunity for emotional indulgence, a selfishness like the child's, permission to cry, to weep her fucking eyes out, while allowing rage-red thoughts of ending everything that makes her existence so exhausting. She can imagine stabbing it with coloured pencils, bright sharpened stakes through the heart, or she can entomb it alive behind a wall of Lego, deliver it poisoned letters that spell doom and destruction in coagulating shapes of spaghetti, maybe take it out for an evening walk and leave it at a crossroads, fantasies of abandonment that have the child disappear like morning mist with the coming of the dawn. And it wouldn't be murder because it would be self-preservation, thoughts she can forgive herself for because it's the moon's fault, it's her monthly cycle. She can cry and be angry and her husband will accept it because he has to and her child will recognize it, her kin of tantrum, and let her bleed a while.

But her period does not come. This is the nightmare she can't wake from.

There is a box in the cupboard that is hers, tucked behind the toilet roll that no one else changes, and she takes it and opens it and dreads what the plastic prophet will tell her.

"*Muuum . . .*"

The vowel sound longer than it needs to be, the word drawing strength from how it makes her cringe. Her withdrawal from it powers its growth.

"In a minute, sweetheart."

She knows that no blood is coming because something else needs it now, and she damns her husband for how he has damned her, curses his nocturnal penetrations, the rare seductions that are desperate attempts to stoke a dead fire, nothing but a tired prodding to keep the embers smouldering because a fire too bright would be dangerous, might burn the child. And she curses herself, too, for wanting the penetrations, yielding to them if not initiating them, seeking the oblivion that comes when she does, the brief reprieve an orgasm offers however stifled it must be.

At the door, as she pees; "Muuuuum . . . *ieeee . . .*"

"In a *minute.*"

And in a minute she might be, might be mummy, might be mummy yet again, so she shakes the stick and waits and hopes she isn't but knows she will be.

There it is. There's the cross that does nothing to keep them at bay, only announces their arrival. Another lives inside her, then, feeding from her as the first one did, taking its sustenance from hers, using her blood, growing, pushing, reshaping her to accommodate its needs. She has not invited it, has in fact taken steps to prevent it, yet here it is, all the stronger for defeating her in its early stages of life, in existing. A girl to supplant her, or a boy to exert its dominance in forcing her to carry a penis.

That banging at the door again, that bastard banging, and she wishes for a miscarriage, a letting of blood and bond, wondering how many mothers have died in childbirth, killed by what they carried, wondering how many others missed out on such mercy to die slow gradual deaths each and every day, revived enough in tiny smiled instalments to do what's wanted. She could scrape or poke her way out of this, drink or smoke or exercise to exorcise herself of the thing that hides inside her, but she knows she won't, knows she can't, because its power has already begun, and here's its blood-brother banging at the door so that the latch loosens and the door swings inward. She gets a foot to it, stops it opening all the way, but she's sitting on the toilet with her shirt clutched in her armpits and a cross she can't bear clutched in her trembling hands. Its face is at the gap between the door and frame, startled by the entry, startled by the abrupt abortion of it, eager to push through regardless, and it gives her a smile, a different smile, one that sees her as she shouldn't be seen, private and vulnerable, but it doesn't care except to mock her for it with a sickle of sharp milk teeth, a smile that's gone before she can decide if it was ever really there.

"Mummy," it says, "I'm *hungry.*"

And she cries, because she knows it always will be.

THE TRAVELLERS STAY

By night the motel was nameless, the stuttering fluorescence of its neon sign only a rectangular outline of where words once were. The light made the shadows of the building darker and gave moths the false hope of somewhere to go, collecting the dust from their broken wings so that a once-vibrant white was now mottled and sulphurous.

By day the place fared no more favourably. The title of its sign was visible, *Travellers Stay*, but so was the fact that it needed a fresh coat of paint twenty years ago. Flakes peeled like scabrous sores. In sunlight, the building behind the sign was more than a dark shape but not much more, the drab monotony of its sun-bleached walls broken only by the repetition of plain numbered doors.

When Matt arrived, the motel was neither of these places but something in between. Dusk was a veil that disguised before and after and the motel looked as good as it ever could. Anyone who came to the *Travellers Stay* came at dusk.

"We're here," Matt said. He made a slow turn and bumped gently up-down an entrance ramp. A sheet of newspaper skittered across his path as an open v, became caught on a wheel, and was turned under it twice before tearing free. He pulled into a spot between a rusting truck and a Ford that sat flat on its tires and noticed neither. "Wake up."

Only when he cranked the handbrake did Ann stir beside him, sitting up from the pillow she'd made of her jacket against the passenger window. The denim had pressed button patterns into her forehead like tiny eyes. A sweep of her fringe and they were gone without her ever knowing they were there.

"Where are we?" Her breath was sour with sleep.

"Motel."

Ann turned to the back seat. "John, honey."

John, her teenage son, mumbled something that spilled a line of drool and woke. He wiped his chin and sat up. "What?" he said. "What?" He sniffed at the saliva drying on the back of his hand.

Matt released the steering wheel and flexed his fingers. He arched his back and shifted in his seat, eager to get out and stretch his legs.

Ann was looking around. "Here? Seriously?"

Matt ignored her.

There was a woman sitting on the porch enjoying a cigarette. She was leaning back on a chair with her feet up on the rail. She was wearing cowboy boots. Cowgirl boots, Matt supposed. Black jeans and a vest top the same, faded grey from too many washes. The door behind her was propped open by a pack of bottled beer.

"Want me to loan you fifty?" Ann said. "She can't be any more than that."

It could have been funny from someone else, but Ann had never mastered that type of humour.

"She's not a hooker," Matt said. He was tired. His words came out the same way.

"And how would you know?"

The woman was attractive. Matt found a lot of young women were, these days. But if he felt any lust it was for the cigarette she held and the beer she drank. Hell, it was for the ease with which she did both. As he watched she brought a hand up to her mouth and inhaled lazily. She chased it with a tip of her drink.

"I *don't* know," Matt said. He got out of the car before he had to say anything else.

The woman looked his way and raised her beer in silent greeting.

"Hi," he called back. Mr. Friendly.

The thump of a car door behind him. Ann.

"We'd like a room," he said to the woman.

"You sure?"

Matt looked at Ann and wondered how much of their conversation the woman might have heard.

"We're sure," Ann said. "You got any?"

Matt sensed some sort of bristling, but only from his wife. The woman in the chair merely shrugged. "Twenty or so, judging by the numbers on the doors."

"We just want one," Matt said.

"Help yourself," she said. She said it differently to most people. Got the inflections all wrong.

"Do we pay by the hour here or what?" John asked, slamming his door at the same time because he wasn't brave enough with the insult. Matt heard him, though, and he'd told him before about slamming the door. Not for the first time he wished Ann's ex had got the custody he'd apparently wanted.

Ann made a show of looking around the parking lot and beyond. It was a show Matt had seen before and it meant she was looking at how he might look at the woman.

"Just one night," he said.

"Hope so," the woman said, getting up and going inside.

That's how you do it, Matt thought, looking at John. *Chicken shit.*

Ann was looking at Matt, eyebrows raised, waiting for him to react somehow to the woman's attitude. He made a show of looking around the parking lot and beyond.

The sky had darkened to something like the colour of the woman's clothes. An occasional breeze tossed litter in small circles and swept grains of sandy dirt across the ground. From far away came the quiet noise of a passing car, a long hush of sound as if the coming night had sighed.

"We're not staying here," Ann said.

"I'm tired," he replied. It meant yes we are and I don't want to fight.

"I'll drive," said John.

"Not my car."

The woman returned with a large disk of white plastic declaring 8 in big bold black. It looked like a giant eye with twin pupils, the key dangling like a metal tear.

"Thanks," Matt said, stepping up to take it.

"Clean sheets, towels, TV." She pointed across the lot. "Vending machines are over there."

"Thanks," Matt said again. He gave the key to Ann and grabbed the bags from the trunk. John kicked at a crushed can and sent it clattering. The woman sat back in her chair and retrieved her bottle. She brought it to her mouth slowly. Swapped it for the cigarette.

"Quit staring." Ann took one of her bags from him, more for the impact of snatching it than from any desire to help. She gave the room key back to him so whatever it opened up would be his fault.

"Good night," the woman said quietly as they walked away. And in a dry tone, addressed to the floor, "Don't let the bed bugs bite."

"It's gonna be a shit hole," John said.

Matt smacked him across the back of the head with his free hand. Thought, *fuck it.*

"Hey!" John and Ann said together, John rubbing at where he'd been struck.

"Language," was all Matt said, but mostly he'd struck out because he was fed up with the boy. And there was no need to state the obvious—of course it would be a shit hole.

"You can't hit me," John said. "You're not my dad."

"Thank God."

"Matt—" Ann started.

"Sorry. I'm just tired, okay? Sorry."

He wasn't tired, though, not really. Tired of driving, and tired of taking John's crap, but not tired like he wanted sleep. In fact, what he wanted was a beer and a smoke and a few minutes on his own to enjoy both.

Ann gestured at the door. A brass 8 that was probably plastic, a peephole beneath like a dropping.

Matt fumbled with the key. The overlarge fob made it a handful. It was the old-fashioned type of key, one you turned in a lock. It turned easily enough; he could have opened the door with a toothpick. He pushed the door open.

There were whispers in there, whispers in the darkness. He reached around the frame for the light switch.

The first thing he saw when the light came on was the usual motel scenery. A large bed, nearly-white sheets tight across it with a tatty blanket on top, and a bedside table with one drawer. The drawer would have contained a bible in the old days but now probably held dried balls of gum and cigarette burns. A TV angled down from the wall so it could be seen from the twin room as well, though the door to that was closed. Somewhere there'd be a tiny bathroom that didn't have a bath.

The second thing he saw was movement as a number of cockroaches scurried for cover. Their shiny bodies glistened in the light they tried to run from. One sped for the shadows under the bed while another moved as if lost. One made straight for the open door.

John brought his foot down hard but missed. The insect dropped down between two boards of the porch.

"Beautiful room, dear," said Ann. But she went in, slinging her bag onto the bed. Fearless city girl that once was.

John went in ahead of Matt, knocking him as he passed. He said sorry as if it was an accident and Matt had to fight the urge to kick the back of his feet into a tangle that would send him sprawling to all fours.

John put the TV on and sat on the bed, looking up at a commercial.

Ann opened and closed the drawer.

"Picture's shit," John told them. He glanced at Matt and added, "Shot," as an alternative.

Matt dumped the bags and went to find the bathroom. He expected to find it between the two bedrooms.

He found it between the two bedrooms.

There was nothing there to scare away with the light. Just a sink and a toilet and a mirror. The mirror was spotted with neglect that would never wipe away. It distorted Matt's reflection, darkened his face with blotches. Someone had smeared a fingernail of snot on it.

"Nice."

He unzipped, lifted the toilet lid, and pissed, tearing a sheet of tissue to wipe the mirror with. It wasn't until he was shaking dry that he saw the cockroach turning in the bowl. Its body span in a current Matt had just made and its legs kicked at the air. It would never get out.

I know exactly how you feel.

He flushed it away, wondering how it had gotten in there in the first place.

"Matt," Ann called, "can you fix the TV?"

He glanced again at the mirror on his way out, wondering what had happened to the man he saw there.

Back when Matt smoked and drank, when he was single, when he was playing and the band was doing pretty good and could maybe one day do better, he got into a fight with a guy because the man was yelling at a woman. He did it because it was often a sure way to get laid and the woman looked good for that. Red hair, straight and long, good breasts and striking eyes. She wore a top that pushed her tits up and her eyes she showed off with subtle makeup.

"The picture won't stay like it's supposed to," she said as he emerged from the bathroom. She tossed the remote onto the bed and continued pulling things from her bag. Instead of makeup, these days her eyes were lined with tiny wrinkles. She rarely looked at Matt now as she had back then. The way she looked at him now was like he was exactly the way she supposed. Her eyes still lit up when she smiled but that was less frequent, and usually because of some TV show. The first time she came her eyes had been wide and her mouth was a pretty O, as if the orgasm had startled her. He hadn't seen that for years.

Matt reached up and turned the TV off by the main switch. "Fixed," he said.

John muttered something Matt ignored and Ann ignored the both of them.

"I'll get some dinner," Matt said.

John threw himself onto his own bed and stretched out. "Pizza."

"He's not driving tonight," Ann told her son. She didn't use the most supportive tone.

Matt left, closing the door on both of them and resting his hands on the porch rails. He looked at the sky and saw nothing he hadn't seen a hundred times before. The words of the motel sign were invisible now, hidden in the glare of a surrounding neon rectangle. The yellow tubes looked like they'd been white once and then pissed on.

Across the lot, on the shorter length of an L-shaped porch, the woman continued to smoke and drink. Occasionally she'd look at the end of what she smoked but mostly she looked at the ground.

Matt took a deep breath. He hadn't had a cigarette in six years (Ann had urged him to quit) and so he hoped for some second-hand smoke. What he smelt instead, carried to him on the dusty air, was the welcome tang of marijuana. He filled his lungs with it, slight as it was. He watched as the woman released another mouthful of smoke, wishing he was near enough to breath it in.

He went to the vending machines instead.

A couple of cockroaches, alarmed by his approach, hurried out from beneath the machine and raced past his foot, slipping under the door of room 12. Others congregated around a nearby garbage sack, bumping into each other and adjusting their course.

The vending machine offered the usual candy and chips as well as some microwave snacks, though he hadn't seen a microwave in the room. He rummaged in his pocket for money and found only a couple of folded bills. The readout told him NO CHANGE.

He'd see if the woman could help him.

She heard him coming and puffed a final time on her joint. She was stubbing it out and chasing the last toke with beer when he offered his money and said he needed change.

"Of course," she said. "Change." But she made no move to give him any. He leant closer with the cash and she took it with a sigh. She stood up and stretched, pushing out her chest in a way that was all the more alluring for being unintentional, her hands at the small of her back until it clicked. He wondered how long she'd been sitting out here. Before he could ask, or make any kind of conversation, she was stepping into the office behind her.

"For the machine?" she asked, calling it slowly. Lazily. The same way she drank her beer.

"Yeah."

She returned with a handful. "It's kinda picky with what it likes," she said, explaining all the coins.

"Great. Thanks."

She puffed her hair out of her face, brushed it aside when that didn't work. "Anything else?"

"Yes, actually. Do you have a microwave back there? Only I saw—"

"Yeah, we got one," she said, sitting again. "Just bring whatever you get and I'll nuke it." The gulp she took of her beer was an obvious goodbye.

Matt went back to the machine. He fed it coins until it served him his choices and took them back to the woman.

"Can I help you?" she asked. It wasn't like she'd forgotten seeing him already. And it was disconcertingly earnest.

"Sure," he said. "You can nuke these." He tried a smile.

"That's it?"

He wondered if she was a hooker after all.

"Er . . ."

She took the food from him and carried it back in, sidestepping over a cockroach that sped across the floor. It turned a circle and went back the other way.

"Where you heading?" she asked, tossing the packets into the microwave. For a ridiculous moment he thought she was talking to the roach.

"Nowhere."

She looked at him, started the microwave. "You got two minutes," she said over its hum.

Matt laughed politely. "Home," he said. "Picked the boy up from his dad's, saw the in-laws. They want to give me a job."

"Not good?"

"No."

"What do you do?"

He said it for the first time in years. "I'm a musician." Words that used to impress every girl he ever said them to. Some pretended otherwise, but it always worked.

"Not any more," she said.

"What?"

"Not if ma and pa get their way."

"Oh. Yeah. Exactly."

"They just want what's best," she said. It was what Ann had told him, several times, until the drive lulled her to sleep. He'd probably end up taking the damn job.

They were quiet until the microwave dinged.

"What do *you* want?" she asked.

"I want them to leave me the fuck alone."

Matt's surprise registered only when he saw hers. She offered food that looked as plastic as its wrapping. "I meant which of these is yours?"

He took it all without specifying, muttered, "Thanks," and hurried back to his room.

He expected Ann to give him shit about how long he'd been. Wouldn't have been surprised if she'd spied on him from behind the blinds. He braced himself for it. He opened the door and went in, dropped the lukewarm food on the bed, shut the door, said, "Dinner," and then saw John.

The boy was standing in the middle of the room and at first Matt thought he was attempting some kind of prank. He wore a black cloak draped over his shoulders and had wound dark tape around his chest and waist. He flailed his arms around in cardboard tubes that he'd stretched black socks over. This was how Matt rationalized it. John's curved back was a shiny black that glistened in the room's light. Matt could see Ann's reflection in it, saw how she cowered in the corner of the room.

"Ann? What's going on?"

Ann shook her head and made wordless noise. She was rocking from side to side, looking at the thing in the middle of the room.

"John?"

He had wires sticking up from some sort of black hat. He was screeching, rubbing his extended arms up and down his legs as he crouched and then knelt. He leant forward on his elbows and brought his feet up behind where they seemed to disappear into the cape that draped him. The head wires flicked back and forth like fishing rods casting line, or like antennae. Yeah, antennae, that was it. The boy's knees opened and sprouted bristled limbs. His calves separated, spitting split shins into new feet. And still he was screeching.

Ann screeched with him. Her rocking had become easier thanks to something like a large curved shield she had on her back. Her clothes were disappearing as if melting into her skin, only to be replaced by an oil spreading from her pores. Matt watched as her breasts distended and spread into a single band of blackened flesh. He heard things cracking in her chest. Her stomach swelled then flattened and split into sections and her newly segmented body fell forward, face down to the floor. The glossy shield she wore on her back separated for a moment and shook thin wings before settling back into place. Her hair fell away as two protrusions sprouted from her head, dancing back and forth erratically as they grew. Claws burst from her palms as she reached for John. For Matt.

Matt retreated until he felt the door handle press against his back.

John was now a huddled shape the size of a suitcase. He bumped his way around the room, striking furniture and hissing. Ann was turning tight circles on the spot.

Matt opened the door behind him and rolled around it out of the room, slamming it shut. When a cockroach fled from beneath he brought his boot down quick and hard without thinking. There was a satisfying crunch. He slid his foot back, wiping the mess into a streak. The creatures in the room were hissing and fluttering and banging into things.

Matt stepped back from the door, waiting for it to bump with an impact. The porch rail stopped him stumbling into the parking lot. He leant against it and waited.

Eventually the sounds inside subsided.

He wiped his mouth, his stubbled chin, and glanced around to see who'd been alerted by the noise.

Across from him, in a chair pushed back against the doorframe, the woman sat drinking beer. She lowered the bottle and wiped her mouth as he had done. He stared at her for a long moment before she beckoned him over.

He went with a quick walk that wasn't quite running, glancing back only once.

"Everything alright?" she said as he turned the corner into her section of the porch.

"My wife . . ."

He didn't know how to finish.

"John. He . . ."

She nodded, got up, and went inside. By the time Matt was at her chair she had returned with another for him. She put it down beside hers and sat. "Yeah," she said. "That happens sometimes."

She gestured for him to sit. He did. When she picked up her beer she hooked another bottle with it and passed it over.

Matt looked briefly at the bottle and took his first mouthful of real beer in five years. Ann had made him quit, or rather she bought near-beer which was the same thing. He gulped until his mouth was awash with it. It was delicious.

"How did you find this place?" said the woman.

"I just turned off the freeway. I was tired. What's happening?"

"It doesn't matter." She raised a leg and pushed against the rail to tip her chair back. She kept her foot on the rail and took another swallow of beer, leaning back in a comfortable balance. "Even if I *could* tell you."

"They're fucking cockroaches," Matt said. He'd finally pushed the words from his mouth.

"I don't think they're at the fucking stage yet," the woman said. "Gotta get used to it first."

Matt shook his head. He was calmer than he should've been, but he wasn't ready for jokes. "They *are* cockroaches?"

"Mm. Tough little critters. But then so are we, right?" She drained the last of her beer and set the bottle down with the row of other empties. From her angled position on the chair she couldn't quite set it down properly and it fell, spinning. Matt watched as it slowed to a stop, the neck pointing his way, and thought of games he'd played as a teenager.

"So the kid's not yours?" she said.

"No. God, no. He's a—"

"Cockroach." She sniggered the abrupt laugh of someone drunk. She had been looking out into the dark but faced him to say, "Sorry."

He shrugged. "I was going to say asshole."

"Like his father?"

She asked the questions without seeming to care for answers. Like they were rehearsed, or lines she knew well from a familiar movie. Matt answered her anyway with another shrug, adding, "You know, she didn't even tell me she had a kid until we'd been together a year? Can you believe that?"

The woman handed him another beer and he slapped the top off against the railing. He brought it up to his mouth so quick for the foam he hit his teeth. The woman winced for him as he gulped it down. She looked back into the darkness.

"You wanna be a rock star, huh?" she said. She smiled when she said it, looked his way so he could see it before it went. "The bright lights of fame and fortune."

"Sounds stupid now," he admitted.

They watched the moths beating themselves against the motel sign. Closer, Matt could see the words within the neon. He noticed the lack of apostrophe, *Travellers Stay*, and wondered if it was true for everyone.

"What are you doing here?" he asked her.

"Nice girl like me in a place like this?" She spat an arcing stream of beer into the parking lot. "Hiding. Deciding what I want to be. I'm allowed to do that, you know."

He held his hands up in surrender, though her tone hadn't been entirely aggressive.

The woman set her chair down and rummaged in the front pocket of her jeans for a crumpled packet of cigarettes. Matt hoped she'd offer him one and she did. When he looked inside he saw a row of ready-made joints.

"You're a musician, right?" she said, seeing his hesitation as reluctance.

He took one and gave the packet back. "It's been a long time."

She returned the pack to her jeans without taking another. "If it's your first in a while, we'll share." She pointed to where the lighter lay next to scattered cigarette butts. A couple were joints smoked down to fingertip length. Roaches, they were called, Matt remembered. This was a roach motel. He snorted a laugh.

"You gotta smoke it first," the woman said.

He glanced over at room 8 and wiped his lips dry. He sparked a flame from the lighter. The paper pinched between his fingers crackled and glowed as he sucked the flame down. He shook the lighter out, a habit he'd had long ago, and exhaled smoke in one, two, three little puffs.

"Good man," the woman said.

"Used to be." He felt light-headed. It *had* been a long time. He passed the joint over.

"Thanks."

"My name's Matt."

"Amber."

A cockroach ran a straight line across the edge of the porch then turned and made for them on the chairs. Amber toed it aside gently and it hurried back the way it had come.

Matt seems to dream the sex and when he wakes he pulls her over and onto him so he can watch this girl with long un-red hair fuck him again, and she does, and this time slowly, but then he's kneeling at the bedside pulling her jeans down and her panties and he realizes maybe he's still drunk or still dreaming or remembering or something because this happened already. He kneels at the bedside and she opens her legs to him and he stares at her sex, but this time before he can stand, plunge, enter her, before he can feel that welcoming wet warmth of a new woman, a torrent of cockroaches spills from inside, a swarm that flows from between her legs to flood the room, dropping from the bed to the floor in inky waves, scurrying over his thighs and groin and tangling themselves in his pubic hair. When he tries to scream, something scampers up across his neck and chin and into his mouth, bristled legs tickling his lips and tongue, wings fluttering against his teeth, and when the squat weight of it slips down his throat he wakes up gagging.

She was at the window, looking out through the blinds. The light coming in was early morning and neon. It made her look hazy.

"You can go now," she said.

She had dressed back into her jeans and vest, her arms folded over her chest and a cigarette between her fingers. He had seen that chest, kissed it, squeezed each breast. Even remembering Ann, what she had become, he felt little regret. He wanted to do it all again. He hardened under the covers thinking about it.

"I want to stay here for a while."

Outside, the motel sign flickered and blinked out.

Amber brought the cigarette to her lips and blew smoke into the weak sunlight coming in between the blinds. It curled and spread there, grey and slow. "Maybe this is my fault," she said to it.

He tried to sit up, to say something.

"No," she said. "You should go. Be a rock star or something."

He brought his arm out from under the covers to reach for her but knocked a lamp down and it smashed. He felt clumsy, like his arm was too long.

She merely glanced sidelong at him and smoked some more. "Too late," she said quietly, and pulled the cord at the window.

The blinds gathered up in a rush and bright sunlight streamed into the room, blinding him. He cried out and crossed his arms over his eyes, thinking this was the worst hangover he'd ever had until he felt how horribly bristly his flailing arms were, how slender. Maybe it wasn't a hangover, maybe he was still drunk or still dreaming or remembering or something, but oh that fucking light hurt!

He rolled from the bed, marvelling at how easy it was; there was a strange new curve to his back and, oh God, he'd seen something like it before, hadn't he? He slid into the darkness beneath the bed, the shade like cool water on his thickening skin.

She was saying something about how he'd had a chance, but it was hard to hear the words over the high noise he was making, and when she said something about his chance or choice or whatever, he had no idea what she was talking about because all he could do was hiss and turn on the spot as his back split and opened and new spiny limbs burst from old ones.

I'm a moth, I'm a moth, I'm a fucking moth!

But of course he wasn't, he never had been. It was easier to hide from the light than to seek it out, easier to blame others for his lack of happiness than to risk being burned in the pursuit of it. The bed above shifted and bumped with him as he changed, but it grew more distant as he diminished and decided and became what he'd always been.

"I guess you'll stay a while," someone said. Someone who knew the way, once, but lost herself on purpose to avoid choices. She'd never be anyone or anything.

He didn't care. There were things with him beneath the bed, nudging the dust and scavenging waste. They had faces, these things. Human faces, looking down at the ground as they bumbled around. He'd never noticed them before.

He remembered, then, the one he'd crushed from room 8. Had it a face like these? And whose face had it been?

He flexed the wings he'd never use and scurried back to his room to find out, hoping whoever he found there would accept him for what he was.

Behind him came the call of tiny voices he pretended not to under-stand.

NO MORE WEST

He was as old, worn, and weary as the barren landscape, and just as dusty. So was his horse. But whereas the rider sat tall and alert, the horse was flagging, head hung low with every slow step.

"C'mon," the man tried, but his throat was as parched as the cracked ground beneath them. Then, because his tongue was too dry to cluck encouragement, and his spurs little more than blunt silver coins, he took off his hat and swiped at the animal's flanks. He steered with his thighs, heading for a rock formation the sinking sun had made silhouette. They'd rest there.

As the sun dipped and bled its last into the sky, rider and mount were finally amongst the rocks. The shadows felt like damp cloths on the cowboy's skin and he relished them. There was a standing pool of water, too. Not ideal, but when your skins are empty it's plenty good enough.

He dismounted without flourish and crouched close enough to wet his knees. He cupped water to his mouth slowly but swallowed with greed, lowering his water-skin into the pool. The horse lapped at it without enthusiasm.

"She looks about ready to die."

The cowboy turned and drew both guns in one motion, but he didn't fire. There was a woman, sitting on the steps of a wagon he hadn't noticed. The shadows, maybe. His eagerness to drink, most likely. She wasn't startled by his swiftness, though at his age it must have been surprising, and she didn't shy from his aim neither.

The horse made a weak whinnying and fell into the dust and shuddered. The cowboy went to the animal quickly but it was already dead.

"Told you."

He straight-armed his aim, suddenly superstitious, and took steps forward. She was unconcerned.

"Weren't me," she said.

He looked at the water, then the skin he'd filled. He kicked it into the pool.

"Weren't no poison, neither."

The woman stood, smoothing her hooped skirt, and came down from her wagon. Travel Trade and Cure Alls, it said on painted boards. She was dressed more for trade at Kitty's than for travel, all skirt and lace and sweat-wet cleavage. She waved his guns away as if swatting flies. "Ain't no good on me, you know that."

They were empty, but at this distance how could she know? Still, he holstered them.

She nodded. "Got food if you're wantin."

They sat around a fire, him spooning beans and meat into his mouth, she simply holding her food and watching. The only sounds were his; slurping, chewing, swallowing. That, and the crackle of the fire.

"What's your name, cowboy?"

He looked up from his food but said nothing.

"Mine's Delia. Madame Delia, here to deal ya. I got anything you need, from bullets to balms."

"Got a horse?"

She laughed. "No more than you have."

"How'd you get here?"

She patted the wagon steps behind her. "You blind? Too much sun can do that to a man, bouncing off this damned dry dirt."

He scraped at the bottom of his tin, then ran his fingers round the juice and licked them clean. "Got no need for bottled miracles," he told her.

She laughed. It had the sound of blown desert sand. "Miracles? No, no miracles. Where you headin?" She offered him her own food by way of encouraging an answer.

"West."

"Ain't no more west."

He looked at her but said nothing. He ate.

"No more cowboys. No more west. It's all gone," she said. "Few more miles that way, then nothin. Go. You'll see."

"What will I see?"

"Nothin."

He finished eating, cast the tin down, and patted at his pockets.

"Need somethin?"

He looked at her. "I need to go west."

She stared at him. He returned it. It was like staring at the darkness of the sky.

"I got what you need," she said. She got up slowly and climbed into the wagon.

If he was meant to follow her, she'd have to wait. He'd smoke first. He rolled his tobacco, tapped it firm on his thigh.

She returned soon enough with a shawl and something else. The shawl she cast around her shoulders, stepping down from the wagon steps. The something else she held out for him. Something on a chain. Jewellery? No. He leaned to see. A watch? It looked the right size. Right shape.

"Compass," she said, pressing it into his palm. He hadn't realized he'd reached for it. The chain coiled on his wrist like a small silver serpent.

"What do I need a compass for? Stars ain't broke."

"Open her up. See where she'll lead you."

He did. It pointed west. It pointed back the way he'd come. He turned it in his hands. It pointed west. He looked at the sky and thought maybe the stars were broke after all.

"It'll take you west for as long as you want."

"How much?"

She smiled. "They say men are for killin 'n commerce, but the female form has its uses, too, don't it? And sometimes it needs a man." She shrugged her shawl away and unfastened the corset she wore beneath to show him what she meant.

"How much?" he said again, pocketing his new treasure. He wouldn't pay for more than the compass.

"Give yourself to me and it's yours."

"I'm old enough to be your grand-pappy."

"No you ain't, and it don't matter none."

He went to her and pulled at the rest of her clothes. She pulled roughly at his. He took one of her breasts in his mouth and she held him there, laying down beneath him with a satisfied sigh. His hand went between her thighs.

"Open her up," she said into his ear. "See where she'll lead you."

He spread her legs with his and pushed inside and didn't care for anything else she whispered.

He fucked her, then he slept.

§

He woke by the ashes of the fire. The sun wasn't up but the colour of the sky said it was coming.

A horse snorted. A black one was harnessed to the wagon. The sound of hooves behind him made the cowboy turn but there was just a man with water-skins in his hands. They bulged full and steamed where he gripped them. "Mornin."

The cowboy grabbed his clothes not for modesty, not for his guns, but for the compass. He felt the reassuring weight of it in his pocket and with less haste shook it into his hand.

"Where's Madam Delia?"

The man made a show of looking around. He held his arms out wide. "Just us."

"What's *your* name?"

The man smiled Delia's smile. "Pick one."

The cowboy didn't care to. He dressed himself.

The stranger clambered up to the seat of the wagon. "Heading west, I hear," he said, scooping up the reins. "Going somewhere else, myself, but I'll take you with me now if it suits."

The cowboy looked to his compass. It was warm in his hands. "No."

"Well, you come back when you're done," the man said. "Part of the deal. But you knew that."

The cowboy nodded. He slapped ash from his hat but didn't put it on.

"Here. Somethin else for your travels."

The cowboy expected one of the water-skins but the man tossed him a belt of bullets. That was the way of the west. He strapped it on without thanks.

"Been some pleasure," the man said with a grin, then—"Yah!"—he was trundling away, a cloud of dust rising behind.

The cowboy looked to the rising sun, opened his compass, and was pleased with what he saw.

He headed west, loading his guns as he went, eager to make dust of his own.

BEACHCOMBING

The day was grey when Tommy saw the man looking out to sea, the sky either cloudless or made entirely of one large cloud without end or beginning. It seemed to Tommy that even the sand was grey that day, dampened by a drizzle that fell in the night and by surf the colour of old washing-up water. Slow waves lapped at the shore, leaving long wet curves in their wake, constantly renewed. This was where Tommy liked to walk, leaving his prints behind where others had before and knowing he could do it again tomorrow without getting confused.

The man was standing within the limits of one of these wet curves himself. Occasionally a wave would wash up around his ankles and drag away again, pulling at the cuffs of his trousers. The man didn't seem to notice. He clutched the collar of his long coat around his throat and looked out to the thin horizon where grey sea met grey sky, a pencil line on tracing paper.

Tommy stopped where he was. He didn't like to get too close to people in case they touched him. The man was still far away, but Tommy would wait until he was gone. Instead of continuing to where the rocks curled into the cove, he examined the stretch of beach around him, looking for treasures.

A bottle peeked from a shallow grave of sand, its neck outstretched and filling with water as the tide washed over it. Usually Tommy wouldn't collect his treasures until the return journey so he didn't have to carry them to the rocks and back again, but as he was waiting and the bottle was there, he pulled one of the plastic bin liners from his pocket and went to it.

The bottle was brown. There wasn't much label showing but it was red and Tommy thought it was probably called Bud. He shook out the bin liner, letting it parachute full with the tang of salt air, and knelt in the wet sand. He dug around the bottle first, it *was* Bud, and then he took it up into his hands and closed his eyes.

Before Tommy, the bottle had belonged to a teenage boy. He was happy, slightly muddled because of Bud, coming to the beach with a girl with red hair. He had held the girl's hand and it was warm. He had tried to hold other parts of her—Tommy didn't know why—but she had slapped him away laughing—Tommy didn't know why. When Tommy brought his fingers up over the lip of the bottle he felt where the boy's had been. He had touched the girl and he had kissed her and sometimes she liked it and sometimes she didn't and he had left the bottle behind afterwards.

It wasn't much and it wasn't all good. Tommy put the bottle in his bag and carried it in his right hand because it would be the rubbish bag.

The wind smacked the plastic bag as he walked around in a circle where the bottle had been. It made a *thwicker-thwicker-thwicker* noise that sounded in a hurry but Tommy took his time. The man was still there and it was still early in the morning so he had ages.

He found a polystyrene food box but it was soaked and gave him nothing so he put that in the rubbish bag as well. He liked to tidy the beach when he looked for treasure because Sally said neatness showed a strength of character and although he didn't really know what that meant he knew it was good and that Sally admired it and so he was tidy. Anyway, if he didn't pick up the rubbish as he went he would only pick it up again tomorrow and waste time.

Sally was nice. She looked after Tommy and the house he lived in and she knew not to touch him but he wouldn't have minded if she did because he knew she was nice. He had touched some of her things. The only time he felt anything bad was when he touched one of the wrappers he found in the bathroom. Sally was scared and confused and ashamed and he felt those things even if he couldn't explain them and he'd cried like she had done. But later, when he went to the toilet and tore off some paper to wipe himself he felt from the first square that she was happy again and relieved and disappointed too, which was confusing but better than before.

In the sand at his feet was a key ring. Tommy was excited. Keys were good, keys were definitely treasures, and even though he'd have to give these to Sally to hand in he could hold them for a while first and find out all sorts of things. He dropped to his knees and dug a trench with both hands, letting the weight of the bottle keep the bag from blowing away. He made neat piles with the sand he dug because neatness showed a strength of character but quickly discovered the key ring was just a key ring. There were no keys. He shook sand from his hands and rubbed them together and looked at what he'd found.

It was a chunky pink plastic heart with a short length of chain and a double hoop of metal at the end where the keys should be. Tommy snatched it up grinning because hearts were good and what he felt made him laugh with joy. A man had given this to a woman because he knew he loved her and he had put a ring where the keys were supposed to go. The man thought it was a funny kind of joke. The woman had smiled politely when he gave it to her, pleased and disappointed like Sally had been, and then she'd seen the ring and screamed but wasn't frightened. She had taken the ring off with trembling fingers, even though she wasn't frightened, and said yes with a trembling voice, and the key ring had been forgotten.

Tommy hugged it close to his chest and pretended the man and woman were his parents. They couldn't be because if the heart was theirs it would be washed empty by now.

He put the heart in his pocket. It was the best treasure in his collection so he didn't want to put it in a bin bag.

The man on the beach was gone. Tommy smiled again and ran the length of the beach before the man could change his mind and come back. He was so happy with the heart he didn't think about the man's footprints and when he remembered on the way back they were already gone.

The man was there again the next day. Tommy could see him even before he got to the beach. Climbing over the little fence at the end of the car park, he saw the man standing and looking at the sea. The sea looked the same as yesterday, grey and mostly flat, and Tommy wondered what was worth looking at. Maybe he had better eyesight and could see a ship or something. Or maybe he couldn't see at all, like the man with the special dog Tommy had petted once.

He went down the few steps to the sand by standing on the very edges and without touching the railing because it had too many people on it. Pavements were the same, even with shoes on, but if you walked carefully a car park was okay. He jumped the last three steps to the sand. The sand was always okay because the sea came and washed it everyday.

The first treasure was right there at the bottom of the steps. It was a little spade, bright green like a jelly bean. Even though the sun stayed away yesterday someone must have come to the beach to make sandcastles. Tommy picked it up and closed his eyes.

The little girl who used it was very happy even though the dentist had just put metal on her teeth because her daddy brought her to the beach instead of taking her back to school and she loved the beach. She wasn't very good at digging. Tommy felt how she held the handle in the middle and tipped the spade to the sand and flicked it instead of pushing it in deep and lifting it or turning it. He felt how her daddy had helped. His hands were low and high on the handle like they were supposed to be. He dug the sand and the girl put handfuls into a bucket, he knew because the daddy knew, and the two of them were very happy. The daddy was glad she was still a child, and so was the girl but in a more muddled up way.

Tommy opened up a bin bag and put the green spade inside. He gathered the top together and carried it in his left hand because it was the treasure bag; things that people lost and Tommy found and took his joy from.

The man was still there. His long coat was open a little bit and the wind filled it up sometimes, puffing it like a dark sail. The man was like the mast of a ship that wasn't going anywhere. He wore a scarf, too, burgundy like beetroot which Tommy didn't like but ate because it was good for you, and the wind blew the scarf back like a flag.

Tommy took off his sandals to feel the sand better and because today he would remember to check the man's footprints.

He found a whole carrier bag full of litter and went through it but put it all in the rubbish because he didn't like the people. They were messy and angry and one of them was bullying the other one about his girlfriend. He also found a hairclip and even though it was quite a way from the sea it must have been there a while because it was clean so that went in the rubbish bag too.

Further along the beach he found one of the small balloon things he wasn't allowed to touch. It was gritty with sand stuck all over it. He nearly touched it anyway because the feeling he got was so good but Sally had found one on his treasure shelf once and was very angry and disgusted and upset about it. She said they were for adults even though Tommy knew it belonged to someone still at school and she took it away in a bundle of tissues and threw it away. He looked for the square wrapper he sometimes found nearby because Sally didn't say he couldn't touch those and they felt good too, all excited and nervous and excited and excited, but he couldn't find it.

He did find a comb. He thought it was funny whenever he found a comb because Sally and the people who looked after him said he was a beachcomber which was someone who collected treasures from the beach. He closed his eyes and reached for it. The man who had lost it carried it in his back pocket but never used it because he had no hair. He carried it because that's what his father used to do. Father was the adult word for daddy. This man loved his daddy even though he was gone, which made him a bit like Tommy. He put it in the treasure bag after using it to make tiny little grooves in the sand.

The man was still there and Tommy only had a little bit of beach left to go before he was too close. He didn't want the man to touch him in case he wasn't nice. You could drop a thing that wasn't nice but it could hurt and hurt if it was a person and you couldn't drop them or make them let go if they didn't want to.

The man said something. Tommy heard it snatched away by the wind and brought to him in a tangle of sounds that didn't make sense anymore because they were unravelled. He wasn't talking to Tommy which was good because he wouldn't be able to talk back because he was a stranger. He was talking to the sea, or to himself. Then he wiped his face like he had sand in his eyes and he left. He walked to the other end of the beach where there was another car park.

Tommy waited for him to be gone completely and then he rushed down to where the man had stood.

The footprints moved away from the sea, long ovals with half-circles following behind, a line of exclamation marks calling out to be noticed. Tommy thought the man should have taken his shoes off because he saw the sea come up over his legs sometimes and now his feet and socks will be soaked and his shoes will squelch all the way home. If there was someone like Sally there she might be angry, especially if he traipsed sand into the house, which was when you made a mess. Plus if he got sand in his shoes it would itch between his toes later when they dried.

Tommy put his own toes over one of the prints, balancing on one foot and lowering the other one slowly. The man's feet were much bigger than Tommy's. He lined his heel up with the curve of the half circle and brought his foot down completely, filling only half, the sand squirming up between his toes but not itching because it was wet.

The man did not want to go home because it didn't have someone like

Sally there. That was all Tommy felt. He stepped forward into the next footprint to make sure. He needed to lunge a bit to make it in one step.

The man was going home because he was sad but he would come back tomorrow. He would come back very early in the morning. For a moment Tommy felt something of himself there, too, and that felt weird and confused him at first. The man had seen him, that was all, but Tommy didn't think of that straight away. The man didn't want Tommy to be there standing around all day but it was Tommy's beach first. Maybe the man was shy.

There was a shell near one of the prints. He knew it didn't count as treasure because there would be nothing on it but he took it anyway and put it in the treasure bag because Sally liked it when he made her things out of shells. He suddenly felt very lucky to have someone like Sally so he spent the rest of the morning looking for more shells to make her something special.

§

The next morning he got up very early, much earlier than usual, and the man was not there.

The day was a darker grey than usual because there was more night left in it, and it was quieter than usual because the air had sleep in it with the salt and the seagulls. Tommy had his bags already out of his pockets but not open and he ran the beach so he could start collecting treasure before the man got there. He held the bags out and they made noises like machine guns in the wind coming in off the sea, so he pretended to be a plane from one of the big wars. He had a medal at home from one of the wars and it used to be his favourite treasure until the key ring.

The black plastic streamed behind him from each fist and he thought it looked a bit like smoke if you pretended hard enough so he spiralled as if he'd been shot by Nazi bastards even though he didn't know what they were and collapsed to the ground in a spectacular explosion of sand.

He found a pile of clothes.

Tommy found clothes on the beach sometimes. He found swimming clothes and t-shirts and underwear like pants or the funny tops that girls wore. Sometimes he found those balloons with the underwear. When he found clothes he usually only found one at a time, but here in the sand was a folded pile of one two three four five *six* things. Seven if you counted the shoes. Nine if you counted the socks and shoes separately.

He'd never found so many all at once and never in a neat and tidy pile that suggested a strength of character. The shoes had the socks inside and sat on top of a pair of shorts on a folded shirt on some trousers rolled up on a coat with a dark red scarf poking out like a tongue. There was an envelope sticking out from under one of the shoes but it wasn't addressed to Tommy. It wasn't addressed to anybody, but Tommy knew unless it had his name on it he couldn't look.

He recognized the coat, even bunched up, and the scarf. The shoes had sand on them and some had fallen off onto the clothes folded underneath. None of them were wet so maybe the man had learnt his lesson about getting too close to the water. Maybe he took his clothes off to go for a swim.

Tommy looked out to sea but as usual there was nothing there but the bumps that were the waves and some seagulls bobbing on the top of them. It looked very cold.

He wouldn't take the clothes even if they were treasures but he would touch them and he did.

Sobs burst from Tommy the moment his fingers felt the stiff linen of the trousers that were nowhere near as soft as his tracksuit bottoms but that was not why he cried. His chest heaved with the man's pain and his head swam with a darkness he couldn't put into words. The man was so lonely and sad and empty like a flat tire. He was on his own all the time like Tommy except Tommy had Sally and he had people that came and cared for him sometimes and this man had nobody at all. He had gone somewhere to be lost and never found because it was the only way he could let go of something bad.

Tommy wailed and pulled away and rubbed his hands in the sand. He fell on his back and stared at a sky that had no moon and no sun and was somewhere in between. He could feel the pain spreading out from the shoes and socks and shorts and shirt and trousers and coat and scarf. He rolled away from them but he could still feel it.

He ran home faster than he ever had.

He came back running even faster, even with the black sack slung over his back *bumpbumpbump*ing him all the way. The man was still not there and that was good because Tommy still didn't want to be touched or talked to, but he did want to help the man. He skidded to a stop in an abrupt slide, landing on his side and kicking up a puff of sand that settled on the plastic bag with a sound like telling off even though he was doing something good.

He opened the bag and all his treasures were inside, every one of them, all the things people had lost and he had found and that held good things, happy things, inside. He took them out in handfuls, smiling at how they tingled and tickled in his head, and he dropped them on the clothes so when the man came back he would see them. He left coins and bottle tops and jewellery he didn't need to hand in, toys and lolly sticks and lipstick. He scooped postcards and pens and sweet wrappers from the treasure bag and left them on the clothes as well. It didn't show a strength of character like he wanted to because it wasn't tidy because he didn't want to touch the clothes again. He wanted to bury them with everything he had that was good. The man would pick up the comic book, the train ticket, the broken phone with all its conversations, and he would see that he could be okay if he felt things that were nice. Tommy gathered all that he had and piled it high, careful not to cover the clothes completely and careful not to cover the letter because he didn't want the man to be lost and not found.

He saved the best for last, putting the chunky pink plastic heart on the top like a shell on a sandcastle. Then he got up and went to where the man would have stood if he'd been there.

One set of footprints came down the wet sand, all curves and circles because the man had no shoes on. They didn't come back. The man must be in the sea. The sea washes things clean and the man would know that because he was older than Tommy.

Tommy looked out to sea and watched for a long time and then he went home because maybe the man was shy and wouldn't come back with Tommy standing around all day.

Tommy's heart would wait for him.

STORY NOTES

A personal indulgence just because I like these things when I read a collection or anthology. Just a few words about each story. If you want to know more you can always reach me via my blog, **probablymonsters.wordpress.com**. There may be spoilers below, so consider yourself warned (though really? You skipped ahead?)

ALL CHANGE

This story is my love letter to the horror genre, particularly the literature. It's also meant to tackle the whole "horror as a bad influence" thing that comes up again and again but I figured "why get defensive?" and went the other way instead, suggesting perhaps yes, these books have had something of a negative effect on Robert. Unless, of course, he's right about who (and what) he meets at the train station. Does he imagine such horrors because they're easier to face than real ones, or are they a way of justifying his own dark impulses? Is he perhaps an unsung hero, defending the rest of the world from monsters they can't even comprehend? I know what I think, but you can make up your own mind.

I HAVE HEARD THE MERMAIDS SINGING

I got a little bit personal here. Not too much, but there's more me in this story than in any of my others so far. It was also a genuine attempt to raise awareness of the serious diving safety issue in Nicaragua—the facts presented here are all too true, I'm afraid. I love diving stories though, and one day I plan to try it myself (preferably somewhere warm, and preferably with the appropriate safety precautions in place). I plan to return to this story with a sequel of sorts because I don't think Eliot has said everything he has to say on the subject yet . . . .

THE FESTERING

This time I aimed for creepy. Not so much the thing in the drawer, but the shuddery Mr. Browning. The drawer came first, though. I wanted to write something weird that just . . . was. Without explanation. I do allow for a certain level of ambiguity, something more psychological than an actual blobby pulsating icky thing, but to be honest I kinda hope both readings work. I wanted to write something about destructive cycles, addressing the horror of repetition. Ruby has a little more strength than her mother, perhaps, but maybe that's merely the ferocity and cunning of her youth. Her youth is certainly important to the story, as are the masks we wear or force upon others for our own convenience. It's possibly one of the most bleak stories in here, suggesting we're all rotten (or rotting) somewhere inside, but hey—it's just a story, right?

AT NIGHT, WHEN
THE DEMONS COME

This one is me having a blast with demons and guns and stuff and it gave me the chance to go all post-apocalyptic (I love that oxymoron) on the world. I also went for a bit of a comic-book vibe (which I'd love to see done, by the way—got a script/panel plan and everything, just saying.). It's also one of a few stories where I tackle issues of gender overtly, and hopefully in a way that's a bit different. Okay, so the persecuted women in a patriarchal setting might be a little familiar but I had fun modifying the damsel in distress trope and with a bit of luck this story shines a murkier light on that whole "patriarchal" thing I just mentioned anyway. I was thrilled to get this picked up by Ellen Datlow for her *Best Horror of the Year* series, and it marks my first appearance in a "best of" anthology. So I love it.

NIGHT FISHING

I love the sea and have written quite a few stories about it, but this is one of the first ones. It's also one of the first that deals with a topic that is rather personal, namely coping (or not coping) with the suicide of a loved one. At the time of drafting this story I was teaching Thom Gunn's poetry and in one of those twists of fate that happen very occasionally, a student introduced me to the film *The Bridge* and suddenly everything fell into place all at once. Terrence and Bobby were already gay anyway so that, coupled with Gunn's own sexuality and love for San Francisco, gave me (I think) a pretty solid story. It certainly seemed to work for some people; it's brought me more emotional comments from readers than any of my other stories except "Beachcombing," and Steve Berman was kind enough to pick it up for his *Wilde Stories* "best of" as well.

KNOCK-KNOCK

My ghost story that isn't a ghost story, and then kind of is. There's stuff here you're meant to figure out on your own, and unless you're J-J it shouldn't be too difficult. I love J-J, he's got another story too when he's older but maybe that'll appear in the next collection.

THE DEATH DRIVE OF RITA, NEE CARINA

The statistics concerning car accidents . . . man, have you seen them? So much can go wrong on the roads. So, so much. I just upped the ante and made some of that deliberate. I'm hoping it wrong-foots the reader a bit, too, so that while you're meant to feel some sympathy for Rita it should develop into something different pretty quickly (and then maybe back again). What also horrifies me is the calm with which we accept these accidents. Worse, we grow *impatient* when a road is closed and traffic delayed because of an accident instead of remembering that someone might have just been packed flat between sheets of metal. From this thoughtless disregard of our fellow humans it was easy to step into the territory of the gods . . . .

THE MAN WHO WAS

I loved writing this. I mean, I love writing everything (mostly), but this gave me a chance to play with Poe, the grand master of horror. The story was originally written for an anthology edited by Steve Berman which looked at the work of Edgar Allan Poe from a different perspective regarding sexuality. I chose a less familiar story to rework, "The Man That Was Used Up," and used it to do more than simply recast the characters according to their gender preferences. Partly I explore masculinity as a construct, something perhaps done a lot when it comes to stories concerning homosexuality, but here I was able to take a more literal approach too, focusing on the horrors of war as well. Not that I can take much credit for that—Poe got there first (as he did for so many other stories).

SHARK! SHARK!

Ah, "Shark! Shark!" I am very fond of this story. Not just because of the British Fantasy Award it won (see how casually I got that in there?) but because it was the first story in a while that I wrote just for me, just for fun. I had been writing a lot for specific audiences or specific anthology criteria at the time and while those stories are still "me" they felt a little pre-determined and restricted, more consciously constructed. This one had no planning or forethought at all, I just started writing and had a great time doing it. I'd always wanted to do something with sharks

(I love them, they scare the crap out of me—as do most things in the sea), but I also knew there'd be problems with any shark story thanks to *Jaws*. My solution was to tackle that head on. And then I thought, hey, while I'm at it, why not address the writing process, the whole construct thing, head on as well? Hence the slightly intrusive narrator. The voice is pretty much me, with just a little tweaking to suit the story. I had no idea what to do with it when it was done, but thankfully Andy Cox took it for *Black Static*. It's been reprinted in Polish, too, which is pretty awesome and makes me very happy.

BLOODCLOTH

Every writer needs to do a vampire story (it's like a rule or something) and this is one of mine. I was inspired by a wonderful film called *The Fall*, directed by Tarsem Singh and based on Valeri Petrov's Bulgarian screenplay. There's this one scene where a character wipes blood from his hands onto a giant curtain and it begins to soak up the fabric in long streaks, which makes for a very striking image. I wondered, what if the blood was his own? And what if this was how you fed the curtain? The title was originally some awful punny thing, "The Curtain's Call" or something, but I changed it to "Bloodcloth" for more impact and it made me think of, well, certain feminine products, shall we say? I kept it though, and redrafted the story to give it a very female focus. You could also read this as a political story, I suppose, regarding the tributes and the colour red, maybe. That said, I'm sort of with Jack Finney regarding this kind of thing—I think Stephen King wrote somewhere that when Finney was asked about the communist symbolism in *Invasion of the Body Snatchers* he apparently said he just wanted to write a cool story with aliens in it. I've tried to do that, too.

THE TILT

A trip to Carcassonne inspired this one, can you tell? And the very real, very disturbing, torture museum they have there. That, plus an awful story I'd read ages ago (thankfully mostly forgotten now) about a man becoming gay, the homosexuality providing the horror element of the story. I just flipped it, looking at the horrors of heterosexuality. Okay, maybe not—it's supposed to look at the complexities of sexuality in general really, as well as what can happen if you (try to) cross that invisible friendship line with someone. I went a bit Freudian with some of the sexual imagery and symbolism but hopefully it doesn't get in the way of the story.

By the way, Carcassonne really is gorgeous.

BONES OF CROW

I'm not a big fan of urban stories but I thought I'd have a go and this is what happened. I'd been toying with an idea based around a nest made of street debris that I'd found but it kept stalling. Then I read Ted Hughes's 'Crow' poems and *voila*, it all came together. I'm hoping there's enough ambiguity here to suggest the bird might not be real, that it's all in her mind, just as it's also supposed to represent a distorted and monstrous home life. At the same time I thought I'd use it on a metaphorical level for the cancer spreading inside her. Plus a group of crows is called a murder, right? So it also provides another possibility regarding Maggie's involvement in her father's death. This story was picked up by Ellen Datlow for *Best Horror of the Year*.

PINS AND NEEDLES

This one was a while coming together as well. It was inspired by an event at work where I saw a drawing pin quite deliberately left pin-side up on a wall where people often sat and I thought—there's a story there. It was only when I was thinking about another story I was struggling with about a guy obsessed with rocket ships that I realized the two ideas belonged together. It received some very good feedback when it first came out, but was also the first of my stories to receive some really bad comments too (the poor reader EVEN USED BLOCK CAPITALS AND EVERYTHING TO TELL ME HOW CRAP IT WAS!). I think it's because of the presentation of James. The thing is, he's a little bit of me, that guy (just a little, of course, I've never done . . . *that*), and I was writing very much with my tongue in my cheek regarding the stereotypes I exploited. Guess you can't please everybody (as James well knows).

GATOR MOON

I love this part of America. At least, I love the look of it and how it's used in fiction. I wrote this after a bit of a James Lee Burke phase. I didn't even *try* to do what he does of course (the man's brilliant—read some if you haven't already), I just thought I'd have a go with the setting.

Nate and Bo came to life pretty much whole and immediately, while the ambiguity regarding the ending kind of evolved. I originally planned to play it as a straight swamp-noir but I just can't help adding a (potentially) supernatural possibility, it seems.

WHERE THE SALMON RUN

National Geographic inspired this one. It was going to be a crime story originally, Ana found dead with her belly open and stuffed with roe, but the story wanted to go somewhere else and any effort to change it would've been, well, like swimming upstream. I couldn't kill Ana in the end anyway, I liked her too much. So it became a story about a phantom pregnancy, a woman haunted by the loss of her child. The supernatural element is only slight, but it's there if you want it to be.

I learnt *waaay* too much about salmon researching this, but thankfully my brain does this thing where it dumps all the info once I've written the story. Gotta say, though, Kamchatka looks like an absolutely amazing place. There are images of that landscape I hope to remember for a long time, and maybe one day I'll even go and see some of it.

INDIAN GIVER

A bit of a break from the norm. I wanted to write one of those "gentlemen's club" style stories (but not, you know, in a gentlemen's club) and this is what happened. I blame Charles Frazier a bit because I'd just read *Cold Mountain* and *Thirteen Moons* and that's why I stole his name for the story. My Frazier, though, that's Sam Elliott. Ain't nothing gonna change that in my head.

A MOTHER'S BLOOD

My genuine absolute fear of children. Not in general—other people's are oka*aay* (though usually never as great as the parents seem to think)—but the thought of having any of my own? Makes me shudder just to think about it.

I'm kidding. They're adorable.

I'm not kidding.

THE TRAVELLERS STAY

Dreams versus reality via insect transformation while tipping an antenna to Kafka. It was the term "roach motel" that brought this one scurrying out of my brain and once I'd added moths I had my tension between those who run from the light and those who fly to it. I'd become one of those people who talked about their dreams (writing) but didn't try as hard as they could or should to make a proper go of it. This is the story I wrote to explore what I saw as a personal flaw, one that I have since learned to address.

NO MORE WEST

I love weird westerns. Funny thing, but growing up I used to hate westerns with a passion. Now that I'm older I rather love them. There's a simplicity to them that appeals which also allows for a stripped down form of story telling. And I like that.

BEACHCOMBING

Possibly my favourite story, for a few reasons. It was the easiest to write, for starters. I sat down with no idea other than a pile of folded clothes on a beach and all of a sudden Tommy came running to say hello (though he's usually quite shy). A few hours later I had a complete first draft, all in one sitting, and over the next day or two merely tidied it up a little. That had never happened before (or since, for that matter, but fingers crossed . . .). Tommy, though, is the main reason I love it so much; he returns in my novel *Sullivan Dunn*. "Beachcombing" was the first story to get me direct emails from readers who liked it, and that was a massive boost that I very much needed at the time. So thanks, Tommy. And everyone who sent such kind words.

ACKNOWLEDGEMENTS

Many thanks go to various people for helping me bring this collection to life ("It's alive! It's aliiiiive!"). The "writing club" that is Mitch Larney and Victoria Leslie played a major part in pulling this together. Between them they have read almost all of these stories, so if there's one here you didn't like, chances are good it's one I didn't give them first. Thanks you two. I forget whose turn it is for the coffees but the next round's on me.

Thanks as well go to all the editors who have published or republished my stories; you've all encouraged me in ways you may not have realized. Particular thanks go to Andy Cox of TTA Press for getting me started and for keeping me going, and to Michael Kelly of Undertow Books who gave insightful advice and whose introduction to ChiZine made this book possible. Ellen Datlow and Steve Berman have both selected material for "best of" anthologies and I'm very grateful to them for that. Benoît Domis selected one for translation into French, which was a huge thrill—*merci*—while Miroslaw Obarski translated another into Polish—*dzięki*. I still think that's pretty cool.

A big "thank you" goes to Chizine's Sandra Kasturi, Brett Savory, Klaudia Bednarczyk, and Courtney Kelly for helpful emails, persuasive prodding, and great editing, Dominik Parisien for proof-reading, and thanks to Erik Mohr as well for producing such gorgeous cover art—I love it. Adore it. Want it on my wall. Thanks also to anyone who provided positive comments about the book. I don't know who you are yet (I hope *someone* said something nice) but I really do thank you. Especially if you're really respected and have some persuasive pull on readers.

Of course, very special thanks go to Jess Jordan. She motivates me to finish the tasks I set myself, encourages me to dream the impossible, yet keeps me grounded enough to avoid any delusions of grandeur (usually via her uncanny ability to reduce any one of my stories to a single line—I'm not yet convinced this is a good thing but it does secretly amuse me). Your computer skills and dual-screen draft comparisons were also very much appreciated, as was that cup of tea you made that one time. I love you, Key Lime. The next book's for you.

Finally, thanks go to you, reader. Thank you for choosing to spend your time with (and perhaps your money on) *Probably Monsters*. I hope you've enjoyed the stories.

ABOUT THE AUTHOR

Ray Cluley has pretty much been writing stories ever since he could hold a pencil. His first successful story was about sharks and pirates and buried treasure and was broadcast on Australian radio when he was seven. Since then he has been published and re-published in various places, many of them dark places, including *Black Static*, *Interzone*, *Crimewave*, *Shadows & Tall Trees*, *Icarus*, *This is Horror*, and a fair few anthologies. His story "Shark! Shark!" won the British Fantasy Award for Best Short Story. He wants another one now and is no doubt writing something else as you read this. His latest stories are "Water For Drowning" and "Within the Wind, Beneath the Snow," available from This is Horror and Spectral Press, respectively.

For more precise details regarding his published work and current projects, you can visit **www.probablymonsters.wordpress.com**

PUBLICATION DATES

"All Change"
  Black Static, TTA Press, 2012

"I Have Heard the Mermaids Singing"
  Black Static, TTA Press, 2011

"The Festering"
  Black Static, TTA Press, 2013

"At Night, When the Demons Come"
  Black Static, TTA Press, 2010

"Night Fishing"
  Shadows & Tall Trees, Undertow Press, 2012

"Knock-Knock"
  Previously unpublished

"The Death Drive of Rita, nee Carina"
  Black Static, TTA Press, 2013

"The Man Who Was"
  Where Thy Dark Eye Glances, Lethe Press, 2013

"Shark! Shark!"
  Black Static, TTA Press, 2012

"Bloodcloth"
  Interzone, TTA Press, 2012

"The Tilt"
  Icarus, Lethe Press, 2013

"Bones of Crow"
  Black Static, TTA Press, 2013

"Pins and Needles"
    Black Static, TTA Press, 2011

"Gator Moon"
    Crimewave, TTA Press, 2013

"Where the Salmon Run"
    Previously unpublished

"Indian Giver"
    Previously unpublished

"A Mother's Blood"
    This Is Horror, www.thisishorror.co.uk, 2012

"The Travellers Stay"
    Black Static, TTA Press, 2011

"No More West"
    How the West was Wicked, Pill Hill Press, 2011

"Beachcombing"
    Black Static, TTA Press, 2010

EMB
RACE
THE
ODD

KNIFE FIGHT AND OTHER STRUGGLES
DAVID NICKLE

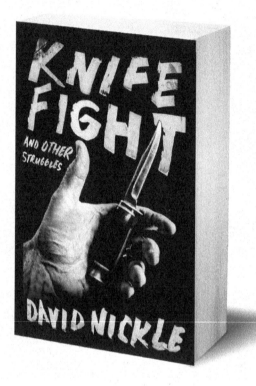

A young man at loose ends finds he cannot look away from his new lover's alien gaze. A young woman out of time seeks her old lover in the cold spaces between the stars. The fleeing worshippers of an ancient and jealous deity seek solace in an unsuspecting New World congregation. In a suburban nursery, a demon with a grudge and a lonely exorcist face off for what could be the last time.

In *Knife Fight and Other Struggles*, David Nickle follows his award-winning debut collection *Monstrous Affections* with a new set of dark tales that span space, time, and genre.

AVAILABLE NOW
ISBN 978-1-77148-304-9

THE YELLOW WOOD

MELANIE TEM

For Alexandra Kove, the path of her life took her far from the claustrophobic forest where her father raised her. She believed that she had to escape, that her only road was away from the family and circumstances of her birth. Now, her road has turned back, converged with the paths of the family she thought was safely in her past.

AVAILABLE NOW
ISBN 978-1-77148-314-8

ANGELS & EXILES
YVES MEYNARD

In these twelve sombre tales, ranging from baroque science fiction to bleak fantasy, Yves Meynard brings to life wonders and horrors. From space travellers who must rid themselves of the sins their souls accumulate in transit, to a young man whose love transcends time; from refugees in a frozen hold at the end of space, to a city drowning under the Qweight of its architectural prayer; from an alien Jerusalem that has corrupted the Earth, to a land still bleeding from the scars of a supernatural war; here are windows opened onto astonishing vistas, stories written with a scientist's laser focus alloyed with a poet's sensibilities.

AVAILABLE NOW
ISBN 978-1-77148-308-7

POINT HOLLOW
RIO YOUERS

Point Hollow, NY. A town with unspeakable secrets. To the tourists that visit each summer, it is quintessential America. They stroll through its picturesque streets and hike its stunning trails. No one sees the cracks in the town's veneer. No one knows its terrible history: a secret that has been buried—forgotten. But Abraham's Faith, the mountain that overshadows Point Hollow, doesn't forget so easily. It booms, wicked and controlling. It is filled with the bones of children. Oliver Wray is Point Hollow's favourite son, its most generous benefactor, admired by all. But Oliver, like the town, has a secret: Abraham's Faith speaks to him, and he has spent a lifetime serving its cruel needs. He believes his secret is safe, but one person has glimpsed the darkness in his heart . . . Matthew Bridge hasn't set foot in Point Hollow for twenty-six years. Something horrifying happened to him there. Memories of an ordeal that flicker and taunt, but cannot be recalled. Now, trying to find the answers to his failed marriage and failing life, Matthew is coming home. Back to Point Hollow. Back to Abraham's Faith.

AVAILABLE NOW
ISBN 978-1-77148-330-8

AGAINST A DARKENING SKY

LAUREN B. DAVIS

A new novel from one of Canada's most acclaimed and celebrated writers, *Against a Darkening Sky* is set in 7th century Northumbria and is the story of Wilona, a seeress and healer whose life and way of being in the world are threatened by the coming of Christianity; and Egan, a young monk from Eire whose visions may have brought him to Christ, but whose experience of the sacred puts him at odds with the Roman church. Full of magic and mystery, Davis's new work explores what happens when one's experience and beliefs clash with those of the people in power.

AVAILABLE APRIL 2015

ISBN 978-1-77148-318-6

CHIZINEPUB.COM

THE ACOLYTE
CRAIG DAVIDSON

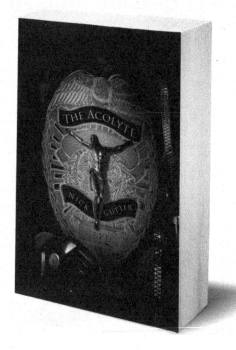

Jonah Murtag is an Acolyte on the New Bethlehem police force. His job: eradicate all heretical religious faiths, their practitioners, and artefacts. Murtag's got problems—one of his partners is a zealot, and he's in love with the other one. Trouble at work, trouble at home. Murtag realizes that you can rob a citizenry of almost anything, but you can't take away its faith. When a string of bombings paralyzes the city, religious fanatics are initially suspected, but startling clues point to a far more ominous perpetrator. If Murtag doesn't get things sorted out, the Divine Council will dispatch The Quints, aka: Heaven's Own Bagmen. The clock is ticking towards doomsday for the Chosen of New Bethlehem. And Jonah Murtag's got another problem. The biggest and most worrisome . . . Jonah isn't a believer anymore.

AVAILABLE APRIL 2015
ISBN 978-1-77148-328-5